THE YEAR'S 25 FINEST

CRIME AND MYSTERY STORIES

THE YEAR'S 25 FINEST
CRIME AND MYSTERY STORIES

Second Annual Edition

Edited by the Staff of *Mystery Scene*

With an introduction by Jon L. Breen

Carroll & Graf Publishers, Inc.
New York

First Carroll & Graf edition 1993

Carroll & Graf Publishers, Inc.
260 Fifth Avenue
New York, NY 10001

ISBN: 0-88184-999-5

Manufactured in the United States of America

OCT 26 1993

The editors would like to thank Larry Segriff, Nevenah Smith, and John Klima for their help in putting this book together. Also, thanks are due to Janet Hutchings, editor of *Ellery Queen's Mystery Magazine*, and Kathleen Jordan, editor of *Alfred Hitchcock Mystery Magazine*, for their help in gathering materials. Thanks also to all the other publishers, editors, authors, and agents who helped make this book possible.

For permission to reprint the stories in this anthology, grateful acknowledgment is made to:

"Someday I'll Plant More Walnut Trees" by Lawrence Block. Copyright © 1993 by Lawrence Block. First published in *Some Days You Get the Bear* William Morrow & Co. Inc. Reprinted by permission of the author.

"The Winfield Trade" by Jeremiah Healy. Copyright © 1992 by Jeremiah Healy. First published in *Cat Crimes II* edited by Martin H. Greenberg and Ed Gorman, Donald I. Fine, Inc. Reprinted by permission of Jed Mattes, Inc.

"Liar's Dice" by Bill Pronzini. Copyright © 1992 by Bill Pronzini. First published in *Ellery Queen's Mystery Magazine*, November 1992 issue. Reprinted by permission of the author.

"Long Live the Queen" by Ruth Rendell. Copyright © 1991 by Ruth Rendell. First published in *Ellery Queen's Mystery Magazine*, July 1991 issue. Reprinted by permission of the author and her agent, Sterling Lord Literistic, Inc.

"Lazy Susan" by Nancy Pickard. Copyright © 1991 by Nancy Pickard. First published in *Sisters in Crime 4* edited by Marilyn Wallace, Berkley Books. Reprinted by permission of the author.

"A Hotel in Bucharest" by Robert Barnard. Copyright © 1992 by Robert Barnard. First published in *Ellery Queen's Mystery Magazine*, Mid-December 1992 issue. Reprinted by permission of the author.

"The Crime of Miss Oyster Brown" by Peter Lovesey. Copyright © 1991 by Peter Lovesey. First published in *Ellery Queen's Mystery Magazine*, May 1991 issue. Reprinted by permission of Jane Gelfman, Gelfman-Schneider.

"Secrets" by June Thomson. Copyright © 1992 by June Thomson. First published in *Ellery Queen's Mystery Magazine*, March 1992 issue. Reprinted by permission of the author and her agent, Curtis Brown, Ltd.

"Whatever Has to Be Done" by Jan Grape. Copyright © 1991 by Jan Grape. First published in *Deadly Allies* edited by Bob Randisi, Bantam Books. Reprinted by permission of the author.

"Stop, Thief!" by Barbara D'Amato. Copyright © 1991 by Barbara D'Amato. First published in *Sisters in Crime 4* edited by Marilyn Wallace, Berkley Books. Reprinted by permission of the author.

"While She Was Out" by Ed Bryant. Copyright © 1988 by Ed Bryant. First published in *Pulphouse: The Hardback Magazine*. Reprinted by permission of the author.

"True Faces" by Pat Cadigan. Copyright © 1992 by Pat Cadigan. First published in *The Magazine of Fantasy and Science Fiction*, April 1992 issue. Reprinted by permission of the author.

Contents

The Mystery in 1992

JON L. BREEN

Though 1992 was widely called the Year of the Woman, that tag won't do in the mystery field, where the 1990s were already the *Decade* of the Woman. In crime fiction, 1992 was the Year of the Lawyer—unless they want to lay claim to the whole decade, too.

Ever since Scott Turow's best-seller *Presumed Innocent* appeared in 1987, lawyer novelists have become an increasingly hot property, and the overwhelming success of John Grisham, whose *The Pelican Brief* (Doubleday) was one of the top-selling fiction titles of 1992, has only accelerated the rush from courtroom to publishers' lists. While the tradition of mystery writing lawyers goes back at least as far as Wilkie Collins, there may never have been so many active in the field at one time, some taking their shots at the next Big Trial best-seller, others foregoing the busman's holiday to produce mysteries that don't rely on legal backgrounds. Aside from the names mentioned later in this article, including at least three on my favored fifteen list, included among the many currently active crime-writing lawyers are Michael Bowen, Warwick Downing, Philip Friedman, Stephen Greenleaf, William Harrington, Jeremiah Healy, Joe L. Hensley, Paul Levine, Steve Martini, Lia Matera, Michael Nava, Francis M. Nevins, Jr., Richard North Patterson, Carolyn Wheat, and William P. Wood.

I also associate the year 1992 with longevity. The eightieth birthday of Julian Symons, equally prominent in the crime fiction field as author, critic, and historian, was a cause of national celebration in the British literary world. William Campbell Gault, age 82, reappeared with a new adventure of private eye Brock Callahan, *Dead Pigeon* (Mystery Scene/Carroll & Graf). And no fewer than three authors whose books I reviewed during the year will turn 90 in 1993: Phyllis A. Whitney (see the best-of-the-year list below); Lawrence Treat, still another law-trained mystery writer, who collaborated with Norbert Ehrenfreund to produce the lively and thought-provoking *You the Jury* (Holt), a collection of courtroom case studies for young adults; and forensic psychiatrist David Abrahamsen, author of the nonfiction study *Murder & Madness: The Secret Life of Jack the Ripper* (Fine).

It was another healthy year statistically. Though the state of the economy and the frenzy of mystery buying by publishers in recent years combined to narrow the pipeline somewhat for writers, the reader (and reviewer) if anything saw an increase in the number of new books pouring forth. In M. S. Cappadonna's listings in *The Armchair Detective* for the first three quarters of 1992, I roughly counted 272 new hardcovers and 53 paperback originals. Extrapolate those figures over a full year and you get 366 and 62, which exceeds the 1991 totals of about 350 and 50. (Note that the hardcover count may miss some volumes that are crime or mystery fiction but not promoted as such, while the paperback original counts are invariably low: for one thing, they don't include the Harlequin Intrigue line, in which dozens of romantic mysteries are published each year.)

It was a good year at the movies for mystery buffs, with such films as *A Few Good Men*, *The Player*, *Sneakers*, and even the Oscar-winning Clint Eastwood western *Unforgiven* seen as criminous enough to merit Edgar nominations. Probably the best movie mystery of the year was the fifth nominee, *The Crying Game*, which included a Big Surprise that viewers, critics, and commentators labored mightily to keep a secret. In a few years, though, it will be as difficult to find anyone ignorant of the *Crying Game* secret as to find someone who can still be surprised by *Psycho*. A pity.

It was also a year of controversy. Michael Crichton's riveting police procedural *Rising Sun* (Knopf) was the target of Japan-bashing charges. I think the charges were unwarranted, but they made for some lively discussions. A number of mystery commentators were wrestling—in the Bouchercon at Toronto and in the pages of *Mystery Scene* among other venues—with the problem of violence in mysteries, especially toward women, and disagreeing over what constitutes censorship. A case of *real* censorship reared its head when the publisher of *Wilson Library Bulletin*, taking umbrage at columnist Will Manley's satirical article on librarians and sex, not only fired the offending writer but ordered remaining copies of the issue destroyed. This item is relevant to the mystery field because reviewer Kathleen L. Maio, who several years ago succeeded the present writer in the magazine's "Murder in Print" department, was one of the principled *WLB* contributors who resigned in protest, along with the editor.

Best Novels of the Year 1992

After repeating once again that *nobody*, save possibly the Edgar best novel committee (and even they have their doubters), has read so voluminously as to make grand pronouncements about the whole mystery genre in any given year, here are the fifteen books that gave me the most pleasure of the crop of 1992:

Lawrence Block, *A Walk Among the Tombstones* (Morrow). New York private eye Matt Scudder, looking for the kidnapped wife of a drug dealer, again proves himself one of the best in the business—and his creator one of those infuriating professionals who can do almost anything and make it look easy.

Jay Brandon, *Rules of Evidence* (Pocket). Though an earlier Brandon courtroom thriller, *Fade the Heat* (1990), was an Edgar nominee, I don't think it was anywhere near as good as this gripping account of an African-American lawyer defending a possibly bigoted white cop on a charge of murder in San Antonio.

Lindsey Davis, *Venus in Copper* (Crown). This is the third entry in one of at least four current mystery series set in ancient Rome (see also the work of Steven Saylor, John Maddox Roberts, and Ron Burns.) It's a well-constructed problem, and Marcus Didius Falco is a superlative guide to the underside of Roman society.

James Ellroy, *White Jazz* (Knopf). The fourth in Ellroy's series about L.A. crime in the forties and fifties clearly won't appeal to every taste: both the telegraphic writing style and the relentlessly downbeat worldview take some adjusting to. But Ellroy is a writer of rare originality and power.

Joe Gores, *32 Cadillacs* (Mysterious). The private-eye procedurals about Daniel Kearny Associates are infrequent—this is the first at book length since 1978—but worth waiting for. Much the best in the series, this one involves repossessing the Caddies from some Gypsies and suggests the criminous comedy of Donald E. Westlake—in fact, it shares a chapter with Westlake's *Drowned Hopes* (1990).

Sue Grafton, *"I" is for Innocent* (Holt). This is surely one of the best (maybe *the* best) in the series about Santa Teresa, California, private eye Kinsey Millhone, combining the usual charming and humorous narration with an unusually good pure puzzle.

David C. Hall, *Return Trip Ticket* (St. Martin's). When you get a load of Donald E. Westlake's introduction to this short private eye novel, the first to be published in his own country by an American writer based in Spain, you'll wonder if the fulsomeness of the praise can possibly be justified. Read it and see.

Robert Harris, *Fatherland* (Random). This alternate-universe political thriller was the best first novel I read in 1992. The setting is Berlin in the early 1960s. It's the world we have known with one small difference; the Nazis won World War II.

Reginald Hill, *Recalled to Life* (Delacorte). Hill is among the most inventive and versatile writers of crime fiction now active. The latest case for Yorkshire cops Dalziel and Pascoe even manages to surpass its Dagger-award winning and Edgar-nominated predecessor, *Bones and Silence* (1990), in its depth of characterization and its creative rearrangement of genre conventions.

John Katzenbach, *Just Cause* (Putnam). Some long "mainstream" crime novels are merely bloated exercises that would be better with their pretensions and page counts cut in half. Not so this four-hundred-pager, a consistently involving and surprising story of a reporter's efforts on behalf of a possibly innocent Death Row inmate—and the aftermath.

Walter Mosley, *White Butterfly* (Norton). It remains to be seen if President Clinton's endorsement of Mosley's work will have the same effect as President Kennedy's championing of Ian Fleming, but it certainly demonstrated the Chief Executive's good taste in mysteries. The third case for African-American Easy Rawlins, unofficial private eye operating in fifties Los Angeles, is well-plotted, well-told, and (most of all) well-peopled.

Anne Perry, *Defend and Betray* (Fawcett Columbine). I may someday compile a best-of-the-year list without a book by Perry, but not just yet. In their third adventure, Victorian sleuths William Monk (cop-turned-private-investigator) and Hester Latterly (nurse) look into the murder of a Crimean War general.

Grif Stockley, *Probable Cause* (Simon and Schuster). The second novel about Arkansas attorney Gideon Page is one of the finest fruits of the current vogue for lawyer fiction. Excellent as the trial scenes are, the book may be most notable for the hero's relationship with his daughter and for its view of southern race relations in the nineties.

Robert K. Tanenbaum, *Reversible Error* (Dutton). The earlier novels about New York assistant D.A. Butch Karp were always enjoyable, if sometimes a bit too movie-ish. In this fourth entry, the gritty series hits full stride. It's one of the best of the year and a surprising non-Edgar nominee.

Phyllis A. Whitney, *The Ebony Swan* (Doubleday). Whitney is as formidable a suspense novelist as ever in this latest book set on Virginia's Northern Neck and varying the pattern in featuring two virtually coequal heroines, one young and the other less young.

I should note that the fact that the above fifteen came from fifteen different publishers is purely coincidental—and also an indication of how widely excellent mystery fiction is being published.

Short Stories

Single-author collections were far less plentiful in 1992 than in the couple of years preceding, but there were still some highlights. Deadheating for book of the year were the first mystery collections of two of the genre's most versatile writers, both of whom (not coincidentally) have a background of publication in mainstream literary magazines. Michael Collins's (Dennis Lynds's) *Crime, Punishment, and Resurrection* (Fine) brings together some of the short stories about New-York-to-California private eye Dan Fortune, including a previously unpublished novella. Ed Gorman's *Prisoners & Other Stories* (CD Publications, P.O. Box 18433, Baltimore, MD 21237) is a highly varied gathering with an afterword by Dean R. Koontz. Others with new collections in 1992 included Joe Gores, with *Mostly Murder* (Mystery Scene/ Pulphouse, Box 1227, Eugene, OR 97440), and John Mortimer (yet another lawyer!) with *Rumpole on Trial* (Viking).

I think the number of multi-author collections may also have been down somewhat, though certainly some series of original anthologies must remian healthy, coming as they do with numbers attached like movie sequels or Super Bowls: Martin H. Greenbery and Ed Gorman's *Cat Crimes II* and *III* (both Fine); Peter Sellers's *Cold Blood IV* (Mosaic), which was among the freebies for those attending the Bouchercon in Toronto; Maxim Jakubowski's *New Crimes 3* (Carroll & Graf), and Marilyn Wallace's *Sisters in Crime 5* (Berkley). In series but without numerals were the Adams Round Table's third collection, *Missing in Manhattan* (Longmeadow), Edward D. Hoch's annual *Year's Best Mystery and Suspense Stories* (Walker), and the present volume's predecessor (Carroll & Graf). Sisters in Crime and the Private Eye Writers of America joined forces for a volume one supposes *could* develop into a series, *Deadly Allies* (Doubleday/Perfect Crime), edited by Marilyn Wallace and Robert J. Randisi. A notable original anthology not in a series was Gorman and Greenberg's *Invitation to Murder* (Dark Harvest).

Reference Books and Secondary Sources

The year's two most notable secondary sources were one that aimed for a wide audience and another that is indispensable to a much narrower company of mystery specialists. John Loughery's *Alias S. S. Van Dine* (Scribners) is the first full-length biography of one of the most significant American figures of the Golden Age of Detection. Van Dine, who was an eminent art and cultural critic under his real name of Willard Huntington Wright, has the right combination of achievement, personal quirks, and notable associates to make an ideal subject for biography. Ellen Nehr's *Doubleday Crime Club Compendium 1928–1991* (Offspring Press, 75 Millthwait Dr., Martinez, CA 94553) is a most valuable guide to all the publications under the mystery field's most durable imprint, which was launched with a bang in 1928 and expired with a whimper in 1991.

Valuable for prospective writers in the genre is *Writing Mysteries: A Handbook by the Mystery Writers of America* (Writer's Digest), edited by Sue Grafton. And fans of the old mystery radio shows should not miss Jim Harmon's *Radio Mystery and Adventure and its Appearances in Film, Television, and Other Media* (McFarland, Box 611, Jefferson, NC 28640).

Sub-genres

I. Private Eyes.

It was a good year for the shamus. Apart from the novels by Block, Gores, Grafton, Hall, and Mosely that make up a third of my top fifteen, there were strong new cases for Depression-era character Carl Wilcox, certainly *sort of* a private eye if (in common with the characters of Block and Mosely) not officially licensed, in Harold Adams's *The Man Who Was Taller Than God* (Walker); New Orleans op Micah Dunn in M. K. Shuman's cunningly plotted *The Last Man to Die* (St. Martin's); Mexico's Hector Belascoaran Shayne in Paco Ignacio Taibo's *Some Clouds* (Viking); Floridian Fred Carver in John Lutz's *Hot* (Holt); Albany, New York's Donald Strachey in Richard

Stevenson's *Third Man Out* (St. Martin's); and Salt Lake City sleuth Moroni Traveler in Robert Irvine's *The Spoken Word* (St. Martin's). Though it's probably time to stop segregating the female ops, I'll do it one more time in undersocoring what a good year they had, with strong cases for Sharon McCone in Marcia Muller's *Pennies on a Dead Woman's Eyes* (Mysterious), Anna Lee in Liza Cody's Edgar-nominated *Backhand* (Doubleday/Perfect Crime), V. I. Warshawski in Sara Paretsky's *Guardian Angel* (Delacorte), and Devon MacDonald in Nancy Baker Jacobs's *A Slash of Scarlet* (Putnam).

II. Formal Detection.

The classicists were also in good form in 1992, though they are less prominent on my list of fiteen than I might normally expect. A husband and wife combination made their fans happy: William L. DeAndrea's *The Vampire Murders* (Doubleday/Perfect Crime) had some of the years cleverest clues and misdirections, while Jane Haddam (Orania Popazoglou) continued her holiday mystery series in the Christmas tale *A Stillness in Bethlehem* (Bantam). Other good books in the grand tradition included Harry Kemelman's *The Day the Rabbi Resigned* (Fawcett Columbine), James Yaffe's *Mom Among the Liars* (St. Martin's), Sharyn McCrumb's *Zombies of the Gene Pool* (Simon and Schuster), M. D. Lake's *A Gift for Murder* (Avon), Colin Dexter's *The Jewel that Was Ours* (Crown), Aaron Elkins's *Make No Bones* (Mysterious), Ronald Lewitsky's *The Wisdom of Serpents* (Scribners), and E. X. Ferrars's *Danger from the Dead* Doubleday/Perfect Crime).

III. Police procedurals.

Apart from the works of Crichton and Hill, discussed above, some of the better procedurals included Ed McBain's *Kiss* (Morrow), latest in the long-running 87th Precinct saga; J. A. Jance's Seattle-based *Without Due Process* (Morrow); Anne Wingate's *Exception to Murder* (Walker); and Lillian O'Donnell's *Pushover* (Putnam). I don't know if they can really be called procedural characters, but Sharyn McCrumb's Spencer Arrowood, in *The Hangman's Beautiful Daughter* (Scribners), and James Lee Burke's Dave Robichaux, in *A Stained White Radiance* (Hyperion), both had notable cases during the year.

IV. Sherlockiana.

Though it's been reported that the Conan Doyle estate will authorize no more Sherlock Holmes pastiches, they nevertheless continue to appear. Edward Hanna's *The Whitechapel Horrors* (Carroll & Graf) is possibly the longest and certainly one of the best executed of the ersatz Holmes volumes, one of many to set him on the trail of Jack the Ripper. All that's lacking, sadly, is a solution to the case, though at least one interesting new suspect is considered. The year's other notable new case for Holmes, Peter Rowland's

The Disappearance of Edwin Drood (St. Martin's), gives the Baker Street sleuth a literary rather than a true-crime problem to solve. (The Italian duo of Carlo Fruttero and Franco Lucentini also tackle the mystery of Dickens's unfinished novel in *The D Case* [Harcourt].)

V. Unclassifiable.

Tired of all this pigeonholing? Some of the other interesting 1992 books don't fit quite as neatly into a category but still deserve mention. Mary Higgins Clark's tricky *All Around the Town* (Simon and Schuster) overcame my usual resistance to this enormously successful writer's works. Leonard Tourney's *Witness of Bones* (St. Martin's) made good use of its Elizabethan background, while Martha Grimes used an American background for the first time in *The End of the Pier* (Knopf). Also notable were Celia Fremlin's *Dangerous Thoughts* (Doubleday/Perfect Crime), Robert Barnard's *A Fatal Attachment* (Scribners), Kevin Robinson's *Mall Rats* (Walker), Randy Russell's *Doll Eyes* (Doubleday/Perfect Crime), and Daniel Ransom's *The Serpent's Kiss* (Dell).

Debutantes

The best first mystery novel I read in 1992 was British: Robert Harris's *Fatherland* (see the list of fifteen). Some notable American firsts were David Berlinsky's determinedly politically incorrect Bay Area private eye novel *A Clean Sweep* (St. Martin's), Miriam Grace Monfredo's feminist historical *Seneca Falls Inheritance* (St. Martin's), and the work of one of those ubiquitous lawyer-novelists, William Bernhardt's *Primary Justice* (Ballantine). That all of these managed to escape the notice of the Edgar selectors suggest an outstanding year indeed for debuts. (Bernhardt, who produced a second book later in the year, *Blind Justice* [Ballantine], also was inexplicably overlooked by the best-paperback selectors.)

Others Mentioned in Dispatches

Other well-known writers with new books in 1992 included a flock of best-seller-list habitués—Evelyn Anthony, Joseph Wambaugh, Lawerence Sanders, Jonathan Kellerman, Lilian Jackson Braun, Patricia D. Cornwell, Barbara Michaels—plus such notables as Ross Thomas, Peter Dickinson, E. Howard Hunt, Faye Kellerman, Stuart Kaminsky, Rita Mae Brown, Carolyn G. Hart, Bill Pronzini, Charlotte MacLeod, William McIlvanney, Anthony Olcott, Simon Brett, Loren D. Estleman, and John Wainwright. Joining the well-established members of the mystery-writing-political-relatives club, Margaret Truman and the late Elliott Roosevelt, was Marilyn Quayle, who produced a thriller with sister Nancy T. Northcott.

A Sense of History

Most notable reprinting of the year was Bantam's ongoing reissue of Rex Stout's original Nero Wolfe novels, each with an introduction by a well-known contemporary mystery writer. And one of the most historically important but least reprinted of writers, Carroll John Daly, was revived in a pair of titles from HarperPerennial, *The Hidden Hand* and *The Snarl of the Beast.*

Closing Admonition

It's never wise to make hasty judgments or form unyielding prejudices in choosing what mystery to read, any more than in any other department of existence. It's a long-standing axiom that no matter how threadbare a particular situation or subject or plot element seems to be from overuse, someone will come along with a fresh angle. Think of this the next time you pick up a novel whose jacket promises you—

• a dedicated big-city cop obsessed with capturing a psychotic serial killer who whenever there is a full moon offs another radio shrink; or
• the adventures of a terminally precious detecting pussycat; or
• Sherlock Holmes's efforts to determine which of three remaining suspects—Oscar Wilde, George Bernard Shaw, and Queen Victoria—is really Jack the Ripper; or
• thrills and laughs in the Florida narcotic trade; or
• murder at the brownie bakeoff; or
• neo-Nazis on the rise in (fill in name of city, state, or country); or
• long-hidden revelations that the famous (fill in name of long dead actor, athlete, politician, social reformer, scientist, author, composer, artist) was really a Great Detective—maybe you should read it instead of passing it by. Maybe *this* one will be really good.

Award Winners for 1992

Edgar Allan Poe Awards
(Mystery Writers of America)

Best novel: Margaret Maron, *Bootlegger's Daughter* (Mysterious)
Best first novel by an American author: Michael Connelly, *The Black Echo* (Little, Brown)
Best original paperback: Dana Stabenow, *A Cold Day for Murder* (Berkley)
Best fact crime book: Harry Farrell, *Swift Justice* (St. Martin's)
Best critical/biographical work: John Loughery, Alias S.S. Van Dine (Scribners)
Best short story: Benjamin J. Schutz, "Mary, Mary, Shut the Door" *(Deadly Allies* Doubleday/ Perfect Crime)
Best young adult mystery: Chap Reaver, *A Little Bit Dead* (Delacorte)
Best juvenile mystery: Eve Bunting, *Coffin on a Case* (Harper/Collins)
Best episode in a TV series: Michael S. Chernuchin and Rene Balcer, "Conspiracy" *(Law and Order*, Universal)
Best TV feature or miniseries: Lynda La Plant, *Prime Suspect (Mystery*, PBS)
Best motion picture: Michael Tolkin, *The Player* (Fineline Features)
Grand master: Donald E. Westlake
Robert L. Fish award (best first story): Steven Saylor, "A Will is a Way" *(Ellery Queen's Mystery Magazine*, March)
Reader of the Year: President Bill Clinton

Agatha Awards
(Malice Domestic Mystery Convention)

Best novel: Margaret Maron, *Bootlegger's Daughter* (Mysterious)
Best first novel: Barbara Neely, *Blanche on the Lam* (St. Martin's)
Best short story: Aaron and Charlotte Elkins, "Nice Gorilla" (*Malice Domestic I* Pocket)

Anthony Awards
(Bouchercon World Mystery Convention)

Best novel: Peter Lovesey, *The Last Detective* (Doubleday/Perfect Crime)
Best first novel: Sue Henry, *Murder on the Iditarod Trail* (Atlantic)
Best true crime: David Simon, *Homicide: A Year on the Killing Streets* (Houghton Mifflin) 1990
Best short story: Liza Cody, "The Lucky Dip," *A Woman's Eye* (Delacorte)
Best short story collection or anthology: Sara Paretsky, ed., *A Woman's Eye* (Delacorte)
Best critical work: Maxim Jakubowsky, ed., *100 Great Detectives* (Carroll & Graf)

Shamus Awards
(Private Eye Writer of America)

Best novel: Max Allan Collins, *Stolen Away* (Bantam)
Best first novel: Thomas D. Davis, *Suffer Little Children* (Walker)
Best original paperback novel: Paul Kemprecos, *Cool Blue Tomb* (Bantam)
Best short story: Nancy Pickard, "Dust Devil" (*The Armchair Detective*, Spring)
Lifetime achievement award: Joseph Hansen

Dagger Awards
(Crime Writers' Association, Great Britain)

Gold Dagger: Colin Dexter, *The Way Through the Wood* (Macmillan)
Silver Dagger: Liza Cody, *Bucket Nut* (Chatto)
John Creasey Memorial Award (best first novel): Minette Walters, *The Ice House* (Macmillan)
Last Laugh Award (best humorous crime novel): Carl Hiassen, *Native Tongue* (Macmillan)

'92 Award (best crime novel set in Continental Europe): Timothy Williams, *Black August* (Gollancz)

Rumpole Award (best crime novel portraying British legal procedure): Peter Rawlinson, *Hatred and Contempt* (Chapmans)

Macavity Awards
(Mystery Readers International)

Best novel: Nancy Pickard, *I.O.U.* (Pocket)

Best first novel (a tie): Sue Henry, *Murder on the Iditarod Trail* (Atlantic), Mary Willis Walker, *Zero at the Bone* (St. Martin's)

Best nonfiction or critical work: Tony Hillerman and Ernie Bulow, *Talking Mysteries* (University of New Mexico Press)

Arthur Ellis Awards
(Crime Writers of Canada)

Best novel: Peter Robinson, *Past Reason Hated* (Viking/Penguin)

Best first novel: Paul Grescoe, *Flesh Wound* (Douglas & McIntyre)

Best true crime: William Lowther, *Arms and the Man: Dr. Gerald Bull, Iraq and the Supergun* (Doubleday Canada)

Best short story: Eric Wright, "Two in the Bush" (*Christmas Stalkings* [Mysterious])

Best genre criticism/reference: Wesley K. Wark, *Spy Fiction, Spy Films, and Real Intelligence* (Frank Cass)

Derrick Murdoch Award: William Bankier, James Powell, Peter Sellers

THE YEAR'S 25 FINEST
CRIME AND MYSTERY STORIES

Lawrence Block, author of Matt Scudder novels such as *A Dance at the Slaughterhouse,* has won the Edgar and many other major mystery awards. For a number of years he's been among the top rank of suspense writers. Here, without lurid effects or grisly detail, he cuts to the human core of a desperate situation, fixing the reader's attention on the natural drama. The story is reprinted from Block's recent collection, *Some Days You Get the Bear.* *

Someday I'll Plant More Walnut Trees
LAWRENCE BLOCK

There is a silence that is just stillness, just the absence of sound, and there is a deeper silence that is more than that. It is the antithesis, the aggressive opposite, of sound. It is to sound as antimatter is to matter, an auditory black hole that reaches out to swallow up and nullify the sounds of others.

My mother can give off such a silence. She is a master at it. That morning at breakfast she was thus silent, silent as she cooked eggs and made coffee, silent while I spooned baby oatmeal into Livia's little mouth, silent while Dan fed himself and while he smoked the day's first cigarette along with his coffee. He had his own silence, sitting there behind his newspaper, but all it did was insulate him. It couldn't reach out beyond that paper shield to snatch other sound out of the air.

He finished and put out his cigarette, folded his paper. He said it was supposed to be hot today, with rain forecast for late afternoon. He patted Livia's head, and with his forefinger drew aside a strand of hair that had fallen across her forehead.

* All introductory story notes were written by James Frenkel.

I can see that now, his hand so gentle, and her beaming up at him, wide-eyed, gurgling.

Then he turned to me, and with the same finger and the same softness he reached to touch the side of my face. I did not draw away. His finger touched me, ever so lightly, and then he reached to draw me into the circle of his arms. I smelled his shirt, freshly washed and sun-dried, and under it the clean male scent of him.

We looked at each other, both of us silent, the whole room silent. And then Livia cooed and he smiled quickly and chucked me under the chin and left. I heard the screen door slam, and then the sounds of the car as he drove to town. When I could not hear it anymore I went over to the radio and switched it on. They were playing a Tammy Wynette song. "Stand by your man," Tammy urged, and my mother's silence swallowed up the words.

While the radio played unheard I changed Livia and put her in for her nap. I came back to the kitchen and cleared the table. My mother waved a hand at the air in front of her face.

"He smokes," I said.

"I didn't say anything," she said.

We did the dishes together. There is a dishwasher but we never use it for the breakfast dishes. She prefers to run it only once a day, after the evening meal. It could hold all the day's dishes, they would not amount to more than one load in the machine, but she does not like to let the breakfast and lunch dishes stand. It seems wasteful to me, of time and effort, and even of water, although our well furnishes more than we ever need. But it is her house, after all, and her dishwasher, and hers the decision as to when it is to be used.

Silently she washed the dishes, silently I wiped them. As I reached to stack plates in a cupboard I caught her looking at me. Her eyes were on my cheek, and I could feel her gaze right where I had felt Dan's finger. His touch had been light. Hers was firmer.

I said, "It's nothing."

"All right."

"Dammit, Mama!"

"I didn't say anything, Tildie."

I was named Matilda for my father's mother. I never knew her, she died before I was born, before my parents met. I was never called Matilda. It was the name on my college diploma, on my driver's license, on Livia's birth certificate, but no one ever used it.

"He can't help it," I said. "It's not his fault."

Her silence devoured my words. On the radio Tammy Wynette sang a song about divorce, spelling out the word. Why were they playing all her records this morning? Was it her birthday? Or an anniversary of some failed romance?

"It's not," I said. I moved to her right so that I could talk to her good ear.

"It's a pattern. His father was abusive to his mother. Dan grew up around that. His father drank and was free with his hands. Dan swore he would never be like that, but patterns like that are almost impossible to throw off. It's what he knows, can you understand that? On a deep level, deeper than intellect, bone deep, that's how he knows to behave as a man, as a husband."

"He marked your face. He hasn't done that before, Tildie."

My hand flew to the spot. "You knew that—"

"Sounds travel. Even with my door closed, even with my good ear on the pillow. I've heard things."

"You never said anything."

"I didn't say anything today," she reminded me.

"He can't help it," I said. "You have to understand that. Didn't you see him this morning?"

"I saw him."

"It hurts him more than it hurts me. And it's my fault as much as it's his."

"For allowing it?"

"For provoking him."

She looked at me. Her eyes are a pale blue, like mine, and at times there is accusation in them. My gaze must have the same quality. I have been told that it is penetrating. "Don't look at me like that," my husband has said, raising a hand as much to ward off my gaze as to threaten me. "Damn you, don't you look at me like that!"

Like what? I'd wondered. How was I looking at him? What was I doing wrong?

"I do provoke him," I told her. "I make him hit me."

"How?"

"By saying the wrong thing."

"What sort of thing?"

"Things that upset him."

"And then he has to hit you, Tildie? Because of what you say?"

"It's a *pattern*," I said. "It's the way he grew up. Men who drink have sons who drink. Men who beat their wives have sons who beat their wives. It's passed on over the generations like a genetic illness. Mama, Dan's a good man. You see how he is with Livia, how he loves her, how she loves him."

"Yes."

"And he loves me, Mama. Don't you think it tears him up when something like this happens? Don't you think it eats at him?"

"It must."

"It does!" I thought how he'd cried last night, how he'd held me and touched the mark on my cheek and cried. "And we're going to try to do something about it," I said. "To break the pattern. There's a clinic in Fulton City where you can go for counseling. It's not expensive, either."

"And you're going?"

"We've talked about it. We're considering it."

She looked at me and I made myself meet her eyes. After a moment she looked away. "Well, you would know more about this sort of thing than I do," she said. "You went to college, you studied, you learned things."

I studied art history. I can tell you about the Italian Renaissance, although I have already forgotten much of what I learned. I took one psychology course in my freshman year and we observed the behavior of white rats in mazes.

"Mama," I said, "I know you disapprove."

"Oh, no," she said. "Tildie, that's not so."

"It's not?"

She shook her head. "I just hurt for you," she said. "That's all."

We live on 220 acres, only a third of them level. The farm has been in our family since the land was cleared early in the last century. It has been years since we farmed it. The MacNaughtons run sheep in our north pastures, and Mr. Parkhill leases forty acres, planting alfalfa one year and field corn the next. Mama has some bank stock and some utilities, and the dividends plus what she's paid for the land rent are enough to keep her. There's no mortgage on the land and the taxes have stayed low. And she has a big kitchen garden. We eat out of it all summer long and put up enough in the fall to carry us through the winter.

Dan studied comparative lit while I studied art history. He got a master's and did half the course work for a doctorate and then knew he couldn't do it anymore. He got a job driving a taxi and I worked waiting tables at Paddy Mac's, where we used to come for beer and hamburgers when we were students. When I got pregnant with Livia he didn't want me on my feet all day but we couldn't make ends meet on his earnings as a cabdriver. Rents were high in that city, and everything cost a fortune.

And we both loved country living, and knew the city was no place to bring up Livia. So we moved here, and Dan got work right away with a construction company in Caldwell. That's the nearest town, just six miles from us on country roads, and Fulton City is only twenty-two miles.

After that conversation with Mama I went outside and walked back beyond the garden and the pear and apple orchard. There's a stream runs diagonally across our land, and just beyond it is the spot I always liked the best, where the walnut trees are. We have a whole grove of black walnuts, twenty-six trees in all. I know because Dan counted them. He was trying to estimate what they'd bring.

Walnut is valuable. People will pay thousands of dollars for a mature tree. They make veneer from it, because it's too costly to use as solid wood.

"We ought to sell these off," Dan said. "Your mama's got an untapped resource here. Somebody could come in, cut 'em down, and steal 'em. Like poachers in Kenya, killing the elephants for their ivory."

"No one's going to come onto our land."

"You never know. Anyway, it's a waste. You can't even see this spot from the house. And nobody does anything with the nuts."

When I was a girl my mama and I used to gather the walnuts after they fell in early autumn. Thousands fell from the trees. We would just gather a basketful and crack them with a hammer and pick the meat out. My hands always got black from the husks and stayed that way for weeks.

We only did this a few times. It was after Daddy left, but while Grandma Yount was still alive. I don't remember Grandma bothering with the walnuts, but she did lots of other things. When the cherries came in we would all pick them and she would bake pies and put up jars of the rest, and she'd boil the pits to clean them and sew scraps of cloth to make beanbags. There are still beanbags in the attic that Grandma Yount made. I'd brought one down for Livia and fancied I could still smell cherries through the cloth.

"We could harvest the walnuts," I told Dan. "If you want."

"What for? You can't get anything for them. Too much trouble to open and hardly any meat in them. I'd sooner harvest the trees."

"Mama likes having them here."

"They're worth a fortune. And they're a renewable resource. You could cut them and plant more and someday they'd put your grandchildren through college."

"You don't need to cut them to plant more. There's other land we could use."

"No point planting more if you're not going to cut these, is there? What do we need them for?"

"What do our grandchildren need college for?"

"What's that supposed to mean?"

"Nothing," I'd said, backing away.

And hours later he'd taken it up again. "You meant I wasted my education," he said. "That's what you meant by that crack, isn't it?"

"No."

"Then what did you mean? What do I need a master's for to hammer a nail? That's what you meant."

"It's not, but evidently that's how you'd rather hear it."

He hit me for that. I guess I had it coming. I don't know if I deserved it, I don't know if a woman deserves to get hit, but I guess I provoked it. Something makes me say things I shouldn't, things he'll take amiss. I don't know why.

Except I do know why, and I'd walked out of the kitchen and across to the walnut grove to keep from talking about it to Mama. Because he had his pattern and I had mine.

His was what he'd learned from his daddy, which was to abuse a woman, to slap her, to strike her with his fists. And mine was a pattern I'd learned from my mama, which was to make a man leave you, to taunt him with your mouth until one day he put his clothes in a suitcase and walked out the door.

In the mornings it tore at me to hear the screen door slam. Because I thought, Tildie, one day you'll hear that sound and it'll be for the last time. One day you'll do what your mother managed to do, and he'll do like your father did and you'll never see him again. And Livia will grow up as you did, in a house with her mother and her grandmother, and she'll have cherry-pit beanbags to play with and she'll pick the meat out of black walnuts, but what will she do for a daddy? And what will you do for a man?

All the rest of that week he never raised his hand to me. One night Mama stayed with Livia while Dan and I went to a movie in Fulton City. Afterward we went to a place that reminded us both of Paddy Mac's, and we drank beer and got silly. Driving home, we rolled down the car windows and sang songs at the top of our lungs. By the time we got home the beer had worn off but we were still happy and we hurried upstairs to our room.

Mama didn't say anything next morning but I caught her looking at me and knew she'd heard the old iron bedstead. I thought, *You hear a lot, even with your good ear pressed against the pillow.* Well, if she had to hear the fighting, let her hear the loving, too.

She could have heard the bed that night, too, although it was a quieter and gentler lovemaking than the night before. There were no knowing glances the next day, but after the screen door closed behind Dan and after Livia was in for her nap, there was a nice easiness between us as we stood side by side doing the breakfast dishes.

Afterward she said, "I'm so glad you're back home, Tildie."

"So you don't have to do the dishes all by yourself."

She smiled. "I knew you'd be back," she said.

"Did you? I wonder if I knew. I don't think so. I thought I wanted to live in a city, or in a college town. I thought I wanted to be a professor's wife and have earnest conversations about literature and politics and art. I guess I was just a country girl all along."

"You always loved it here," she said. "Of course it will be yours when I'm gone, and I had it in mind that you'd come back to it then. But I hoped you wouldn't wait that long."

She had never left. She and her mother lived here, and when she married my father he just moved in. It's a big old house, with different wings added over the years. He moved in, and then he left, and she just stayed on.

I remembered something. "I don't know if I thought I'd live here again," I said, "but I always thought I would die here." She looked at me, and I said, "Not so much die here as be buried here. When we buried Grandma I thought, *Well, this is where they'll bury me someday.* And I always thought that."

Grandma Yount's grave is on our land, just to the east of the pear and apple orchard. There are graves there dating back to when our people first lived here. The two children Mama lost are laid to rest there, and Grandma Yount's mother, and a great many children. It wasn't that long ago that people would have four or five children to raise one. You can't read what's cut into most of the stones, it's worn away with time, and it wears faster now that we have the acid rain, but the stones are there, the graves are there, and I always knew I'd be there, too.

"Well, I'll be there, too," Mama said. "But not too soon, I hope."

"No, not soon at all," I said. "Let's live a long time. Let's be old ladies together."

I thought it was a sweet conversation, a beautiful conversation. But when I told Dan about it we wound up fighting.

"When she goes," he said, "that's when those walnuts go to market."

"That's all you can think about," I said. "Turning a beautiful grove into dollars."

"That timber's money in the bank," he said, "except it's not in the bank because anybody could come in and haul it out of there behind our backs."

"Nobody's going to do that."

"And other things could happen. It's no good for a tree to let it grow beyond its prime. Insects can get it, or disease. There's one tree already that was struck by lightning."

"It didn't hurt it much."

"When they're my trees," he said, "they're coming down."

"They won't be your trees."

"What's that supposed to mean?"

"Mama's not leaving the place to you, Dan."

"I thought what's mine is yours and what's yours is mine."

"I love those trees," I said. "I'm not going to see them cut." His face darkened, and a muscle worked in his jaw. This was a warning sign, and I knew it as such, but I was stuck in a pattern, God help me, and I couldn't leave it alone. "First you'd sell off the timber," I said, "and then you'd sell off the acreage."

"I wouldn't do that."

"Why? Your daddy did."

Dan grew up on a farm that came down through his father's father. Unable to make a living farming, first his grandfather and then his father had sold off parcels of land little by little, whittling away at their holdings and each time reducing the potential income of what remained. After Dan's mother died his father had stopped farming altogether and drank full time, and the farm was auctioned for back taxes while Dan was still in high school.

I knew what it would do to him and yet I threw that in his face all the same. I couldn't seem to help it, any more than he could help what followed.

At breakfast the next day the silence made me want to scream. Dan read the paper while he ate, then hurried out the door without a word. I couldn't hear the screen door when it banged shut or the car engine when it started up. Mama's silence—and his, and mine—drowned out everything else.

I thought I'd burst when we were doing the dishes. She didn't say a word and neither did I. Afterward she turned to me and said, "I didn't go to college so I don't know about patterns, or what you do and what it makes him do."

The *quattrocento* and rats in a maze, that's all I learned in college. What I know about patterns and family violence I learned watching Oprah and Phil Donahue, and she watched the same programs I did. ("He blacked your eye and broke your nose. He kicked you in the stomach while you were pregnant. How can you stay with a brute like this?" "But I love him, Geraldo. And I know he loves me.")

"I just know one thing," she said. "It won't get better. And it will get worse."

"No."

"Yes. And you know it, Tildie."

"No."

He hadn't blacked my eye or broken my nose, but he had hammered my face with his fists and it was swollen and discolored. He hadn't kicked me in the stomach but he had shoved me from him. I had been clinging to his arm. That was stupid, I knew better than to do that, it drove him crazy to have me hang on him like that. He had shoved me and I'd gone sprawling, wrenching my leg when I fell on it. My knee ached now, and the muscles in the front of that thigh were sore. And my rib cage was sore where he'd punched me.

But I love him, Geraldo, Oprah, Phil. And I know he loves me.

That night he didn't come home.

I couldn't sit still, couldn't catch my breath. Livia caught my anxiety and wouldn't sleep, couldn't sleep. I held her in my arms and paced the floor in front of the television set. Back and forth, back and forth.

At midnight finally I put her in her crib and she slept. Mama was playing solitaire at the pine table. Only the top is pine, the base is maple. An antique, Dan pronounced it when he first saw it, and better than the ones in the shops. I suppose he had it priced in his mind, along with the walnut trees.

I pointed out a move. Mama said, "I know about that. I just haven't decided whether I want to do it, that's all." But she always says that. I don't believe she saw it.

At one I heard our car turn off the road and onto the gravel. She heard it, too, and gathered up the cards and said she was tired now, she'd just turn in. She was out of the room and up the stairs before he came in the door.

He was drunk. He lurched into the room, his shirt open halfway to his waist, his eyes unfocused. He said, "Oh, Jesus, Tildie, what's happening to us?"

"Shhh," I said. "You'll wake the baby."

"I'm sorry, Tildie," he said. "I'm sorry, I'm so goddam sorry."

Going up the stairs, he spun away from me and staggered into the railing. It held. I got him upstairs and into our room, but he passed out the minute he lay down on our bed. I got his shoes off, and his shirt and pants, and let him sleep in his socks and underwear.

In the morning he was still sleeping when I got up to take care of Livia. Mama had his breakfast on the table, his coffee poured, the newspaper at his place. He rushed through the kitchen without a word to anybody, tore out the door and was gone. I moved toward the door but Mama was in my path.

I cried, "Mama, he's leaving! He'll never be back!"

She glanced meaningfully at Livia. I stepped back, lowered my voice. "He's leaving," I said, helpless. He had started the car, he was driving away. "I'll never see him again."

"He'll be back."

"Just like my daddy," I said. "Livvy, your father's gone, we'll never see him again."

"Stop that," Mama said. "You don't know how much sticks in their minds. You mind what you say in front of her."

"But it's true."

"It's not," she said. "You won't lose him that easy. He'll be back."

In the afternoon I took Livia with me while I picked pole beans and summer squash. Then we went back to the pear and apple orchard and played in the shade. After a while I took her over to Grandma Yount's grave. We'll all be here someday, I wanted to say, your grandma and your daddy and your mama, too. And you'll be here when your time comes. This is our land, this is where we all end up.

I might have said this, it wouldn't hurt for her to hear it, but for what Mama said. I guess it's true you don't know what sticks in their minds, or what they'll make of it.

She liked it out there, Livia did. She crawled right up to Grandma Yount's stone and ran her hand over it. You'd have thought she was trying to read it that way, like a blind person with Braille.

* * *

31

He didn't come home for dinner. It was going on ten when I heard the car on the gravel. Mama and I were watching television. I got up and went into the kitchen to be there when he came in.

He was sober. He stood in the doorway and looked at me. Every emotion a man could have was there on his face.

"Look at you," he said. "I did that to you."

My face was worse than the day before. Bruises and swellings are like that, taking their time to ripen.

"You missed dinner," I said, "but I saved some for you. I'll heat up a plate for you."

"I already ate. Tildie, I don't know what to say."

"You don't have to say anything."

"No," he said. "That's not right. We have to talk."

We slipped up to our room, leaving Mama to the television set. With our door closed we talked about the patterns we were caught in and how we seemed to have no control, like actors in a play with all their lines written for them by someone else. We could improvise, we could invent movements and gestures, we could read our lines in any of a number of ways, but the script was all written down and we couldn't get away from it.

I mentioned counseling. He said, "I called that place in Fulton City. I wouldn't tell them my name. Can you feature that? I called them for help but I was too ashamed to tell them my name."

"What did they say?"

"They would want to see us once a week as a couple, and each of us individually once a week. Total price for the three sessions would be eighty dollars."

"For how long?"

"I asked. They couldn't say. They said it's not the sort of change you can expect to make overnight."

I said, "Eighty dollars a week. We can't afford that."

"I had the feeling they might reduce it some."

"Did you make an appointment?"

"No. I thought I'd call tomorrow."

"I don't want to cut the trees," I said. He looked at me. "To pay for it. I don't want to cut Mama's walnut trees."

"Tildie, who brought up the damn trees?"

"We could sell the table," I said.

"What are you talking about?"

"In the kitchen. The pine-top table, didn't you say it was an antique? We could sell that."

"Why would I want to sell the table?"

"You want to sell those trees bad enough. You as much as said that as soon as my mama dies you'll be out back with a chain saw."

"Don't start with me," he said. "Don't you start with me, Tildie."

"Or what? Or you'll hit me? Oh, God, Dan, what are we doing? Fighting over how to pay for the counseling to keep from fighting. Dan, what's the matter with us?"

I went to embrace him but he backed away from me. "Honey," he said, "we better be real careful with this. They were telling me about escalating patterns of violence. I'm afraid of what could happen. I'm going to do what they said to do."

"What's that?"

"I want to pack some things," he said. "That's what I came home to do. There's that Welcome Inn Motel outside of Caldwell, they say it's not so bad and I believe they have weekly rates."

"No," I said. "No."

"They said it's best. Especially if we're going to start counseling, because that brings everything up and out into the open, and it threatens the part of us that wants to be in this pattern. Tildie, from what they said it'd be danger-ous for us to be together right now."

"You can't leave," I said.

"I wouldn't be five miles away. I'd be coming for dinner some nights, we'd be going to a movie now and then. It's not like—"

"We can't afford it," I said. "Dan, how can we afford it? Eighty dollars a week for the counseling and God knows how much for the motel, and you'd be having most of your meals out, and how can we afford it? You've got a decent job but you don't make that kind of money."

His eyes hardened but he breathed in and out, in and out, and said, "Tildie, just talking like this is a strain, don't you see that? We can afford it, we'll find a way to afford it. Tildie, don't grab on to my arm like that, you know what it does to me. Tildie, stop it, will you for God's sake stop it?"

I put my arms around my own self and hugged myself. I was shaking. My hands just wanted to take hold of his arm. What was so bad about holding on to your husband's arm? What was wrong with that?

"Don't go," I said.

"I have to."

"Not now. It's late, they won't have any rooms left anyhow. Wait until morning. Can't you wait until morning?"

"I was just going to get some of my things and go."

"Go in the morning. Don't you want to see Livvy before you go? She's your daughter, don't you want to say good-bye to her?"

"I'm not leaving, Tildie. I'm just staying a few miles from here so we'll have a chance to keep from destroying ourselves. My God, Tildie, I don't want to leave you. That's the whole point, don't you see that?"

"Stay until morning," I said. "Please?"

"And will we go through this again in the morning?"

"No," I said. "I promise."

We were both restless, but then we made love and that settled him, and soon he was sleeping. I couldn't sleep, though. I lay there for a time, and then I put a robe on and went down to the kitchen and sat there for a long time, thinking of patterns, thinking of ways to escape them. And then I went back up the stairs to the bedroom again.

I was in the kitchen the next morning before Livia woke up. I was there when Mama came down, and her eyes widened at the sight of me. She started to say something but then I guess she saw something in my eyes and she stayed silent.

I said, "Mama, we have to call the police. You'll mind the baby when they come for me. Will you do that?"

"Oh, Tildie," she said.

I led her up the stairs again and into our bedroom. Dan lay facedown, the way he always slept. I drew the sheet down and showed her where I'd stabbed him, slipping the kitchen knife between two ribs and into the heart. The knife lay on the table beside the bed. I had wiped the blood from it. There had not been very much blood to wipe.

"He was going to leave," I said, "and I couldn't bear it, Mama. And I thought, Now he won't leave, now he'll never leave me. I thought, This is a way to break the pattern. Isn't that crazy, Mama? It doesn't make any sense, does it?"

"My poor Tildie."

"Do you want to know something? I feel safe now, Mama. He won't hit me anymore and I never have to worry about him leaving me. He can't leave me, can he?" Something caught in my throat. "Oh, and he'll never hold me again, either. In the circle of his arms."

I broke then, and it was Mama who held me, stroking my forehead, soothing me. I was all right then, and I stood up straight and told her she had better call the police.

"Livia'll be up any minute now," she said. "I think she's awake, I think I heard her fussing a minute ago. Change her and bring her down and feed her her breakfast."

"And then?"

"And then put her in for her nap."

After I put Livia back in her crib for her nap Mama told me that we weren't going to call the police. "Now that you're back where you belong," she said, "I'm not about to see them take you away. Your baby needs her mama and I need you, too."

"But Dan—"

"Bring the big wheelbarrow around to the kitchen door. Between the two of us we can get him down the stairs. We'll dig his grave in the back, we'll bury him here on our land. People won't suspect anything. They'll just think he went off, the way men do."

"The way my daddy did," I said.

Somehow we got him down the stairs and out through the kitchen. The hardest part was getting him into the old wheelbarrow. I checked Livia and made sure she was sleeping soundly, and then we took turns with the barrow, wheeling it out beyond the kitchen garden.

"What I keep thinking," I said, "is at least I broke the pattern."

She didn't say anything, and what she didn't say became one of her famous silences, sucking up all the sound around us. The barrow's wheel squeaked, the birds sang in the trees, but now I couldn't hear any of that.

Suddenly she said, "Patterns." Then she didn't say anything more, and I tried to hear the squeak of the wheel.

Then she said, "He never would have left you. If he left he'd only come back again. And he never would have quit hitting you. And each time would be a little worse than the last."

"It's not always like it is on *Oprah*, Mama."

"There's things you don't know," she said.

"Like what?"

The squeaking of the wheel, the song of birds. She said, "You know how I lost the hearing in the one ear?"

"You had an infection."

"That's what I always told you. It's not true. Your daddy cupped his hands and boxed my ears. He deafened me on the one side. I was lucky, nothing happened to the other ear. I still hear as good as ever out of it."

"I don't believe it," I said.

"It's the truth, Tildie."

"Daddy never hit you."

"Your daddy hit me all the time," she said. "All the time. He used his hands, he used his feet. He used his belt."

I felt a tightening in my throat. "I don't remember," I said.

"You didn't know. You were little. What do you think Livia knows? What do you think she'll remember?"

We walked on a ways. I said, "I just remember the two of you hollering. I thought you hollered and finally he left. That's what I always thought."

"That's what I let you think. It's what I wanted you to think. I had a broken jaw, I had broken ribs, I had to keep telling the doctor I was clumsy, I kept falling down. He believed me, too. I guess he had lots of women told him the same thing." We switched, and I took over the wheelbarrow. She said, "Dan would have done the same to you, if you hadn't done what you did."

"He wanted to stop."

"They can't stop, Tildie. No, not that way. To your left."

35

"Aren't we going to bury him alongside Grandma Yount?"

"No," she said. "That's too near the house. We'll dig his grave across the stream, where the walnut grove is."

"It's beautiful there."

"You always liked it."

"So did Dan," I said. I felt so funny, so light-headed. My world was turned upside down and yet it felt safe, it felt solid. I thought how Dan had itched to cut down those walnut trees. Now he'd lie forever at their feet, and I could come back here whenever I wanted to feel close to him.

"But he'll be lonely here," I said. "Won't he? Mama, won't he?"

The walnut trees lose their leaves early in the fall, and they put on less of a color show than the other hardwoods. But I like to come to the grove even when the trees are bare. Sometimes I bring Livia. More often I come by myself.

I always liked it here. I love our whole 220 acres, every square foot of it, but this is my favorite place, among these trees. I like it even better than the graveyard over by the pear and apple orchard. Where the graves have stones, and where the women and children of our family are buried.

Jeremiah Healy has written a number of keenly observed, pithy stories about police and Private Investigators alike. Winner of the Edgar for short fiction, author of a growing list of novels, he and his protagonist, Cuddy, obviously know their way around the high and the low of Boston. In this story from *Cat Crimes II,* he spins an unexpected tale. Red Sox fans might call it a pitchout.

The Winfield Trade
JEREMIAH HEALY

ONE

Venetia Scott said, "Slow down a bit and take this next right."

I looked over to her. "Much farther?"

She shook her head. "Not more than a mile now. I really *do* appreciate your driving me from work, Mr. Cuddy."

My new client said it like she was thanking a waiter for bringing her an extra cocktail napkin. About five-five and mid-thirties, Scott looked trim in a gray herringbone suit with a ruffled white blouse and two-inch heels. Her face was thin, but she had big green eyes and generous lips and auburn hair drawn back into a bun that hinted at shoulder length once loosened.

Scott had called me at my office. A lawyer who represented her bank in major loan deals had recommended me as a private investigator who could be trusted on a confidential matter. I told her I'd call her back, then dialed the lawyer. Venetia Scott had checked out as a recently promoted vice-president in charge of computer lease agreements for one of the few Boston financial institutions still taking nourishment without government receivership. I'd picked her up just fifteen minutes ago outside one of the bank's branches, filling up the time more with small talk than business as she gave me directions to her home address.

"Ms. Scott, I take it whatever you want me to work on has to do with your house?"

"It does."

"Just what, exactly?"

My client took a deep breath. "Beginning about a month ago, someone has been staying there while I've been away on weekends."

It was Thursday as we were talking. "How do you know?"

"Little things. And feelings. I'm *very* sensitive that way."

Jesus. "Do you live alone?"

An icy tone. "What difference does that make?"

"What I mean is, could somebody else in the house be responsible?"

"No. Since my divorce, I live alone except for Winfield."

"Winfield?"

"My cat."

I smiled. "Named after Dave?"

"I beg your pardon?"

"Dave Winfield. Yankee outfielder who was unhappy in New York, moved to a couple of other teams since."

The icy tone again. "Winfield is not named after an *athlete*. He is named after Winfield Scott, a general in the Mexican-American War. I'm a traceable descendant."

"Oh."

The cat turned out to be a tubby orange tabby with yellow eyes and long whiskers. He was affectionate enough, brushing against my pant cuffs and purring like a snoring lumberjack when I scratched between his ears.

We were in the foyer of Scott's modest Cape Cod, the smallest house in a good neighborhood. A terrific investment in the mid-eighties, it was probably holding its value as well as could be expected now. I'd checked the front door on our way in. No sign of forced entry.

Scott walked me through a living room with colonial furniture, including an old-fashioned slider chair, to a kitchen extended via a deck into the backyard. The back door lock and jamb looked fine, too.

"You keep your windows locked?"

"Always."

"Security system?"

"No."

I stepped out onto the deck and looked left, then right. Each bordering house was nestled on about an acre, hers only a half-acre by the looks of the landscaping that acted as boundary lines.

"Neighbors?"

Scott pointed left. "That place has been empty for three months. Foreclosure, but not by my bank." She swung right. "The couple on the other side have been in Florida for six weeks. Which is my point, really."

"Your point?"

"Yes. If someone simply wanted to break into a house and occupy it like a *squatter,* there are better choices within easy reach. No, Mr. Cuddy, this is harassment."

"Harassment."

"Yes. Subtle, but clear."

"Could you share some of the subtleties with me?"

A labored sigh. "Toilet paper roll just *slightly* out of kilter."

I looked down at Winfield, who had followed us from room to room. "Maybe the cat, toying with it?"

The icy tone a third time. "Water glasses rinsed and dried, leaving no spots. Forks placed in drawer tines down rather than tines up."

"Forks."

"I beg your—"

"Forks plural, or just one each time?"

"Just one."

"Same for glasses?"

"Yes."

We moved back into the living room. "You think it's harassment, you must have somebody in mind."

"*Three* somebodies. Do you wish to take notes?"

I sat down in the slider chair. Comfortable and silent.

Scott used her left hand to tick off names on her right, as though she were vigorously polishing her nails. "First, Chris Murphy, my ex-husband. He's a police officer in the next town."

Uh-oh. "He still have a set of keys to this place?"

"No. The locks have been changed twice."

"Twice?"

"Yes. Once after the judge ordered him out during the divorce three years ago, and again five weeks ago."

"Just before you noticed the 'subtle harassment.' "

"Exactly. That brings me to the second—what would you call it, 'suspect'?"

"The second person will do fine."

"Second is Luther Dane, my assistant at the bank. I lost my keys at work, which was the reason I had the locks changed again. Luther would have access to my new key."

"This Dane have any motive?"

"Yes. He would love to see me foul up due to pressure here so that he could get my job."

"Is that realistic?"

"It's how I got *my* promotion."

"By forcing out a boss?"

"Precisely. Which brings us to number three, Irene Presker."

"Your former boss."

A nod. "I'm sure she has it in for me after I nudged her out."

I found myself rooting for Presker but fought it. "She have access to your keys?"

"Not that I know of."

"Who was the locksmith this last time?"

A wave of the hand. "A nice man, got on *famously* with Winfield. Vietnamese, I think. He came by to change the locks on a Friday just as I was leaving."

"And the next week, the live-in stuff began happening."

"The next weekend."

"Why is it that you go away weekends, Ms. Scott?"

She glanced involuntarily toward a shelf on the wall. I could see a framed photo of Scott in casual clothes, hugging a handsome man of about fifty with gray hair that looked carefully styled even in the breeze that lifted it.

My client said, "I'm seeing a man who's allergic to cat dander, so I spend weekends at his home."

"Name?"

"I don't want you approaching him."

"I'd just like his name in case it comes up."

"Evan Speidel."

I looked at the photo again and took a guess. "Also in banking?"

"Yes. He'll be the next president of Ridgeview Savings and Loan, a *solid* institution."

Scott put more into "solid" than I could have with a hammer.

"Speidel have a key to your house?"

The icy tone got glacial. "I keep a spare at his home."

I glanced down at the cat. "Why not just give Winfield away?"

My client glared at me. "I bought him for Chris originally, but Winfield stayed with me as part of the divorce settlement."

I chewed on that awhile.

"If you're thinking that Evan has anything to do with this, forget it."

Actually, I was thinking that Venetia Scott might have been better off with the cop that liked cats than the banker who couldn't, but I kept it to myself.

TWO

On Friday morning I got up early and went over the addresses Venetia Scott had given me. Then I drove to the downtown area nearest her house.

The sign over the glass door said MAIN STREET LOCKSMITH in tin-type. The walls of the six-by-seven shop were lined with brass knobs and sturdy plates and imposing deadbolts. A skinny man with Southeast Asian features sat behind a steel counter with an English-language newspaper open in front of him. His black hair hung over his forehead almost to his eyebrows, and he worked a bony index finger one word at a time through a column that had the phrase "Khmer Rouge" in its headline. Behind him, purple beads, strung vertically on wire, curtained entry to the back of the shop. The beads shimmered a little as I closed the front door.

The man looked up at me, smiled and said, "Can I help, sir?"

I said, "Mr. . . ."

"Hun is my name."

I showed him my ID. He looked at it a long time, reading "John Francis Cuddy" as carefully as he had the newspaper.

"What you want?"

I pocketed the leather holder and explained that I was asking questions for Venetia Scott.

Hun's eyes grew wary. "Ms. Scott?"

"Yes."

"What is problem?"

"No problem for you. I'd just like to ask you a few questions."

Hun looked resigned. "Ask."

I pointed at the article he'd been reading. "You're from Cambodia originally?"

"Why that matter?"

"No reason, except you're reading an article about the Khmer Rouge."

Hun's jaw clenched. "I no need to read about Khmer Rouge. I live through Khmer Rouge. In Phnom Penh, then in camp, then in jungle." He stabbed the paper with the tip of his finger. "Newspaper used to say two million people kill by Pol Pot. Now say only one million. How can this be?"

I didn't have an answer for him. "You changed the locks at Ms. Scott's house?"

"Yes, I do that for her."

"Anybody ever ask you for keys to the house?"

Hun's eyes widened. "Ask me?"

"Yes."

"Nobody."

I went through the names I had, including the new boyfriend, Evan Speidel. Hun shook his head no, the eyes stony at each one. I got the feeling that other interrogators hadn't treated him so well in the past.

"Anyone else here I could talk to?"

Hun's eyes went back down to the article. "Is nobody else. Only me."

Chris Murphy, about six-two and two hundred pounds, looked like a surfer who was losing his dishwater blond hair. And his temper at me.

"Cuddy, I don't get why you're asking me all these questions."

"I'm hired to ask questions. These are simple ones."

"Simple, huh? Like am I harassing my ex-wife and you won't even tell me what I'm supposed to be doing?"

I'd called Murphy at police headquarters in the neighboring town, then waited for him outside, as he'd asked me to. We were standing next to a dented, five-year-old Corvette that I took to be his car. Murphy had his arms crossed, beefy hands working on the outside of his sport coat.

"Murphy—"

"I mean, what the hell position am I in with the department, I get accused of harassing my ex, this day and age?"

"So you haven't been in any kind of contact with Venetia Scott."

"No, I told you. Not her, not the bank, not the house. Not since the restraining order way back when."

I hadn't mentioned the house.

Murphy said, "You think I'm nuts or something, a cop violating a re- straining order?"

I didn't think he was nuts. I did wonder how he and Venetia Scott ever got together, but I wasn't sure I wanted to find out.

"Seen your cat lately?"

"My—Winfield? Hell, that little bugger still around?"

"How do you mean?"

"Aw, Venny, she never cared much one way or the other for the cat. Just like another pawn in the chess game between her lawyer and me."

"Because you wanted him back?"

Murphy looked exasperated. "Cuddy, she held onto him because I made her *think* I wanted him back."

"Why would you do that?"

"So I could get what *I* wanted, like this car, some other stuff to set myself up in a new place."

"While she got the house."

"Right, right. Hell, it was like a negotiating tactic on my part. What do you think, I'm stupid?"

I let that one pass, too.

Irene Presker had answered her own telephone and now answered her own door. The condo complex was a nice one, low and by the sea about eight miles south of Boston. From the parking lot, I'd seen a little skyline through the smog in the distance and a couple of playful sailboats through the mist in the foreground.

Presker, however, did not look playful herself. About five feet tall, she was pushing a hundred fifty, mostly through the hips and thighs. Her hair was curly and too black to be natural, the make-up overdone considering she was apparently working at home that day.

Staring at my ID, Presker said, "Which would be easier for me, to talk with you or call the cops?"

"Calling the cops, definitely."

The hint of a grin. "You're really a private investigator?"

"Really and truly."

"All right, come in."

The living room was a little box without fireplace or harbor view, a small, open kitchen cloistered with it. A corridor ran off in one direction toward two closed doors, I assumed a bedroom and a bath. Presker took one barrel chair, me the other, there not being space enough for couch or even loveseat.

"So, what's this about?"

"A former associate of yours is being harassed. Your name came up."

"I'm supposed to know something about 'a former associate' being harassed?"

"That's what I'm here to find out."

"Hah. You wasted your gas. The only one I could . . ." Presker's eyes did grow playful. "Not Venetia Scott?"

"Yes."

"There is a God. I must thank Him."

"Ms. Presker—"

"So, is Venny going nuts?"

Venny. The nickname her ex-husband had used. "You're not even curious about what the harassment is?"

"Not unless it's really awful. I'd rather use my imagination."

"Why so down on Scott?"

"Down. Down, now there's a great word for Venny. Put down, shut down, shot down. Lots of possibilities there."

"Possibilities?"

"For who's harassing her. Let me tell you something about your client, Mr. Cuddy. Venny, basically speaking, is a witch. An absolute witch. She begged me to take her on as my assistant at the bank, and her resumé wasn't in the personnel folder before she was laying the groundwork to replace me. Venny sucked up to people, slept with people, whatever it took. Oh, yeah, one other thing, too. She really did master the job."

"Which is?"

"Doing loan papers on complicated computer leases. You know the jargon?"

"None of it."

"Then I'll spare you. Just figure that she can understand complicated relationships, technical and financial, then protect the bank as to them."

"And you taught her?"

"That's right."

"And now she's in your office in a downtown skyscraper and you're working out of your house."

"Oh, but I'm con-*sult*-ing." A thick layer of sarcasm coated Presker's voice. "My own *home* office. It's really much *so* much more meaningful and satisfying than a *mere* salary and stock options."

It took me a minute to appreciate that Presker was lampooning Scott's speech patterns.

"Anything you can tell me about who might be after her?"

Presker laughed, not a pleasant sound. "Try the guy who replaced her. Maybe he's learning at the witch's knee."

Luther Dane was a young black man with horn-rimmed glasses. I met him sitting at a desk outside Venetia Scott's office in the skyscraper. He looked studious in a blue suit, white button-down shirt and quiet tie. At least until he started talking. Then he both looked and sounded studious.

"I don't have any idea what could be behind this, Mr. Cuddy."

Scott was at a meeting, so Dane and I had moved into her office, a nice view of the beige and gray airport and a verdant harbor island through a window that I was sure couldn't be opened. Dane had taken Scott's desk chair without seeming to think about it. I tried one of the captain's chairs, my shoulders covering the emblem of a local business school emblazoned on the backrest.

"No reason for anyone you know of to be harassing Ms. Scott?"

"Venetia Scott is a warm and wonderful human being."

Dane's words would have sounded fine to a bug planted in the office. His face and body language told a different story, like a Mideast hostage giving a canned television interview.

"You're not interested in scaring her out of her job?"

"Ms. V. Scott does not scare."

"Rattle her then. Enough so she starts to make mistakes here at work."

"Her mistakes would be looked upon as my mistakes, too."

"Not if you created the record correctly."

Dane smiled. "Law school, Mr. Cuddy?"

"A year, nights. You?"

"Four years, nights. Worked long and hard to get this far. I'm not about to pollute my own well."

"So, if you're not interested in scaring or rattling your boss, how do you plan to get ahead?"

"By outworking her. Her and anybody else I'm competing with."

"And you figure you can outwork Ms. Scott."

"The way she's spending her weekends? You bet."

I hadn't said anything about weekends. "How's that?"

"Her weekends, man. She's spending them somewhere else."

"How do you know?"

Dane spread his hands wide, encompassing Scott's office. "Because I come in every Saturday and half a day on Sunday, Mr. Cuddy. I'm here, and she isn't, and that means she's off somewhere."

"Like at her house?"

"Not when I try to reach her there."

"Why would you try to do that?"

Dane shrugged. "Even on weekends, questions come up that I'm not good enough to answer."

"Yet."

Just a smile.

THREE

After speaking with Luther Dane, I didn't wait for Venetia Scott to come back from her meeting. Instead I got my car out of hock at the parking garage next to the bank and drove to the suburban town where Ridgeview Savings and Loan had its offices.

I sat outside the red-bricked and gold-domed building for an hour before being rewarded by the appearance of Evan Speidel. He shook two sets of hands on his way from the main entrance to a black Lincoln Continental. Inside the Lincoln, Speidel drove sedately about three miles to a butcher block and ferns saloon just off a busy mall. I parked three slanting rows away from his car and followed him into the restaurant.

When he shook a few more hands and took a table, I slid onto a stool at the bar, the mirror above the top shelf bottles allowing me to watch Speidel in reflection. After a waiter presented him with a *Wall Street Journal* to skim, a cocktail waitress brought him what looked like a dry manhattan without his having to order it. He glanced up a couple of times, like a man watching for someone to join him.

Someone did.

Irene Presker swooshed through the place, still made up but now dressed like Venetia Scott had been in bankers' tweeds. Speidel took one of Presker's hands in both of his as greeting. Then they sat down across from each other and began talking. I couldn't see any way of getting out of there without her spotting me, so I sat still and nursed a beer.

They talked through a drink and lunch and were about to order dessert when Presker caught me out of the corner of her eye. She barely paused, covering it with a palm-up gesture to support her chins. Waving off coffee, the consultant waited until Speidel covered the tab by signing for it, then shook hands goodbye with him as he moved toward the exit and she toward the rest rooms.

Presker made sure Speidel was gone before reversing direction and steaming up to the bar. "What's the idea of following me?"

"Maybe I didn't believe everything I heard at your condo."

"Does that mean you have to give me a heart attack in the middle of an interview?"

"Interview?"

"The man who just left is—"

Presker stopped, but I hadn't interrupted her.

I said, "Who is he?"

She tapped a stubby finger on my left arm. "He left before I did, but he was here before I was. I would have noticed you taking this stool if you came in after me. That means you were here before me." Presker looked playful again. "And that means that either you've tapped my phone, in which case you wouldn't have bothered covering this little meeting, or you're following my lunch date. But why?"

I got up before telling Presker anything else, feeling my client might be a little disappointed in me.

I sat in my car until Irene Presker came out. She noticed me, as I'd hoped she would, but just blew me a kiss, which meant I wasn't fooling her at all.

I started up and drove back toward the city, thinking as best I could. Chris Murphy might have intimidated Hun the locksmith into giving him the new key to Venetia Scott's house. Murphy also could have used a skeleton master from his department, but where was his motive three years after the divorce? Luther Dane could have lifted the new key sometime at work, had it copied, and returned it before Scott realized it was missing, but he really didn't seem to think he needed to reduce his boss to supplant her. Irene

Presker might have gotten the spare key to the house from Evan Speidel, in which case her bluff at the bar was one for the record books. Speidel might be able to slip away from Scott on one of their weekends at his place, but why go to her place to do, essentially, nothing?

Shaking my head, I focused on the traffic. At least I knew where that was going.

Luther Dane's voice said, "Ms. Scott's office."
I said, "May I speak with her?"
"I'll see, Mr. Cuddy."
Good at recognizing voices, Mr. Dane.
"Venetia Scott."
"Can Dane hear us?"
"No."
"You're positive?"
"Yes. What is it?"
"Given that it's Friday, are you going to Speidel's place?"
"Yes. Why?"
"I have an idea."

It was something I'd hoped I could avoid. Solo, you can't really watch a house completely from the street or the back or the sides. Short of a high perch, there are just too many blind spots created by the building itself. But, owner willing, you can cover it pretty thoroughly from one place.

Inside it.

In the dark, I sat on the slider in the living room, Winfield curled up on my lap. I'd paced off the strides to both front and back doors. The slider was almost exactly equidistant from each.

It was barely eight o'clock when I heard something at the back door. Winfield jumped off my lap and did his rotund best to scamper out there. I moved to the wall by the kitchen, hoping I wasn't going to need a weapon. I heard the faint sound of the door opening, then closing, then nothing.

I waited five seconds. Then ten. At fifteen, I went into the kitchen.

Nobody. Not even Winfield.

I looked out the windows, but didn't see anything. I went back to the living room and sank into the slider. I thought about it, then thought some more. About what I'd told people, and what I hadn't told them.

And eventually I believed I saw it.

I knocked on the door to the mini-mansion a second time. Evan Speidel opened it. He was wearing a silk robe that probably cost more than my rent.

"Yes?" Nice baritone voice, too.

"I need to speak with Venetia Scott."

47

"At this hour?"

"Tell her it's John Cuddy."

The door closed in my face. Two minutes later, Scott reopened it.

Her robe matched Speidel's, her auburn hair indeed tumbling onto her shoulders. "This had better be important."

I stepped inside the house. "It won't take long. There's bad news and good news."

"What's the bad news?"

"I think we've lost Winfield."

I heard Speidel chuckle from the other room, but Scott's face stayed neutral. "That I can live with, I guess. What's the good news?"

"If you'll trust me to guarantee that it's over, I can end it tonight, nobody getting hurt or in trouble."

The executive in Scott stiffened. "Guaranteed?"

"Absolutely. But I keep everything I've learned to myself."

My client took ten seconds to weigh that. "Do it."

This time I kept knocking until a shadow loomed in the weak light behind the purple beads. Hun's head peered out, shook, then came forward slowly with the rest of his body as he let me into the shop.

I said, "Where's the cat?"

He thought about toughing it out, then said, "In the back. Where I live."

"Tied up?"

Hun gave me a derisive look and spat out a word I didn't understand. Winfield came running, slowed only a little by the bead curtain, most of which he could get under. He regarded me but cuddled up to Hun.

The locksmith said, "How you know it was me?"

"The other people I talked to, the other names I asked you about, I didn't tell any of them the problem had something to do with Ms. Scott's house."

Hun shook his head. "That is not enough."

"No, but Scott said you really liked the cat. And at her house only the smallest things were disturbed, like someone was visiting, not intimidating."

I stopped, but Hun nodded.

I said, "Only the things you would need to give him food and yourself water and relief."

"I like to give him food. I like to visit him."

"And based on what I told you, you might miss the chance to see him again."

"You tell me problem with house, maybe problem with locks. Maybe Ms. Scott not use me next time to change locks. Maybe I cannot see Winfield again without break in."

"Which you didn't want to do."

"I am locksmith! I do not break in houses!"

"But you'd risk your business to see the cat."

Hun reached down to stroke Winfield's head. "I lose my whole family, Khmer Rouge. This cat only creature all United States nice to me."

"So you were willing to trade your profession for being able to have him."

The stony look. "Yes."

"Ever hear of Dave Winfield?"

"Who?"

"Skip it."

Bill Pronzini's novels and short stories have won him awards and respect in mystery fiction. His "Nameless Detective" is justly famous; in addition to solo work he collaborates, most notably with Marcia Muller, whose work is also represented here.

In this story from the pages of *Ellery Queen's Mystery Magazine,* Pronzini offers up a short, sharp dose of reality for the reader: one is put in mind of the clarity and bite of *Strangers on a Train* . . . both that piece and this one are chilling, plausible tales of memorably clever and dangerous characters.

Liar's Dice
BILL PRONZINI

"Excuse me. Do you play liar's dice?"

I looked over at the man two stools to my right. He was about my age, early forties; average height, average weight, brown hair, medium complexion —really a pretty nondescript sort except for a pleasant and disarming smile. Expensively dressed in an Armani suit and a silk jacquard tie. Drinking white wine. I had never seen him before. Or had I? There was something familiar about him, as if our paths *had* crossed somewhere or other, once or twice.

Not here in Tony's, though. Tony's is a suburban-mall bar that caters to the shopping trade from the big department and grocery stores surrounding it. I stopped in no more than a couple of times a month, usually when Connie asked me to pick up something at Safeway on my way home from San Francisco, occasionally when I had a Saturday errand to run. I knew the few regulars by sight, and it was never very crowded anyway. There were only four patrons at the moment: the nondescript gent and myself on stools, and a young couple in a booth at the rear.

"I do play, as a matter of fact," I said to the fellow. Fairly well too, though I wasn't about to admit that. Liar's dice and I were old acquaintances.

"Would you care to shake for a drink?"

"Well, my usual limit is one . . ."

"For a chit for your next visit, then."

"All right, why not? I feel lucky tonight."

"Do you? Good. I should warn you, I'm very good at the game."

"I'm not so bad myself."

"No, I mean I'm *very* good. I seldom lose."

It was the kind of remark that would have nettled me if it had been said with even a modicum of conceit. But he wasn't bragging; he was merely stating a fact, mentioning a special skill of which he felt justifiably proud. So instead of annoying me, his comment made me eager to test him.

We introduced ourselves; his name was Jones. Then I called to Tony for the dice cups. He brought them down, winked at me, said, "No gambling now," and went back to the other end of the bar. Strictly speaking, shaking dice for drinks and/or money is illegal in California. But nobody pays much attention to nuisance laws like that, and most bar owners keep dice cups on hand for their customers. The game stimulates business. I know because I've been involved in some spirited liar's dice tournaments in my time.

Like all good games, liar's dice is fairly simple—at least in its rules. Each player has a cup containing five dice, which he shakes out but keeps covered so only he can see what is showing face up. Then each makes a declaration or "call" in turn: one of a kind, two of a kind, three of a kind, and so on. Each call has to be higher than the previous one, and is based on what the player *knows* is in his hand and what he *thinks* is in the other fellow's—the combined total of the ten dice. He can lie or tell the truth, whichever suits him; but the better liar he is, the better his chances of winning. When one player decides the other is either lying or has simply exceeded the laws of probability, he says, "Come up," and then both reveal their hands. If he's right, he wins.

In addition to being a clever liar, you also need a good grasp of mathematical odds and the ability to "read" your opponent's facial expressions, the inflection in his voice, his body language. The same skills an experienced poker player has to have, which is one reason the game is also called liar's poker.

Jones and I each rolled one die to determine who would go first; mine was the highest. Then we shook all five dice in our cups, banged them down on the bar. What I had showing was four treys and a deuce.

"Your call, Mr. Quint."

"One five," I said.

"One six."

"Two deuces."

"Two fives."

"Three treys."

"Three sixes."

I considered calling him up, since I had no sixes and he would need three showing to win. But I didn't know his methods and I couldn't read him at all. I decided to keep playing.

"Four treys."

"Five treys."

"Six treys."

Jones smiled and said, "Come up." And he had just one trey (and no sixes). I'd called six treys and there were only five in our combined hands; he was the winner.

"So much for feeling lucky," I said, and signaled Tony to bring another white wine for Mr. Jones. On impulse I decided a second Manhattan wouldn't hurt me and ordered that too.

Jones said, "Shall we play again?"

"Two drinks is definitely my limit."

"For dimes, then? Nickels or pennies, if you prefer."

"Oh, I don't know . . ."

"You're a good player, Mr. Quint, and I don't often find someone who can challenge me. Besides, I have a passion as well as an affinity for liar's dice. Won't you indulge me?"

I didn't see any harm in it. If he'd wanted to play for larger stakes, even a dollar a hand, I might have taken him for a hustler despite his Armani suit and silk tie. But how much could you win or lose playing for a nickel or a dime a hand? So I said, "Your call first this time," and picked up my dice cup.

We played for better than half an hour. And Jones wasn't just good; he was uncanny. Out of nearly twenty-five hands, I won two—*two*. You could chalk up some of the disparity to luck, but not enough to change the fact that his skill was remarkable. Certainly he was the best I'd ever locked horns with. I would have backed him in a tournament anywhere, anytime.

He was a good winner, too: no gloating or chiding. And a good listener, the sort who seems genuinely (if superficially) interested in other people. I'm not often gregarious, especially with strangers, but I found myself opening up to Jones—and this in spite of him beating the pants off me the whole time.

I told him about Connie, how we met and the second honeymoon trip we'd taken to Lake Louise three years ago and what we were planning for our twentieth wedding anniversary in August. I told him about Lisa, who was eighteen and a freshman studying film at UCLA. I told him about Kevin, sixteen now and captain of his high-school baseball team, and the five-hit, two home run game he'd had last week. I told him what it was like working as a design engineer for one of the largest engineering firms in the country, the nagging dissatisfaction and the desire to be my own boss someday, when I had enough money saved so I could afford to take the risk. I told him about remodeling our home, the boat I was thinking of buying, the fact that I'd always wanted to try hang-gliding but never had the courage.

Lord knows what else I might have told him if I hadn't noticed the polite but faintly bored expression on his face, as if I were imparting facts he already knew. It made me realize just how much I'd been nattering on, and embarrassed me a bit. I've never liked people who talk incessantly about themselves, as though they're the focal point of the entire universe. I can be a good listener myself; and for all I knew, Jones was a lot more interesting than bland Jeff Quint.

I said, "Well, that's more than enough about me. It's your turn, Jones. Tell me about yourself."

"If you like, Mr. Quint." Still very formal. I'd told him a couple of times to call me Jeff but he wouldn't do it. Now that I thought about it, he hadn't mentioned his own first name.

"What is it you do?"

He laid his dice cup to one side. I was relieved to see that; I'd had enough of losing but I hadn't wanted to be the one to quit. And it was getting late—dark outside already—and Connie would be wondering where I was. A few minutes of listening to the story of his life, I thought, just to be polite, and then—

"To begin with," Jones was saying, "I travel."

"Sales job?"

"No. I travel because I enjoy traveling. And because I can afford it. I have independent means."

"Lucky you. In more ways than one."

"Yes."

"Europe, the South Pacific—all the exotic places?"

"Actually, no. I prefer the U.S."

"Any particular part?"

"Wherever my fancy leads me."

"Hard to imagine anyone's fancy leading him to Bayport," I said. "You have friends or relatives here?"

"No, I have business in Bayport."

"Business? I thought you said you didn't need to work. . . ."

"Independent means, Mr. Quint. That doesn't preclude a purpose, a direction in one's life."

"You do have a profession, then?"

"You might say that. A profession and a hobby combined."

"Lucky you," I said again. "What is it?"

"I kill people," he said.

I thought I'd misheard him. "You . . . what?"

"I kill people."

"Good God. Is that supposed to be a joke?"

"Not at all. I'm quite serious."

"What do you mean, you *kill* people?"

"Just what I said."

"Are you trying to tell me you're . . . some kind of paid assassin?"

"Not at all. I've never killed anyone for money."

"Then why . . . ?"

"Can't you guess?"

"No, I can't guess. I don't want to guess."

"Call it personal satisfaction," he said.

"What people? Who?"

"No one in particular," Jones said. "My selection process is completely random. I'm very good at it too. I've been killing people for . . . let's see, nine and a half years now. Eighteen victims in thirteen states. And, oh yes, Puerto Rico—one in Puerto Rico. I don't mind saying that I've never even come close to being caught."

I stared at him. My mouth was open; I knew it but I couldn't seem to unlock my jaw. I felt as if reality had suddenly slipped away from me, as if Tony had dropped some sort of mind-altering drug into my second Manhattan and it was just now taking effect. Jones and I were still sitting companionably, on adjacent stools now, he smiling and speaking in the same low, friendly voice. At the other end of the bar Tony was slicing lemons and limes into wedges. Three of the booths were occupied now, with people laughing and enjoying themselves. Everything was just as it had been two minutes ago, except that instead of me telling Jones about being a dissatisfied design engineer, he was calmly telling me he was a serial murderer.

I got my mouth shut finally, just long enough to swallow into a dry throat. Then I said, "You're crazy, Jones. You must be insane."

"Hardly, Mr. Quint. I'm as sane as you are."

"I don't believe you killed eighteen people."

"Nineteen," he said. "Soon to be twenty."

"Twenty? You mean . . . someone in Bayport?"

"Right here in Bayport."

"You expect me to believe you intend to pick somebody at random and just . . . murder him in cold blood?"

"Oh no, there's more to it than that. Much more."

"More?" I said blankly.

"I choose a person at random, yes, but carefully. Very carefully. I study my target, follow him as he goes about his daily business, learn everything I can about him down to the minutest detail. Then the cat and mouse begins. I don't murder him right away; that wouldn't give sufficient, ah, satisfaction. I wait . . . observe . . . plan. Perhaps, for added spice, I reveal myself to him. I might even be so bold as to tell him to his face that he's my next victim."

My scalp began to crawl.

"Days, weeks . . . then, when the victim least expects it, a gunshot, a push out of nowhere in front of an oncoming car, a hypodermic filled with digitalin and jabbed into the body on a crowded street, simulating heart failure. There are many ways to kill a man. Did you ever stop to consider just how many different ways there are?"

"You . . . you're not saying—"

"What, Mr. Quint? That I've chosen *you?*"

"Jones, for God's sake!"

"But I have," he said. "You are to be number twenty."

One of my hands jerked upward, struck his arm. Involuntary spasm; I'm not a violent man. He didn't even flinch. I pulled my hand back, saw that it was shaking, and clutched the fingers tight around the beveled edge of the bar.

Jones took a sip of wine. Then he smiled—and winked at me.

"Or then again," he said, "I might be lying."

". . . What?"

"Everything I've just told you might be a lie. I might not have killed nineteen people over the past nine and a half years; I might not have killed anyone, ever."

"I don't . . . I don't know what you—"

"Or I might have told you part of the truth . . . that's another possibility, isn't it? Part fact, part fiction. But in that case, which is which? And to what degree? Am I a deadly threat to you, or am I nothing more than a man in a bar playing a game?"

"Game? What kind of sick—"

"The same one we've been playing all along. Liar's dice."

"Liar's dice?"

"My own special version," he said, "developed and refined through years of practice. The perfect form of the game, if I do say so myself—exciting, unpredictable, filled with intrigue and mortal danger for myself as well as my opponent."

I shook my head. My mind was a seething muddle; I couldn't seem to fully grasp what he was saying.

"I don't know any more than you do at this moment how you'll play your part of the hand, Mr. Quint. That's where the excitement and the danger lies. Will you treat what I've said as you would a bluff? Can you afford to take that risk? Or will you act on the assumption that I've told the monstrous truth, or at least part of it?"

"Damn you . . ." Weak and ineffectual words, even in my own ears.

"And if you do believe me," he said, "what course of action will you take? Attack me before I can harm you, attempt to kill me . . . here and now in this public place, perhaps, in front of witnesses who will swear the attack was unprovoked? Try to follow me when I leave, attack me elsewhere? I might well be armed, and an excellent shot with a handgun. Go to the police . . . with a wild-sounding and unsubstantiated story that they surely wouldn't believe?

Hire a detective to track me down? Attempt to track me down yourself? Jones isn't my real name, of course, and I've taken precautions against anyone finding out my true identity. Arm yourself and remain on guard until, if and when, I make a move against you? How long could you live under such intense pressure without making a fatal mistake?"

He paused dramatically. "Or—and this is the most exciting prospect of all, the one I hope you choose—will you mount a clever counterattack, composed of lies and deceptions of your own devising? Can you actually hope to beat me at my own game? Do you dare to try?"

He adjusted the knot in his tie with quick, deft movements, smiling at me in the back-bar mirror—not the same pleasant smile as before. This one had shark's teeth in it. "Whatever you do, I'll know about it soon afterward. I'll be waiting . . . watching . . . and I'll know. And then it will be my turn again."

He slid off his stool, stood poised behind me. I just sat there; it was as if I were paralyzed.

"Your call, Mr. Quint," he said. And he was gone into the night.

Acclaimed on both sides of the Atlantic, winner of multiple Edgars and Silver Daggers, Ruth Rendell has, both under her own name and as Barbara Vine, been writing superlative novels and short fiction for years. In the following story a feline proves to be the object of obsession . . . and the focus of a most difficult negotiation, one which devolves into an outright power struggle.

Long Live the Queen
RUTH RENDELL

It was over in an instant. A flash of orange out of the green hedge, a streak across the road, a thud. The impact was felt as a surprisingly heavy jarring. There was no cry. Anna had braked, but too late and the car had been going fast. She pulled in to the side of the road, got out, walked back.

An effort was needed before she could look. The cat had been flung against the grass verge which separated road from narrow walkway. It was dead. She knew before she knelt down and felt its side that it was dead. A little blood came from its mouth. Its eyes were already glazing. It had been a fine cat of the kind called marmalade because the color is two-tone, the stripes like dark slices of peel among the clear orange. Paws, chest, and part of its face were white, the eyes gooseberry green.

It was an unfamiliar road, one she had only taken to avoid roadworks on the bridge. Anna thought, I was going too fast. There is no speed limit here but it's a country road with cottages and I shouldn't have been going so fast. The poor cat. Now she must go and admit what she had done, confront an angry or distressed owner, an owner who presumably lived in the house behind that hedge.

She opened the gate and went up the path. It was a cottage, but not a pretty one: of red brick with a low slate roof, bay windows downstairs with a green front door between them. In each bay window sat a cat, one black, one orange and white like the cat which had run in front of her car. They stared at her, unblinking, inscrutable, as if they did not see her, as if she was not there. She could still see the black one when she was at the front door. When she put her finger to the bell and rang it, the cat did not move, nor even blink its eyes.

No one came to the door. She rang the bell again. It occurred to her that the owner might be in the back garden and she walked round the side of the house. It wasn't really a garden but a wilderness of long grass and tall weeds and wild trees. There was no one. She looked through a window into a kitchen where a tortoiseshell cat sat on top of the fridge in the sphinx position and on the floor, on a strip of matting, a brown tabby rolled sensuously, its striped paws stroking the air.

There were no cats outside as far as she could see, not living ones at least. In the left-hand corner, past a kind of lean-to coalshed and a clump of bushes, three small wooden crosses were just visible among the long grass. Anna had no doubt they were cat graves.

She looked in her bag and, finding a hairdresser's appointment card, wrote on the blank back of it her name, her parents' address and their phone number, and added, *Your cat ran out in front of my car. I'm sorry, I'm sure death was instantaneous.* Back at the front door, the black cat and the orange-and-white cat still staring out, she put the card through the letter box.

It was then that she looked in the window where the black cat was sitting. Inside was a small overfurnished living room which looked as if it smelt. Two cats lay on the hearthrug, two more were curled up together in an armchair. At either end of the mantelpiece sat a china cat, white and red with gilt whiskers. Anna thought there ought to have been another one between them, in the center of the shelf, because this was the only clear space in the room, every other corner and surface being crowded with objects, many of which had some association with the feline: cat ashtrays, cat vases, photographs of cats in silver frames, postcards of cats, mugs with cat faces on them, and ceramic, brass, silver, and glass kittens. Above the fireplace was a portrait of a marmalade-and-white cat done in oils and on the wall to the left hung a cat calendar.

Anna had an uneasy feeling that the cat in the portrait was the one that lay dead in the road. At any rate, it was very like. She could not leave the dead cat where it was. In the boot of her car were two plastic carrier bags, some sheets of newspaper, and a blanket she sometimes used for padding things she didn't want to strike against each other while she was driving. As wrapping for the cat's body, the plastic bags would look callous, the newspapers worse. She would sacrifice the blanket. It was a clean dark-blue blanket, single size, quite decent and decorous.

The cat's body wrapped in this blanket, she carried it up the path. The black cat had moved from the left-hand bay and had taken up a similar position in one of the upstairs windows. Anna took another look into the living room. A second examination of the portrait confirmed her guess that its subject was the one she was carrying. She backed away. The black cat stared down at her, turned its head, and yawned hugely. Of course it did not know she carried one of its companions, dead and now cold, wrapped in an old car blanket, having met a violent death. She had an uncomfortable feeling, a ridiculous feeling, that it would have behaved in precisely the same way if it had known.

She laid the cat's body on the roof of the coalshed. As she came back round the house, she saw a woman in the garden next door. This was a neat and tidy garden with flowers and a lawn. The woman was in her fifties, white-haired, slim, wearing a twin set.

"One of the cats ran out in front of my car," Anna said. "I'm afraid it's dead."

"Oh, dear."

"I've put the—body, the body on the coalshed. Do you know when they'll be back?"

"It's just her," the woman said. "It's just her on her own."

"Oh, well. I've written a note for her. With my name and address."

The woman was giving her an odd look. "You're very honest. Most would have just driven on. You don't have to report running over a cat, you know. It's not the same as a dog."

"I couldn't have just gone on."

"If I were you, I'd tear that note up. You can leave it to me, I'll tell her I saw you."

"I've already put it through the door," said Anna.

She said goodbye to the woman and got back into her car. She was on her way to her parents' house, where she would be staying for the next two weeks. Anna had a flat on the other side of the town, but she had promised to look after her parents' house while they were away on holiday, and—it now seemed a curious irony—her parents' cat.

If her journey had gone according to plan, if she had not been delayed for half an hour by the accident and the cat's death, she would have been in time to see her mother and father before they left for the airport. But when she got there, they had gone. On the hall table was a note for her in her mother's hand to say that they had had to leave, the cat had been fed, and there was a cold roast chicken in the fridge for Anna's supper. The cat would probably like some, too, to comfort it for missing them.

Anna did not think her mother's cat, a huge fluffy creature of a ghostly whitish-grey tabbyness named Griselda, was capable of missing anyone. She couldn't believe it had affections. It seemed to her without personality or charm, to lack endearing ways. To her knowledge, it had never uttered beyond giving an occasional thin squeak that signified hunger. It had never been known to rub its body against human legs, or even against the legs of the furniture. Anna knew that it was absurd to call an animal selfish—an animal naturally put its survival first, self-preservation being its prime instinct—yet she thought of Griselda as deeply, intensely, callously selfish. When it was not eating, it slept, and it slept in those most comfortable places where the people that owned it would have liked to sit but from which they could not bring themselves to dislodge it. At night it lay on their bed and, if they moved, dug its long sharp claws through the bedclothes into their legs.

Anna's mother didn't like hearing Griselda referred to as "it." She corrected Anna and stroked Griselda's head. Griselda, who purred a lot when recently fed and ensconced among cushions, always stopped purring at the touch of a human hand. This would have amused Anna if she had not seen that her mother seemed hurt by it, withdrew her hand and gave an unhappy little laugh.

When she had unpacked the case she brought with her, had prepared and eaten her meal and given Griselda a chicken leg, she began to wonder if the owner of the cat she had run over would phone. The owner might feel, as people bereaved in great or small ways sometimes did feel, that nothing could bring back the dead. Discussion was useless, and so, certainly, was recrimination. It had not in fact been her fault. She had been driving fast, but not *illegally* fast, and even if she had been driving at thirty miles an hour she doubted if she could have avoided the cat which streaked so swiftly out of the hedge.

It would be better to stop thinking about it. A night's sleep, a day at work, and the memory of it would recede. She had done all she could. She was very glad she had not just driven on as the next-door neighbor had seemed to advocate. It had been some consolation to know that the woman had many cats, not just the one, so that perhaps losing one would be less of a blow.

When she had washed the dishes and phoned her friend Kate, wondered if Richard, the man who had taken her out three times and to whom she had given this number, would phone and had decided he would not, she sat down beside Griselda—not *with* Griselda but on the same sofa as she was on—and watched television. It got to ten and she thought it unlikely the cat woman— she had begun thinking of her as that—would phone now.

There was a phone extension in her parents' room but not in the spare room where she would be sleeping. It was nearly eleven-thirty and she was getting into bed when the phone rang. The chance of its being Richard, who was capable of phoning late, especially if he thought she was alone, made her go into her parents' bedroom and answer it.

A voice that sounded strange, thin, and cracked said what sounded like "Maria Yackle."

"Yes?" Anna said.

"This is Maria Yackle. It was my cat that you killed."

Anna swallowed. "Yes. I'm glad you found my note. I'm very sorry, I'm very sorry. It was an accident. The cat ran out in front of my car."

"You were going too fast."

It was a blunt statement, harshly made. Anna could not refute it. She said, "I'm very sorry about your cat."

"They don't go out much, they're happier indoors. It was a chance in a million. I should like to see you. I think you should make amends. It wouldn't be right for you just to get away with it."

Anna was very taken aback. Up till then the woman's remarks had seemed reasonable. She didn't know what to say.

"I think you should compensate me, don't you? I loved her, I love all my cats. I expect you thought that because I had so many cats it wouldn't hurt me so much to lose one."

That was so near what Anna had thought that she felt a kind of shock, as if this Maria Yackle or whatever she was called had read her mind. "I've told you I'm sorry. I am sorry, I was very upset, I *hated* it happening. I don't know what more I can say."

"We must meet."

"What would be the use of that?" Anna knew she sounded rude, but she was shaken by the woman's tone, her blunt, direct sentences.

There was a break in the voice, something very like a sob. "It would be of use to me."

The phone went down. Anna could hardly believe it. She had heard it go down but still she said several times over, "Hallo? Hallo?" and "Are you still there?"

She went downstairs and found the telephone directory for the area and looked up Yackle. It wasn't there. She sat down and worked her way through all the Ys. There weren't many pages of Ys, apart from Youngs, but there was no one with a name beginning with Y at that address on the rustic road among the cottages.

She couldn't get to sleep. She expected the phone to ring again, Maria Yackle to ring back. After a while, she put the bedlamp on and lay there in the light. It must have been three, and still she had not slept, when Griselda came in, got on the bed, and stretched her length along Anna's legs. She put out the light, deciding not to answer the phone if it did ring, to relax, forget the run-over cat, concentrate on nice things. As she turned face-downward and stretched her body straight, she felt Griselda's claws prickle her calves. As she shrank away from contact, curled up her legs, and left Griselda a good half of the bed, a thick rough purring began.

The first thing she thought of when she woke up was how upset that poor cat woman had been. She expected her to phone back at breakfast time but nothing happened. Anna fed Griselda, left her to her house, her cat flap, her garden and wider territory, and drove to work. Richard phoned as soon as she got in. Could they meet the following evening? She agreed, obscurely wishing he had said that night, suggesting that evening herself only to be told he had to work late, had a dinner with a client.

She had been home for ten minutes when a car drew up outside. It was an old car, at least ten years old, and not only dented and scratched but with some of the worst scars painted or sprayed over in a different shade of red. Anna, who saw it arrive from a front window, watched the woman get out of it and approach the house. She was old, or at least elderly—is elderly older than old or old older than elderly?—but dressed like a teenager. Anna got a closer look at her clothes, her hair, and her face when she opened the front door.

It was a wrinkled face, the color and texture of a chicken's wattles. Small blue eyes were buried somewhere in the strawberry redness. The bright white hair next to it was as much of a contrast as snow against scarlet cloth. She wore tight jeans with socks pulled up over the bottoms of them, dirty white trainers, and a big loose sweatshirt with a cat's face on it, a painted smiling bewhiskered mask, orange and white and green-eyed.

Anna had read somewhere the comment made by a young girl on an older woman's boast that she could wear a miniskirt because she had good legs: "It's not your legs, it's your face." She thought of this as she looked at Maria Yackle, but that was the last time for a long while she thought of anything like that.

"I've come early because we shall have a lot to talk about," Maria Yackle said and walked in. She did this in such a way as to compel Anna to open the door farther and stand aside.

"This is *your* house?"

She might have meant because Anna was so young or perhaps there was some more offensive reason for asking.

"My parents'. I'm just staying here."

"Is it this room?" She was already on the threshold of Anna's mother's living room.

Anna nodded. She had been taken aback but only for a moment. It was best to get this over. But she did not care to be dictated to. "You could have let me know. I might not have been here."

There was no reply because Maria Yackle had seen Griselda.

The cat had been sitting on the back of a wing chair between the wings, an apparently uncomfortable place though a favorite, but at sight of the newcomer had stretched, got down, and was walking toward her. Maria Yackle put out her hand. It was a horrible hand, large and red with ropelike blue veins standing out above the bones, the palm calloused, the nails black and broken and the sides of the forefinger and thumb ingrained with brownish dirt. Griselda approached and put her smoky whitish muzzle and pink nose into this hand.

"I shouldn't," Anna said rather sharply, for Maria Yackle was bending over to pick the cat up. "She isn't very nice. She doesn't like people."

"She'll like me."

And the amazing thing was that Griselda did. Maria Yackle sat down and Griselda sat on her lap. Griselda the unfriendly, the cold-hearted, the cat who purred when alone and who ceased to purr when touched, the ice-eyed, the standoffish walker-by-herself, settled down on this unknown, untried lap, having first climbed up Maria Yackle's chest and onto her shoulders and rubbed her ears and plump furry cheeks against the sweatshirt with the painted cat face.

"You seem surprised."

Anna said, "You could say that."

"There's no mystery. The explanation's simple." It was a shrill, harsh voice, cracked by the onset of old age, articulate, the usage grammatical but the accent raw cockney. "You and your mum and dad, too, no doubt, you all think you smell very nice and pretty. You have your bath every morning with bath essence and scented soap. You put talcum powder on and spray stuff in your armpits, you rub cream on your bodies and squirt on perfume. Maybe you've washed your hair, too, with shampoo and conditioner and—what-do-they-call-it?—mousse. You clean your teeth and wash your mouth, put a drop more perfume behind your ears, paint your faces—well, I daresay your dad doesn't paint his face, but he shaves, doesn't he? More mousse and then aftershave.

"You put on your clothes. All of them clean, spotless. They've either just come back from the dry-cleaners or else out of the washing machine with biological soap and spring-fresh fabric softener. Oh, I know, I may not do it myself but I see it on the TV.

"It all smells very fine to you, but it doesn't to her. Oh, no. To her it's just chemicals, like gas might be to you or paraffin. A nasty strong chemical smell that puts her right off and makes her shrink up in her furry skin. What's her name?"

This question was uttered on a sharp bark. "Griselda," said Anna, and, "How did you know it's a she?"

"Face," said Maria Yackle. "Look—see her little nose. See her smiley mouth and her little nose and her fat cheeks? Tomcats got a big nose, got a long muzzle. Never mind if he's been neutered, still got a big nose."

"What did you come here to say to me?" said Anna.

Griselda had curled up on the cat woman's lap, burying her head, slightly upward turned, in the crease between stomach and thigh. "I don't go in for all that stuff, you see." The big red hand stroked Griselda's head, the stripy bit between her ears. "Cat likes the smell of me because I haven't got my clothes in soapy water every day, I have a bath once a week, always have and always shall, and I don't waste my money on odorizers and deodorizers. I wash my hands when I get up in the morning and that's enough for me."

At the mention of the weekly bath, Anna had reacted instinctively and edged her chair a little farther away. Maria Yackle saw, Anna was sure she saw, but her response to this recoil was to begin on what she had in fact come about: her compensation.

"The cat you killed, she was five years old and the queen of the cats, her name was Melusina. I always have a queen. The one before was Juliana and she lived to be twelve. I wept, I mourned her, but life has to go on. 'The queen is dead,' I said, 'long live the queen!' I never promote one, I always get a new kitten. Some cats are queens, you see, and some are not. Melusina was eight weeks old when I got her from the Animal Rescue people, and I gave them a donation of twenty pounds. The vet charged me twenty-seven pounds fifty for her injections—all my cats are immunized against feline enteritis and leptospirosis—so that makes forty-seven pounds fifty. And she had her booster at age two, which was another twenty-seven fifty. I can show you the receipted bills, I always keep everything, and that makes seventy-five pounds. Then there was my petrol getting her to the vet—we'll say a straight five pounds, though it was more—and then we come to the crunch, her food. She was a good little trencherwoman."

Anna would have been inclined to laugh at this ridiculous word, but she saw to her horror that the tears were running down Maria Yackle's cheeks. They were running unchecked out of her eyes, over the rough red wrinkled skin, and one dripped unheeded onto Griselda's silvery fur.

"Take no notice. I do cry whenever I have to talk about her. I loved that cat. She was the queen of the cats. She had her own place, her throne—she used to sit in the middle of the mantelpiece with her two china ladies-in-waiting on each side of her. You'll see one day, when you come to my house.

"But we were talking about her food. She ate a large can a day—it was too much, more than she should have had, but she loved her food, she was a good little eater. Well, cat food's gone up over the years, of course, what hasn't, and I'm paying fifty pee a can now, but I reckon it'd be fair to average it out at forty pee. She was eight weeks old when I got her, so we can't say five times three hundred and sixty-five. We'll say five times three fifty-five and that's doing you a favor. I've already worked it out at home, I'm not that much of a wizard at mental arithmetic. Five three-hundred and fifty-fives are one thousand, seven hundred and seventy-five, which multiplied by forty makes seventy-one thousand pee or seven hundred and ten pounds. Add to that the seventy-five plus the vet's bill of fourteen pounds when she had a tapeworm and we get a final figure of seven hundred and ninety-nine pounds."

Anna stared at her. "You're asking me to give you nearly eight hundred pounds?"

"That's right. Of course, we'll write it down and do it properly."

"Because your cat ran under the wheels of my car?"

"You murdered her," said Maria Yackle.

"That's absurd. Of course I didn't murder her." On shaky ground, she said, "You can't murder an animal."

"You did. You said you were going too fast."

Had she? She had been, but had she said so?

Maria Yackle got up, still holding Griselda, cuddling Griselda, who nestled purring in her arms. Anna watched with distaste. You thought of cats as fastidious creatures but they were not. Only something insensitive and undiscerning would put its face against that face, nuzzle those rough grimy hands. The black fingernails brought to mind a phrase, now unpleasantly appropriate, that her grandmother had used to children with dirty hands: in mourning for the cat.

"I don't expect you to give me a check now. Is that what you thought I meant? I don't suppose you have that amount in your current account. I'll come back tomorrow or the next day."

"I'm not going to give you eight hundred pounds," said Anna.

She might as well not have spoken.

"I won't come back tomorrow, I'll come back on Wednesday." Griselda was tenderly placed on the seat of an armchair. The tears had dried on Maria Yackle's face, leaving salt trails. She took herself out into the hall and to the front door. "You'll have thought about it by then. Anyway, I hope you'll come to the funeral. I hope there won't be any hard feelings."

That was when Anna decided Maria Yackle was mad. In one way, this was disquieting—in another, a comfort. It meant she wasn't serious about the compensation, the seven hundred and ninety-nine pounds. Sane people don't invite you to their cat's funeral. Mad people do not sue you for compensation.

"No, I shouldn't think she'd do that," said Richard when they were having dinner together. He wasn't a lawyer but had studied law. "You didn't admit you were exceeding the speed limit, did you?"

"I don't remember."

"At any rate, you didn't admit it in front of witnesses. You say she didn't threaten you?"

"Oh, no. She wasn't unpleasant. She cried, poor thing."

"Well, let's forget her, shall we, and have a nice time?"

Although no note awaited her on the doorstep, no letter came, and there were no phone calls, Anna knew the cat woman would come back on the following evening. Richard had advised her to go to the police if any threats were made. There would be no need to tell them she had been driving very fast. Anna thought the whole idea of going to the police bizarre. She rang up her friend Kate and told her all about it and Kate agreed that telling the police would be going too far.

The battered red car arrived at seven. Maria Yackle was dressed as she had been for her previous visit, but, because it was rather cold, wore a jacket made of synthetic fur as well. From its harsh, too-shiny texture there was no doubt it was synthetic, but from a distance it looked like a black cat's pelt.

She had brought an album of photographs of her cats for Anna to see. Anna looked through it—what else could she do? Some were recognizably of those she had seen through the windows. Those that were not, she supposed might be of animals now at rest under the wooden crosses in Maria Yackle's back garden. While she was looking at the pictures, Griselda came in and jumped onto the cat woman's lap.

"They're very nice, very interesting," Anna said. "I can see you're devoted to your cats."

"They're my life."

A little humoring might be in order. "When is the funeral to be?"

"I thought on Friday. Two o'clock on Friday. My sister will be there with her two. Cats don't usually take to car travel, that's why I don't often take any of mine with me, and shutting them up in cages goes against the grain—but my sister's two Burmese love the car, they'll go and sit in the car when it's parked. My friend from the Animal Rescue will come if she can get away and I've asked our vet, but I don't hold out much hope there. He has his goat clinic on Fridays. I hope you'll come along."

"I'm afraid I'll be at work."

"It's no flowers by request. Donations to the Cats' Protection League instead. Any sum, no matter how small, gratefully received. Which brings me to money. You've got a check for me."

"No, I haven't, Mrs. Yackle."

"Miss. And it's Yakob. J-A-K-O-B. You've got a check for me for seven hundred and ninety-nine pounds."

"I'm not giving you any money, Miss Jakob. I'm very, very sorry about your cat, about Melusina, I know how fond you were of her, but giving you compensation is out of the question. I'm sorry."

The tears had come once more into Maria Jakob's eyes, had spilled over. Her face contorted with misery. It was the mention of the wretched thing's name, Anna thought. That was the trigger that started the weeping. A tear splashed onto one of the coarse red hands. Griselda opened her eyes and licked up the tear.

Maria Jakob pushed her other hand across her eyes. She blinked. "We'll have to think of something else then," she said.

"I beg your pardon?" Anna wondered if she had really heard. Things couldn't be solved so simply.

"We shall have to think of something else. A way for you to make up to me for murder."

"Look, I will give a donation to the Cats' Protection League. I'm quite prepared to give them—say, twenty pounds." Richard would be furious, but perhaps she wouldn't tell Richard. "I'll give it to you, shall I, and then you can pass it on to them?"

"I certainly hope you will. Especially if you can't come to the funeral."

That was the end of it, then. Anna felt a great sense of relief. It was only now that it was over that she realized quite how it had got to her. It had actually kept her from sleeping properly. She phoned Kate and told her about the funeral and the goat clinic, and Kate laughed and said Poor old thing. Anna slept so well that night that she didn't notice the arrival of Griselda who, when she woke, was asleep on the pillow next to her face but out of touching distance.

Richard phoned and she told him about it, omitting the part about her offer of a donation. He told her that being firm, sticking to one's guns in situations of this kind, always paid off. In the evening, she wrote a check for twenty pounds but, instead of the Cats' Protection League, made it out to Maria Jakob. If the cat woman quietly held onto it, no harm would be done. Anna went down the road to post her letter, for she had written a letter to accompany the check, in which she reiterated her sorrow about the death of the cat and added that if there was anything she could do Miss Jakob had only to let her know. Richard would have been furious.

Unlike the Jakob cats, Griselda spent a good deal of time out of doors. She was often out all evening and did not reappear until the small hours, so that it was not until the next day, not until the next evening, that Anna began to be alarmed at her absence. As far as she knew, Griselda had never been away so long before. For herself, she was unconcerned—she had never liked the cat, did not particularly like any cats, and found this one obnoxiously self-centered and cold. It was for her mother, who unaccountably loved the creature, that she was worried. She walked up and down the street calling Griselda, though the cat had never been known to come when it was called.

It did not come now. Anna walked up and down the next street, calling, and around the block and farther afield. She half expected to find Griselda's body, guessing that it might have met the same fate as Melusina. Hadn't she read somewhere that nearly forty thousand cats are killed on British roads annually?

On Saturday morning, she wrote one of those melancholy lost-cat notices and attached it to a lamp standard, wishing she had a photograph. But her mother had taken no photographs of Griselda.

* * *

Richard took her to a friend's party and afterward, when they were driving home, he said, "You know what's happened, don't you? It's been killed by that old mad woman. An eye for an eye, a cat for a cat."

"Oh, no, she wouldn't do that. She loves cats."

"Murderers love people. They just don't love the people they murder."

"I'm sure you're wrong," said Anna, but she remembered how Maria Jakob had said that if the money was not forthcoming, she must think of something else—a way to make up to her for Melusina's death. And she had not meant a donation to the Cats' Protection League.

"What shall I do?"

"I don't see that you can do anything. It's most unlikely you could prove it, she'll have seen to that. You can look at it this way—she's had her pound of flesh."

"Fifteen pounds of flesh," said Anna. Griselda had been a large, heavy cat.

"Okay, fifteen pounds. She's had that, she's had her revenge. It hasn't actually caused you any grief—you'll just have to make up some story for your mother."

Anna's mother was upset, but nowhere near as upset as Maria Jakob had been over the death of Melusina. To avoid too much fuss, Anna had gone further than she intended, told her mother that she had seen Griselda's corpse and talked to the offending motorist, who had been very distressed.

A month or so later, Anna's mother got a kitten, a grey tabby tomkitten, who was very affectionate from the start, sat on her lap, purred loudly when stroked, and snuggled up in her arms, though Anna was sure her mother had not stopped having baths or using perfume. So much for the Jakob theories.

Nearly a year had gone by before she again drove down the road where Maria Jakob's house was. She had not intended to go that way. Directions had been given her to a smallholding where they sold early strawberries on a roadside stall but she must have missed her way, taken a wrong turning, and come out here.

If Maria Jakob's car had been parked in the front, she would not have stopped. There was no garage for it to be in and it was not outside, therefore the cat woman must be out. Anna thought of the funeral she had not been to —she had often thought about it, the strange people and strange cats who had attended it.

In each of the bay windows sat a cat, a tortoiseshell and a brown tabby. The black cat was eyeing her from upstairs. Anna didn't go to the front door but round the back. There, among the long grass, as she had expected, were four graves instead of three, four wooden crosses, and on the fourth was printed in black gloss paint: MELUSINA, THE QUEEN OF THE CATS, MURDERED IN HER SIXTH YEAR. RIP.

That "murdered" did not please Anna. It brought back all the resentment at the unjust accusations of eleven months before. She felt much older, she felt wiser. One thing was certain, ethics or no ethics, if she ever ran over a cat again she'd drive on—the last thing she'd do was go and confess.

She came round the side of the house and looked in at the bay window. If the tortoiseshell had still been on the windowsill, she probably would not have looked in, but the tortoiseshell had removed itself to the hearthrug.

A white cat and the marmalade-and-white lay curled up side by side in an armchair. The portrait of Melusina hung above the fireplace and this year's cat calendar was up on the left-hand wall. Light gleamed on the china cats' gilt whiskers—and between them, in the empty space that was no longer vacant, sat Griselda.

Griselda was sitting in the queen's place in the middle of the mantelpiece. She sat in the sphinx position with her eyes closed. Anna tapped on the glass and Griselda opened her eyes, stared with cold indifference, and closed them again.

The queen is dead, long live the queen!

Nancy Pickard, author of the popular Jenny Cain novels, including the Anthony Award winner *Say No to Murder,* has won the Macavity, the American Mystery Award, and the Agatha; she's been nominated for the Edgar and many other awards. "Lazy Susan," first published in *Sisters in Crime 4,* deftly explores the fine line that sometimes—but not always—separates predators and prey . . .

Lazy Susan
NANCY PICKARD

"I want you to teach me how to shoot a gun," Susan Carpenter said to her husband over breakfast.

"You want me to do *what?*"

Stan Carpenter's mouth, which he had only just opened to insert a big bite of toast, hung empty of everything but incredulity.

"Take me to a shooting range."

As Susan spoke, she piled two pieces of bacon and a fried egg onto her muffin so she could eat it all at once like a sandwich. It seemed to her a silly waste of effort to eat only one thing at a time.

Her husband's astonishment turned into delight.

"Honey, I think that's a wonderful idea, you know I do."

Indeed, she did. Ever since she'd been robbed the week before on a dark night in the parking lot of the Mulberry Street Shopping Center, Stanley had pestered her to learn how to protect herself, preferably with a gun.

"I can't believe it." He shook his head. Grape jelly dripped over the edge of his toast into his coffee with a faint splash that he didn't notice. "You've always hated guns."

"Well, you know what they say." Susan's smile was rueful. "A conservative is a liberal who's been mugged. I guess you win, dear."

"We'll go to a range tonight," Stan promised.

*   *   *

Susan had been more angry than scared when she was robbed. The mugger hadn't hurt her much, just a little tap on the head with his handgun to remind her who was boss. It hadn't even broken the skin and it certainly didn't knock her out. It was only a little injury added to the greater insult. And about that insult she was so darn mad! Furious, incensed, fit to be tied and so darn mad!

"Fifty dollars!" she ranted to the nice patrolman. "One minute I had fifty dollars in my purse and the next minute I had zilch. Fifty hard-earned dollars gone, just gone! I have to work *hours* to earn that much money, and he comes along and takes it—" She'd snapped her fingers in the policeman's face. "—just like that!"

She was right, of course, except possibly about the "hard-earned" part. That might have been a bit of an exaggeration. True, she did have a job as a receptionist in a sales office, but in a more calm and candid moment, Susan would have been the first to admit that she didn't exactly work hard for her money. Oh, she showed up at the job every day, more or less on time. And she put in her eight hours, give or take a few, and she smiled at all the customers, and her bosses liked her, most people couldn't help but like her. But there was more work that didn't get done on her desk than did. As she was always saying to her friends, "Oh, well, you know me . . . Lazy Susan."

"How does it feel?"

Susan shrugged in reply to Stanley's question.

Actually, the little gun was surprisingly pleasant to hold, with a satisfying weight and a smooth, sensuous feel. She hefted it in her right hand, cocked it with her left, aimed it as Stanley had instructed her, felt infuriated all over again at the thought of the mugging, and pulled the trigger.

"Hey, that's darned good!" Stan shouted.

She'd never heard him raise his voice before, but then that was the only possible means of communication at the Target Shooting Range. Not even the ear protectors they wore could completely muffle the shocking blast of constant gunfire at the indoor range.

Susan resisted the urge to point the gun barrel toward her mouth and blow the smoke away like John Wayne.

"I want to shoot another round," she said, and swaggered just the tiniest bit.

"Good evening, ladies."

The expert in self-defense stood beside a slide projection screen, a "clicker" in his hand. He started right in by saying, "Your basic victim of a mugging looks like this . . ."

He clicked, and a color slide appeared on the screen. It showed a frail old woman who carried a shopping bag in one hand and a purse in the other.

"Your basic muggee, shall we say, just plain looks vulnerable. Like this lady. She looks hesitant, timid, kind of lost. Your basic mugger likes the looks of her. She'll make it easy for him to grab, push and run. He's not as likely to pick on a victim who looks as if she might fight back."

Click. This time, a picture of a younger woman appeared. She looked strong and fit, and her hands were free.

"So if you want to avoid being mugged, walk confidently! Keep that head up. Pull those shoulders back. Let those arms swing. And don't load yourself up with a lot of packages that render you helpless. Tuck your purse under your armpit, excuse the expression, or grasp it firmly with both hands. Look as if you know where you're going, even if you don't. Make that mugger think you're one tough cookie."

He winked at them. "Any questions so far?"

Susan raised her hand. "Is there any way to spot a potential mugger?"

"Sure." The instructor grinned. "He's the one in the dark clothes, hiding in the bushes."

Everyone but Susan laughed.

This was the third evening of the series. At the first session, they'd learned to scream like hell and run like a bat out of. At the second, they'd examined the merits of doorkeys and fingernail files as weapons. This night the topic had been, "Who Is a Likely Mugging Victim?"

The ladies who filed out of the community center at the end of class were an unusually well-postured bunch who didn't walk by any bushes.

Stan was astonished at how much stronger and more confident Susan seemed after only three weeks of self-defense training.

"You're really sticking to it," he said, and planted a kiss atop her light brown curls. "I've never seen you put so much energy into anything, honey."

"Well, some things are worth taking trouble over," Susan said, a shade righteously, all things considered. "Besides, I'm still so darned mad!"

She took judo lessons, just a few, and practiced walking so she looked taller and more powerful. She even tried talking in a lower octave. Nobody was going to mess with *her!*

The stores were closed when the last movie-goers filed out into the vast dark reaches of the Mulberry Street Shopping Center parking lot. It had been one of the Superman films. After two-and-a-half hours of watching him bend steel and leap tall buildings, Susan felt inspired. Like one tough cookie.

Stan would not have approved of her going to the movie alone, of course, especially not back to the scene of the crime, as it were. But he was out of town and besides, she'd had all those lessons. Now she knew a thing or two.

A dark cluster of bushes stood between her and her car. She walked confidently straight to and through them, then she turned around and crouched down a little, to peer carefully behind her.

She saw the man before he noticed her.

Everything she'd learned at her self-protection classes passed through her mind: she examined his walk, the look on his shadowed face, the object he held in his hands. Her breath quickened. She thought of those hours she'd had to work to earn those fifty dollars and of the so-and-so who had stolen it from her so easily.

She took from her pocket the little gun that Stan had taught her to use. Then, just as the man stepped past the bushes, she jumped behind him so he couldn't see her.

She put the gun to his head.

"I don't want to hurt you," Susan said in her confident new voice, pitched an octave lower than normal. "I just want your money."

The little old man dropped his shopping bag in a heap beside one leg of Susan's black trousers.

"My goodness, there's been another mugging at the shopping center!" Stan folded back the local news section of the morning paper. The edges dragged through his poached eggs, and yolk dripped onto his lap. "That just proves my point. You should never go there alone at night. You won't, will you, Susan?"

"You're getting egg on your trousers, dear."

"What? Oh gosh, I am, and all over the floor, too."

"Don't worry about it." Susan casually waved a hand. "I'll take care of it. I have lots of extra time now."

Stan smiled a little nervously. He was glad she had quit that low-paying receptionist's job, but he was worried that his adorable but admittedly lazy Susan might not try very hard to find another job.

"Now you'll have time to train for something better," he said, hope in his voice. "I'm sure you can find something that offers an easy way to make good money."

Lazily, Susan stirred her coffee.

"Yes, dear." She smiled. "I probably can."

Robert Barnard, the popular author of many sharp stories and novels, weighs in here with a story that starts with an issue—illegal adoption—but doesn't stop there. Nicely unpredictable, this story, first published in *Ellery Queen's Mystery Magazine,* is a pleasure for its surprises and the way Barnard handles his intriguing characters.

A Hotel in Bucharest
ROBERT BARNARD

The lift in the Harmonia had seemed slightly suspect when he had arrived the evening before, but Gerald risked it. He got to the first floor without mishap, and in the breakfast room he found a long table spread with cold meats and fish, two kinds of rolls and plenty of bread, several different jams, and a toaster. It was not unlike the breakfast provided in any Scandinavian hotel. Gerald got a plateful of this and that, poured himself a cup of thick, black coffee, and settled down at a table.

"Is your wife not feeling up to breakfast?"

The question, startling him out of his thoughts, came from a woman at the table to his right. She had soft, brown hair, waved in a rather old-fashioned style, and a sympathetic smile. The man facing her across the table watched in a detached manner, as if he was used to her approaching strangers.

"I'm afraid I don't actually have a wife. I'm a widower."

"Oh—I *am* sorry. I do apologize. Robbie said there was another couple arriving yesterday evening, and I thought . . . Well, Tarom do their best, but they somehow don't manage to make people feel confident. And the airport is just a bit scary after dark."

"I'd certainly agree about *that*. . . . You said another couple?"

"Wanting to adopt one of the orphans. We always call them that, though most of them are abandoned, poor little mites."

Light had dawned on Gerald. He had expected, having chosen a middle-priced hotel, that some of the guests there would be on that sad quest.

"Are there a lot of people here looking for a child to adopt?"

"Oh yes—quite a lot. All nationalities—French, German, Scandinavian. But the Harmonia prides itself on its British connections, going back to before the war. There are other sorts of British guests here too: journalists, business-men, tourist people. . . ."

"Ah, I'm a tourist person," said Gerald, spreading a second roll with the rich, sweet jam that he had found very palatable. "And a journalist too. I'm going to do a series of articles for the *Yorkshire Post* on Romania—I live near York, by the way. What I'm really here for, though, is to scout around hotels and tourist venues. I'm thinking of starting up a specialist travel firm. Every-one who's been here since the revolution says the tourist potential is im-mense."

"Peasants," said the man unexpectedly. "The Balkans are the last place in Europe where you can find peasants."

He was in his late forties, wearing an anonymous suit and a college tie Gerald could not place. But the air of detachment, even of being nothing-very-much, was belied by sharp, living eyes.

"I don't think the Romanian government would be happy if we pushed the 'peasant' line too far," Gerald explained. "Though the folk element could come into it—in fact it always does in package tours. For some reason it makes people feel better about mass tourism."

"Well, it's nice to have met you," said the woman, standing up. "We must get on to another day of being passed from pillar to post. I'm Eileen Kershaw, by the way, and this is my husband Roland."

"How do you do. I'm Gerald Coutts."

"If you're not doing anything tonight, come up to the bar. We usually meet in the bar, to discuss progress, or lack of it. The Panorama Bar's on the top floor, and Radu the barman is very sweet, and knows us all."

"If I don't have anything on I'll come up," Gerald promised.

When he had finished the last drop of a second cup of coffee Gerald went back to the foyer and decided not to risk the lift back to the third floor. He still considered himself a young man: forty-two, and very little sign of running to fat. Gradually, though, as he trudged up the dimly lit stairwell, he became gripped by a feeling that he had known he was going to get at some time or other in Romania: the feeling of being watched. It persisted when he pushed the door through to the equally murky corridor on the third floor: one imagined Securitate men in rooms noting comings and goings, clocking up meetings in the corridors, playing through bugged conversations of hotel guests—everything managed, manipulated, as if the guests were forced to dance some ludicrous minuet to music from a manic party headquarters.

A door opened at the far end of the corridor. A young couple emerged, talking and laughing—she blonde, healthy, and tall, with a Valkyrie figure, he tanned, athletic, and handsome. The perfect Siegmund and Sieglinde, such as you can only conceive in your mind's eye, never see on the operatic stage. As they passed him Gerald heard the man say: "I've had worse at the Majestic in Tunbridge Wells," and their laughter echoed in the stairwell.

He shook off his feeling of oppression, of sinister watchers. Things had changed: this was now a world of normal people, a part of the new Europe.

His morning was spent with Ministry people and with people lower down in the tourist business. Everyone tried to be cooperative, though Gerald felt this was something new for them and they didn't really know how. The weather was glorious for October, and he ate lunch outside at the Athenée Palace. When he got back at late evening to the Harmonia he collected his passport from Reception along with his key.

"I'm sorry, we still 'ave to check—just like the old days."

The clerk who handed it over was a broad, plump man with a jolly smile that seemed to hide a congenital melancholy.

"Don't mention it. Hotels in most European countries check passports."

"Really? We do not know, you see."

"Dare I risk the lift up to the Panorama Bar?"

" 'E's been mended today. Use 'im while 'e is 'ealthy!"

The lift opened straight out into the bar, which had a splendid view over the uncertain lights of Bucharest, and which was ringing with laughter and conversation. The presiding genius was Radu, the roly-poly barman, who seemed to set the relaxed tone of the place. English couples were mixing and swapping experiences with couples of other nationalities, and the single people—doubtless the businessmen and journalists the Kershaws had mentioned—formed their own little groups. Eileen and Roland Kershaw hailed him, and he went over to talk to them. They were round a table with the Wagnerian couple he had passed in the corridor.

"We saw our baby today!" said Eileen triumphantly. "I held her!"

"Has she got a name?"

"Elena. It's a lovely name, isn't it? We're not going to change it to Helen. We want her to know she's Romanian. We'll bring her back here when she's older, so she always feels at home. Oh—this is Ursula Upjohn and Edward Upjohn."

"Ed," said the Siegmund young man. He didn't seem like an Ed. They both were so young and vital and healthy that it was odd to think of them as unable to have children—and difficult to think of a reason why they shouldn't adopt. Perhaps they wanted a baby—there were very few of those available for adoption in Britain, Gerald knew. Anyway, it hardly seemed polite to ask.

"How are things going with you?" he asked Ursula.

"Oh, we're at about the same stage as Eileen and Roland. We *hope*—fingers crossed—to be able to take Mihai home next visit."

"I suppose things are never certain, never clear-cut."

"Never, ever," said Ed feelingly.

"That's why we're so lucky to have Robbie," said Ursula. "He's fantastic. If there's a way of getting round problems, or a way of cutting through red tape, Robbie will find it."

"There he is now," said Roland. "That must be the new couple."

When Robbie had emerged from the lift, half the heads in the room had turned in his direction—some with a sort of starved hope in their eyes, rather as those with a need for faith will feast on some cut-price messiah. But there was nothing shifty or bargain-basement about Robbie. He was a clean-cut man in his mid-forties, in a smart, claret-colored blazer, carrying five or six files. He had smiles all round, but he made initially for a couple sitting a little aside from the rest, not yet fully integrated. The man was cherubic, almost boyish, with blond curly hair and a wicked smile. Certainly he could be no more than thirty. His wife was a woman of forty-odd, hair cut short and starting to go gray, dressed in a severely cut suit. Something executive in local government, Gerald guessed.

"That's Laura Perceval," said Ursula. "And Terry. They were out at the Ploesti orphanage this afternoon."

"You should have brought them over and introduced them," said Eileen. "You're not doing your duty."

"Yes, I should. They seemed awfully nice. From Derbyshire, I think."

Tactfully nobody mentioned the discrepancy in their ages. No prizes for guessing why they couldn't adopt in Britain, Gerald thought. Robbie was questioning them—first one, then the other, turning his face to look into theirs, the couple leaning forward, interested, concerned, questioning in their turn.

"Robbie always takes new couples to the Ministry on their first morning," said Ed. "They're used to people from Romchild—that's our organization. Then he leaves them on their own—with a little sheet of suggested steps. It's a sort of throwing-in at the deep end."

"We've seen one! We've found one, we think!"

The cry was from another new couple, and was the signal for congratulations, backslappings, toasts. The groupings were breaking up, and Gerald took advantage of the interruption to slip away. The new couple was a thick-set, rubicund Yorkshire businessman, Mike Lawson, with a strong but pleasant accent, and his wife Mareeka, a beautiful Indian woman, wearing a sari, with a sophisticated Southern accent and limitless charm.

"He's a champion little fellow," Gerald heard Mike say, grinning happily.

"Well, you've *really* got reason to wear your sari tonight," Eileen said to Mareeka. So she didn't always, Gerald thought: she was in that interesting hinterland between East and West. Hinterlands were always fascinating. Come to that, post-Ceausescu's Romania was one. Gerald introduced himself to one of the journalists and was soon chatting to him and a London businesswoman who joined them about topics of common interest. But he was fascinated by the couples and kept his eye on them all evening, watching Robbie go from one couple to another—interested, encouraging, concerned—and finally end up the center of an adoring, immensely jolly group. He was, it seemed, a source of hope, a beacon of light.

In the next few days Gerald seemed to get busier and busier, and was soon taking off from Bucharest in a hired car, earmarking possible routes and goals for future trips. There was, as he had expected, immense tourist potential, combined with next to no knowledge of the imperatives of mass tourism. There were possibilities everywhere he went that kept him constantly excited. But he usually found himself back at the Harmonia in the evening and enjoying a drink in the Panorama Bar. Here he could follow the progress and disappointments of the various couples, and admire the way Robbie would go around raising spirits and suggesting ways round or through the roadblocks that officialdom erected.

"You do a wonderful job," he said to him one evening.

"I'm a Northerner," said Robbie. "In Pontefract we don't take no for an answer."

"How often does it take a bribe to change a 'no' to 'yes'?"

Robbie winked.

"It's the last resort. Officially it's against Romchild's principles. We don't like doing it because if we did it too readily we'd be doing it all the time. But now and then . . ."

Gerald spoke to the newest couple one morning over breakfast. Laura and Terry Perceval, he had noticed, were always very purposeful, eating and drinking while they were planning their day and their next moves, and making notes in a little black book. If Terry had the looks of a toyboy, he didn't seem to behave like one.

"The trouble with social services people in Britain," said Laura briskly, after they had chatted for a bit and got round to the inevitable topic, "is that they can't see beyond their noses. And because of the press they're scared stiff of making the slightest mistake. They don't want to know about anything outside their own little boundaries. You tell them that the situation for orphans here is desperate and they shrug."

"And believe me, it is desperate," said Terry. "We've only scraped the surface, but we *know*."

"Because they're so scared of the press they try to live in an ideal world," Laura went on. "Model two-parent families, him older than her, he in a job, she at home, black parents for black children. . . ."

"Life is a lot messier than that," said Terry. "There are different sorts of relationships. And people with no relationships who would make excellent parents."

"But you have to have some kind of certificate of fitness to take your baby into Britain when the time comes, don't you?" Gerald asked.

"Oh yes," said Terry. "Usually."

"We have ours," said Laura firmly.

"I suppose you suffered a lot of prying to get it?"

"Sheer bloody impertinence," she replied, her mouth set in a grim line.

Most of the couples seemed to spend two or three weeks at a time in Romania, then return home and consolidate their position by postal or telephone contacts (though the latter were very difficult). The more experienced ones like Eileen and Roland Kershaw obviously had a whole lot of other couples in England to contact, compare notes with, support. While they were in Romania much of the couples' time was spent waiting, or was just filled up in some way or other. Gerald went to a concert at the Atheneum and in the interval, when it was the done thing to promenade around the entrance hall under the great dome, Gerald met up with Mike Lawson and Edward Upjohn.

"Mareeka wouldn't come," said Mike, in his broad Yorkshire accent. "Says that every movement in Mahler's too long by ten minutes."

"She'd be well advised not to say that anywhere near the Festival Hall," said Gerald. "She might get lynched."

"Ursula's a medieval music freak," said Ed. "And I'm a philistine. I jog to Nigel Kennedy pops on my personal stereo, and lift weights to the best of James Last. I came along because there was a spare ticket."

"I think of you as a rather Wagnerian couple," said Gerald. "Fighting dragons and defending holy grails."

"Sorry to disappoint you. A propos, do you want to walk back with us? The streets are so dark, and there've been a lot of muggings."

"Really? I've felt perfectly safe. But I'd be happy to walk back with you."

When they got back to the Harmonia they found Robbie poring over passports and papers with the friendly receptionist, both very serious as befitted people engaged in satisfying the diktats of bureaucracy. Robbie waved.

"See you in the Panorama," he shouted.

"You missed Mahler's Sixth," said Gerald to Mareeka in the bar, where she was sipping a brandy. "It was very good."

"I'm rather like Ursula," said Mareeka coolly. "Anything later than Haydn is a bit suspect. Beethoven was a big mistake, and even Mozart sometimes went too far."

The next day Gerald directed his car up to Sinaia. Everyone had told him it was one of the inevitable goals of any package tour he might put together, and they were right. The summer palace of the Hohenzollern kings was the copywriter's dream: a series of buildings in baronial-feudal style, set in the mountain's side, the interiors darkly wooden but grandiose—the headquarters of Herne the Hunter. The place was, Gerald noted, quite innocent of the needs of tourism: there was not a postcard in sight, nor a guidebook, and supervision was minimal. He felt both wonder and some compunction at the changes tours like the ones he was planning would bring.

As he came out blinking into the sunlight and headed toward the lodge which had served as a writers' retreat for the hymners of Ceausescu's greatness, Gerald suddenly paused in his stride: that feeling had come upon him again, that feeling of being watched. Eerie. He shook himself: probably it was some sort of transference from the old days, for the writers when they were up here must have had a close eye kept on them for any sign of backsliding from a posture of total devotion to the Great Conductor.

The feeling evaporated as soon as it came. He saw Eileen Kershaw approaching from the lodge and waving.

"Hello! You never said you were coming up here."

"Oh, I'm going all over."

"Mareeka's around somewhere. She hasn't seen it. This is my second visit. Isn't it wonderful?"

"Absolutely wonderful."

"And just waiting for package tourists."

Gerald smiled wryly.

"You make it sound rather dreadful. I'm hoping to have small, discriminating groups."

"I'm sure you are. And it will do so much good to the economy. But it won't be quite the same, will it?"

"Not quite. But Romania has been so cut off. The more connections it has with the rest of Europe, the better."

"That's right," said Mareeka, who had just strolled over from the direction of the palace. "We need to get people interested in the place. They were at the time of the revolution, but then it sort of tailed off. People's attention span seems to get shorter and shorter. But the Romanians are so anxious to learn how things are done in the West."

"That's not absolutely an unmixed blessing," said Eileen. "Somebody had her handbag snatched back near the restaurant an hour ago. Just like Florence or Rome. They say things like that hardly ever happened before the revolution."

"Under Ceausescu nobody had anything worth stealing," said Gerald. "I still feel a lot safer here in Romania than I would on the streets of London or Edinburgh."

But the topic of crime pursued him during his remaining days in Romania—tales of muggings in the nearly unlit streets of nighttime Bucharest, tales of the illegal money-changers turning nasty and demanding Western currency with menaces, rumors that the miners were poised to come back to the capital, with stories of what they had done the last time they took over the streets there. The couples were becoming more uneasy, or perhaps using the stories to justify themselves in taking children from that environment. Gerald saw no evidence himself of any rising tide of crime, and rather mocked all their stories. Then, two days before he was due to return home, he heard that the receptionist at the Harmonia, the man he had spoken to on his second day, had been knifed on his way home and killed.

"It's not as though he was likely to be carrying the takings home with him," said Mike Lawson. "It's just horrible and senseless."

For Gerald, though, the trip had gone well. Officialdom, slowly and uncertainly, had opened up under his persistent negotiating techniques: arrangements had been come to, promises made, itineraries scheduled. The more he had seen of the country, the more wonderful it seemed. Whatever one's doubts about mass tourism, it had to be a good thing to open up such beauty and interest to sympathetic travelers.

For some of the couples, too, things were going well. Roland and Eileen, as they had hoped, were firming in on their prospects of adopting Elena. They had been assured that their next trip would be their last, and they could then take her home with them. Terry and Laura Perceval—perhaps aided by Laura's experience in government, which was in fact at national level rather than the local level which Gerald had guessed at—had a definite prospect of adoption on their first trip, something of a record. They showed round photographs in the Panorama Bar of Laura holding the tiny baby girl at the door of the orphanage, with Terry leaning over her shoulder and tweaking the laughing baby's nose. It all seemed so good, so beneficial, so normal. Gerald left with many good wishes and some promises that at some time in the future many of them, with their children, would come on one of his tours.

In the months that followed, Gerald went several times to Romania, but he never spent more than one night at the Harmonia. He was investigating Cluj, Timisoara, Constanta, and he always flew on to one or other of the towns next day, after the ritual meetings with Ministry or tourism officials. On one of his overnight stays he found Laura and Terry Perceval at the Harmonia, and heard that things were progressing well with their adoption. On another occasion he found Robbie there, but he was so busy with the affairs of new couples whom he was helping over the difficult first hurdles that Gerald didn't manage to do more than swap a few words of greeting with him. On his last visit before the first of the tours was scheduled to take place, he found Mike Lawson behind him in the airport queue to take the plane home.

"Great to see you again. Where's Mareeka?" he asked.

"She didn't come this time. This was just a quick 'sorting-out' visit, to see some Ministry troublemakers."

"Successful?"

"Very. The next trip is going to be *the* one."

When he'd gone through the formalities Gerald waited for Mike as he checked his luggage through, but Mike opted to go Smoking.

"Didn't realize you did," said Gerald.

"We Yorkshiremen have all the vices, and damn the busybodies who want to make us live healthily and forever. Actually, it's the strain of this business. I was down to one or two a day, but I'm well up again now."

It was after his first tour had taken place, and been a glorious success, that Gerald found a brief lull in his life. The topic of the Romanian "orphans," though no longer hot news, was never entirely out of it: obstructive local authorities in Britain who regarded the adoptions with disapproval; a couple who had found "bonding" impossible with their adopted child; a couple who had smuggled their baby in. The journalist in Gerald had been dormant for a time, and it now reasserted itself. How had the couples that he had come to know so well fared with their adopted children? There was certainly a story there, maybe three or four.

It was just a question of getting in touch, because there had been no exchange of addresses. Robbie, he knew, came from Pontefract, but as his surname was Taylor tracking him down might be difficult. He seemed to remember the Percevals came from Derbyshire, but he wasn't sure which town. The Kershaws he thought came from Luton (how awful—to adopt a child and bring it up in Luton!), and the Upjohns from London somewhere. Mike Lawson's luggage he had seen at the airport in Bucharest. He could not remember the address, but it had been Huddersfield, and he knew Mike was in the carpet business. It was with Mike, obviously, that he should make a start. When he drove to Huddersfield a couple of days later he found the firm in the Yellow Pages, but when he rang he was told that Mike was away on a buying trip to London.

"Stupid of me. I should have rung in advance. Do you think you could give me his home number?"

The reason he had not tried to contact Mike and Mareeka in advance was his journalist's instinct that the truest picture comes from a surprise visit: no time to prepare a false impression. He knew from all those press reports that some of the adoptions had been deliriously successful, others less so. He compared the number with the four M. Lawsons in the telephone book and drove out to the address. There was a good chance, he felt, that Mareeka, with the new baby, would be at home.

The house was a substantial stone one, probably late-Victorian, with a small front garden onto the street, land stretching out to the back, and a row of semis forming the rest of the street. Not at all a bad place in which to bring up a child. Gerald was disappointed, though, to get no response to his ring on the doorbell.

"They're both out," came a cry from next door. An elderly man, wrinkled and weather-beaten, was clipping his hedge in the nearest of the semis. "I think Mike is in London for a few days."

Gerald went over.

"Yes, they told me he was away on business at the shop. I thought his wife might be in."

The man stopped clipping.

"His wife? Mr. Lawson doesn't have a wife."

"But Mareeka . . . Oh, perhaps they're not married."

"Who? Never heard of a name like that. Mr. Lawson's never been married, and there's no woman has lived here since his mother died. Oh—it wouldn't be young Edward's wife you'd be looking for, would it?"

"Edward?"

"His nephew Ed. He's been living with Mike for a bit. He's divorced from his wife, Mike says, and he's just got custody of their child. He's home most of the day since the little boy came, but he's shopping in Leeds today. Was it his wife you were looking for? She's never lived here, to my knowledge."

"No, it . . . it wasn't her. I think I've made a mistake."

On the way home Gerald stopped at a pub on the outskirts of the town, bought lunch and a pint, and tried to think things through. What he had seen in Bucharest had been an elaborate facade and charade. Robbie Taylor was running an organization to help people—well-heeled people, no doubt—who had no chance, or next to none, of adopting in Britain. So Mike and Ed were partners, and had set up a quite different facade here in Huddersfield to account for their lives together. And if they—seen at the concert—were partners, most probably Eileen and Mareeka—seen at Sinaia—were partners too. And the rest? Was it Roland Kershaw and Terry, and Laura Perceval and Ursula? Gerald sat pondering.

He had felt great sympathy for the couples. He and his wife had had no children, though they were only beginning to talk of adoption or fostering when his wife became ill. But adoption of the kind that Robbie was organizing presented issues of conscience that he had never considered except in passing, and he recognized that now he was forced to wrestle with them in earnest. Was it in the child's interest—even granted the dreadful conditions in some of the orphanages—to be adopted by a homosexual couple? What if, in some cases, they were pedophiles?

He was still muddled, thrashing around, when he got home. It seemed like an omen to find a thick Ministry letter from Romania on his doormat, and more of an omen still when he opened it: the Ministry officials were impressed and delighted by the success of the tour, and wanted to have discussions aimed at publicizing them more widely and making them more frequent. It was all Gerald needed to make up his mind: he checked his diary, then got on to Tarom at once to book a flight and a room at the Harmonia.

The plane was late out of Heathrow as usual. When Gerald finally made it to his hotel room he had little energy left for a visit to the Panorama. The next day was spent in talks at the Ministry, talks which alternated between the exhilarating and the frustrating as usual, but there was the difference this time that the atmosphere was notably more friendly. He ate early at the

Athenée Palace, hoping in vain to avoid the cabaret, and then went back to the Harmonia.

"Is Mr. Taylor staying here at the moment?" he asked the new clerk at Reception, handsome and smiling.

"Robbie? Oh yes, he's here. He's always coming and going. It's room four-oh-eight."

Upstairs the Panorama Bar was full of couples, and Radu welcomed him as a returned friend. Gerald found a businessman he knew to talk to, and watched. All the couples—or "couples," as he thought of them now—were new, but they were going through the same routines which by now Gerald knew so well: welcoming newcomers, encouraging the downhearted, comparing notes. And there too was Robbie, smartly dressed as always, going from couple to couple, files in hand, helping, directing, cheering. This was not the place, Gerald thought, to talk to him.

It was after eleven, when all the couples had accepted his benediction and exhortation and drifted off, that Robbie left the bar. Gerald gave him ten minutes, then went down to 408. The "Come in" was firm and confident.

"Oh, hello. I saw you were back."

"I wonder if we could have a chat."

"Sure."

"You see, I went over to Huddersfield to see Mike and Mareeka."

There was barely a flicker of the eyelids. Robbie looked up at him guilelessly, a small smile playing on his lips, utterly confident. Godlike, Gerald thought suddenly.

"Oh yes. Mike phoned and told me that someone had been there. Why don't you sit down?"

Tentatively Gerald took the other chair.

"So you see, I know all about this outfit of yours."

"Do you?"

"Know that it's all a sham. How do you manage it? Forged passports?"

"Yes."

"Forged certificates of suitability for adopting?"

"Sometimes. There are other ways with the private agencies, and sometimes with the Social Services people as well."

"All to put through dubious adoptions for your own profit. I suppose Eileen and Mareeka are a couple, are they?"

"They are, as a matter of fact. Does it bother you?"

"No, it doesn't. But that's not the point. And Roland and Terry. I suppose? And Laura and Ursula?"

Robbie laughed out loud.

"Sorry, old boy. You really don't know all about us after all. No, no: Laura and Terry are a couple."

Gerald was nonplussed for a moment.

"Oh? Why can't they adopt in Britain? The age difference?"

"Not exactly. You see, they are brother and sister."

"Oh. . . . And Roland?"

"Roland is a bachelor—a quiet man who's lived alone all his life, and would now like to adopt a child. And Ursula is married—to a man with multiple sclerosis. They are comfortably off, and Ursula doesn't see why she should forego the pleasure of having a child. So you see, it's not as simple as you thought."

"No."

And yet Gerald was not sure that this new information made him feel less uneasy. Not with Robbie sitting there, that smile of self-approval playing on his lips. He was playing God: reversing nature, righting wrongs, changing woe to bliss. And doing so to immense applause—from the people he aided, but also from himself. What sort of effect did playing God have on a man's character? Gerald brought the matter bluntly into the open.

"What gives you the right to play God?"

"You get me wrong. I don't play God." But he brushed aside the accusation with a scorn that was Olympian. "I am simply the facilitator. I make things possible."

"So what makes you think you know better than the trained social worker?"

"I know better because I don't have their narrow view of human potential."

"How wonderful that sounds! But you do it for money."

"Partly. Romchild does make a modest profit. But mostly I do it to make people happy. There's too little happiness around."

"And if you found that one of your . . . clients was a pedophile? Or a sadist?"

"I'd call the whole thing off. I do have a policeman friend who is very good about checking if I have that suspicion. . . ." He leaned forward and raised his voice, like a politician. "But when you think how many heads of children's homes and foster parents have been found to have abused the children in their care in recent years, do you think your famous 'trained social workers' do so very much better than me?"

It was a telling point. Gerald acknowledged it by standing up, irresolute, uneasy.

"I don't know . . . I'll have to think."

"And what might you do?"

"Go to the British police. You've done several things that are against British law."

Robbie shook his head.

"I don't really think you're the sort of person who's so hidebound and prejudiced that you'd want to stop me taking these children from the dreadful conditions they're living in. Have you seen any of them? They're vegetables where they are. And in Britain, in the homes I find for them, they're happy, laughing, normal children. I've seen it. Women of forty-odd have children every day the world over. Why shouldn't they adopt? Men bring up children on their own all the time when their wives die or run out on them. Why shouldn't they adopt? Yes, and homosexual couples too—why should they be denied that joy?"

It all made so much sense. It was just that Gerald, leaning against the hotel room door, distrusted that air of omniscience, that limitless self-appro-bation, that God-like confidence.

And as he leaned his head against the door another picture came into Gerald's mind: of Robbie at the Reception desk, his head and the Reception clerk's bent over, studying passports, serious, worried. And he remembered all that talk—orchestrated? a sort of preparation?—about a rising tide of crime. And he remembered that genial, sad, ordinary man, knifed in the dark streets as he went home from work.

"You're quite right," he said, keeping his voice as steady as possible. "You're doing work that needs doing. You won't hear any more from me."

Once clear of the room, in the dark stairwell that had given him such an eerie sensation of being watched even on his first day, he stopped and put his forehead against the stone wall. He had still no idea what he was going to do. He did not know whether he had been believed or not. And if he had not been, he did not know how far Robbie would go to keep him quiet. He had entered one of those hinterlands which once he had found so interesting, so exciting. And he did so very much wish he hadn't.

One is sometimes tempted to think of Peter Lovesey as being from another age. He has been writing for many years, always with the result of pleasurable tales, be they short or long. The following story, from *Ellery Queen's Mystery Magazine,* is a perfect example of his consummate skill in bringing the reader through a maze of divertingly delivered details, leaving fair clues, and yet completely flamboozling the poor reader, who can only gasp and laugh and cry out with discovery and satisfied surprise.

The Crime of
Miss Oyster Brown
PETER LOVESEY

Miss Oyster Brown, a devout member of the Church of England, joined passionately each Sunday in every prayer of the Morning Service—except for the general Confession, when, in all honesty, she found it difficult to class herself as a lost sheep. She was willing to believe that everyone else in church had erred and strayed. In certain cases she knew exactly how, and with whom, and she would say a prayer for them. On her own account, however, she could seldom think of anything to confess. She tried strenuously, more strenuously —dare I say it?—than you or me to lead an untainted life. She managed conspicuously well. Very occasionally, as the rest of congregation joined in the Confession, she would own up to some trifling sin.

You may imagine what a fall from grace it was when this virtuous woman committed not merely a sin, but a crime. She lived more than half her life before it happened.

She resided in a Berkshire town with her twin sister Pearl, who was a mere three minutes her senior. Oyster and Pearl—a flamboyance in forenames that owed something to the fact that their parents had been plain John and Mary Brown. Up to the moment of birth the Browns had been led to expect one child, who, if female, was to be named Pearl. In the turmoil created by a second, unscheduled, daughter, John Brown jokingly suggested naming her Oyster. Mary, bosky from morphine, seized on the name as an inspiration, a delight to the ear when said in front of dreary old Brown.

Of course the charm was never so apparent to the twins, who got to dread being introduced to people. Even in infancy, they were aware that their parents' friends found the names amusing. At school they were taunted as much by the teachers as the children. The names never ceased to amuse. Fifty years on, things were still said just out of earshot and laced with pretended sympathy. "Here come Pearl and Oyster, poor old ducks. Fancy being stuck with names like that."

No wonder they faced the world defiantly. In middle age, they were a formidable duo, stalwarts of the choir, the Bible-reading Circle, the Townswomen's Guild, and the Magistrates' Bench. Neither sister had married. They lived together in Lime Tree Avenue, in the mock-Tudor house where they were born. They were not short of money.

There are certain things people always want to know about twins, the more so in mystery stories. I can reassure the wary reader that Oyster and Pearl were not identical. Oyster was an inch taller, more sturdy in build than her sister and slower of speech. They dressed individually, Oyster as a rule in tweed skirts and check blouses that she made herself, always from the same Butterick pattern; Pearl in a variety of mail-order suits in pastel blues and greens. No one confused them.

As for that other question so often asked about twins, neither sister could be characterized as "dominant." Each possessed a forceful personality by any standard. To avoid disputes they had established a household routine, a division of the duties that worked pretty harmoniously, all things considered. Oyster did most of the cooking and the gardening, for example, and Pearl attended to the housework and paid the bills when they became due. They both enjoyed shopping, so they shared it. They did the church flowers together when their turn came, and they always ran the bottle stall at the church fete. Five vicars had held the living at St. Saviour's in the twins' time as worshipers there. Each new incumbent was advised by his predecessor that Pearl and Oyster were the mainstays of the parish. Better to fall foul of the diocesan bishop himself than the Brown twins.

All of this was observed from a distance, for no one, not even a vicar making his social rounds, was allowed inside the house in Lime Tree Avenue. The twins didn't entertain, and that was final. They were polite to their neighbors without once inviting them in. When one twin was ill, the other would transport her to the surgery in a state of high fever rather than call the doctor on a visit.

It followed that people's knowledge of Pearl and Oyster was limited. No one could doubt that they lived an orderly existence; there were no complaints about undue noise or unwashed windows or neglected paintwork. The hedge was trimmed and the garden mown. But what really bubbled and boiled behind the regularly washed net curtains—the secret passion that was to have such a dire result—was unsuspected until Oyster committed her crime.

She acted out of desperation. On the last Saturday in July, 1990, her well ordered life suffered a seismic shock. She was parted from her twin sister. The parting was sudden, traumatic, and had to be shrouded in secrecy. The prospect of anyone finding out what had occurred was unthinkable.

So for the first time in her life Oyster had no Pearl to change the light bulbs, pay the bills, and check that all the doors were locked. Oyster—let it be understood—was not incapable or dim-witted. Bereft as she was, she managed tolerably well until the Friday afternoon, when she had a letter to post, a letter of surpassing importance, capable—God willing—of easing her desolation. She had agonized over it for hours. Now it was crucial that the letter caught the last post of the day. Saturday would be too late. She went to the drawer where Pearl always kept the postage stamps and—calamity—not one was left.

Stamps had always been Pearl's responsibility. To be fair, the error was Oyster's; she had written more letters than usual and gone through the supply. She should have called at the Post Office when she was doing the shopping.

It was too late. There wasn't time to get there before the last post at 5:15. She tried to remain calm and consider her options. It was out of the question to ask a neighbor for a stamp; she and Pearl had made it a point of honor never to be beholden to anyone else. Neither could she countenance the disgrace of dispatching the letter without a stamp in the hope that it would get by, or the recipient would pay the amount due.

This left one remedy, and it was criminal.

Behind one of the Staffordshire dogs on the mantelpiece was a bank statement. She had put it there for the time being because she had been too busy to check where Pearl normally stored such things. The significant point for Oyster at this minute was not the statement, but the envelope containing it. More precisely, the top right-hand corner of the envelope, because the first-class stamp had somehow escaped being canceled.

Temptation stirred and uncoiled itself.

Oyster had never in her life steamed an unfranked stamp from an envelope and used it again. Nor, to her knowledge, had Pearl. Stamp collectors sometimes removed used specimens for their collections, but what Oyster was contemplating could in no way be confused with philately. It was against the law. Defrauding the Post Office. A crime.

There was under twenty minutes before the last collection.

I couldn't, she told herself. *I'm on the Parochial Church Council. I'm on the Bench.*

Temptation reminded her that she was due for a cup of tea in any case. She filled the kettle and pressed the switch. While waiting, watching the first wisp of steam rise from the spout, she weighed the necessity of posting the letter against the wickedness of reusing a stamp. It wasn't the most heinous of crimes, Temptation whispered. And once Oyster began to think about the chances of getting away with it, she was lost. The kettle sang, the steam gushed, and she snatched up the envelope and jammed it against the spout. Merely, Temptation reassured her, to satisfy her curiosity as to whether stamps could be separated from envelopes by this method.

Those who believe in retribution will not be in the least surprised that the steam was deflected by the surface of the envelope and scalded three of Oyster's fingers quite severely. She cried out in pain and dropped the envelope. She ran the cold tap and plunged her hand under it. Then she wrapped the sore fingers in a piece of kitchen towel.

Her first action after that was to turn off the kettle. Her second was to pick up the envelope and test the corner of the stamp with the tip of her fingernail. It still adhered to some extent, but with extreme care she was able to ease it free, consoled that her discomfort had not been entirely without result. The minor accident failed to deter her from the crime. On the contrary, it acted like a prod from Old Nick.

There was a bottle of gum in the writing desk and she applied some to the back of the stamp, taking care not to use too much, which might have oozed out at the edges and discolored the envelope. When she had positioned the stamp neatly on her letter, it would have passed the most rigorous inspection. She felt a wicked frisson of satisfaction at having committed an undetectable crime. Just in time, she remembered the post and had to hurry to catch it.

There we leave Miss Oyster Brown to come to terms with her conscience for a couple of days.

We meet her again on the Monday morning in the local chemist's shop. The owner and pharmacist was John Trigger, whom the Brown twins had known for getting on for thirty years, a decent, obliging man with a huge mustache who took a personal interest in his customers. In the face of strong competition from a national chain of pharmacists, John Trigger had persevered with his old-fashioned service from behind a counter, believing that some customers still preferred it to filling a wire basket themselves. But to stay in business, he had been forced to diversify by offering some electrical goods.

When Oyster Brown came in and showed him three badly scalded fingers out in blisters, Trigger was sympathetic as well as willing to suggest a remedy. Understandably, he inquired how Oyster had come by such a painful injury. She was expecting the question and had her answer ready, adhering to the truth as closely as a God-fearing woman should.

"An accident with the kettle."

Trigger looked genuinely alarmed. "An electric kettle? Not the one you bought here last year?"

"I didn't," said Oyster at once.

"Must have been your sister. A Steamquick. Is that what you've got?"

"Er, yes."

"If there's a fault—"

"I'm not here to complain, Mr. Trigger. So you think this ointment will do the trick?"

"I'm sure of it. Apply it evenly, and don't attempt to pierce the blisters, will you?" John Trigger's conscience was troubling him. "This is quite a nasty scalding, Miss Brown. Where exactly did the steam come from?"

"The kettle."

"I know that. I mean was it the spout?"

"It really doesn't matter," said Oyster sharply. "It's done."

"The lid, then? Sometimes if you're holding the handle you get a rush of steam from that little slot in the lid. I expect it was that."

"I couldn't say," Oyster fudged, in the hope that it would satisfy Mr. Trigger.

It did not. "The reason I asked is that there may be a design fault."

"The fault was mine, I'm quite sure."

"Perhaps I ought to mention it to the manufacturers."

"Absolutely not," Oyster said in alarm. "I was careless, that's all. And now, if you'll excuse me—" She started backing away and then Mr. Trigger ambushed her with another question.

"What does your sister say about it?"

"My sister?" From the way she spoke, she might never have had one.

"Miss Pearl."

"Oh, nothing. We haven't discussed it," Oyster truthfully stated.

"But she must have noticed your fingers."

"Er, no. How much is the ointment?"

Trigger told her and she dropped the money on the counter and almost rushed from the shop. He stared after her, bewildered.

The next time Oyster Brown was passing, Trigger took the trouble to go to the door of his shop and inquire whether the hand was any better. Clearly she wasn't overjoyed to see him. She assured him without much gratitude that the ointment was working. "It was nothing. It's going to clear up in a couple of days."

"May I see?"

She held out her hand.

Trigger agreed that it was definitely on the mend. "Keep it dry, if you possibly can. Who does the washing up?"

"What do you mean?"

"You or your sister? It's well known that you divide the chores between you. If it's your job, I'm sure Miss Pearl won't mind taking over for a few days. If I see her, I'll suggest it myself."

Oyster reddened and said nothing.

"I was going to remark that I haven't seen her for a week or so," Trigger went on. "She isn't unwell, I hope?"

"No," said Oyster. "Not unwell."

Sensing correctly that this was not an avenue of conversation to venture along at this time, he said instead, "The Steamquick rep was in yesterday afternoon, so I mentioned what happened with your kettle."

She was outraged. "You had no business!"

"Pardon me, Miss Brown, but it *is* my business. You were badly scalded. I can't have my customers being injured by the products I sell. The rep was very concerned, as I am. He asked if you would be so good as to bring the kettle in next time you come so that he can check if there's a fault."

"Absolutely not," said Oyster. "I told you I haven't the slightest intention of complaining."

Trigger tried to be reasonable. "It isn't just your kettle. I've sold the same model to other customers."

"Then they'll complain if they get hurt."

"What if their children get hurt?"

She had no answer.

"If it's inconvenient to bring it in, perhaps I could call at your house."

"No," she said at once.

"I can bring a replacement. In fact, Miss Brown, I'm more than a little concerned about this whole episode. I'd like you to have another kettle with my compliments. A different model. Frankly, the modern trend is for jug kettles that couldn't possibly scald you as yours did. If you'll kindly step into the shop, I'll give you one now to take home."

The offer didn't appeal to Oyster Brown in the least. "For the last time, Mr. Trigger," she said in a tight, clipped voice, "I don't require another kettle." With that, she walked away up the high street.

Trigger, from the motives he had mentioned, was not content to leave the matter there. He wasn't a churchgoer, but he believed in conducting his life on humanitarian principles. On this issue, he was resolved to be just as stubborn as she. He went back into the shop and straight to the phone. While Oyster Brown was out of the house, he would speak to Pearl Brown, the sister, and see if he could get better cooperation from her.

Nobody answered the phone.

At lunchtime, he called in to see Ted Collins, who ran the garden shop next door, and asked if he had seen anything of Pearl Brown lately.

"I had Oyster in this morning," Collins told him.

"But you haven't seen Pearl?"

"Not in my shop. Oyster does all the gardening, you know. They divide the work."

"I know."

"I can't think what came over her today. Do you know what she bought? Six bottles of Rapidrot."

"What's that?"

"It's a new product. An activator for composting. You dilute it and water your compost heap and it speeds up the process. They're doing a special promotion to launch it. Six bottles are far too much, and I tried to tell her, but she wouldn't be told."

"Those two often buy in bulk," said Trigger. "I've sold Pearl a dozen tubes of toothpaste at a go, and they must be awash with Dettol."

"They won't use six bottles of Rapidrot in twenty years," Collins pointed out. "It's concentrated stuff, and it won't keep all that well. It's sure to solidify after a time. I told her one's plenty to be going on with. She's wasted her money, obstinate old bird. I don't know what Pearl would say. Is she ill, do you think?"

"I've no idea," said Trigger, although in reality an idea was beginning to form in his brain. A disturbing idea. "Do they get on all right with each other? Daft question," he said before Collins could answer it. "They're twins. They've spent all their lives in each other's company."

For the present he dismissed the thought and gave his attention to the matter of the electric kettles. He'd already withdrawn the Steamquick kettles from sale. He got on the phone to Steamquick and had an acrimonious conversation with some little Hitler from their public-relations department who insisted that thousands of the kettles had been sold and the design was faultless.

"The lady's injury isn't imagined, I can tell you," Trigger insisted.

"She must have been careless. Anyone can hurt themselves if they're not careful. People are far too ready to put the blame on the manufacturer."

"People, as you put it, are your livelihood."

There was a heavy sigh. "Send us the offending kettle, and we'll test it."

"That isn't so simple."

"Have you offered to replace it?"

The man's whole tone was so condescending that Trigger had an impulse to frighten him rigid. "She won't let the kettle out of her possession. I think she may be keeping it as evidence."

"Evidence?" There was a pause while the implication dawned. "Blimey."

On his end of the phone, Trigger permitted himself to grin.

"You mean she might take us to court over this?"

"I didn't say that."

"Ah."

"But she does know the law. She's a magistrate."

An audible gasp followed, then: "Listen, Mr., er—"

"Trigger."

"Mr. Trigger. I think we'd better send someone to meet this lady and deal with the matter personally. Yes, that's what we'll do."

Trigger worked late that evening, stocktaking. He left the shop about 10:30. Out of curiosity he took a route home via Lime Tree Avenue and stopped the car opposite the Brown sisters' house and wound down the car window. There were lights upstairs and presently someone drew a curtain. It looked like Oyster Brown.

"Keeping an eye on your customers, Mr. Trigger?" a voice close to him said.

He turned guiltily. A woman's face was six inches from his. He recognized one of his customers, Mrs. Wingate. She said, "She's done that every night this week."

"Oh?"

"Something fishy's going on in there," she said. "I walk my little dog along the verge about this time every night. I live just opposite them, on this side, with the wrought-iron gates. That's Pearl's bedroom at the front. I haven't seen Pearl for a week, but every night Oyster draws the curtains and leaves the light on for half an hour. What's going on, I'd like to know. If Pearl is ill, they ought to call a doctor. They won't, you know."

"That's Pearl's bedroom, you say, with the light on?"

"Yes, I often see her looking out. Not lately."

"And now Oyster switches on the light and draws the curtains?"

"And pulls them back at seven in the morning. I don't know what *you* think, Mr. Trigger, but it looks to me as if she wants everyone to think Pearl's in there, when it's obvious she isn't."

"Why is it obvious?"

"All the windows are closed. Pearl always opens the top window wide, winter and summer."

"That is odd, now you mention it."

"I'll tell you one thing," said Mrs. Wingate, regardless that she had told him several things already, "whatever game she's up to, we won't find out. Nobody ever sets foot inside that house except the twins themselves."

At home and in bed that night, Trigger was troubled by a gruesome idea, one that he'd tried repeatedly to suppress. Suppose the worst had happened a week ago in the house in Lime Tree Avenue, his thinking ran. Suppose Pearl Brown had suffered a heart attack and died. After so many years of living in that house as if it were a fortress, was Oyster capable of dealing with the aftermath of death, calling in the doctor and the undertaker? In her shocked state, mightn't she decide that anything was preferable to having the house invaded, even if the alternative was disposing of the body herself?

How would a middle-aged woman dispose of a body? Oyster didn't drive a car. It wouldn't be easy to bury it in the garden, nor hygienic to keep it in a cupboard in the house. But if there was one thing every well bred English lady knew about, it was gardening.

Oyster was the gardener.

In time, everything rots in a compost heap. If you want to accelerate the process, you buy a preparation like Rapidrot.

Oyster Brown had purchased six bottles of the stuff. And every night she drew the curtains in her sister's bedroom to give the impression that she was there.

He shuddered.

In the fresh light of morning, John Trigger told himself that his morbid imaginings couldn't be true. They were the delusions of a tired brain. He decided to do nothing about them.

Just after 11:30, a short fat man in a dark suit arrived in the shop and announced himself as the Area Manager of Steamquick. His voice was suspiciously like the one Trigger had found so irritating when he had phoned their head office. "I'm here about this allegedly faulty kettle," he announced.

"Miss Brown's?"

"I'm sure there's nothing wrong at all, but we're a responsible firm. We take every complaint seriously."

"You want to see the kettle? You'll be lucky."

The Steamquick man sounded smug. "That's all right. I telephoned Miss Brown this morning and offered to go to the house. She wasn't at all keen on that idea, but I was very firm with the lady and she compromised. We're meeting here at noon. She's agreed to bring the kettle for me to inspect. I don't know why you found her so intractable."

"High noon, eh? Do you want to use my office?"

Trigger had come to a rapid decision. If Oyster was on her way to the shop, he was going out. He had two capable assistants.

This was a heaven-sent opportunity to lay his macabre theory to rest. While Oyster was away from the house in Lime Tree Avenue, he would drive there and let himself into the back garden. Mrs. Wingate or any other curious neighbor watching from behind the lace curtains would have to assume he was trying to deliver something. He kept his white coat on, to reinforce the idea that he was on official business.

Quite probably, he told himself, the compost heap will turn out to be no bigger than a cowpat. The day was sunny and he felt positively cheerful as he turned up the avenue. He checked his watch. Oyster would be making mincemeat of the Steamquick man about now. It would take her twenty minutes, at least, to walk back.

He stopped the car and got out. Nobody was about, but just in case he was being observed he walked boldly up the path to the front door and rang the bell. No one came.

Without appearing in the least furtive, he stepped around the side of the house. The back garden was in a beautiful state. Wide, well stocked, and immaculately weeded borders enclosed a finely trimmed lawn, yellow roses on a trellis, and a kitchen garden beyond. Trigger took it in admiringly, and then remembered why he was there. His throat went dry. At the far end, beyond the kitchen garden, slightly obscured by some runner beans on poles, was the compost heap—as long as a coffin and more than twice as high.

The flesh on his arms prickled.

The compost heap was covered with black-plastic bin liners weighted with stones. They lay across the top, but the sides were exposed. A layer of fresh green garden refuse, perhaps half a meter in depth, was on the top. The lower part graduated in color from a dull yellow to earth-brown. Obvious care had been taken to conserve the shape, to keep the pressure even and assist the composting process.

Trigger wasn't much of a gardener. He didn't have the time for it. He did the minimum and got rid of his garden rubbish with bonfires. Compost heaps were outside his experience, except that as a scientist he understood the principle by which they generated heat in a confined space. Once, years ago, an uncle of his had demonstrated this by pushing a bamboo cane into his heap from the top. A wisp of steam had issued from the hole as he withdrew the cane. Recalling it now, Trigger felt a wave of nausea.

He hadn't the stomach for this.

He knew now that he wasn't going to be able to walk up the garden and probe the compost heap. Disgusted with himself for being so squeamish, he turned to leave, and happened to notice that the kitchen window was ajar, which was odd considering that Oyster wasn't at home. Out of interest, he tried the door handle. The door was unlocked.

He said, "Anyone there?" and got no answer.

From the doorway he could see a number of unopened letters on the kitchen table. After the humiliation of turning his back on the compost heap, this was like a challenge, a chance to regain some self-respect. This, at least, he was capable of doing. He stepped inside and picked up the letters. There were five, all addressed to Miss P. Brown. The postmarks dated from the beginning of the previous week.

Quite clearly, Pearl had not been around to open her letters.

Then his attention was taken by an extraordinary lineup along a shelf. He counted fifteen packets of cornflakes, all open, and recalled his conversation with Ted Collins about the sisters buying in bulk. If Collins had wanted convincing, there was ample evidence here: seven bottles of decaffeinated coffee, nine jars of the same brand of marmalade, and a tall stack of boxes of paper tissues. Eccentric housekeeping, to say the least. Perhaps, he reflected, it meant that the buying of six bottles of Rapidrot had not, after all, been so sinister.

But now that he was in the house, he wasn't going to leave without seeking an answer to the main mystery, the disappearance of Pearl. His mouth was no longer dry and the gooseflesh had gone from his arms. He made up his mind to go upstairs and look into the front bedroom.

On the other side of the kitchen door, more extravagance was revealed. The passage from the kitchen to the stairway was lined on either side with sets of goods that must have overflowed from the kitchen. Numerous tins of cocoa, packets of sugar, pots of jam, gravy powder, and other grocery items were stored as if for a siege, stacked along the skirting boards in groups of at least half a dozen. Trigger began seriously to fear for the mental health of the twins. Nobody had suspected anything like this behind the closed doors. The stacks extended halfway upstairs.

As he stepped upward, obliged to tread close to the banister, he was gripped by the sense of alienation that must have led to hoarding on such a scale. The staid faces that the sisters presented to the world gave no intimation of this strange compulsion. What was the mentality of people who behaved as weirdly as this?

An appalling possibility crept into Trigger's mind. Maybe the strain of so many years of appearing outwardly normal had finally caused Oyster to snap. What if the eccentricity so apparent all around him now were not so harmful as it first appeared? No one could know what resentments, what jealousies lurked in this house, what mean-minded cruelties the sisters may have inflicted on each other. What if Oyster had fallen out with her sister and attacked her? She was a sturdy woman, physically capable of killing.

If she'd murdered Pearl, the compost-heap method of disposal would certainly commend itself.

Come now, he told himself, this is all speculation.

He reached the top stair and discovered that the stockpiling had extended to the landing. Toothpaste, talcum powder, shampoos, and soap were stacked up in profusion. All the doors were closed. It wouldn't have surprised him if when he opened one he was knee-deep in toilet rolls.

First he had to orientate himself. He decided that the front bedroom was to his right. He opened it cautiously and stepped in.

What happened next was swift and devastating. John Trigger heard a piercing scream. He had a sense of movement to his left and a glimpse of a figure in white. Something crashed against his head with a mighty thump, causing him to pitch forward.

* * *

About four, when the Brown twins generally stopped for tea, Oyster filled the new kettle that the Steamquick Area Manager had exchanged for the other one. She plugged it in. It was the newfangled jug type and she wasn't really certain if she was going to like it, but she certainly needed the cup of tea.

"I know it was wrong," she said, "and I'm going to pray for forgiveness, but I didn't expect that steaming a stamp off a letter would lead to this. I suppose it's a judgment."

"Whatever made you do such a wicked thing?" her sister Pearl asked, as she put out the cups and saucers.

"The letter had to catch the post. It was the last possible day for the Kellogg's Cornflakes competition, and I'd thought of such a wonderful slogan. The prize was a fortnight in Venice."

Pearl clicked her tongue in disapproval. "Just because I won the Birds Eye trip to the Bahamas, it didn't mean *you* were going to be lucky. We tried for twenty years and only ever won consolation prizes."

"It isn't really gambling, is it?" said Oyster. "It isn't like betting."

"It's all right in the Lord's eyes," Pearl told her. "It's a harmless pastime. Unfortunately, we both know that people in the church won't take a charitable view. They wouldn't expect us to devote so much of our time and money to competitions. That's why we have to be careful. You didn't tell anyone I was away?"

"Of course not. Nobody knows. For all they know, you were ill, if anyone noticed at all. I drew the curtains in your bedroom every night to make it look as if you were here."

"Thank you. You know I'd do the same for you."

"I *might* win," said Oyster. "Someone always does. I put in fifteen entries altogether, and the last one was a late inspiration."

"And as a result we have fifteen packets of cornflakes with the tops cut off," said Pearl. "They take up a lot of room."

"So do your frozen peas. I had to throw two packets away to make some room in the freezer. Anyway, I felt entitled to try. It wasn't much fun being here alone, thinking of you sunning yourself in the West Indies. To tell you the truth, I didn't really think you'd go and leave me here. It was a shock."

Oyster carefully poured some hot water into the teapot to warm it. "If you want to know, I've also entered the Rapidrot Trip of a Lifetime competition. A week in San Francisco followed by a week in Sydney. I bought six bottles to have a fighting chance."

"What's Rapidrot?"

"Something for the garden." She spooned in some tea and poured on the hot water. "You must be exhausted. Did you get any sleep on the plane?"

"Hardly any," said Pearl. "That's why I went straight to bed when I got in this morning." She poured milk into the teacups. "The next thing I knew was the doorbell going. I ignored it, naturally. It was one of the nastiest shocks I ever had, hearing the footsteps coming up the stairs. I could tell it wasn't you. I'm just thankful that I had the candlestick to defend myself with."

"Is there any sign of life yet?"

"Well, he's breathing, but he hasn't opened his eyes, if that's what you mean. Funny, I would never have thought Mr. Trigger was dangerous to women."

Oyster poured the tea. "What are we going to do if he doesn't recover? We can't have people coming into the house." Even as she was speaking, she put down the teapot and glanced out of the kitchen window toward the end of the garden. She had the answer herself.

Psychologists tell us about the stages of maturation through which children must progress on their way to maturity. And one of their dictums is that each stage of development is apt to be fluid; regression to earlier modes of behavior occurs during times of stress or fatigue. But adolescence is never as simple as the books and doctors would have us believe, and the catch phrases of psychobabble find expression in complex actions and tangled motivations. June Thomson, in this story from *Ellery Queen's Mystery Magazine*, catches a moment, a single awful moment, in which the games and ploys of childhood become the irrevocable reality of death. The reader is free to draw conclusions from the evidence, as to whether it was murder or accident. What is clear is that Thomson is a most skilled and subtle writer.

Secrets
JUNE THOMSON

Yesterday I went to my sister Naomi's funeral. It was a sad little ceremony, attended by only a few people, mostly acquaintances whom she had made in Rochester, where she had lived for the past fifteen years since her second divorce. I had the feeling none of them were close friends. Naomi had never possessed the gift of intimacy, not with either of her husbands and certainly not with me, her younger brother.

As a child, I had both envied and admired her. Thin and long-legged, she could outrun almost any boy of her own age and knew how to bowl overarm like a professional. Nothing frightened her, not even Father. At the same time, I was intimidated by her self-assurance and the intensity of her determination.

It was largely for this reason that we had grown apart, but not entirely.

As her coffin was lowered into the grave, I thought: It's too late now to ask her what really happened all those years ago on the cliff-top in Cornwall.

* * *

It was toward the end of August 1939, shortly before the outbreak of the war, when Naomi was thirteen and I was seven; one of those perfect summers of long, hot days and impeccable skies which one remembers all one's life as part of a vanished childhood. The fear of war seemed only to add an extra dangerous glitter to the sea.

As we did every year, we spent that summer at the small, whitewashed house our parents owned in the fishing village of Portmerron on the North Cornish coast. From its windows, we could look out at the sea and the surrounding cliffs, towering above the little harbor. At night, we went to sleep to the sound of waves slapping up against the rocks or sucking at the sand and, in the morning, we were wakened by the screams of the gulls.

But that summer, there were two changes to our usual holiday routine. For the first time that I could remember, my father wasn't able to join us. Because of the crisis, all leave had been cancelled at the Foreign Office where he worked.

And Edward Wilson came to stay.

"Why does he have to?" Naomi demanded when Mother broke the news to us one morning over breakfast.

Mother laid down the letter from Mrs. Wilson she had been reading.

"Because his father's been called up into the air force and his mother wants Edward to stay with us while she finds somewhere to live near to where he's been posted," she explained in that reasonable voice she often adopted with Naomi, rarely with me. It was only years later, when I heard myself using the same tone, that I realized it was her way of avoiding a confrontation.

"But he's stupid!"

Mother came close to losing her patience.

"I won't have you saying that, Naomi! And please remember you're to be nice to him. He's going to feel lonely here at first without his parents. I want you and Tom to make friends with him."

"I don't care what she says, he is stupid," Naomi asserted when, breakfast over, we walked down to the beach.

I nodded, knowing better than to disagree with her, although I secretly thought that anyone whose father was in the air force couldn't be entirely contemptible. I imagined Mr. Wilson in a leather helmet, like Biggles, flying over vast continents laid out below him and colored red as they were in my school atlas. As for Edward, I had no clear recollection of him. His mother and mine were old childhood friends who had kept in touch, although they rarely met after the Wilsons moved to Reading. The last time I had seen him had been two years before at a Christmas circus in London, but it was the clowns I remembered more vividly than him.

He arrived two days later, accompanied by his mother, who left the same evening to return to Reading.

Even now my memories of him are far from clear for I have difficulty in distinguishing my childhood image of him from my sister's.

To her, he was merely a nuisance, a fat lump of a child who tagged along after us, spoiling our games, who couldn't swim and was hopeless at beach cricket. As if through her eyes, I saw him toiling after us across the sand, his face moist under his linen sunhat, calling out in a constant wail, "Wait for me!" Her private nickname for him was the Vest, because of the white singlet he always wore under his shirt. With her talent for mockery, she made up a song about him to the tune of Bobby Shaftoe:

> Edward Wilson wears a vest,
> He is nothing but a pest,
> Let's lock him in a great big chest,
> Soppy Edward Wilson.

When Mother was present, she would hum the tune under her breath or tap out its rhythm on the table until Mother, not understanding the joke but suspecting it was directed at Edward, told her to stop. After that, she only hummed or tapped in front of him, enticing me with a sideways smile to join in the fun.

My own memories of him, those not influenced by Naomi's attitude, are different. Because the house was small, we had to share a bedroom, which I resented at first until I came to enjoy his company. Generous with his possessions, he let me borrow his Rupert annuals or look through his stamp collection. But I remember him best sitting cross-legged on his bed, a round-faced, fair-haired boy of my own age, wearing blue and white striped pajamas, his teddy bear, Benjy, perched on the pillow beside him, and discussing with me in his grave, adult manner those subjects, such as football and model trains, which small boys of seven find mutually absorbing.

He wanted to be a boffin when he grew up, like his father. At the time, I didn't know what the word meant.

"What's a boffin?" I asked.

Instead of laughing at me for my ignorance as Naomi would have done, he answered me quite seriously.

"It's someone who does research. Daddy's an expert in radio. That's why he's been called up into the air force."

"I thought your father was a pilot."

"Oh, no," he corrected me proudly, as if it was far better to be a boffin than to fly a plane. "He's part of a very special team that's been set up somewhere in Scotland to test out new equipment. Actually, it's terribly secret and I'm not supposed to say anything about it in case the Germans find out. So you must promise not to tell."

In giving him my word, I sealed a bond with him, the true nature of which I wasn't to understand until later.

It was largely on Edward's account that toward the end of the week Mother suggested that the three of us go on the bus that afternoon into Trewarth, the small seaside resort about six miles away.

"Do we have to go?" Naomi cried.

For once, Mother was adamant.

"It'll make a change and besides, Edward hasn't seen anything of Cornwall yet apart from the beach. Now, I've looked up the times of the buses. If you get the one straight after lunch, you'll have two hours to spend in Trewarth before catching the half-past-four bus home."

"But there's nothing to do in Trewarth!"

"Nonsense! Of course there is," Mother said brightly. "There's the promenade and the donkeys and the Punch and Judy show on the beach."

Even Naomi realized that it was useless to argue, although she grumbled under her breath to me that it was all the Vest's fault as we went upstairs to get ready for the excursion.

"Silly idiot!" she muttered, slamming her bedroom door shut behind her.

As we left, Mother called out last instructions to us from the front steps.

"Keep together so you won't lose one another and hold hands when you cross the road. And don't miss the half-past-four bus home. Naomi, did you hear me?"

If she did, Naomi made no sign. Her brow like thunder, she stalked off down the road toward the bus stop outside the Portmerron Arms, her long brown legs flashing in and out under the skirt of the hated dress which Mother had made her wear for the occasion, while Edward and I trotted beside her, in clean shirts and shorts, our hair sleeked back with water.

The bus ride was enjoyable but Naomi was right about Trewarth. Once the temporary excitement of the shops and the holiday crowds had worn off, there was very little to do. Caged in between the breakwaters, the sea seemed tame after Portmerron as it lapped languidly up the beach. There were no rocks here to climb, no hidden pools to discover. There wasn't even room to run about, for the beach was strewn with deckchairs and the slumbering bodies of sunbathers.

There were, however, donkeys—a sullen line of them, heads hanging low in the heat, the sand around them stained with their droppings, on which the blowflies buzzed and feasted. Edward refused a ride on one of them, wrinkling up his nose in disgust at the smell.

As for the Punch and Judy show, we had missed most of the performance. Using this as an excuse, Naomi made us stand at the back among the grownups, although I suspected her pride wouldn't let her join the semicircle of little children seated on the sand in front of the booth. With her arms tightly folded across her chest, her disapproval made itself so apparent that neither Edward nor I dared to join in the laughter, not even when Punch seized the stick and beat the policeman over the head with it.

When the curtains closed and the Punch and Judy man emerged from the back to pass round the hat, she dragged us away.

"What are we going to do now?" Edward asked plaintively as we crunched up the beach toward the promenade.

"I don't know. I said the place was boring," Naomi replied in an I-told-you-so voice.

I was going to suggest that we go to the penny amusement arcade when Edward noticed a sign at the top of the steps, pointing to a museum.

"I want to go there," he said.

"You won't like it," Naomi warned him.

"Yes I will."

He came to a halt in the middle of the pavement and stood there facing her, plump legs set apart and an expression on his face not unlike Naomi's when she was determined to get her own way.

"I want to go," he repeated.

My sister sighed in the same way Mother did when faced with our intractability, usually Naomi's, but, to my surprise, she gave in. Perhaps she realized that she had gone too far in spoiling our afternoon and word might get back to Mother.

"Oh, all right then. Come on!"

Seizing us by the hands, she hurried us across the road at the traffic lights and into a side street where the museum was situated in a gray stone building, up three steps.

It was sixpence each to go in. Naomi clicked her tongue at this exorbitant amount, although I had the feeling that she secretly enjoyed the importance of paying over the half-crown which Mother had given to her for spending money and being handed the tickets by the lady in the kiosk from a big yellow roll.

"I'll look after them," she told us, putting them away, together with the change, into her navy-blue school purse which hung on a strap over the front of her dress and which Mother had made her take with her. She kept us waiting while she snapped the button fastener firmly shut before leading the way inside.

After the heat and glare of the town, the interior was as cool and as dim as a church. Long, cream-colored blinds drawn down over the windows kept out the sun. As we entered, our footsteps rang out on the stone floor.

There were only two rooms, the first devoted to the wildlife of the area, almost entirely stuffed seabirds, perched on pieces of rock or squatting on meager nests of twigs and pebbles. Their malevolent black eyes glared at us through the dusty glass of their cases.

Naomi made us stay together and we trailed after her from one display to the next while she read out loud to us from the explanatory cards fixed to the wall at the side of each exhibit.

" 'The Great Black-Backed Gull, *Larus marinus*,' " she intoned in a loud, clear voice, " ' is common along the North Cornish coast where it nests singly or in colonies. Larger than the Herring Gull, it is distinguished by its heavy bill, its black wings, and pinkish legs. A predator, it will steal the eggs and young of other seabirds.' "

Several people turned round to look, as if we really were in church and ought to be silent, but Naomi only tossed her head and went on with the readings until Edward and I began to fidget and finally even she grew tired of the game. When we moved into the second room, given over to local history, she allowed us to go off on our own, Edward hanging back to look at a case of Roman finds, mostly old coins and bits of broken pottery, while I made straight for one of two large exhibits set up in alcoves on each side at the further end of the room.

It was a tableau depicting a smugglers' cave, lit by only the yellow glow from two lanterns, standing on papier-mâché rocks, which cast eerie shadows over the bearded faces of three men, bending down over brandy casks and large, oilskin-wrapped parcels, labeled "Tobacco" in case there was any doubt about their contents. But I was puzzled by the treasure chest, open and carelessly spilling out ropes of pearls, jeweled coronets, and great handfuls of gold coins which, taken with the black eye-patch one of the figures was wearing, suggested pirates rather than smugglers.

Unless, of course, they were meant to be wreckers as well.

Father had told us about the wreckers, how they stood on the cliffs with lanterns, luring ships onto the rocks, and then plundered their cargoes.

I started to walk toward Naomi in order to ask her opinion.

She was standing, totally absorbed, in front of the other tableau, although I caught only a glimpse of it before she whirled about as I approached.

Behind her, I could see the interior of a darkened room—a hut, perhaps, or a primitive cottage. Curious objects, bundles of dried herbs, leather bottles and crude earthenware jars, hung down from the low, beamed ceiling or were scattered about the floor beside an open fire over which a big, black pot was suspended from a chain. In the lurid glow from a red bulb, not quite concealed under the logs and the scarlet crepe-paper flames, I could dimly discern the silhouette of a woman, crouching beside the hearth, a black cat at her side and a broom made out of sticks propped up in a corner.

There was something sinister about the setting but before I could examine it more closely, Naomi had whisked me round so that I had my back to it.

"What do you want?" she demanded fiercely.

"Nothing," I stammered. "I was only going to ask you about the smugglers."

"There isn't time," she retorted, looking at the boy's watch strapped to her wrist. "We have to go now."

Pushing me in front of her by the shoulder, she collected up Edward and swept the pair of us out of the museum and along the street to the promenade.

We were almost a quarter of an hour too early for the bus. There would have been time for us to go to the penny arcade and to have had a turn on the crane or one of the pin-tables or, better still, the mechanical model of the death of Mary Queen of Scots and to have made the little figures jerk into action, especially the executioner who brought his axe crashing down to send the poor Queen's head tumbling from her shoulders.

Naomi wouldn't let us. We might miss the bus and then Mother would be cross.

But she relented far enough to buy Edward and me each a triangular stick of orange ice cream from the Wall's Stop-Me-And-Buy-One tricycle on the sea-front and then left us by the bus stop, sucking at the sweet, frozen juice which made our teeth ache and which tasted of the cardboard container while she disappeared inside Boot's the Chemist a little way up the street.

She was back within minutes, the pocket of her dress bulging with something in a white paper bag which she refused to show us.

"It's none of your business," she said briskly, just like Mother and then, spitting on her handkerchief, began to scrub our faces clean for the journey home.

We were silent on the bus, too dazed by the sun and the heat to talk. Edward and I sat together, Naomi occupying a seat by herself on the other side of the aisle, as if she had nothing to do with us.

"I think a bath and early bed tonight," Mother said over tea, seeing our flushed faces.

"I'm not tired," Naomi said. Indeed, she looked bursting with energy and purpose. "I was thinking of walking up to the cliff-top with Tom. We haven't been there yet this holiday. Edward needn't come if he doesn't want to."

He took up the challenge as I think he was meant to.

"But I'd like to go, too. I haven't been there either."

Mother looked doubtful.

"I don't know, Edward. It's a long walk and you've had a very busy day."

"I'm not a bit tired, honestly," he assured her, his face stricken. "Oh, please, Mrs. Mortimer!"

Mother capitulated.

"Very well then, you may go, but only if you promise to keep to the path and not go near the edge."

"I promise," he said solemnly. "Cross my heart."

Mother turned to address Naomi, who had been watching this exchange with her head on one side and a little smile on her face, oddly triumphant.

"You heard that, Naomi?"

Naomi nodded, tossing back her hair as she got up from the table.

"I'm going upstairs to take off this stupid dress," she announced.

But she didn't, not straight away, for I heard the back door close behind her and it was several minutes after Edward and I had gone up to our room to change our clothes as well that she finally came upstairs.

Mother must have heard her, too, for she went out into the hall to call up to her.

"Naomi, what are you doing in my bedroom?"

Naomi's voice was raised in reply.

"I'm looking for the nail scissors."

"What do you want them for?"

There followed one of those silences which children use with such effect to draw attention to an adult's obtuseness.

"To cut my nails with."

Of course, silly, was the unspoken rider.

"Then put them back when you've finished with them," Mother said sharply.

Even so, Naomi was ready before us and came banging on our door, calling out impatiently, "Come on, you two! Hurry up!"

The path started at a stile only a few yards from the house and, after crossing a small field of rough grass, began the long, slow climb upward around the side of the cliff.

Naomi went first, striding ahead of us in her boy's khaki shorts and her white aertex blouse, as vigorous and intrepid as an explorer leading an expedition into unknown territory. Scrambling after her, I could see her sharp elbows pumping in and out and her long dark hair, held back by an elastic band, bouncing purposefully between her shoulder blades.

Behind me, Edward puffing up the slope, kept calling out every few yards, "Wait for me!"

I stopped unwillingly for him, torn between a reluctance to abandon him and an eagerness to catch up with my sister, remembering her assertion as we had started off that the last one at the top would be a sissy.

At last, the path rounded the shoulder of the cliff and the view burst upon us in a sudden, dazzling revelation of sky and sea. It was like entering into another world where all the familiar dimensions, seen at ground level, were expanded to new and dizzying proportions. The sky was a vast, circular, blue immensity, extending around us on all sides, unobstructed by rooftops or masts or chimney pots.

As for the sea, it lay below us, almost motionless at that height, its silvery surface, faintly crinkled, stretching out for miles and miles to a far-off smudged purple line which was the horizon.

We could look down not only on the sea but on the gulls, circling beneath or suspended, pinned and screaming, against the wind.

And how it blew up there! It met us head-on as Edward and I came panting around the last bend in the path to find Naomi already on the headland, straining forward into its blast like the figurehead on a sailing ship. It had snatched the band from her hair, which was tossing in wild gusts about her head.

It even tore the words from her mouth as she turned to speak to us until, laughing with exhilaration, she flung herself down on the grass, out of its grasp.

We joined her, I lying prone beside her, Edward sitting more decorously with his legs crossed as he did on his bed at home.

"I said, Isn't it wonderful up here?" Naomi repeated. "Better than horrible old Trewarth and the soppy museum. Aren't you glad you came?"

She was looking directly at Edward who, still breathless from the climb, nodded dumbly.

There was a brilliance about her which had nothing to do with the sunlight or the sea.

And then, as if already bored with sitting still, she leapt to her feet and the wind reclaimed her, whipping at the legs of her shorts and her shirtsleeves so that they cracked like flags.

"Don't you wish you could fly?" she shouted, raising her arms above her head. "I do! I'd fly all over the world, to Africa and Asia and China."

"China's in Asia," Edward pointed out.

He was watching her uneasily, dazzled by her glitter and yet wary of it.

"I know that, stupid!"

Swooping down, she seized him by the shoulders and lugged him to his knees.

"Come on! Let's try!"

"Don't be silly," he said, squirming under her grip. "People can't fly."

"Your father does."

Proud though he was of his father, Edward didn't contradict her and I realized then how seriously he regarded the secret he had confided in me; too precious to be told even to Naomi. It was the first time in my life I had ever shared a secret with anyone other than her.

But he was too honest, or perhaps too naive, to lie and instead he replied obliquely, "That's in an airplane with an engine."

"You don't need an airplane. There's gliders and hot-air balloons. They don't have engines," Naomi retorted.

Even I knew she was right. As for Edward, he was reduced to silence.

Feeling in the pocket of her shorts, she took out a small white jar with a blue lid, its sides still patched with little bits of paper where the label had been scraped off.

"Or there's this," she added.

"What is it?" Edward asked.

"It's flying ointment."

Edward looked at her skeptically.

"There isn't such a thing."

"Yes, there is."

"Where did you get it from then?"

"Never you mind. It's a secret, isn't it, Tom?" she said, inviting me to join in the conspiracy even though I didn't understand it. "Smell it."

Taking off the lid, she thrust the jar under Edward's nose. He drew back, pulling a face.

"It's horrible."

"It's meant to be. It's a very special ointment made from magic herbs which only grow in jungles or on the top of high mountains."

"Can I have a smell?" I pleaded.

She waved the opened jar in front of my face, long enough for me to see that it contained a thick, white substance, with exactly the same appearance and scent as the cold cream Mother used, except it was flecked with green morsels of what looked like leaves, snipped up small, which gave off the sharp, distinct aroma of mint.

For the first time, I began dimly to make the connection between the tableau in the museum and Naomi's visit to the chemist's and the back garden at home. The incident with Mother's nail scissors also fell into place together with scraps of half-remembered knowledge from the children's encyclopedia.

"Didn't witches use flying ointment?" I asked.

Naomi glanced at me approvingly, as if I had said the right thing for once.

"Of course they did. They used to rub it into themselves, like this."

Dipping two fingers into the jar, she smeared the cream onto Edward's bare legs and arms below his shorts and shirt sleeves, rubbing it hard into his skin.

"It tingles," he complained.

"It's meant to," Naomi told him. "That means the magic's working. Now stand up and see if you can fly."

He scrambled reluctantly to his feet, his knees and elbows glistening, stained here and there with the green juice from the little bits of leaves.

"Go on!" Naomi ordered. "Don't just stand there like a ninny. Wave your arms up and down, like me."

Kneeling upright, she began to flap her own arms. As if mesmerized, Edward mimicked her, slowly at first and then more eagerly as the rhythm seized him.

"Harder!" she shouted into the wind. "Harder! That's better. And now run!"

He ran, beating his arms up and down, his legs working like pistons as the wind claimed him and, as if it were a huge hand thrusting against his back, propelled him faster and faster down the slopes.

"Don't go near the edge!" Naomi shrieked.

But the warning came too late.

As the wind caught her words and whirled them away, he, too, arms flailing, went spinning off into space.

I must have jumped to my feet although I wasn't aware of doing so, only of Naomi clutching me by the ankle in so fierce a grip that her fingers burned through my socks down to the skin. I couldn't see her face for the tears that were pouring down mine and a terrible blankness of vision at the horror of it all. But I heard her voice quite distinctly.

"Walk! Don't run!"

I obeyed her numbly, following her across the cliff and copying her when she dropped down to wriggle forward on her stomach for the last few yards.

Lying side by side, we peered down over the edge.

Far, far below was the beach we played on, so diminished in size that it seemed nothing more than a tiny, pale crescent of sand. To the left, something else pale lay on its face in the water, gently lifting and falling in the waves like a piece of flotsam.

"It wasn't our fault," Naomi said. "He tripped."

"Did he?" I asked. I couldn't remember that, only his feet in his brown Clark's sandals slithering frantically over the short, slippery grass.

"Yes, he did. He was running when he tripped and fell. I told him not to go near the edge."

That part at least was true.

"It wasn't our fault," Naomi repeated. "He was stupid. He wouldn't do what he was told. That's what we have to tell Mummy. But you're not to say anything about this," she added. She was holding in her hand the white jar of flying ointment. Getting carefully to her feet, she flung it far out to sea with that powerful overarm action which I so much envied.

"Why not?" I asked, watching as it made a wide arc through the air before disappearing into the dazzle of the sea.

"Because it was a joke," she explained, dropping down again beside me. "Just a joke. But Mummy wouldn't understand and she'd be terribly, terribly angry with both of us. So would Daddy."

And so I was drawn into the conspiracy after all, one of silence, compounded of the fear of adult anger and a sense of awful guilt which I couldn't understand myself and which, for that very reason, I could never have expressed to anyone else.

So the truth, whatever it might have been, never came out, never even at the inquest at which, I learned later, a verdict of accidental death was returned.

Naomi and I didn't go to the funeral; only our parents attended. By that time, war had been declared and we had been sent away to stay with our grandparents in Wiltshire where we remained for the rest of the war, safe from the air raids on London.

Things were never the same again. That was the last summer we spent at the house in Cornwall. Later, it was requisitioned for evacuees from Southampton and, after the war, my parents sold it.

I have never returned to Portmerron; neither, as far as I know, had Naomi, although I can't be certain of that.

As I explained at the beginning, we drifted apart as we grew older, the gap which had always existed between us becoming wider over the years until finally we communicated with each other only out of a sense of duty, exchanging cards at birthdays or Christmas.

Watching as her coffin was lowered into the ground, I thought again of Edward, the first real friend I ever had. But it was too late to find the answer to the question I should have asked Naomi all those years ago on that Cornish cliff-top.

"Did you really mean him to die?"

Jan Grape writes about Texas in a way that is just *different* from non-Texan writers. In particular, her women are the real McCoy, and their lives are complex and conflicted the way life can be, in the real world. Here's a nice little puzzle and a neatly plotted solution, first published in *Deadly Allies*, offered for your delectation.

Whatever Has To Be Done
JAN GRAPE

A fierce lightning and thunderstorm jarred me awake at 5:12 a.m. Autumn storms in Houston, Texas, often give the impression the end of the world is near. The dream I'd been immersed in had been pleasant, but try as I might, I couldn't remember it. The brilliant streaks flashed a sesquicentennial fireworks display and seeped through the top edge of the mini-blinds as Mother Nature declared a moratorium for sleepers.

It's not in my emotional make-up to wake up early; neither alert nor cheerful. Maybe it has to do with one of my past lives or blood pressure slowdown or something. Anyway, I tossed around trying to will myself back to sleep, knowing all the time it wouldn't work. But I waited until seven to crawl out to the shower. "Damn Sam," I said aloud, while dressing and wishing I could have my caffeine intravenously. "Lousy way to start a Friday."

The pyrotechnics were over, but the rain continued steadily, steaming the interior of my car and making the rush hour drive to the LaGrange Building hazardous and hair-raising. Determined to shake off frustration at the lack of sleep and the Gulf Coast monsoon, I paused in front of the fourth floor door and felt a sense of pride as I read the discreet sign - G. & G. Investigations. My partner, Cinnamon Jemima Gunn, and I could be proud, we'd turned a profit the last three months. No one expected it to last. Sometimes, even we had doubts.

There was a message from C.J., as she was known to all except a few close friends, on the answering machine. "Gone to Dallas for the weekend, Jenny.

117

Work today and play tomorrow. Keep outta trouble, Girlfriend." She had a legitimate reason to go, a dying client wanted to find a missing niece and a good lead led to "Big D," but once the work was done, she had a friend playing football for the Cowboys who would show her a fun weekend.

Lucky sister, I thought, ready to feel sorry for myself. "But wait—there's only a half day's work here," I said aloud "and it's rainy—and besides it's Friday." It only took two seconds to decide to finish the paperwork and to blow this joint. I put myself in high gear and was ready to leave by noon.

I had straightened up the lounge/storeroom, grabbed my purse and reset the phone machine, when the outer door opened.

"Oh. No. Don't tell me you're leaving?" the woman said. "Are you Jenny Gordon?"

She was slender with reddish blonde hair, not really pretty. Her eyes were too close together and her mouth too thin, but there was something about her. Vulnerability? She had one of those voices that rise into a whine and grated like fingernails on glass. I hate voices like that. She dropped her dripping umbrella, one of those bubble see-through ones, onto the floor. Her raincoat, after she peeled it off to reveal a blue velour jogging suit, hit the sofa, and slid to the floor. I hate slobs, too. As if your things are not good enough. Maybe people like that just don't care. Or maybe she was used to someone picking up after her.

"I am Jenny Gordon and I was leaving, but what may . . . ?"

"Well, great. That's the way my whole life has been the past twenty-four hours. All screwed up." She walked over and sat on one of the customer chairs, rummaged in her purse for a cigarette and pulled out a lighter encased in a silver and turquoise case. "It's really the shits, you know. Me needing a P.I.," she burst out laughing in a high-pitched nervous tone.

I tried to figure out what was going on without much luck.

She stopped laughing long enough to say, "And who does he send me to? A woman, for Christ's sake." She laughed some more and finished with a cough, then flicked the lighter and lit the cigarette without asking if I minded. I smoke, and didn't mind, yet it's nice to be asked.

I'm not the happy homemaker type, but I couldn't stand the spreading, staining puddles. The woman really was a slob, I thought, picking up her raincoat. I hung it on the coat rack, folded her umbrella and stood it in the wastebasket near the door. There was no sign she noticed what I did and no thanks either. Some people should just stay in their own pig pens and not run around spreading their muck.

I headed across the room, intending to get some paper towels from our lounge/storage room to soak up the mess. "As I started to ask a moment ago, is there something I can do, Miss . . . ?"

"Ms. Loudermilk. Voda Beth Loudermilk."

"Ms. Loudermilk, why do you need an investigator?" I paused momentarily, in the doorway. Her answer stopped me cold.

"I killed my husband last night. Emptied his own gun into him." The whine was gone, and the words came out in monotone, as if she were describing a grocery list. "He died on me." She smashed the cigarette into an ashtray. "Isn't that the silliest thing you ever heard?" She laughed, but sounded close to tears.

If I was surprised because she didn't throw the butt onto the floor, I was totally wiped out by what she said. I was so intent, I didn't noticed someone else had opened the outer door and entered. I blurted out, "Perhaps you need a lawyer, Mrs. Loudermilk, not a detective."

"It was time he hurt someone else instead of me."

A quiet voice interrupted, "Voda Beth. Shut your mouth and keep it shut." He spoke in a quiet even tone.

The speaker was a short wiry man I recognized immediately from his many newspaper photos and television appearances. A shock of steel gray hair, brushed back to emphasize the widow's peak, the piercing blue eyes and every one of his seventy-eight years etched on his face. I'd never met him, of course, but I knew who he was. Hell, everyone knew who "Bulldog" King Porter was— the best criminal lawyer money could buy.

"Oh shit, Bulldog," Voda Beth said. "You know a P.I.'s like a priest. They can't reveal the confidences their clients tell them."

He was dressed like a lawyer would have dressed forty or fifty years ago. Dark charcoal, pinstripe, three piece suit, white shirt with French cuffs peeking out the prerequisite amount, big gold cufflinks. The tie, a shade lighter than the suit, was not a clip-on and was tied with a perfect Windsor knot. A heavy gold link watch chain had a gold Phi Beta Kappa key dangling from one end. "That only applies to P.I.s in dime store novels." Bulldog walked over to me and held out his hand. "Ms. Gordon, I've heard a lot about you. I'm Bulldog Porter."

His hand was soft, but the grip firm. "I'm honored to meet you, sir. I've heard a lot about you, too." Porter had begun his practice in Galveston, during the thirties, when the island city considered itself a free state, allowing drinking, gambling and prostitution. He had even defended members of the "beach gang" who smuggled Canadian booze into the Gulf port and shipped it to places like Chicago and Detroit.

"I'll just bet you have, Ms. Gordon." He chuckled. "And let me tell you up front, most of it is true."

Mrs. Loudermilk stood up. Her curly hair framed the sharp angled face which twisted in anger. "Bulldog . . ."

"Voda Beth, just sit right back down there and keep quiet for a minute."

She glared, but did as he said.

"Now, Ms. Gordon . . ."

"Please call me Jenny, Mr. Porter."

"Only if you call me Bulldog."

"Deal. Now, I'm assuming you have a special reason to be here."

"Good. I like that. Cut the crap and right down to brass tacks." He nodded to our storage/lounge area. "Let's go in here and have a little chat. Voda Beth, you stay put." The woman sent him a lethal look, but didn't get up.

"My client in there," he said as we sat at the kitchen-style table, "was mouthing off when I came in. Let's chalk that up to her current emotional state. To her grief, if you will. You see, her husband was shot and killed around 8:00 p.m. last night. She was questioned for hours, eventually charged by the police and locked up in women's detention over at 61 Reisner, just before dawn. She's been without food or sleep for over twenty-four hours."

"Her lack of sleep," I said, "plus the grief and trauma she's experienced have rendered her incapable of acting correctly or speaking coherently."

"Exactly. I heard you were sharp." He took out a pipe and, within seconds, had asked if I minded and got it lit. Bulldog Porter wasn't known as the plodding, methodical type. "We have great need of an investigator and you were highly recommended by Lieutenant Hays of HPD homicide department."

The fact Larry Hays sent Porter to me was a surprise. Larry was a good friend, but he still thought it was laughable, my being a private detective. My background is medical: an x-ray technologist. I worked ten years detecting the mystery of the human body and knew nothing about real mysteries. Luckily, C.J. had police experience and I'd been a willing pupil.

If what Bulldog said about the woman was true, she needed help. Maybe I was wrong to condemn her casual attitude about her wet things. If I'd just spent the night in jail, I sure as hell wouldn't be worrying about neatness. Besides, the chance to do a job for Porter was worth considering. G. & G. Investigations wasn't doing so well that we could turn down someone with his clout. "Did she kill her husband?"

He didn't answer immediately. "Voda Beth says she has been physically, sexually and emotionally abused her whole married life. She says he was hitting on her and couldn't take it any longer. That she pulled his own gun out from under the mattress and emptied it into him. Her father and I were old school chums and I agreed to take her case because of him. Actually, it shouldn't be hard to prove diminished-capacity." He leaned back, and his eyes zeroed on mine like an electron beam. "What I need from you, Jenny," he smiled, "is to discover if her story of abuse is true."

"Is there any physical evidence of her being beaten; like bruises or anything?"

"Not to my knowledge."

"Has she ever reported to a doctor or to anyone that she was abused?"

"I don't think so. But I'd like you to find out."

"What do you know about Mr. Loudermilk?"

"Another thing for you to look into. J.W. Loudermilk owned a development and construction company which was doing quite well until Houston's oil bust. But you'd need to do a thorough background check on him. I do know he was married before and he has a daughter from that first marriage. The daughter lived with him, until recently, and she'd be the first place to start."

"And next, the ex-wife?"

"Precisely. Her name is Elwanda Watson. Had a second marriage which also didn't last. Four children by Watson. I have addresses and phone numbers for you." He placed the pipe in the ashtray I'd placed near him, reached into his inner coat pocket and held out an index card. "I believe you've already decided to work for me?"

I smiled as I took the card. "I have indeed." I went to get a copy of our standard contract for his signature. Voda Beth didn't look up when I passed through. When I returned, Porter had written out a check and handed it to me. He'd not inquired about fees. I nearly gasped—it was made out for $5,000.

"I need to have as much information as possible by next Tuesday morning for the preliminary hearing," Bulldog said. "That means working through the weekend if necessary. If you can find out the truth about the Loudermilks' relationship, I might be able to get the charges dropped and we won't have to go to trial."

"If the truth is as she says it is."

"Oh. Naturally. But I believe it is." Mr. Porter spent a few seconds with *our* client and left.

It was time to interview the widow. I walked in and sat behind the desk, searching her face. A neon sign flashing "not guilty" did not appear on her forehead.

"Why don't you tell me what happened, Voda Beth?"

Her eyelids were red-rimmed and the pale blue eyes were devoid of life or light. She was holding her body rigid and her mouth tight as if to keep herself from flying apart.

"Look," I said. "I know you're exhausted, you need food and rest. How about telling me a few brief details and if I need something else, we can talk later."

"J.W. and I had been arguing all evening. If I said black, he said white. I can't remember what started this particular one. Finally, I told him I couldn't take anymore tonight, that I wanted to go to bed. I went to our bedroom, took a shower and he sat in the den and drank."

"Did he drink a lot?"

"Sometimes, and even more lately."

"Why lately?"

"Things were bad financially, really bad the past few months." Voda Beth pressed her hands to her temples, then rubbed them slowly. "I remember now. That's what started the argument. Money. I'd bought two new bras yesterday, the underwire on my last one broke that morning."

My partner, C.J., had been a policewoman in Pittsburgh for eight years and one thing she'd taught me about interviewing someone, is it's usually best to not say anything once the person is talking. If you interrupt you can lose them, they'll clam up.

"I had just finished brushing my hair and was ready to get into bed when J.W. came in, yelling about how stupid I was for spending money we didn't have. He was furious. He'd sat in there and drank and got madder and madder.

"He got right in my face, screaming, and when I tried to ignore him, he got even madder. He slapped me. Twice, at least, and the third time he knocked me onto the bed. He kept hitting with his open hand. One blow made me bite my lip, see?"

She showed me a large hematoma inside her cheek. I made appropriate noises of sympathy. "What happened next?"

"He straddled me and started punching me in the stomach and breast with his fists. A blackness came over me, slowly, at first. It got darker and redder. Somehow . . . I really don't know how, I got my hand under the mattress and got hold of his gun. The next thing I knew, he was lying across the bed and . . . and I remembered hearing the gun and there was blood everywhere and . . ."

She began crying, great shuddering sobs. I walked around the desk, handed her a box of Kleenex and patted her shoulder, not really knowing what to say or do. She kept trying to say she didn't mean it, but it was a long time before she got it all out.

When she'd calmed down, and blew her nose, I sat down behind the desk. "This wasn't the first time your husband beat you?"

"No. He didn't do it often and he'd always apologize, say he was sorry and he'd never do it again. That he loved me and didn't want to hurt me. Months would go by and I'd believe everything was fine, then wham." She was back to her monotone voice.

"Did you ever tell anyone? Your doctor maybe?"

"No. I was too ashamed. Besides, whatever I'd done to set him off was all my fault. I was the one who . . ."

"Voda Beth. Whatever you did was no reason to be battered or beaten. But my telling you won't help or make any difference to you. You need to get professional help."

"I will. Bulldog is setting it up."

I walked around to her again and patted her shoulder once more. "It's time you went home. You didn't drive over here, did you?"

"Bulldog brought me. He said he'd send someone to pick me up."

"Come on then, I'll go downstairs with you."

A white stretch limo was waiting in the front circular drive when we reached the lobby and a driver lounging against the front passenger fender saw us and walked over. "Mrs. Loudermilk?" He helped her in and she waved one finger as he closed the door.

I walked to the parking garage. Lowly private investigators have to drive themselves home.

"If that tight-assed bitch thinks she can kill my father and get away with it, she's crazy."

J.W. Loudermilk's daughter was two months over eighteen, but looked twenty-five. Her name was Elizabeth, but she preferred to be called Liz, she said, after inviting me into her condo in far southwest Houston. She mentioned that she was scheduled for a tennis lesson at the nearby YWCA, but said she could spare a few minutes.

I'd been unable to reach her the evening before and had secretly been glad. Voda Beth's story had unnerved me. With a good night's sleep, I'd hoped to be able to think more rationally. Silly me. My dreams had been filled with a faceless someone who punched and slapped me half the night. It was three o'clock before I finally slid into a dreamless sleep.

I showered and dressed in my weekend office attire—Wrangler jeans and a T-shirt—but since it was a cool forty-nine degrees this morning, I pulled on a sweater. My hair had been short and curly permed for summer and as I combed through the tangled dark mop, I decided to let it grow for the cooler weather. I checked out a new wrinkle at one corner of my right eye. "Damn Sam. At thirty-three, you shouldn't be having wrinkles," I said. "Someday, you'll have to pay more attention to such things, but not today."

A tiny smudge of cocoa frost eye shadow added depth to my dark eyes, and a quick swipe of powder was easy and fast and completed my bow to cosmetics. Spending time with creams and moisturizers was not my idea of fun and I intended to fight it as long as possible.

I'd arrived for my appointment with J.W.'s daughter at 10:30 a.m. on the dot.

She had offered me a cold drink. I accepted a Diet Coke and sat down as she bustled around in the kitchen. Her living room was a high-beamed ceiling affair, all mirrors, posters and wicker furniture from Pier One Imports. There wasn't a sofa, just two chairs, and a lamp table between them, set before a fireplace. As a young woman out on her own, she probably couldn't afford much.

I studied her as she brought in the drinks. She was lovely, self-assured and poised. She had a heart-shaped face, blue-black hair, cut shoulder length and curly permed. Her eyes were such a deep indigo they looked violet and there was no doubt her resemblance to a young Liz Taylor was often mentioned. She was dressed in a white tennis skirt and top, showing off her golden tan to great advantage. Oh. To be eighteen again, I thought, but only for a brief second.

"Mrs. Gordon?" She seated herself opposite me.

"Jenny, please."

"Okay, Jenny. Let's get one thing cleared up right now. I never did like Voda Beth. She's a coke-snorting, greedy slut who married my father for his money."

"You know all this for a fact?" The violet eyes narrowed briefly, before looking at me head-on. Maybe she was sincere, but her cliched words sounded like the old evil stepmother routine.

"My father owned his own construction and development company. He built office buildings and shopping malls. When his business suffered reverses, she couldn't stand it." Liz set her glass down on the end table next to her chair, picked up a nail file and began filing her nails. "They argued all the time. Mostly about money. She was always wanting this new dress or that new piece of furniture. Now, with Dad dead, I guess she'll be in high cotton."

"Were their arguments ever violent? Did you see or hear your father hitting her?"

Liz finished the nail she was working on, put that finger to her mouth and began chewing on the cuticle. She shook her head. "Dad did have a temper, but I don't think he ever so much as slapped the bitch."

I sipped on the Diet Coke. "What gave you the idea she'll be in high cotton now? Insurance?"

"She talked him into taking out a policy for two million a few months ago. She killed him to get that money, there's no doubt in my mind."

I made a mental note to check out the insurance. "How did you find out about this policy?"

"She flaunted it in my face. It's one of those big companies, something Mutual. I'm sure you can find a record of it someplace."

"You mentioned she used coke?"

"I've known ever since I was sixteen and she offered it to me." Liz's face contorted with fury. "That bitch came along, turned my father against me, but it only worked a short time."

"What else did they argue about besides the money?"

"The drugs and the men she slept with."

"She slept around?"

"He said she did. I have no knowledge of that personally."

The picture the girl painted was certainly not something to help Mr. Porter. In fact, it was more likely to hang Voda Beth Loudermilk. But it did strike me strange, the girl didn't have one kind word to say about her step-mother. "How old were you when they married?"

"Thirteen." She drained her glass. "My mother couldn't hold on to Dad. She's a silly bitch, too. Sometimes she doesn't have the sense God gave a goose." She stood. "Sorry, Jenny. I do have to get to the Y for my tennis lesson. My fondest hope is that Voda Beth rots in jail."

Thirteen is a difficult age. I knew from losing my own mother when I was twelve that I would have resented it tremendously if my father had remarried. Her remarks about her own mother seemed strangely out of place. Didn't this girl like anyone? I wondered. Placing the unfinished Coke on the table, I got up. "Appreciate your talking to me, Liz." I handed her one of my cards. "If you think of anything else I should know, please call."

Liz preceded me to the door and opened it. "If it's something that'll help convict her, you'll hear from me."

It would be easier to make notes of my interview at my office. When I arrived I was surprised to find C.J. at the front desk, hacking away at the computer. "It's good to see you, but weren't you supposed to stay in Dallas all weekend?"

"Yes, but don't ask any questions, okay?" she said and her tone indicated she wasn't kidding. C.J.'s face, which always reminded me of a darker-skinned Nichelle Nichols, the *Star Trek* actress, was marred by a deep frown of concentration. The new computer we'd recently bought was giving her fits. She continued hitting the buttons and keys like she was working out on a punching bag.

The fun with the football player obviously didn't work out. "Ooo . . . kay," I said and told her about our new client, Voda Beth Loudermilk, brought in by Mr. Bulldog Porter himself. She nodded without comment and I began telling of my interview of Liz Loudermilk. "Liz tried to look and sound sincere, but I'm having a hard time believing her. The hate this girl had was so thick in the room it nearly smothered me."

She paused, and turned to listen. "Sounds like she's definitely jealous of the second wife."

"I've tried to imagine how I would feel, in that situation. I'm sure I would have resented any woman *my* father brought in to take my mother's place."

"Five years is a long time to nurse a grudge. Didn't Voda Beth ever do anything nice for Liz?" C.J. looked down at herself and tried to brush off a minute piece of something white from her bright green sweater, gave up and plucked it with her fingernails and tossed it away. The sweater, trimmed in brown and gold leather, was worn over a slim dark brown skirt and she'd added a bright green leather belt. She was also wearing green tinted pantyhose and dark brown boots. At her six foot height, she looks great in whatever she wears, but a couple of years as a model in Manhattan had set her style forever into the high fashion look.

My taste usually runs to levis or sweats. Of course, no matter what I wore, I still looked just like me, Jenny Gordon, of Houston, Texas. "Liz Loudermilk will cheerfully push the plunger on the syringe if her stepmother is sentenced to die by injection. She ain't too crazy about her own mother, either."

"Maybe she's got a fixation on her father and anyone else is just a big zero in her mind."

"You're probably right. I was madly in love with my father when I was fourteen," I said, thinking back. "About six months later, I hated him."

"That was a normal growing-up process. I did about the same thing." She smiled and leaned the chair back, folding her hands across her stomach. "Girlfriend, you know what strikes me about your conversation with that girl?"

"That insurance policy?"

"Yes. But besides that. She called Voda Beth a tight-assed bitch. That describes someone uptight or morally rigid. It's not something I normally would associate with a woman who used drugs and slept around."

"You're right. It's total contradiction, isn't it?" I lit a cigarette, forgetting for a moment how much C.J. disliked my smoking.

She fanned the smoke with an exaggerated flip of her black hand. "Get out of here with that thing." She turned back to the computer. "Besides, until I figure out how to trace that insurance policy, I don't need you in my hair." She picked up the telephone receiver. "I guess I'd better call the 'old pro' over at Intertect first and find out where to start."

C.J. had a good working relationship with the private investigators over at Intertect, an office which specialized in computers and data bases. Good thing. Computers blow my mind completely. I'd probably never figure this one out.

I went into the lounge and turned on the air purifier and thought about my client. Bulldog Porter had wanted me to find "something" to prove wife abuse. Unfortunately, the talk with Liz Loudermilk had only tightened the noose.

I'd felt sorry for Voda Beth when she told of being beaten. She might even be a greedy slut, but I doubted she was as bad as the girl had tried to make her sound. It's easy to use pop psychology to categorize people, yet the girl did sound like the classic example of a jealous daughter.

I walked back through to the back office to my desk, taking care not to disturb C.J. as she punched keys on the computer and numbers on the telephone. I called to make a late afternoon appointment with the ex-wife, Elwanda Watson. She worked as a waitress at a seafood restaurant out in the Heights area and said we could meet there. I typed up notes of the "Liz" interview on my old IBM Selectric and placed them in the Loudermilk file. I'd never let that machine go, even if I did learn things like Word Perfect programs and networking with modems.

Just before 5:00 p.m., Elwanda Watson called and changed our meeting to her home. I stacked the paperwork on my desk, told C.J. I'd see her tomorrow, not that she heard me—she was still wrestling with the computer. Just before the door closed, however, she called out, "Sunday brunch at my house, okay?"

Saturday afternoon traffic around the LaGrange Building was thicker than bees around molasses, maddening, but normal. The building is located two and a half blocks from the Galleria. Even in the early fifties, this whole area was still part of a dairy farm. Now, a six-block square area of high dollar shopping malls, department and specialty stores, hotels and high rise office buildings, including developer Gerald Hines' sixty-five story Transco Tower, filled the land where Crimson Clover used to grow and cows got fat. From the air, the whole area was filled with concrete, steel and bronzed glass and looked like a city skyline, but it's six miles from downtown Houston in suburbia-land. The lack of zoning laws here makes for some unusual building developments.

Elwanda Watson lived in a story and a half house made of white brick and wood and cedar shakes, four miles west of my office. An older neighborhood built in the late fifties before contractors and architects took a notion to make suburban houses all look alike. These were in a wide range of individual styles and colors. A huge Magnolia tree stood sentinel in front and a pink bicycle lay on its side in the St. Augustine grass. Four baskets of white and burgundy impatiens hung from the eaves.

The woman who answered the door was short, overweight, with ponderous breasts and hips almost scraping the doorway. She had short, dark hair streaked heavily with gray and a startled expression which seemed to be a permanent look. She wore a dingy, white sweat suit, no make-up and said she was Elwanda Watson. It would be difficult to believe Liz Loudermilk came from this woman's womb, if it had not been for the eyes. That unique shade of blue, tingeing to violet. Either Elwanda had lost her beauty long ago, or Liz got her looks from her father.

She led me to a large kitchen/den area, both paneled in knotty pine, and there were children's play noises coming from the back yard. She indicated I should sit in the chair across from the sofa and brought tall glasses of iced tea before settling on the Early American style sofa.

I glanced around. The room had the look of having been hastily picked up. A large entertainment cabinet stood against one wall. Wires and plugs stuck out and dangled from the front and one side, indicating sound and electronics had once been installed and then removed. A small TV set was alone on a shelf. Newspapers, magazines, books, and games: Monopoly, Scrabble, Uncle Wiggly, Yahtzee, Parcheesi, dominoes and cards, were piled on and in the cabinet. The drape hung loose from the rod on one side and dragged on the floor. It was an "I don't care look," much like the woman herself. Two failed marriages had taken their toll. "Ms. Gordon, what . . ." she said.

Smiling at her, I said, "Call me Jenny, please."

"And I'm Elwanda. Well, Jenny, what is it you wish to know? This whole horrible thing is too, too weird. Poor old J.W. dead. And Voda Beth accused of killing him. Unbelievable, I tell you. It just boggles my mind."

"It's hard to believe Voda Beth killed J.W.?"

"I'd just never figure her to do something so awful. She seems like such a nice person. Gracious and polite to me and she's been really kind and generous to my Liz."

"Really? Liz doesn't share your feelings."

"Oh that Liz. She *can* act like a spoiled brat. The things I could tell you would take half the night. But you don't have time for that. She mouths off about Voda Beth something terrible sometimes, but deep down, I know she likes her step-mom."

"That wasn't the impression I got this morning."

"Oh, I know," said Elwanda. "Liz told me how tacky she was this morning and asked me to apologize for the things she said."

"She doesn't owe *me* an apology."

"Well, she did mislead you. Made it seem like Voda Beth was a wicked person when she's not." She rubbed both eyes like a person just waking up. "My daughter is beautiful and brilliant, but she can also act like a two year old when she doesn't get her way. Sooner or later you have to give in. Of course, she's always sorry afterward and will make up for it a hundred ways."

Despite Elwanda's trying to make Liz sound like nothing more than a rebellious and rambunctious child, I had seen the rage Liz had for Voda Beth. It wasn't just a temper tantrum. I'd hate to see that rage turned on anyone. Elwanda was maternally blind to her child's faults. She didn't want to think otherwise, and I thought it best to get off that subject.

"Voda Beth claimed J.W. was beating her when she killed him. Was he ever abusive to you?"

"Oh, my. No. I was married to the man for ten years and he never raised a hand to me." She looked directly at me and her wide-eyed look of astonishment was more pronounced. "And I don't see him abusing Voda Beth, either. He worshiped her. He was always a kind and wonderful husband. And father. Always."

If that was true, I wondered, then why did she divorce this boy scout? I had to ask. "Why did you . . ."

"Divorce him? He left me. For another woman. Not Voda Beth; it was over long before he met her. There were lots of other women. Some men are born womanizers and J.W. was one. That is, until Voda Beth caught him. I don't think he ever strayed from her." Tears welled up in those big violet eyes and this overweight, throw-away wife's voice held a wistful note.

"What about his low boiling point?"

It took her a moment to speak. "He could get angry, real easy-like when he was young, but he'd mellowed out. Even so, his anger never, ever, led to violence."

"Did Voda Beth ever go out on him?"

"I don't think so. He probably would've told me if she had."

I raised an eyebrow.

"It's sounds funny I guess, but after he married her, he and I got real friendly-like. I mean, like close friends. He apologized for hurting me in the past. He was so good when my marriage with Don Watson broke up. Offered me money because he knew I was having a hard time with four little kids."

At their mention, the children's voices outside reached a crescendo and she walked to the patio door to check. Evidently, it was nothing which needed her presence. Mother-like, however, she stuck her head out and told them to stop whatever they were doing and find something else to do. She came back to the sofa and sat. "I think it was because he was finally happy. He said once, Voda Beth had taught him the right way to treat a woman and he'd learned his lesson."

Obviously, Elwanda still had deep feelings for J.W. Loudermilk and she wasn't going to say anything against him. Unfortunately, what she said was detrimental to my client. If J.W. didn't have a history of abusing women, it looked like Voda Beth had lied. I stood. "I appreciate your talking to me."

"Sorry I wasn't more help." We headed to the front door and she said, "Oh, I just thought of something. It's possible they had some fights over Liz. That was one thing he could get angry enough to come to blows over. Although I still don't see it."

"Why not?"

"Liz would have told me about it."

After the way the girl had talked about her mother, I was not sure she'd confide in Elwanda, but what do I know about daughters? Especially teen-age ones.

"Liz was very angry with her father the past few years—for breaking up our marriage, for marrying Voda Beth. For what she saw as him neglecting her. She would gripe and complain how he didn't pay any attention to her, how he was always fawning over Voda Beth. Now that I think on it, she must have been jealous of her father."

That could explain the rage I saw in the girl. "I guess that's normal in young girls who want their fathers all to themselves."

"She could get all worked up about it. Throw fits and scream at him. That's one reason he made her move out of the house."

"He made his own daughter leave?"

"About three months ago. She was working and making good money, but she would stay out all hours and do things to aggravate him—like smoking pot in the house. Anyway, he got fed up and although Voda Beth tried to stop him, he made Liz get a place of her own. She was really bent all out of shape over that for awhile."

"I guess it's hard to be a parent, these days." I thanked her again and left.

I headed back to my apartment, grateful the traffic had slackened off. It gave me time to wonder about my client. Whatever had happened that night in the Loudermilks' home was still muddled, but it looked as if my client had lied through her teeth.

I ate a light dinner—grilled chicken and a big salad—and spent the rest of the evening reading a P.I. novel.

I went to bed and just before drifting off to sleep, I decided tomorrow I'd call Lieutenant Larry Hays of Houston's homicide department. Maybe the police and autopsy reports would give me some fresh insights.

I called Larry Hays on his car phone and caught him as he was driving away from headquarters to go have breakfast. "No rest for the wicked, huh?"

"Not on Sunday," he said. "Meet me at Kay's in twenty minutes."

Kay's was a favorite hang-out of law enforcement personnel. The restaurant's owner, Bert DeLeon, had a thing about listening to the cop's war stories. He really got into that stuff. He'd been especially fond of my late husband, and when Tommy introduced me to him, I figured if Bert had not approved, Tommy would not have proposed. Kay's served family style food and gave better service than the high-priced restaurants.

Lieutenant Hays sat at the back booth on the west side and a mug of coffee was waiting for me. "Are you eating?" he asked.

"Just an English muffin and half a grapefruit."

"Watching your weight again?"

"Always. I weighed 125 this morning."

"That's about your normal, isn't it?"

"Yes, but you know how I love chicken-fried steak and Mexican food and the only way I can indulge is to keep this five feet six inch woman on that 125."

"Poor baby."

Larry is six three and weighs about 185 and never has to watch his weight because he has a great metabolism. It was frustrating and I tried not to think about it. "Just shut up and eat your cholesterol-filled eggs and pancakes and bacon."

"I intend to."

Larry had been my husband's partner and friend from the day they were rookies until politics had caused Tommy to resign and become a private detective. Larry took on a self-appointed task of watching out for me after my husband was killed, and sometimes it was stifling. We'd had several arguments about it, but recently he had weakened. Mostly because I'd learned from C.J. how to handle myself. He was a damn good cop and I respected his opinions. It was easier when he respected mine.

After we'd eaten, he answered my questions about the Loudermilk case. "The medical examiner has some doubts about your client's story."

"What?"

"The angle of the shot for one thing. Mrs. Loudermilk says she was crouched on the bed when she shot him; that doesn't wash. The M.E. says the shooter was standing. If she were as close to him as she says there would have been powder burns on his body. The M.E. says the shooter had to be standing, at least, twelve to fourteen feet away."

"Wow. Bulldog's not going to like that."

Larry ran a big hand through his sandy hair. "Probably a good thing. I don't think he can prove she was abused."

"Why not?"

"I talked to our police psychologist and, although he didn't talk to her, he says she doesn't display the attitude of a battered woman. Immediately after a battering, most woman usually act meek and acquiescent. She came in there full of self-confidence. Almost daring us to believe her." Larry signaled the waitress to bring him more coffee. "She's got all the buzz words and phrases down pat. Like how he got boozed up and how he used his open hand on her face and his fists on her breasts and abdomen."

"Yeah, she gave me those classic statements, too, the ones I've read about; like how he'd say he was sorry and how she deserved it."

His hazel eyes narrowed. "At one point Thursday night, the sex crimes unit took her over to get a medical exam. No evidence of sexual intercourse. They noticed a couple of bruises on her torso, but thought they could have been self-inflicted. She gave us a pretty good story, but she hasn't given us the truth, yet."

"Could she be covering for someone. Like maybe the daughter?"

"Possibly, but the captain and the D.A. want to go ahead with the indictment, anyway. The physical evidence and her confession wrap everything up in a nice neat package with a big bow. I just never have liked neat packages."

"The daughter is seething with rage against the stepmother."

"Rage isn't evidence. Lots of daughters hate their stepparents. You don't have to worry. Bulldog will plead Voda Beth on diminished capacity and get her off or he'll plea bargain." He absently stirred the coffee and then realized he hadn't added the sugar yet. "I do have a funny feeling there's something else."

"I guess I'd better talk to Bulldog. He's not going to be too happy with this."

"Likely not." He grabbed the check and stood. "I hate to eat and run," he said, "but I've got to go interrogate witnesses in a drive-by shooting last night."

"Have fun."

"Oh, yeah," he said harshly, his mind already to the task that lay ahead.

I headed for the office and, for once, the traffic wasn't a problem. Sunday morning is one of the rare good times to drive in this congested Bayou city.

I had talked with C.J. before leaving home and canceled our brunch date. She said she'd go to the office and see what she could turn up on the computer. She wanted to run credit records on all three women, Voda Beth and Liz Loudermilk and Elwanda Watson; and throw in J.W. Loudermilk, too.

She'd made coffee. I poured a cup and sat down next to her desk. She had not found anything unusual on the women's credit records, and the daughter hadn't established any credit yet. We discussed my interview with Elwanda and told her what Larry had said. "I'd better call Bulldog. I don't have one solitary thing to help him. He'll probably want to fire us."

"Okay," she said, "but I've got a couple more checks to make while you're getting us fired."

I walked back to my desk and called Bulldog Porter's office. His answering service said he'd call me back within the hour or, if he didn't, for me to call again.

Twenty minutes later, C.J. came in my office and a gleam was in her dark eyes. "I got it."

"What?" I asked, not remembering what she'd been trying to do. I was still waiting on Bulldog to return my call and was trying to get my reports ready for him and figure out how much I could deduct from the $5,000 he had given me.

"Remember Liz Loudermilk told you about a big insurance policy?" I nodded. "She was right. You're going to love this."

"Uh-oh. Don't tell me you've found another motive for Voda Beth."

"Our client isn't the only one with a motive. Little Miss Liz could inherit it all. All by herself."

"Oh, yeah? How?"

"If Voda Beth dies first or is disqualified, it all goes to the loving daughter."

"All . . . ll rii . . . ii . . . ght. And I guess if ole Voda Beth goes to prison for killing her husband, she'll be disqualified?"

"You got that right, Ms. Gordon, and to help put Liz to the top of the suspect list, you won't believe this, she put money down yesterday on a brand new, fiery red Miata."

"You have got to be kidding."

"If I'm lying, I'm dying. But just don't *forget* one important thing—stepmommy's told you and the police a big lie."

"That's okay. Old Bulldog will say she made that statement under duress," I said. "This is just what he needed. It gives him some ammunition for his reasonable doubt."

"Wonder what the lovely Liz was doing that night?"

I called Lieutenant Hays, knowing he'd need to know what we'd found. Luckily, he was near his car phone and I filled him in on Liz. He wasn't too happy. The case was closed as far as he was concerned, but after he grumbled, said he'd talk with the daughter tomorrow, to see if she had an alibi for the night in question.

"C.J., I think Liz did it and our client confessed, all under some misguided idea to protect Liz. Bulldog can take this and run with it."

"When do I get to meet this mouthpiece anyway?"

"Anytime you say. You'll like him, he's positively charming."

"Unh-unh. No way I'm gonna like a shyster who useta work fo' de mob. Those guys ain't nobody for this li'l black girl to mess wid'." As usual, her slipping into southern black street talk cracked me up. Coming from such a smart and beautiful woman it was funny.

As I laughed, she said, "By the way, while running those credit card histories I did find a few interesting tidbits on old J.W. himself."

"How can someone who sounds like you be so smart? You can check credit card records?"

"If you know the right buttons to push and Intertect does." She handed me the printout of J.W. Loudermilk's Visa and American Express statements for the past year.

I flipped through them. "Holy shit, this is scary. You don't expect any old Jane Blow to be able to run a credit card account check."

"Oh hell," her voice full of pride, "not just any old Jane Blow can do it. It takes a few brains and persistence. I took what I learned from my investigator pals and played around for awhile and was able to come up with a password for a security code."

"My partner—the smartass computer hack." I was scanning the account statements and something caught my attention. Loudermilk had visited three different doctors in the past month and had charged his visits to his AmEx. "Wonder what this medical stuff is all about?"

"Give that girl a gold star. That's what I thought was so interesting."

"I happen to know this Doctor Gaudet is a neurosurgeon. I'm not sure about the other two."

"Think I should check them out?" She grinned.

"Holy shit. Why didn't I think of that?"

"Because you hired me to think for you."

"Someone has to do the important stuff," I said. "I don't want to talk to Voda Beth again. It makes me mad when a client lies to me, but I could go talk to Elwanda Watson again. Maybe J.W. confided some medical problem to her. It's probably not important though."

"Fine. But do it tomorrow. I make a motion we get out of here. Sunday's almost over and we need a little R & R."

"Honey," I said, using one of her favorite expressions, "you ain't never lied."

Monday morning dawned with Houston shrouded in fog. Not unusual this time of year; with cooler air sweeping down across Texas and meeting the warm Gulf air, it was inevitable. It looked like the sun would burn it off around ten, and sure enough, I was right. When I left for Elwanda's around 10:30, there were only a few pockets of misty stuff, although the sky was still hazy.

I had not called first for an appointment; sometimes it's better to catch people when they're not on guard. Turns out Elwanda was not the only one to be surprised. I found my client, Voda Beth Loudermilk, visiting Elwanda. Neither seemed pleased to see me, but I didn't let that stop me. They were both dressed in gowns and robes, but it looked as if neither had slept. What was going on between these two? I wondered.

They sat on the sofa next to each other and I sat in a platform rocker which angled off to their right. After exchanging a few politenesses, I mentioned homicide was interviewing Liz this morning, setting off quite a reaction.

Voda Beth practically yelled at me. "Liz didn't have anything to do with anything. I'm the one who shot J.W. The police already have my statement." She burst out crying and Elwanda moved closer to put her arms around Voda Beth, making soothing sounds as if comforting a baby.

"I resent someone accusing my daughter," Elwanda said. "Was that your idea, Ms. Gordon?"

"Not exactly. But some new information about Liz did come to my attention. Naturally, I had to tell the lieutenant in charge."

"What information?" she asked.

"I'm not at liberty to say."

Voda Beth was crying so hard she began coughing and Elwanda got up to get a glass of water. As she moved to the kitchen, the telephone rang. The receiver was a few feet from her, but when she shot a quick look at Voda Beth, she turned and said, "Jenny, would you mind getting that?"

I walked into the kitchen as Elwanda hurried back to the sofa. "Watson's residence," I said.

"Jenny, is that you? Good. I thought you should know what I found out from Doctor James Gaudet. Seems that Loudermilk had a deep-seated, inoperable brain tumor."

I turned my back to the two women and kept my voice low. "Neuroblastoma?"

"Some big long name," she said. "I'm not sure if that was it, but the doctor said it was bad. Real bad. That he'd never seen a malignancy grow so fast. The man was only weeks away from blindness, paralysis and death."

"Sounds like Loudermilk's luck . . . wait a minute."

"Now. Now, you're thinking. This may have been planned."

"A mercy killing . . . maybe."

"Bingo. Something else you should know. Larry called. Liz has a strong alibi. She and a girlfriend were baby-sitting for her younger brothers and sisters at her mom's house."

"Where did Elwanda go?"

"Liz says she doesn't know, but maybe . . ."

"The Loudermilks'," C.J. and I said in unison. I thought for a moment, then said, "Why don't you call Bulldog Porter? Ask him to come over here immediately. This may get interesting." I hung up the receiver, walked to the coffee pot, and poured a cup, but it was bitter.

I could see Elwanda and Voda Beth still huddled. It looked as if both had been crying, but there were signs of recovery. I rinsed out the coffee pot. The coffee canister was empty and it took me a few minutes to locate a new can, open it and get the pot dripping. I'd just poured three cups when the front doorbell rang.

Elwanda answered it and led Bulldog back into the den. Both women were definitely not expecting him, and wanted to know what was going on, would someone please tell them?

I handed the coffee around and then stood near the glass patio door and began. "I'm presenting a hypothetical case here, Bulldog. If you ladies will, please listen." They turned tear-streaked faces to me. Elwanda's permanent look of astonishment was more pronounced. Voda Beth looked tired. Bone tired.

"I think there was this nice man, who had a nice wife and a nice ex-wife and a not so very nice brain tumor. He knows he doesn't have much time before he will be totally incapacitated and a short time after that, he will die. He doesn't want to die like that. The man also had some business losses. There's the wife and an eighteen-year-old daughter to think about." You could have heard an eye blink, they were so quiet.

"I think this very nice man decided to commit suicide. Everything is planned, but that night for some reason, maybe fear, he was unable to do this alone. He asked his wife for help. She refused. He was on somewhat friendly terms with his ex-wife and he calls her. The ex comes over. He convinces the women time is running out. That the job must be done. The discussion continues, he is adamant, he begs and cajoles and one of them is convinced to help. Maybe it was the ex. But the wife says to the ex-wife 'no,' if anything goes wrong what will happen to your children? You can't go to prison. I won't allow it. But I can't kill the man I love, either. Finally, one woman does it and the wife calls the police."

I looked at each woman, was unable to read the truth. "How does that sound to you ladies? Bulldog?"

No one said anything and I saw big tears running, first down Voda Beth's face and, then, Elwanda's. Silent tears which quietly dripped into their laps, leaving traces on the robes. Their hands were clasped tightly together.

Elwanda said, "That's pretty much what happened. I'm the one who shot him first. Voda Beth took the gun then, and emptied it into him so if the police tested her hands there would be gunpowder traces and her fingerprints would be on the gun."

"No." The anguish was clear and strong in Voda Beth's voice. "I'm the one who fired the gun. She had nothing to do with it. I killed him and I'll take the punishment."

"Bulldog," I said. "Looks like you've got your hands full."

"Oh no," he said, "this one is already won. I doubt there will even be a trial. And if there is, plea bargaining is still an option. Thank you for your help, Jenny. You can expect business from me, now and then, when I have the need of an investigator. Send me an invoice for your expenses."

I walked out of Elwanda Watson's house and drove to the LaGrange, parked and walked inside. When I reached our office, C.J. asked, "Which one did it? Who fired the gun?"

"I don't think it really matters. They just did what they thought had to be done."

Barbara D'Amato, author of the Cat Marsala novels, packs an almost Dickensian sense of Chicago society into "Stop, Thief!," first published in *Sisters in Crime 4*.

Stop, Thief!
BARBARA D'AMATO

Officer Susannah Maria Figueroa lounged back against one of the desks in the roll-call room. She was five feet one, which made her just the right height to be able to rest both buttocks on the desktop.

"See—this woman in a Porsche was driving along, minding her own business, on the way to an afternoon of serious shopping," she said to Officers Hiram Quail and Stanley Mileski, while her partner, Norm Bennis, taller than she was, lounged with one thigh against a neighboring desk, "and *whump!* she hits a cat in the street."

"I would think *moosh!* Not *whump!*" Mileski said. He was a skinny white guy, slightly stooped.

"She gets out," Figueroa said, "looks at the cat, head's okay, tail's okay, but it's flat as a wafer in the middle. Well, it's about three o'clock in the afternoon and she figures the kids'll be coming outa school soon and it's gonna upset the little darlings to see a squashed cat."

"Would," said Mileski. "Some. Then again, some of 'em would love it."

"So she picks it up real careful by the tail and puts it in a Bloomingdale's bag she had in the car and drives on to the mall with it."

"Type o' woman," said Norm Bennis, "who has lotsa extra Bloomie's bags." Bennis was a black man of medium height, built like a wedge. He had slender legs, broad chest, and very, very muscular shoulders.

"Right," said Figueroa, shrugging a little to settle her walkie-talkie more comfortably. "So she pulls up into the mall. Gets out to go in, she should hit Nieman Marcus before the rush starts, but the sun's shinin' down hard and

137

she figures the car's gonna heat up and the cat's gonna get hot and smell up her car."

"Which it would," said Mileski.

"So she takes the bag and puts it up on the hood of the car to wait there while she's shopping. She goes in the mall. Meanwhile, along comes this other woman—"

"Nice lookin' lady," Bennis said. "Named Marietta."

"—who sees the bag there, thinks hah! Fine merchandise unattended, and takes it. Then this woman Marietta with the Bloomie's bag goes into the mall. She's a shoplifter. She's truckin' through the jewelry department at Houston's lookin' for something worth boostin', sees a pearl necklace some clerk didn't put back, picks it up, opens the Bloomie's bag, drops the necklace in, sees the cat, screams like a train whistle, and falls down in a dead faint. The store manager or some such honcho runs over, tries to revive her, slaps her face, but she sits up once, glances at the bag and falls over again in a dead faint, so they call the paramedics. The EMTs arrive, chuck her onto a gurney, put her Bloomie's bag between her feet, which is SOP with personal belongings, and whisk her out to the ambulance."

"Meanwhile," Bennis said, "the clerk at the jewelry counter's seen the pearls are missin'."

"Which is where we come in. By this time the woman's at the hospital, but by astute questioning of the store personnel, we put two and two together—"

"*Experience* and astute questioning, Suze my man," Bennis said. Bennis was thirty-five. Suze was twenty-six.

"—we figure out where the pearls are. So we roll on over to the hospital with lights and siren. Woman's in the emergency room and we just mosey on in and ask if we can dump out the bag. Orderly doesn't know enough to say no—"

"Sometimes you luck out," said Bennis.

"—so we turn the bag upside down and out flops the pearls plus the dead cat. At which point, the *orderly* faints."

"We were kinda surprised ourselves," Bennis said. "Didn't faint, though."

"Too tough," said Figueroa.

"Macho," said Bennis.

"Spent the next two hours in the district on the paper," Figueroa said.

"Odd, you know, when a supposed victim turns into a perp. Kinda felt sorry for her."

Figueroa said, "Not me, Bennis. She's a crook."

Mileski said, "Don't suppose they managed to revive the cat?"

Sergeant Touhy strode in and the third watch crew faded into seats.

Sergeant Touhy said, "Bennis? Figueroa? We've had a complaint from the hospital. Seems they don't like cat guts on their gurneys."

Bennis started to say, "We didn't know about the cat—" but Figueroa kicked him and muttered, "Probable cause!" so he shut up. "But we got our offender, Sarge," Suze Figueroa said.

"Yeah," Bennis said. "Boosts our solved record."

Touhy ignored them. "Next time, look in the bag first. Now let's read some crimes."

"You really need *three* ammo pouches?" Quail whispered at Figueroa. "You expecting a war?"

She whispered back. "Hey! You get in serious shit and I come in as backup you'll kiss my pouches."

Each ammo pouch held six rounds of .38 ammunition for the standard service revolver. You could fit three pouches, max, on your Sam Browne, though most officers didn't. Privately, Figueroa wished she could carry her ammo like the cowboys did, in loops all around the belt. But the department had a regulation that all ammo had to be concealed. Takes half the fun out, Figueroa thought.

She also thought it would be nice if Maintenance would wait to turn on the heat in here until the weather got cold. The roll-call room for the First District was never going to be a photo opportunity for *Architectural Digest*. But why not livable? The smell of hot wool and sweat was practically thick enough to see.

After ten minutes or so Touhy finished up with, "Pick up the new runaway list at the desk. Now, we've been getting more and more complaints from the senior-citizen groups in the neighborhood, and I'll tell you now I don't want the Gray Panthers on my ass. We got a lot of older people out there, they think they're under siege. From teenagers, more than our serious nasties. These are people who're specifically trying to get their grocery shopping done before the schools let out. Get back in their houses before the teenagers are set free. I mean, it's like three-thirty to them is when the Draculas come out. They get pushed, hassled. Yelled at. Called bad names. Get their groceries stolen."

"It happens," Mileski said.

"Not in *my* district it don't, Mileski!"

"Right, boss."

"Okay. Now hit the bricks and clear."

Norm and Suze were in an early car today, so they were on the street by three in the afternoon. They were beat car 1-33, patrolling the north end of the district.

Chicago's First District is unique among the twenty-five district stations in that it operates out of the big central cop-shop at 11th and State. It is also one of the most varied districts. It has world-class hotels of mind-boggling elegance and enough marble to stress the bedrock. It has the most soul-deadening public housing. It has staggeringly expensive jewelry emporiums and meretricious underwear stores where lewd sayings are embroidered on bras and panty bottoms. It has grade schools and premier medical schools and on-the-job training in crime and prostitution.

"One thirty-one?"

One thirty-one was Mileski and his partner, Hiram Quail. Suze and Norm heard Mileski's voice come back, "Thirty-one."

"I've got a car parked on a fire hydrant at 210 W. Grand."

"Ten-four, squad."

A new voice. "One twenty-seven."

"Twenty-seven. Go."

"I need an RD number for an attempted strongarm robbery."

"Uh—your number's gonna be 660932."

"Thanks much."

Norm and Suze rolled south on Wells, Norm driving and Suze doing a good eyeballing of the street. This part of Wells was a patchwork retail mix of run-down cigar and miscellany stores, trendy boutiques, newsstands that specialized in stroke magazines, cheap shoe stores, a Ripley's Believe It or Not Museum, coffee shops with early-bird special dinners and upscale yuppie restaurants where you could pay fifty bucks for a hundred calories. Four black teenagers, three of them boys with Gumby haircuts and one leotard-clad girl, cutting school and throwing shots at each other, lingered around a newsstand. They glanced at the squad car and looked away. A skinny white guy with a wispy beard passed them, cowboy-walking. "One of our known felons," Norm said.

"Brace him?" Suze said.

"He's not breakin' a law."

"Not right *now*."

"Be mellow, my man."

Coming the other way were two women in high heels, wearing fur coats that were hardly necessary, given the mild weather, the coats open in front, heavy gold chains swinging, very high heels, and purses dangling by their straps from one hand. Norm slowed. The white guy and the black kids watched the women peck their way along the street.

"Volunteer victims," Norm said.

The radio said, "Twenty-seven, your VIN is coming back clear."

"Ten-four."

"Thirty-one?"

"Thirty-one."

"We got a maroon Chevy blew the stoplight at—"

Norm shrugged as the women achieved the next block unharmed. He accelerated away from the curb. The radio said, "One thirty-three."

Suze picked up the mike. "Thirty-three."

"We got a shoplifting, Sounds of the Times, 279 Wells, two male whites, fifteen to eighteen years old."

"Somebody holding them?" Suze said.

"Nope. Fled on foot, knocked over an old man. Check on the man, plus see the manager. Mr. Stone."

The address was a block north of their car's beat boundary, but thirty-one was tied up, so it was reasonable for them to slide on over.

Sounds of the Times was one of the seriously trendy ones. The double window display, with glossy chrome-and-ebony frames around the windows and the entry between them, was laid out on sheets of casually rumpled blue denim. "Dance through the Decades" was spelled out in letters cut from sheet music that hung from barely visible threads above the display. There were rows of CDs, and beneath them rows of shoes of the period when the music was popular, starting in the left window with the 1890s, Strauss waltzes and kid pumps with little seed pearls, through Cuban heels and Friml with a gap where a CD had been taken out, and Billy Rose with T-strap dancing shoes, through the early fifties, saddle shoes then penny loafers and Nat "King" Cole. In the right window the late fifties segued into Elvis and then the Beatles, with strap sandals, then Earth shoes, and acid rock, up to 2 Live Crew, and Hammer and in front of these a pair of inflatable Reeboks. A pretty nice window, Figueroa thought, although it would have been nicer-looking if the display hadn't been in such rigid rows.

The old man sat on a bench outside the store, trembling. Like many old men, his face looked like a peach—a three-day growth of soft white beard against an old pink skin. He was dressed in an aged windbreaker. He looked bitterly cold, despite the pleasant weather.

"See if he's hurt. I'll check with the manager," Norm said. The manager was striding toward the front door already. He wore a white shirt with navy and red sleeve garters and a navy vest and pants.

Suze sat down on the bench. "You okay?" she asked.

"I guess."

"What's your name, sir?"

"Minton. Raymond Minton."

"What happened to you, Mr. Minton?"

"Um—" He shook his head as if he wasn't sure.

"How old are you, Mr. Minton?"

"Eighty-seven," he said with some pride and complete clarity.

"And where do you live?"

"Fassbinder House."

Something less than a nursing home, more than a residence hotel. Figueroa knew it. Supervised living it was called, for the indigent elderly. About a block and a half west of here. She had been inside with a walkaway a couple of weeks before. It was functional.

Minton's head bobbed up and down on a skinny neck. The hair was thin and white on top of his head and hadn't been cut recently. Wisps of it moved in the breeze. The man needed a hat, Suze Figueroa thought. A wool hat.

"What happened here?" she said.

"Pushed me down." He was, sadly, not at all amazed. It had probably happened before.

"How? Where?"

"I was going out of the store. Under that alarm arch thing. One of 'em was just ahead of me. The other one was coming through and gave me a shove. Pushed me right down. Like I was—a door or something like that in his way. Just shoved me away. And then the alarm went off."

"You fell?"

"Mmm-mm." He pointed at his knee. The pants leg was roughed and a little blood soaked into the fabric from underneath. Thin blood, Figueroa thought.

"Can you stand on it?"

"Oh sure!" he said and got up to show her. He sat down immediately, a little sheepish at his weakness. But not as if anything was broken, Suze thought with some relief. The hand that lay in his lap was skinned on the palm and the ball of the thumb was bleeding. Caught himself on the hand and knee. Better that than break an elbow. She'd had one of them last week, and he'd screamed so much she could hardly hear the dispatcher to call for an ambulance.

"Wait here, please, Mr. Minton."

Bennis had got the manager calmed down. It wasn't that the guy was scared. Mr. Stone was angry, bright red in the face.

"Slouching around the store! I gotta keep my eyes on all of 'em at once!" he said. "I hate kids. Punks!"

"I guess *mosta* your customers are kids, though, huh?" Bennis said.

"Shit! Yeah!"

Bennis sighed; his mild suggestion that the store profited from teenagers had done nothing to honey up Mr. Stone. "So let me get a description."

"Punks!"

"Yeah, I know. Black punks or white punks?"

"I told you guys that when I called in!"

"Tell me again."

"White, and by the way—"

"Height?"

"Medium. Like five ten. One was maybe a little shorter than that."

"Weight?"

"Skinny. Both of 'em. Brown hair. And skinheads."

"Skinheads! Really?" Chicago didn't have many skinheads. Yet. Let's keep our fingers crossed, Bennis thought.

"Well, not *real* skinheads, but their hair was cut right to the scalp up to here," he said, indicating an inch above the tops of his ears. "I hate that bald haircut they wear."

"Eye color?"

"Hey! How'm I gonna see a thing like that? Sneaky little monsters keep their eyes squinted anyhow!"

Bennis said, "Clothes?"

"Black leather jackets, running shoes, Levi's. Jackets must've cost more than I make a *week*."

At the clothing description, which narrowed it to maybe eighty percent of the teenagers in the city, Bennis sighed again, loud enough for Stone to hear him and frown. "Distinguishing features?"

"Ugly bastards. One was pimply. Other one was trying to grow a mustache. Hah! Smirking at me with five hairs on his upper lip!"

Bennis got on the radio and put out the description. Figueroa sidled over to the window displays. She looked at the gap.

"See which way they went?" Bennis asked Stone.

"Nah. Right into the crowd out there and zip!"

"Mr. Minton," Figueroa said, walking out the door, "did *you* see which way they went?"

"There."

Minton pointed south.

"Fled southbound," Bennis said. "Mr. Stone?"

"Yeah?"

"How many CDs did they have on 'em when they took off?"

"How do I know? Didn't even know there was a problem until the door alarm went off. There's the one missin' outa the window, but probably they loaded up before they boogied. Shit! Anyhow, by the time the alarm goes off they're outa here. Fat lot of good the alarm is. And that old guy's lyin' on the sidewalk. You don't think he's gonna sue us, do ya? The old guy?"

"I wouldn't know, Mr. Stone."

"Better not. His own fault, gettin' in the way."

Figueroa strolled around while Bennis told the dispatcher that the teens could have one or more stolen CDs on them.

"Never catch 'em now," Stone said. "Took you guys five minutes to get here."

"Two," Bennis said. "You called at 3:11. We rolled up at 3:13."

"Well, it's five minutes *now*. They could be anywhere."

Bennis shrugged. Too true.

Outside, Figueroa sat down on the bench next to the old man. "How's that knee now, Mr. Minton?" she said.

"Don't know." He stretched the leg out. The thin fabric of his worn pants pulled back from the blood-stained knee and he winced. He dragged his pants leg up a few inches with one blue-veined hand, picking the fabric loose from the skin. His shinbone looked sharp above the sagging sock.

"Are you married, Mr. Minton?" Figueroa said.

"Was. Her name was Helen. She's dead."

"How long have you been living at Fassbinder House?"

"Four years."

"How do you like it? Pretty Spartan?" For a second she wondered if he'd know what Spartan meant. Or would remember if he had once known. When he answered, she felt as chagrined as if she had been visibly condescending.

"It isn't bad. The food's warm."

And how basic that was, Figueroa thought.

"Mr. Minton, I guess you and your wife used to dance," Figueroa said. "To Friml."

He didn't answer.

"Do they have a CD player at the Fassbinder?"

He didn't answer.

"What do they play on it?"

The old man groaned. "Show tunes," he said. "Broadway shows. From the Forties and Fifties."

"I see."

"Do you? They think—the nice children who run the Fassbinder think—we were young in the Forties and Fifties. They can't imagine anybody being older than that. Young! I was forty-seven in 1950!" He started to laugh, laughed and laughed, showing missing teeth and an old tongue, creased and bluish-pink, laughed until he started to cough. But he caught himself then and quieted.

Figueroa said, "I'll tell the manager it was a mistake."

"Fourteen dollars for one disc!" he said. It could have been fourteen thousand.

"Give it to me, Mr. Minton, and I'll take it back."

He grabbed her arm in a bony grip. "I wouldn't have said the kids did it. I really wouldn't have. If they hadn't pushed me."

Bennis said, "How'd you know?"

"With a missing Friml? Kids these days aren't into that."

"Some could be, Suze my man."

"The kind wearing that sort of outfit? That kind of haircut?"

"Not likely."

"Scholarly types maybe. Plus, these kids were out of here by 3:11."

"So?"

"School's out at 3:30. They were cutting school. These are not your scholars, Bennis. If Hammer had been lifted, okay. But Rudolf Friml?"

Bennis nodded. They got back in the squad car.

"He gonna just skate, Figueroa?"

"Yeah, I cut him loose."

"Um—"

"Hey, Bennis, you figure he's gonna go on to a life of crime? He's eighty-seven years old."

"How we gonna put it down?"

"Unfounded."

"Okay."

"What's the matter?"

"I saw you buy the CD from Stone. For the old guy."

"Shit, don't look at me like that. I saved us two hours in the district handling the paper."

"Figueroa, my man, climb down. You are preaching to the converted. I already called in for fifteen minutes' personal time. I'm gonna buy you a cup of coffee."

"Why me?"

"I figure it'll take you that long to get over bein' human."

Edward Bryant is known to a great number of people as a Hugo and Nebula Award-winning Science Fiction author, but he has written a large number of powerful contemporary suspense stories as well. The following, originally published in *Pulphouse: The Hardback Magazine* and available widely only since last year when it was reprinted in *Dark Crimes 2,* we promise, will forever change your concept of the mall experience.

While She Was Out
EDWARD BRYANT

It was what her husband said then that was the last straw.

"Christ," muttered Kenneth disgustedly from the family room. He grasped a Bud longneck in one red-knuckled hand, the cable remote tight in the other. This was the time of night when he generally fell into the largest number of stereotypes. "I swear to God you're on the rag three weeks out of every month. PMS, my ass."

Della Myers deliberately bit down on what she wanted to answer. PXMS, she thought. That's what the twins' teacher had called it last week over coffee after the parent-teacher conference Kenneth had skipped. Pre-holiday syndrome. It took a genuine effort not to pick up the cordless Northwestern Bell phone and brain Kenneth with one savage, cathartic swipe. "I'm going out."

"So?" said her husband. "This is Thursday. Can't be the auto mechanics made simple for wusses. Self defense?" He shook his head. "That's every other Tuesday. Something new, honey? Maybe a therapy group?"

"I'm going to Southeast Plaza. I need to pick up some things."

"Get the extra-absorbent ones," said her husband. He grinned and thumbed up the volume. ESPN was bringing in wide shots of something that looked vaguely like group tennis from some sweaty-looking third-world country.

"Wrapping paper," she said. "I'm getting some gift-wrap and ribbon." Were there fourth-world countries? she wondered. Would they accept political refugees from America? "Will you put the twins to bed by nine?"

"Stallone's on HBO at nine," Kenneth said. "I'll bag 'em out by half-past eight."

"Fine." She didn't argue.

"I'll give them a good bedtime story." He paused. "The Princess and the Pea."

"Fine." Della shrugged on her long down-filled coat. Anymore, she did her best not to swallow the bait. "I told them they could each have a chocolate chip cookie with their milk."

"Christ, Della. Why the hell don't we just adopt the dentist? Maybe give him an automatic monthly debit from the checking account?"

"One cookie apiece," she said, implacable.

Kenneth shrugged, apparently resigned.

She picked up the keys to the Subaru. "I won't be long."

"Just be back by breakfast."

Della stared at him. What if I don't come back at all? She had actually said that once. Kenneth had smiled and asked whether she was going to run away with the gypsies, or maybe go off to join some pirates. It had been a temptation to say yes, dammit, yes, I'm going. But there were the twins. Della suspected pirates didn't take along their children. "Don't worry," she said. I've got nowhere else to go. But she didn't say that aloud.

Della turned and went upstairs to the twins' room to tell them good night. Naturally they both wanted to go with her to the mall. Each was afraid she wasn't going to get the hottest item in the Christmas doll department— the Little BeeDee Birth Defect Baby. There had been a run on the BeeDees, but Della had shopped for the twins early. "Daddy's going to tell you a story," she promised. The pair wasn't impressed.

"I want to see Santa," Terri said, with dogged, five-year-old insistence.

"You both saw Santa. Remember?"

"I forgot some things. An' I want to tell him again about BeeDee."

"Me, too," said Tammi. With Tammi, it was always "me too."

"Maybe this weekend," said Della.

"Will Daddy remember our cookies?" said Terri.

Before she exited the front door, Della took the chocolate chip cookies from the kitchen closet and set the sack on the stairstep where Kenneth could not fail to stumble over it.

"So long," she called.

"Bring me back something great from the mall," he said. His only other response was to heighten the crowd noise from Upper Zambo-somewhere-or-other.

* * *

Sleety snow was falling, the accumulation beginning to freeze on the streets. Della was glad she had the Subaru. So far this winter, she hadn't needed to use the four-wheel drive, but tonight the reality of having it reassured her.

Southeast Plaza was a mess. This close to Christmas, the normally spacious parking lots were jammed. Della took a chance and circled the row of spaces nearest to the mall entrances. If she were lucky, she'd be able to react instantly to someone's backup lights and snaffle a parking place within five seconds of its being vacated. That didn't happen. She cruised the second row, the third. Then—There! She reacted without thinking, seeing the vacant spot just beyond a metallic blue van. She swung the Subaru to the left.

And stamped down hard on the brake.

Some moron had parked an enormous barge of an ancient Plymouth so that it overlapped two diagonal spaces.

The Subaru slid to a stop with its nose about half an inch from the Plymouth's dinosaurian bumper. In the midst of her shock and sudden anger, Della saw the chrome was pocked with rust. The Subaru's headlights reflected back at her.

She said something unpleasant, the kind of language she usually only thought in dark silence. Then she backed her car out of the truncated space and resumed the search for parking. What Della eventually found was a free space on the extreme perimeter of the lot. She resigned herself to trudging a quarter mile through the slush. She hadn't worn boots. The icy water crept into her flats, soaked her toes.

"Shit," she said. "Shit shit shit."

Her shortest-distance-between-two-points course took her past the Plymouth hogging the two parking spots. Della stopped a moment, contemplating the darkened behemoth. It was a dirty gold with the remnants of a vinyl roof peeling away like the flaking of a scabrous scalp. In the glare of the mercury vapor lamp, she could see that the rocker panels were riddled with rust holes. Odd. So much corrosion didn't happen in the dry Colorado air. She glanced curiously at the rear license plate. It was obscured with dirty snow.

She stared at the huge old car and realized she was getting angry. Not just irritated. Real, honest-to-god, hardcore pissed off. What kind of imbeciles would take up two parking spaces on a rotten night just two weeks before Christmas?

Ones that drove a vintage, not-terribly-kept-up Plymouth, obviously.

Without even thinking about what she was doing, Della took out the spiral notebook from her handbag. She flipped to the black page past tomorrow's grocery list and uncapped the fine-tip marker (it was supposed to write across anything—in this snow, it had *better*) and scrawled a message:

DEAR JERK, IT'S GREAT YOU COULD USE UP TWO PARKING SPACES ON A NIGHT LIKE THIS. EVER HEAR OF THE JOY OF SHARING?

She paused, considering: then appended:

—A CONCERNED FRIEND

Della folded the paper as many times as she could, to protect it from the wet, then slipped it under the driver's-side wiper blade.

It wouldn't do any good—she was sure this was the sort of driver who ordinarily would have parked illegally in the handicapped zone—but it made her feel better. Della walked on to the mall entrance and realized she was smiling.

She bought some rolls of foil wrapping paper for the adult gifts—assuming she actually gave Kenneth anything she'd bought for him—and an ample supply of Strawberry Shortcake pattern for the twins' presents. Della decided to splurge—she realized she was getting tired—and selected a package of pre-tied ribbon bows rather than simply taking a roll. She also bought a package of tampons.

Della wandered the mall for a little while, checking out the shoe stores, looking for something on sale in deep blue, a pair she could wear to Kenneth's office party for staff and spouses. What she *really* wanted were some new boots. Time enough for those after the holiday when the prices went down. Nothing appealed to her. Della knew she should be shopping for Kenneth's family in Nebraska. She couldn't wait forever to mail off their packages.

The hell with it. Della realized she was simply delaying returning home. Maybe she *did* need a therapy group, she thought. There was no relish to the thought of spending another night sleeping beside Kenneth, listening to the snoring that was interrupted only by the grinding of teeth. She thought that the sound of Kenneth's jaws moving against one another must be like hearing a speeded-up recording of continental drift.

She looked at her watch. A little after nine. No use waiting any longer. She did up the front of her coat and joined the flow of shoppers out into the snow.

Della realized, as she passed the rusted old Plymouth, that something wasn't the same. *What's wrong with this picture?* It was the note. It wasn't there. Probably it had slipped out from under the wiper blade with the wind and the water. Maybe the flimsy notebook paper had simply dissolved.

She no longer felt like writing another note. She dismissed the irritating lumber barge from her reality and walked on to her car.

* * *

Della let the Subaru warm up for thirty seconds (the consumer auto mechanics class had told her not to let the engine idle for the long minutes she had once believed necessary) and then slipped the shift into reverse.

The passenger compartment flooded with light.

She glanced into the rearview mirror and looked quickly away. A bright, glaring eye had stared back. Another quivered in the side mirror.

"Jesus Christ," she said under her breath. "The crazies are out tonight." She hit the clutch with one foot, the brake with the other, and waited for the car behind her to remove itself. Nothing happened. The headlights in the mirror flicked to bright. "Dammit." Della left the Subaru in neutral and got out of the car.

She shaded her eyes and squinted. The front of the car behind hers looked familiar. It was the gold Plymouth.

Two unseen car-doors clicked open and chunked shut again.

The lights abruptly went out and Della blinked, her eyes trying to adjust to the dim mercury vapor illumination from the pole a few car-lengths away.

She felt a cold thrill of unease in her belly and turned back toward the car.

"I've got a gun," said a voice. "Really." It sounded male and young. "I'll aim at your snatch first."

Someone else giggled, high and shrill.

Della froze in place. This couldn't be happening. It absolutely could not.

Her eyes were adjusting, the glare-phantoms drifting out to the limit of her peripheral vision and vanishing. She saw three figures in front of her, then a fourth. She didn't see a gun.

"Just what do you think you're doing?" she said.

"Not doing *nothin'*, yet." That, she saw, was the black one. He stood to the left of the white kid who had claimed to have a gun. The pair was bracketed by a boy who looked Chinese or Vietnamese and a young man with dark, Hispanic good looks. All four looked to be in their late teens or very early twenties. Four young men. Four ethnic groups represented. Della repressed a giggle she thought might be the first step toward hysteria.

"So what are you guys? Working on your merit badge in tolerance? Maybe selling magazine subscriptions?" Della immediately regretted saying that. Her husband was always riding her for smarting off.

"Funny lady," said the Hispanic. "We just happen to get along." He glanced to his left. "You laughing, Huey?"

The black shook his head. "Too cold. I'm shiverin' out here. I didn't bring no clothes for this."

"Easy way to fix that, man," said the white boy. To Della, he said, "Vinh, Tomas, Huey, me, we all got similar interests, you know?"

"Listen—" Della started to say.

"Chuckie," said the black Della now assumed was Huey, "let's us just shag out of here, okay?"

"*Chuckie?*" said Della.

"Shut up!" said Chuckie. To Huey, he said, "Look, we came up here for a vacation, right? The word is fun." He said to Della, "Listen, we were having a good time until we saw you stick the note under the wiper." His eyes glistened in the vapor-lamp glow. "I don't like getting any static from some 'burb-bitch just 'cause she's on the rag."

"For God's sake," said Della disgustedly. She decided he didn't really have a gun. "Screw off!" The exhaust vapor from the Subaru spiraled up around her. "I'm leaving, boys."

"Any trouble here, Miss?" said a new voice. Everyone looked. It was one of the mall rent-a-cops, bulky in his fur-trimmed jacket and Russian-styled cap. His hand lay casually across the unsnapped holster flap at his hip.

"Not if these underage creeps move their barge so I can back out," said Della.

"How about it, guys?" said the rent-a-cop.

Now there *was* a gun, a dark pistol, in Chuckie's hand, and he pointed it at the rent-a-cop's face. "Naw," Chuckie said. "This was gonna be a vacation, but what the heck. No witnesses, I reckon."

"For God's sake," said the rent-a-cop, starting to back away.

Chuckie grinned and glanced aside at his friends. "Remember the security guy at the mall in Tucson?" To Della, he said, "Most of these rent-a-pig companies don't give their guys any ammo. Liability laws and all that shit. Too bad." He lifted the gun purposefully.

The rent-a-cop went for his pistol anyway. Chuckie shot him in the face. Red pulp sprayed out the back of his skull and stained the slush as the man's body flopped back and forth, spasming.

"For chrissake," said Chuckie in exasperation. "Enough already. Relax, man." He leaned over his victim and deliberately aimed and fired, aimed and fired. The second shot entered the rent-a-cop's left eye. The third shattered his teeth.

Della's eyes recorded everything as though she were a movie camera. Everything was moving in slow motion and she was numb. She tried to make things speed up. Without thinking about the decision, she spun and made for her car door. She knew it was hopeless.

"Chuckie!"

"So? Where's she gonna go? We got her blocked. I'll just put one through her windshield and we can go out and pick up a couple of sixpacks, maybe hit the late show at some other mall."

Della heard him fire one more time. Nothing tore through the back of her skull. He was still blowing apart the rent-a-cop's head.

She slammed into the Subaru's driver seat and punched the door-lock switch, for all the good that would do. Della hit the four-wheel-drive switch. *That* was what Chuckie hadn't thought about. She jammed the gearshift into first, gunned the engine, and popped the clutch. The Subaru barely protested as the front tires clawed and bounded over the six-inch concrete row barrier. The barrier screeched along the underside of the frame. Then the rear wheels were over and the Subaru fishtailed momentarily.

Don't over-correct, she thought. It was a prayer.

The Subaru straightened out and Della was accelerating down the mall's outer perimeter service road, slush spraying to either side. Now what? she thought. People must have heard the shots. The lot would be crawling with cops.

But in the meantime—

The lights, bright and blinding, blasted against her mirrors.

Della stamped the accelerator to the floor.

This was crazy! This didn't happen to people—not to *real* people. The mall security man's blood in the snow had been real enough.

In the rearview, there was a sudden flash just above the left-side head-light, then another. It was a muzzle-blast, Della realized. They were shooting at her. It was just like on TV. The scalp on the back of her head itched. Would she feel it when the bullet crashed through?

The twins! Kenneth. She wanted to see them all, to be safely with them. Just be anywhere but here!

Della spun the wheel, ignoring the stop sign and realizing that the access road dead-ended. She could go right or left, so went right. She thought it was the direction of home. Not a good choice. The lights were all behind her now; she could see nothing but darkness ahead. Della tried to remember what lay beyond the mall on this side. There were housing developments, both completed and under construction.

There had to be a 7-Eleven, a filling station, *something*. Anything. But there wasn't, and then the pavement ended. At first the road was suddenly rougher, the potholes yawning deeper. Then the slush-marked asphalt stopped. The Subaru bounced across the gravel; within thirty yards, the gravel deteriorated to roughly graded dirt. The dirt surface more properly could be called mud.

A wooden barrier loomed ahead, the reflective stripes and lightly falling snow glittering in the headlights.

It *was* like on TV, Della thought. She gunned the engine and ducked sideways, even with the dash, as the Subaru plowed into the barrier. She heard a sickening *crack* and shattered windshield glass sprayed down around her. Della felt the car veer. She tried to sit upright again, but the auto was spinning too fast.

The Subaru swung a final time and smacked firm against a low grove of young pine. The engine coughed and stalled. Della hit the light switch. She smelled the overwhelming tang of crushed pine needles flooding with the snow through the space where the windshield had been. The engine groaned when she twisted the key, didn't start.

Della risked a quick look around. The Plymouth's lights were visible, but the car was farther back than she had dared hope. The size of the lights wasn't increasing and the beams pointed up at a steep angle. Probably the heavy Plymouth had slid in the slush, gone off the road, was stuck for good.

She tried the key, and again the engine didn't catch. She heard something else—voices getting closer. Della took the key out of the ignition and glanced around the dark passenger compartment. Was there anything she could use? Anything at all? Not in the glovebox. She knew there was nothing there but the owner's manual and a large pack of sugarless spearmint gum.

The voices neared.

Della reached under the dash and tugged the trunk release. Then she rolled down the window and slipped out into the darkness. She wasn't too stunned to forget that the overhead light would go on if she opened the door.

At least one of the boys had a flashlight. The beam flickered and danced along the snow.

Della stumbled to the rear of the Subaru. By feel, she found the toolbox. With her other hand, she sought out the lug wrench. Then she moved away from the car.

She wished she had a gun. She wished she had learned to *use* a gun. That had been something tagged for a vague future when she'd finished her consumer mechanics course and the self defense workshop, and had some time again to take another night course. It wasn't, she had reminded herself, that she was paranoid. Della simply wanted to be better prepared for the exigencies of living in the city. The suburbs weren't *the city* to Kenneth, but if you were a girl from rural Montana, they were.

She hadn't expected *this*.

She hunched down. Her nose told her the shelter she had found was a hefty clump of sagebrush. She was perhaps twenty yards from the Subaru now. The boys were making no attempt at stealth. She heard them talking to each other as the flashlight beam bobbed around her stalled car.

"So, she in there chilled with her brains all over the wheel?" said Tomas, the Hispanic kid.

"You an optimist?" said Chuckie. He laughed, a high-pitched giggle. "No, she ain't here, you dumb shit. This one's a tough lady." Then he said, "Hey, lookie there!"

"What you doin'?" said Huey. "We ain't got time for that."

"Don't be too sure. Maybe we can use this."

What had he found? Della wondered.

"Now we do what?" said Vinh. He had a slight accent.

"This be the West," said Huey. "I guess now we're mountain men, just like in the movies."

"Right," said Chuckie. "Track her. There's mud. There's snow. How far can she get?"

"There's the trail," said Tomas. "Shine the light over there. She must be pretty close."

Della turned. Hugging the toolbox, trying not to let it clink or clatter, she fled into the night.

They cornered her a few minutes later.

Or it could have been an hour. There was no way she could read her watch. All Della knew was that she had run; she had run and she had attempted circling around to where she might have a shot at making it to the distant lights of the shopping mall. Along the way, she'd felt the brush clawing at her denim jeans and the mud and slush attempting to suck down her shoes. She tried to make out shapes in the clouded-over dark, evaluating every murky form as a potential hiding place.

"Hey, baby," said Huey from right in front of her.

Della recoiled, feinted to the side, collided painfully with a wooden fence. The boards gave only slightly. She felt a long splinter drive through the down coat and spear into her shoulder. When Della jerked away, she felt the splinter tear away from its board and then break off.

The flashlight snapped on, the beam at first blinding her, then lowering to focus on her upper body. From their voices, she knew all four were there. Della wanted a free hand to pull the splinter loose from her shoulder. Instead she continued cradling the blue plastic toolbox.

"Hey," said Chuckie, "what's in that thing? Family treasure, maybe?"

Della remained mute. She'd already gotten into trouble enough, wising off.

"Let's see," said Chuckie. "Show us, Della-honey."

She stared at his invisible face.

Chuckie giggled. "Your driver's license, babe. In your purse. In the car."

Shit, she thought.

"Lousy picture." Chuckie. "I think maybe we're gonna make your face match it." Again, that ghastly laugh. "Meantime, let's see what's in the box, okay?"

"Jewels, you think?" said Vinh.

"Naw, I don't think," said his leader. "But maybe she was makin' the bank deposit or something." He addressed Della. "You got enough goodies for us, maybe we can be bought off."

No chance, she thought. They want everything. My money, my rings, my watch. She tried to swallow, but her throat was too dry. My life.

"Open the box," said Chuckie, voice mean now.

"Open the box," said Tomas. Huey echoed him. The four started chanting, "Open the box, open the box, open the box."

"All right," she almost screamed. "I'll do it." They stopped their chorus. Someone snickered. Her hands moving slowly, Della's brain raced. Do it, she thought. But be careful. So careful. She let the lug wrench rest across her palm below the toolbox. With her other hand, she unsnapped the catch and slid up the lid toward the four. She didn't think any of them could see in, though the flashlight beam was focused now on the toolbox lid.

Della reached inside, as deliberately as she could, trying to betray nothing of what she hoped to do. It all depended upon what lay on top. Her bare fingertips touched the cold steel of the crescent wrench. Her fingers curled around the handle.

"This is pretty dull," said Tomas. "Let's just rape her."

Now!

She withdrew the wrench, cocked her wrist back and hurled the tool about two feet above the flashlight's glare. Della snapped it just like her daddy had taught her to throw a hardball. She hadn't liked baseball all that much. But now—

The wrench crunched something and Chuckie screamed. The flashlight dropped to the snow.

Snapping shut the toolbox, Della sprinted between Chuckie and the one she guessed was Huey.

The black kid lunged for her and slipped in the muck, toppling face-first into the slush. Della had a peripheral glimpse of Tomas leaping toward her, but his leading foot came down on the back of Huey's head, grinding the boy's face into the mud. Huey's scream bubbled; Tomas cursed and tumbled forward, trying to stop himself with out-thrust arms.

All Della could think as she gained the darkness was, I should have grabbed the light.

She heard the one she thought was Vinh, laughing. "Cripes, guys, neat. Just like Moe and Curley and that other one."

"Shut up," said Chuckie's voice. It sounded pinched and in pain. "Shut the fuck up." The timbre squeaked and broke. "Get up, you dorks. Get the bitch."

Sticks and stones—Della thought. Was she getting hysterical? There was no good reason not to.

As she ran—and stumbled—across the nightscape, Della could feel the long splinter moving with the movement of the muscles in her shoulder. The feeling of it, not just the pain, but the sheer, physical sensation of intrusion, nauseated her.

I've got to stop, she thought. I've got to rest. I've got to think.

Della stumbled down the side of a shallow gulch and found she was splashing across a shallow, frigid stream. Water. It triggered something. Disregarding the cold soaking her flats and numbing her feet, she turned and started upstream, attempting to splash as little as possible. This had worked, she seemed to recall, in *Uncle Tom's Cabin*, as well as a lot of bad prison escape movies.

The boys were hardly experienced mountain men. They weren't Indian trackers. This ought to take care of her trail.

After what she estimated to be at least a hundred yards, when her feet felt like blocks of wood and she felt she was losing her balance, Della clambered out of the stream and struggled up the side of the gulch. She found herself in groves of pine, much like the trees where her Subaru had ended its skid. At least the pungent evergreens supplied some shelter against the prairie wind that had started to rise.

She heard noise from down in the gulch. It was music. It made her think of the twins.

"What the *fuck* are you doing?" Chuckie's voice.

"It's a tribute, man. A gesture." Vinh. "It's his blaster."

Della recognized the tape. Rap music. Run DMC, the Beastie Boys, one of those groups.

"Christ, I didn't mean it." Tomas. "It's her fault."

"Well, he's dead," said Chuckie, "and that's it for him. Now turn that shit off. Somebody might hear."

"Who's going to hear?" said Vinh. "Nobody can hear out here. Just us, and her."

"That's the point. She can."

"So what?" said Tomas. "We got the gun, we got the light. She's got nothin' but that stupid box."

"We *had* Huey," said Chuckie. "Now we don't. Shut off the blaster, dammit."

"Okay." Vinh's voice sounded sullen. There was a loud click and the rap echo died.

Della huddled against the rough bark of a pine trunk, hugging the box and herself. The boy's dead, she thought. So? said her common sense. He would have killed you, maybe raped you, tortured you before pulling the trigger. The rest are going to have to die too.

No.

Yes, said her practical side. You have no choice. They started this.

I put the note under the wiper blade.

Get serious. That was harmless. These three are going to kill you. They will hurt you first, then they'll put the gun inside your mouth and—

Della wanted to cry, to scream. She knew she could not. It was absolutely necessary that she not break now.

Terri, she thought, Tammi. I love you. After a while, she remembered Kenneth. Even you. I love you too. Not much, but some.

"Let's look up above," came the voice from the gully. Chuckie. Della heard the wet scrabbling sounds as the trio scratched and pulled their way up from the stream-bed. As it caught the falling snow, the flashlight looked like the beam from a searchlight at a movie premiere.

Della edged back behind the pine and slowly moved to where the trees were closer together. Boughs laced together, screening her.

"Now what?" said Tomas.

"We split up." Chuckie gestured; the flashlight beam swung wide. "You go through the middle. Vinh and me'll take the sides."

"Then why don't you give me the light?" said Tomas.

"I stole the sucker. It's mine."

"Shit, I could just walk past her."

Chuckie laughed. "Get real, dude, You'll smell her, hear her, somethin'. Trust me."

Tomas said something Della couldn't make out, but the tone was unconvinced.

"Now *do* it," said Chuckie. The light moved off to Della's left. She heard the squelching of wet shoes moving toward her. Evidently Tomas had done some wading in the gully. Either that or the slush was taking its toll.

Tomas couldn't have done better with radar. He came straight for her.

Della guessed the boy was ten feet away from her, five feet, just the other side of the pine. The lug wrench was the spider type, in the shape of a cross. She clutched the black steel of the longest arm and brought her hand back. When she detected movement around the edge of the trunk, she swung with hysterical strength, aiming at his head.

Tomas staggered back. The sharp arm of the lug wrench had caught him under the nose, driving the cartilage back up into his face. About a third of the steel was hidden in flesh. "Unh!" He tried to cry out, but all he could utter was, "Unh, unh!"

"Tomas?" Chuckie was yelling. "What the hell are you doing?"

The flashlight flickered across the grove. Della caught a momentary glimpse of Tomas lurching backward with the lug wrench impaled in his face as though he were wearing some hideous Halloween accessory.

"Unh!" said Tomas once more. He backed into a tree, then slid down the trunk until he was seated in the snow. The flashlight beam jerked across that part of the grove again and Della saw Tomas' eyes stare wide open, dark and blank. Blood was running off the ends of the perpendicular lug wrench arms.

"I see her!" someone yelled. "I think she got Tomas. She's a devil!" Vinh.

"So chill her!"

Della heard branches and brush crashing off to her side. She jerked open the plastic toolbox, but her fingers were frozen and the container crashed to the ground. She tried to catch the contents as they cascaded into the slush and the darkness. Her fingers closed on something, one thing.

The handle felt good. It was the wooden-hafted screwdriver, the sharp one with the slot head. Her auto mechanics teacher had approved. Insulated handle, he'd said. Good forged steel shaft. You could use this hummer to pry a tire off its rim.

She didn't have time to lift it as Vinh crashed into her. His arms and legs wound around her like eels.

"Got her!" he screamed. "Chuckie, come here and shoot her."

They rolled in the viscid, muddy slush. Della worked an arm free. Her good arm. The one with the screwdriver.

There was no question of asking him nicely to let go, of giving warning, of simply aiming to disable. Her self-defense teacher had drilled into all the students the basic dictum of do what you can, do what you have to do. No rules, no apologies.

With all her strength, Della drove the screwdriver up into the base of his skull. She thrust and twisted the tool until she felt her knuckles dig into his stiff hair. Vinh screamed, a high keening wail that cracked and shattered as blood spurted out of his nose and mouth, splattering against Della's neck. The Vietnamese boy's arms and legs tensed and then let go as his body vibrated spastically in some sort of fit.

Della pushed him away from her and staggered to her feet. Her nose was full of the odor she remembered from the twins' diaper pail.

She knew she should retrieve the screwdriver, grasp the handle tightly and twist it loose from Vinh's head. She couldn't. All she could do at this point was simply turn and run. Run again. And hope the survivor of the four boys didn't catch her.

But Chuckie had the light, and Chuckie had the gun. She had a feeling Chuckie was in no mood to give up. Chuckie would find her. He would make her pay for the loss of his friends.

But if she had to pay, Della thought, the price would be dear.

Prices, she soon discovered, were subject to change without warning.

With only one remaining pursuer, Della thought she ought to be able to get away. Maybe not easily, but now there was no crossfire of spying eyes, no ganging-up of assailants. There was just one boy left, even if he *was* a psychopath carrying a loaded pistol.

Della was shaking. It was fatigue, she realized. The endless epinephrine rush of flight and fight. Probably, too, the letdown from just having killed two other human beings. She didn't want to have to think about the momentary sight of blood flowing off the shining ends of the lug wrench, the sensation of how it *felt* when the slot-headed screwdriver drove up into Vinh's brain. But she couldn't order herself to forget these things. It was akin to someone telling her not, under any circumstances, to think about milking a purple cow.

Della tried. No, she thought. Don't think about it at all. She thought about dismembering the purple cow with a chain saw. Then she heard Chuckie's voice. The boy was still distant, obviously casting around virtually at random in the pine groves. Della stiffened.

"They're cute, Della-honey. I'll give 'em that." He giggled. "Terri and Tammi. God, didn't you and your husband have any more imagination than that?"

No, Della thought. We each had too much imagination. Tammi and Terri were simply the names we finally could agree on. The names of compromise.

"You know something?" Chuckie raised his voice. "Now that I know where they live, I could drive over there in a while and say howdy. They wouldn't know a thing about what was going on, about what happened to their mom while she was out at the mall."

Oh God! thought Della.

"You want me to pass on any messages?"

"You little bastard!" She cried it out without thinking.

"Touchy, huh?" Chuckie slopped across the wet snow in her direction. "Come on out of the trees, Della-honey."

Della said nothing. She crouched behind a deadfall of brush and dead limbs. She was perfectly still.

Chuckie stood equally still, not more than twenty feet away. He stared directly at her hiding place, as though he could see through the night and brush. "Listen," he said. "This is getting real, you know, *boring*." He waited. "We could be out here all night, you know? All my buddies are gone now, and it's thanks to you, lady. Who the hell you think you are, Clint Eastwood?"

Della assumed that was a rhetorical question.

Chuckie hawked deep in his throat and spat on the ground. He rubbed the base of his throat gingerly with a free hand. "You hurt me, Della-honey. I think you busted my collarbone." He giggled. "But I don't hold grudges. In fact—" He paused contemplatively. "Listen now, I've got an idea. You know about droogs? You know, like in that movie?"

Clockwork Orange, she thought. Della didn't respond.

"Ending was stupid, but the start was pretty cool." Chuckie's personality seemed to have mutated into a manic stage. "Well, me droogs is all gone. I need a new gang, and you're real good, Della-honey. I want you should join me."

"Give me a break," said Della in the darkness.

"No, really," Chuckie said. "You're a born killer. I can tell. You and me, we'd be perfect. We'll blow this popsicle stand and have some real fun. Whaddaya say?"

He's serious, she thought. There was a ring of complete honesty in his voice. She floundered for some answer. "I've got kids," she said.

"We'll take 'em along," said Chuckie. "I like kids, always took care of my brothers and sisters." He paused. "Listen, I'll bet you're on the outs with your old man."

Della said nothing. It would be like running away to be a pirate. Wouldn't it?

Chuckie hawked and spat again. "Yeah, I figured. When we pick up your kids, we can waste him. You like that? I can do it, or you can. Your choice."

You're crazy, she thought. "*I* want to," she found herself saying aloud.

"So come out and we'll talk about it."

"You'll kill me."

"Hey," he said, "I'll kill you if you *don't* come out. I got the light and the gun, remember? This way we can learn to trust each other right from the start. I won't kill you. I won't do nothing. Just talk."

"Okay." Why not, she thought. Sooner or later, he'll find his way in here and put the gun in my mouth and—Della stood up—but maybe, just maybe —Agony lanced through her knees.

Chuckie cocked his head, staring her way. "Leave the tools."

"I already did. The ones I didn't use."

"Yeah," said Chuckie. "The ones you used, you used real good." He lowered the beam of the flashlight. "Here you go. I don't want you stumbling and falling and maybe breaking your neck."

Della stepped around the deadfall and slowly walked toward him. His hands were at his sides. She couldn't see if he was holding the gun. She stopped when she was a few feet away.

"Hell of a night, huh?" said Chuckie. "It'll be really good to go inside where it's warm and get some coffee." He held the flashlight so that the beam speared into the sky between them.

Della could make out his thin, pain-pinched features. She imagined he could see hers. "I was only going out to the mall for a few things," she said.

Chuckie laughed. "Shit happens."

"What now?" Della said.

"Time for the horror show." His teeth showed ferally as his lips drew back in a smile. "Guess maybe I sort of fibbed." He brought up his hand, glinting of metal.

"That's what I thought," she said, feeling a cold and distant sense of loss. "Huey, there, going to help?" She nodded to a point past his shoulder.

"Huey?" Chuckie looked puzzled just for a second as he glanced to the side. "Huey's—"

Della leapt with all the spring left in her legs. Her fingers closed around his wrist and the hand with the gun. "Christ!" Chuckie screamed, as her shoulder crashed against the spongy place where his broken collarbone pushed out against the skin.

They tumbled on the December ground, Chuckie underneath, Della wrapping her legs around him as though pulling a lover tight. She burrowed her chin into the area of his collarbone and he screamed again. Kenneth had always joked about the sharpness of her chin.

The gun went off. The flash was blinding, the report hurt her ears. Wet snow plumped down from the overhanging pine branches, a large chunk plopping into Chuckie's wide-open mouth. He started to choke.

Then the pistol was in Della's hands. She pulled back from him, getting to her feet, back-pedaling furiously to get out of his reach. She stared down at him along the blued-steel barrel. The pirate captain struggled to his knees.

"Back to the original deal," he said. "Okay?"

I wish, she almost said. Della pulled the trigger. Again. And again.

"Where the hell have you been?" said Kenneth as she closed the front door behind her. "You've been gone for close to three hours." He inspected her more closely. "Della, honey, are you all right?"

"Don't call me that," she said. "Please." She had hoped she would look better, more normal. Unruffled. Once Della had pulled the Subaru up to the drive beside the house, she had spent several minutes using spit and Kleenex trying to fix her mascara. Such makeup as she'd had along was in her handbag, and she had no idea where that was. Probably the police had it; three cruisers with lights flashing had passed her, going the other way, as she was driving north of Southeast Plaza.

"Your clothes." Kenneth gestured. He stood where he was.

Della looked down at herself. She'd tried to wash off the mud, using snow and a rag from the trunk. There was blood too, some of it Chuckie's, the rest doubtless from Vinh and Tomas.

"Honey, was there an accident?"

She had looked at the driver's side of the Subaru for a long minute after getting home. At least the car drove; it must just have been flooded before. But the insurance company wouldn't be happy. The entire side would need a new paint job.

"Sort of," she said.

"Are you hurt?"

To top it all off, she had felt the slow stickiness between her legs as she'd come up the walk. Terrific. She could hardly wait for the cramps to intensify.

"Hurt?" She shook her head. No. "How are the twins?"

"Oh, they're in bed. I checked a half hour ago. They're asleep."

"Good." Della heard sirens in the distance, getting louder, nearing the neighborhood. Probably the police had found her driver's license in Chuckie's pocket. She'd forgotten that.

"So," said Kenneth. It was obvious to Della that he didn't know at this point whether to be angry, solicitous or funny. "What'd you bring me from the mall?"

Della's right hand was nestled in her jacket pocket. She felt the solid bulk, the cool grip of the pistol.

Outside, the volume of sirens increased.

She touched the trigger. She withdrew her hand from the pocket and aimed the pistol at Kenneth. He looked back at her strangely.

The sirens went past. Through the window, Della caught a glimpse of a speeding ambulance. The sound Dopplered down to a silence as distant as the dream that flashed through her head.

Della pulled the trigger and the *click* seemed to echo through the entire house.

Shocked, Kenneth stared at the barrel of the gun, then up at her eyes. It was okay. She'd counted the shots. Just like in the movies.

"I think," Della said to her husband, "that we need to talk."

Pat Cadigan is another author well known to science fiction readers. Her work consistently focuses on the psychological reality of difficult situations made more difficult by strong people placed into conflict. Her stories have dealt with humans, vampires, aliens . . . all of your best friends and some of your worst nightmares. "True Faces," first published in *The Magazine of Fantasy and Science Fiction,* is one of the most cleverly scripted and fascinating procedurals we've seen in quite a long time.

True Faces
PAT CADIGAN

A human diplomat is found murdered in an alien embassy. Seventeen aliens are present. Each claims to be the sole murderer, and because of their psychological makeup, each passes a lie detector test.
1. Are any of them telling the truth?
2. Why was the human killed?
3. How do you question aliens who are congenital liars?

"I *told* you I wasn't in the mood for this," Stilton whispered.

I gave him an elbow in the ribs without looking away from the body of the woman lying on the floor of the large room. I'm never much in the mood for a strangulation murder myself, but it didn't pay to advertise. Not in this company. History, I thought; I'm looking at history in the making right there in front of me. People had been strangled before and they'd get strangled again, but this was the first time one had ever been strangled in an alien embassy. The first alien embassy, no less. Two firsts. And we were the first law enforcement officers on the scene, so that was three firsts. The day was definitely running hot.

On my other side, the tall man in the retro-tuxedo swallowed loudly for the millionth time. He'd said his name was Farber and given his occupation as secretary to the dead woman. I wasn't sure which was more striking, his old-fashioned getup or his noisy peristaltic action. I'd never met anyone who could swallow loudly before—did that make it five firsts? I shoved the thought aside. The room was so quiet, I probably could have heard him digesting his food if I listened closely enough. The Lazarians either observed quiet as a religion, or they were as much in shock as the human employees, who were all huddled together on the far side of the room, too spooked even to whisper to each other.

There was only one Lazarian on this side of the room. The rest were gathered in a semicircle around the corpse. There were about twenty of them and the grouping had this very odd formality to it, as if they'd all gathered there to seek an audience with the woman.

I turned to Farber, who reacted by swallowing again and then blotting his forehead with his sleeve. "One more time?" I gave Stilton another jab in the ribs.

"Ready," Stilton said sourly, moving so that I could see he had the interviewer aimed.

"Migod, I always thought it was just in the hollies that the police made you tell a story over and over," Farber said, glancing at the 'viewer's flat lens in a furtive way. I didn't make anything of that—the only people who never got nervous about having a 'viewer trained on them were dead or inhuman. Of course, it was hard to tell with the Lazarians—they looked a lot like scarecrows and I'd never seen a nervous scarecrow, or even an extraterrestrial facsimile.

"You can give us the 'viewer's digest condensed version," I told him. "The third recording doesn't need as much."

Farber swallowed. "Fine. I came in here and found Ms. Entwater just as you see her now, with the Lazarians gathered around her. Just as you see *them* now. The other human employees were elsewhere in the building, but the one Lazarian rounded them all up, brought them in here, and hasn't allowed anyone to leave since. Then I called you. From here. Since I'm not allowed to leave, either."

I glanced at Stilton, who nodded. "And you say that Ms. Entwater's relationship with the Lazarians was . . . what?"

Swallow. His Adam's apple bounded up and down above his collar. "Cordial. Friendly. Very good. She liked them. She liked her work. If she had any enemies among the Lazarians, she never told me about it and she told me close to everything."

"Care to speculate on what she didn't tell you?" I asked.

He thought about that for a moment, swallowing. "She didn't tell me there was a Pilot in the building."

"Why not?"

"Either she didn't have a chance or she didn't think to." Swallow. "It's hardly necessary for the secretary to be updated hourly as to who drops by for a social visit and who doesn't."

"You're sure it was a social visit?"

Swallow. "Pilots come by all the time to visit the Lazarians. The Lazarians trained them in Interstellar Resonance Travel, so they feel a certain kinship to them, much more than to other humans, I think."

"Why do you think that?" I asked.

"Because they seldom have any interactions with any of the humans here. Except for Ms. Entwater, who sees them in and sees them out again." Swallow. "*Saw* them in. And out again."

"She always did, personally? Isn't that more of a job for a receptionist or a secretary?"

"Dallette or I would see to other visits. The Pilots Ms. Entwater always saw to personally."

"Then she wouldn't have had to tell you in so many words that a Pilot was in the building," I said. "You'd know by whatever she was doing."

Swallow. "*If* I knew what she was doing. I was busy with press releases for most of the morning, so I was in the translation room."

"The Lazarians' press releases?"

Swallow, followed by a nod. "They like to alert the media themselves. About everything. Today it was various things about hollies they'd seen and what they thought about them and the dissolution of three-bond—"

"Wait a minute," I said. "You didn't mention that before." The old ways never failed. Get someone to tell a story over and over and something new was bound to show up.

Swallow. "I'm sorry. I wasn't hiding it—" a glance at the 'viewer—"I'd just forgotten. It's like a—a marriage breaking up, or maybe a long engagement. The Lazarians are—well, there are similarities, but there are always strange little differences embedded in them. In any case, it didn't concern Ms. Entwater."

"Are you sure?" I said.

"Absolutely." Swallow. "Ms. Entwater never, ah, intruded into their private lives."

I couldn't help laughing a little. "Come on. Celie Entwater's job was to gain improved understanding of the Lazarians. How could she do that unless she was acquainted with their private lives?"

"Ms. Entwater considered herself a diplomat engaged in deep study of another culture. She was rigorous in observing customs and taboos, all that sort of thing. She knew that if we offended them, they might close down and go back to Lazarus—"

"Lah-ah . . . ZA-AHR . . . eesh," came a deep, nasal-sounding voice behind me, enunciating each syllable as if it were a separate word, with a bit of a gargle on the ZA-AHR.

Farber swallowed and bowed from the waist. I turned around. The one free-ranging Lazarian in the room was standing as close as possible to Stilton, who rolled his eyes. The Lazarian custom of space-density had gotten old for him very quickly. I found it pretty off-putting myself—it was like dealing with a race of people who had been raised in crowded elevators, unable to be comfortable unless they were all on top of each other.

Which made the half-circle formation around Entwater's corpse doubly odd, I thought suddenly. They weren't as close to each other or to her as they could get. Because she was dead? Or for some other Lazarian reason I had yet to find out?

"I need to question all the humans here," I said to the Lazarian. "If one of them killed Ms. Entwater, that person must be punished according to our law."

"Trrrried and punished if found guilty," the Lazarian corrected. "Question."

Farber moved to my side, swallowing. "Thinta-ah requests permission to inquire something of you," he said to me, sounding ceremonial. I repressed the urge to sigh heavily; I'm no diplomat, and the six years I'd spent on the gang squad had made me tired of ritual. Maybe it should have prepared me for the more byzantine protocols of extraterrestrials, but I've got a bad attitude. Twenty years ago, when the Lazarians had first arrived, maybe I'd have been much more excited, but then, I've always had low blood pressure anyway.

"Ask your question," I said.

"Say 'please,' " Farber whispered.

I smiled as broadly as I could. "Please."

The Lazarian put its six-digit hands on top of its sacklike head. "If Entwa-ahter is dead by one of us, wha-aht then?"

I glanced at Entwater again. From this distance, it was hard to see the details of the marks on her throat, but they could have been made by one of those Lazarian hands. One would have been enough—like the rest of their limbs, those digits were long and multijointed, and could have gone all the way around a human neck easily. "This is your embassy," I said, "which means to us, it is a piece of your nation. We would trust you to serve your own justice in this matter."

Stilton was looking at me like I was crazy. I didn't blame him. All of a sudden, I was talking like a hollie version of a diplomat. I couldn't help it; something about the Lazarians was making me go into awkward-formal mode.

The Lazarian put a hand on top of the 'viewer, much to Stilton's shock. "Truth ma-ah-chine."

I gave Farber a sidelong glance. "What now?"

Farber swallowed twice. "It would seem that Thinta-ah wants you to use the 'viewer on them." He gestured at the Lazarians standing around Entwater.

Stilton coughed. "I don't think it'll work. We're—ah—" he turned to the Lazarian—"we're too different." I could tell he was trying to imagine how those sackheads would register. The 'viewer worked on interpreting a lot of little things—facial expression, blood flow, temperature, eye and muscle movements, pulse, respiration, vocal quality and inflection, choice of words, context, and some other things I didn't have to bother remembering. It wasn't infallible, we'd all been told, but in my experience, I have yet to see anyone beat it, not even the most hardened pathological liars. We were only allowed to use it to determine probable cause for search and/or arrest, not to determine official guilt or innocence, so it wasn't any more admissible in court than the old lie detector results had been, but it was useful enough.

"Can convert," said the Lazarian. "Ha-ahve progra-ahms to converrrt for our species."

Stilton held the 'viewer protectively close to his chest, giving me a desperate look.

"I don't know," I said. "I'd have to call—"

Farber swallowed. "Weren't you told to take every measure necessary to wrap this up as quickly as possible?" He leaned closer and lowered his voice. "Do you want to think about the repercussions of having an unsolved murder in the Lazarian embassy? They'll have to call out the National Guard to protect this place, and all of us *will still be trapped inside of it*. And that includes you and your partner. The door is *booby-trapped*. Something sonic. Break the plane from this side and you'll drop like a rock. When you wake up, you'll have the worst headache of your life." He jerked his head at the group of humans. "Some of *them* tried it. Ask them if they'll try it again. Get it through your head, no one is going to leave here until this is settled, and if it takes months, that's not Thinta-ah's problem."

"All right," I said. All right for now. Call in a siege team? I'd never get that okayed. I'd have to see about locating the control for the doorway knockout and figure out how to disable it later. That would probably cause an international incident—interstellar incident?—but not as major an incident as a siege team storming the place.

I looked at the Lazarian, but that face was unreadable. As usual. It was actually the outer surface of a kind of flexible exoskeleton that covered the whole head, featureless except for irregular, opaque black patches where the eyes and mouth would be. I'd read somewhere that the exoskeleton thickened and then thinned out again on some cycle that was individual to each Lazarian, but no one knew what caused it or what it meant to the Lazarians, except that they referred to what lay beneath it as the "true face," which was never to be shown to another living being, not even if its owner were dead.

Which I thought begged the question: what was the point of having a so-called "true face" if nobody could ever see it?

Something teased at the edge of my mind. I looked over at the Lazarians still motionless around the corpse. Was the penalty for seeing a "true face" immediate death?

Everyone was staring at me expectantly. "I should still probably call in for authorization," I said weakly.

"Ca-ahll," said the Lazarian, and it wasn't granting me permission, but giving me an order.

I took the cellular off my belt and punched the speed-dial for the direct line to the captain. The subsequent conversation was almost as brief.

"She says it's a go," I said, clipping the phone back onto my belt. Stilton looked outraged for half a second and then wiped all expression from his face. For some reason, 'viewer operators get extremely possessive about their babies. Normally, Stilton wouldn't even let me hold his. "Let's get the program and convert the 'viewer for Lazarians."

Farber looked distressed as he swallowed. "Well, I've just thought of a problem."

I winced. "Only one. What a relief."

"It's a big one. The problem is in Ms. Entwater's office upstairs. Everyone who was in the embassy at the time of Ms. Entwater's death is now here in this room, Lazarians and humans alike. We may not leave this room, not any of us."

"Why not?" I said, looking at Thinta-ah.

"Bee-cauzzzeh," the Lazarian replied, still using the command voice.

"Oh," I said, hoping I didn't sound sarcastic and looked at Farber. "Any ideas?"

He took a long time swallowing. "We could call a courier to fetch the program for us. Of course, the courier will have to stay here with us afterward."

"We'll charge the overtime to the embassy," I said, reaching for my cellular again.

The courier business took a little longer, since the courier made the mistake of entering the room we were all in first, forcing me to call out for another. Forewarned, the second courier put the program chips in an envelope and tossed it to me through the open doorway.

"Go to it," I said, handing the envelope to Stilton. His face had a slightly greenish cast to it.

"Before I fool with the 'viewer and quite possibly break it, maybe we should talk to the humans," he said.

"Our species *firrrrrrst*," said Thinta-ah, and it was another command. I wanted to object. Across the room, the half dozen human employees were still huddled together, albeit less closely. Except for the Pilot, who had gotten tired of sitting and was now leaning against the wall behind the others, smoking a cigarette in a long holder. She looked happy, but all Pilots look happy all the time. It's something that happens to them as a result of their training. Maybe after that first trip, they never really "come back," so to speak.

"Do as you're told," Farber said to Stilton, managing to sound apologetic. "I've got a wife, a husband, and three children I'd like to see again before I'm much older, and I imagine you both have families as well."

I cleared my throat. In Stilton's case, that had been the wrong appeal to make; his significant others had voted him out three weeks before and he was still stinging from it.

But instead of giving Farber the evil eye, he went to work on the 'viewer, even allowing me to steady it for him while he changed chips.

It took Stilton about half an hour to get everything synchronized and in phase and whatever else—I'm no more of a techie than I am a diplomat, though I suspected the last fifteen minutes he spent on running tests and diagnostics was nothing but pure stalling.

"I guess it's ready," he said at last. "But even with all these adjustments and conversions for Lazarian biology, I don't know how well it's going to work with an exoskeleton."

"No ex-oh," said Thinta-ah, coming over to stand too close again. "True faaaa-aice."

The Lazarians gathered around Entwater made no perceptible physical movements, but something in the air changed. Everybody felt it, even the humans on the other side of the room. It was similar to the sudden presence of ozone before a lightning strike (don't ask me how I know about that unless you're ready for a story longer than this one), and for a moment, I thought I could actually feel my hair stand on end.

"I know your custom of not showing the true face," I said to Thinta-ah. "How—"

Thinta-ah made Stilton cringe by touching the 'viewer again. "Not a-ahlive."

"You'll allow me a recording that we can look at?" Stilton said, amazed.

"A-ahllow to look a-aht recording *one time*," the Lazarian said, making a strange movement something like a full body shrug. The clothing, as loose, mismatched, and wrinkled as anything that ever came out of a Good Will free bin, seemed to readjust itself on the Lazarian's loose-jointed body, somehow acquiring even more wrinkles. Wrinkles seemed to be their fashion statement. The Lazarians around the corpse still didn't move, but I knew they were unhappy. Not just unhappy, but unhappier than they had ever been in their lives. I tried to imagine an equivalent for myself—being forced to strip naked in public seemed obvious, but I knew this was a lot more than a nudity taboo.

My gaze fell on the 'viewer. Maybe more like being exposed with one of these things? "One time," I said to Stilton. "We'd better make it a good look, then."

Thinta-ah did some fast organizing. The humans were to sit directly behind and with their backs to the group in the center of the room so they couldn't possibly see their true faces while they were speaking to the 'viewer. Very simple solution—just the sort of thing that signals some major complication is imminent.

Stilton and I found a chair for the 'viewer. He got it aimed at the first Lazarian, fiddled with the focus for a few seconds, and then turned it on. "Any time," he told the Lazarian and turned away, crowding close to me as Thinta-ah crowded close to him.

In the long pause that followed, I could hear the Lazarian removing the exoskeleton. It was a ghastly sound, like cloth ripping and I wondered if it hurt. Anything that made a noise like that seemed like it *had* to hurt.

"You a-ahsk," said Thinta-ah.

I cleared my throat. "What is your name?"

"Simeer-ah," said the Lazarian. I felt Thinta-ah stiffen. The last syllable indicated this was some relative of Thinta-ah's, but not which kind.

"How are you connected to—"

"A-ahsk only about Entwa-ahter!" Thinta-ah practically shouted.

I hesitated, wanting to explain about establishing a pattern and knowing at the same time that Thinta-ah wasn't buying. A Lazarian's true face was exposed in the presence, if not the sight, of others, and to them, this was much more urgent than a murder. Any murder.

I could have sworn I heard Farber swallow from across the room. "Do as you're told," he called from where he and the courier stood facing the now closed door.

Behind me, the exposed Lazarian made a small noise. I'd never heard the sound before, but I knew instinctively that the alien was weeping. A wave of compassion mixed with shame swept through me—not the best thing for a cop to feel during a murder investigation. If I'd felt sorry for everyone who'd ever cried during questioning, there'd have been a few more hardheads running free who had gotten away with murder and worse.

I took a deep breath. "What do you know about the death of Celie Entwater?"

"I a-ahm responsible."

My shamed compassion turned to cold water. "Are you saying you killed her?"

"It is my fault."

"Are you saying you killed her?" I asked again.

Stilton shrugged. "First time's a charm, I guess," he whispered.

"You strangled Celie Entwater?" I persisted.

"I ha-ahve the blaaaaaa-aimmeh."

"Stop now," said Thinta-ah, softly. "Next."

I gave up. "All right. We'll wait while you cover yourself."

Damnedest thing—the exoskeleton made the same ripping-cloth sound going back on as it had coming off. My nerves felt sandpapered. And I only had to hear that noise nineteen more times.

No, sixteen more times, I discovered after it was safe to turn around again. Stilton aimed the 'viewer at the next Lazarian. The first one looked no worse for the experience—outwardly, anyway. There was nothing like sweat or blood, the exoskeleton appeared unchanged. But the Lazarian's body looked a little more relaxed, the kind of posture you see in people who finally confess to a crime and find they're more relieved at being able to get it off their chests than they are frightened of being punished. Maybe the first time really had been a charm.

Then the second Lazarian said exactly the same thing and the world rearranged itself into the form it always took during a criminal investigation. The world is full of liars, liars who say they didn't do it and liars who say they did, liars who say they're sorry and liars who say they're not, liars who swear they've never done it before, liars who promise they'll never do it again. Apparently some things were universal—literally.

By the time the sixth one confessed, Stilton had taken over the questioning and my cynicism felt like a drug reaching toxic levels in my system. The only thing I actually listened to after number seven was that ripping-cloth sound. There was some kind of cosmic irony at work here, I thought; expose your true face and then tell a lie. Gave a deeper meaning to the term *barefaced liar*, that was for sure.

What I wasn't sure about was why it was affecting me so intensely. Maybe because I secretly suffered from the ailment of poor species self-image, believing that aliens must be truly superior forms of life to flaw-ridden humanity, and they'd shattered my illusions of their being closer to the angels. What was that old joke that had made the rounds back when the Lazarians had first arrived? An optimist thinks humans could be the highest form of life in the universe, a pessimist knows they are. Right. Try this one, I thought bitterly—an optimist thinks all beings are siblings, a pessimist knows they are. And the name of the first sibling, in any language anywhere, was Cain.

"Still awake?" Stilton asked me suddenly.

I managed not to jump at the sound of his voice. "Yeah. Just."

"Good. Last confession coming up," he said, fiddling with the 'viewer on the chair. Without my noticing, the lights in the room had come up in response to the waning daylight. Through the frosted windows, I could see that it was nearly dark. With any luck, we might get out by dawn, I thought wearily. And when we did, I was going to ask for a transfer out of homicide and go chase burglars for a while, or drug addicts or people who never paid their parking tickets.

"One more time," Stilton said, assuming the position.

The sound of ripping cloth. If this one was going to lie about Entwater, too, then I hoped it hurt.

But number seventeen was apparently the rebel in the group. "Fa-ahr-ber," the last Lazarian said. "Fa-ahr-ber is at fault."

"What a relief," I said. "I was afraid sixteen Lazarians had taken turns choking someone to death. But it turns out that the man dressed like a butler did it. Can't wait to alert the media."

Thinta-ah suddenly came back to life and told Farber to send out for pizza. Apparently pizza was the closest thing we had to a Lazarian native dish. That didn't cheer me, or even give me an appetite, though I knew I should have been hungry.

And thirsty. The humans were. They all looked as if they'd spent the day in a desert, except for the Pilot, who seemed as completely detached and unaffected as ever. And yet, it was the Pilot who informed us that there were new problems developing with the humans.

She came over while we were setting up the 'viewer on a side table so we could go over the recordings. "We have people in very serious need," she said, pointing her cigarette holder at them.

"Of what?" As soon as the words were out of my mouth, I knew the answer, but the Pilot was already telling me.

"Of toilets. Some are in real pain," she added cheerfully. I wanted to hit her.

Instead, I talked to Farber. His response made me want to hit *him*. "Thinta-ah knows," he said. "Arrangements were made before you got here." He pointed at a large ornamental flowerpot in the corner. "It only looks like a flowerpot," he added, as if reading my mind. "It's a, ah, Lazarian waste receptacle. The Lazarians are, ah—" swallow—"*casual* about this kind of function."

"Oh, really?" I said. "I sure haven't seen any of *them* use it."

Swallow. "They only need to every other week. This isn't the week."

I went to the humans and broke it to them myself. One of them, a middle-aged man, shook his head stubbornly without looking up at me. But a woman of about sixty shrugged, marched over to the receptacle and pointedly turned her back. The anger was almost palpable and I knew what kind of stories they were all going to tell when they were finally allowed to leave. Lazarian-human diplomatic relations could well end up being harmed more by the bathroom arrangements than by a murder, I thought, going back to Stilton. Even terrorists would take their hostages to the bathroom.

Or, I thought, looking at Thinta-ah who was being careful to look anywhere but toward the corner, had humans just come that much closer to understanding the experience of exposing the true face?

Understanding? I doubted it. They'd remember it, but it wasn't the sort of thing that would generate much empathy.

"*One* look," Thinta-ah reminded us when we were ready to look at the recordings.

"Only one," Stilton said. He had half a pizza next to him and he was feeling better, much better than the delivery person who had come into the room before we could warn her. She sat sulking with the first courier. I wondered if anyone besides the employees' families, a courier service, and a pizza parlor had picked up on the fact that there was something funny happening at the Lazarian embassy. My cellular had been strangely silent, no one calling for an update or a statement or anything at all. Maybe we were sitting under a governmental belljar, families, courier service, pizza parlor, and all.

"I'll need to freeze each image sometimes," Stilton told Thinta-ah. "Is that all right?"

The answer was so long in coming that I thought Thinta-ah had gone to sleep standing up again. "Yes. A-ahll right. One time through."

Stilton sighed with relief, turned on the 'viewer, and picked up a slice of double shitake mushroom. The screen lit up and he dropped the pizza in his lap. If I'd had an appetite, I'd have had pizza in my own lap.

The face on the screen was Entwater's.

Stilton slammed down the freeze button. "What did you *do?*" I whispered angrily. "Did you get the focus upside down and put it on *her?*"

"You can see I didn't," he said, too spooked to be offended. "That's not the image of a dead person. That face is animated, it's moving, talking. Look at the readings." He pointed at the box on the left side of the screen. "They say living, not dead."

I looked from the screen to Thinta-ah on the other side of the table. "Could this possibly be this Lazarian's true face?"

"I maaaaaa-aiy not look," Thinta-ah said. "But wha-aht faaaa-aice you see must be the true one."

I got up and went around the table to the alien. "Listen," I whispered. "The face on the screen is—"

"Do *not* tell me," said Thinta-ah. "I maaaaaaaay *not* know. Wha-aht faaaaaaa-aice is there is true."

I tried to think. It was hard with the heavy garlic smell drifting over from the platter next to Stilton. "Okay. The face on the screen cannot possibly belong to one of your species, but to another one entirely, and to a certain being—"

"*I maaaaaay not know!*" Thinta-ah's voice echoed in the room, not the command voice this time but a cry of anguish. Everything stopped. Over by the Rockwell-esque mural of the first meeting between human and Lazarian, Farber straightened up from a whispered conversation with the courier and the pizza delivery person to glare at me.

"I'm sorry," I said to Thinta-ah and bowed. "I was . . . I was ignorant."

The Lazarian refused to look at me. I went back around the other side of the table next to Stilton, feeling as if I had just defiled somebody else's church with a rite from my own. And I didn't even go to church.

The association caught in my mind like a burr. *Was* this religious? Discounting hobby-killers and for-hires, people tend to take a life over matters to do with love/sex and personal offenses, real or imagined. *Our* people . . . but the Lazarians?

I beckoned impatiently to Farber, who hurried over. "Can I ask Thinta-ah about Lazarian psychology?"

Swallow (of course). "No."

I groaned. "Why not?"

"You're not a psychologist. Besides, they don't actually have any."

"What are you talking about? They must. *Everybody* has psychology. *Animals* have psychology."

"Well, yes, they *have* it—" swallow—"but they don't have it as a science or a discipline or whatever you want to call it. The study of psychology is unknown on their world."

"But they must have *something*."

Farber nodded. "They do. They have true faces."

"That's a big mother's help," I said. "You want to know what true face that Lazarian on the end over there has?"

He started to protest that he wasn't allowed to look and I waved his words away.

"Never mind. You wouldn't believe it if you did see it." He started to walk away and I caught his arm. "Hey, stay close, will you? I'm working without a net here."

"We all are," he murmured.

"The verdict is in," Stilton said, sitting back. "According to the 'viewer, this alien is telling the truth."

I stared at Entwater's image, still frozen on the screen. She had been a very attractive woman; at least one of her parents had had relatives from Japan and whatever else was mixed with it had blessed her with the kind of features that age well. Damned shame they wouldn't have a chance to age any further —or would they? Did true faces age? Supposedly, no one knew. *Supposedly.* But someone must have. There had to be some Lazarian keeper of forbidden knowledge . . . didn't there?

I gave up that line of thought as futile. If there were any such Lazarians, they were most likely back on Lazarus, or La-ah-ZA-AHR-eesh, or whatever the hell it was.

"What do you want to do?" Stilton asked me. "You want me to let this picture go and see the next?"

"Are you done looking at it?"

"Are you?" He ran a hand through his black curls. "Remember, we're never going to see it again, so make sure you've seen your fill."

"I'm not so sure about that," I said as he unfroze the image. The corresponding readings in the box were holding, waiting for the video to catch up.

"What do you mean?" Stilton said.

I pointed at the 'viewer. "That's what I mean."

I could actually see Stilton break into a sweat as Entwater's face reappeared.

"Why are you surprised?" I said. "They all *said* the same thing." I looked at Farber. "All except one."

Farber gazed back at me, swallowing without comprehension. Apparently, the last Lazarian's voice hadn't carried over to him. Or he hadn't been paying attention.

This time we ran the video concurrent with the lie detector program; I watched the face while Stilton kept track of the readings. I wanted to imprint that face on my mind. It wasn't *quite* identical to the other one, but the differences were minor—the width of the face, the length of the nose, the size of the chin. That figured—each Lazarian's head would be a different size, so the face on it would be sized to fit. The Procrustean face. No, the true face on the Procrustean head.

Stilton sighed unhappily. "This one's telling the truth, too. Or so it says here. The program must be defective, though how we'd ever be able to tell—" he sighed again.

"Keep going," I said. "Maybe we'll see a variation somewhere."

Stilton gave me a dirty look. "Yah."

"We've already seen some." I leaned close and whispered. "That face isn't completely identical to the first one. There *are* variations, almost too minor to see, but they *are* there. What about the readings?"

He called back the first set for comparison. "You're right. But the variations are all physiological. They have two pulses, and they have respiration and skin temperature and they show the same degrees of variation from one Lazarian to another that we show one human to another. In all standard healthy people, anyway."

"So let's see if maybe someone *isn't* standard healthy."

Now he almost smiled. "I like you better than I used to, all of a sudden," he said and focused his attention on the 'viewer again.

But of course, I had just been overly optimistic. Entwater's face appeared, confessed, disappeared, and reappeared over and over without any telling variations. That *was* probably telling, except we couldn't understand *what* it was telling.

At least the seventeenth Lazarian looked like Farber. I took great consolation in the fact that my certainty had been correct. It didn't make up for the fact that the 'viewer said that Lazarian was also telling the truth, the whole truth, and nothing but the truth, but you can't have everything.

"The program's got to be defective," Stilton said, replacing Farber's facsimile with the seventeen readings. "We might as well switch programs, record all the humans, and then get comfortable in our new home. We're going to be here quite a while and we might as well get over our potty shyness as soon as possible."

"No," I said, standing up and looking at Thinta-ah. Farber took a step toward me and Stilton rose to his feet in response, moving to protect my left.

"I understand your feelings about the toilet," he said, "but don't go losing your head over it now."

"I mean no, the program's not defective, not no, I won't use the toilet." I went over and stood as close as possible to the Lazarian, who didn't move away. "The program's *incomplete*. We don't have a control."

"A what?" said Farber suspiciously.

"A control," I said, staring up at Thinta-ah. "A standard to measure the other Lazarians against."

Stilton practically jumped over the table.

"Same arrangements as for the other Lazarians," I said. "Thinta-ah, it's your turn in the barrel."

"It's already been Thinta-ah's turn," said Stilton, sounding scared.

The Lazarian lunged past me for the table, but Stilton already had the 'viewer in his arms. "Back off," he said, moving away, "or I'll turn this around and show everyone in the room what's on the screen."

Stretched out across the table, Thinta-ah hesitated and then straightened up slowly. "You maaaaaaaay not see."

"I've seen," Stilton said. "You didn't say every Lazarian but you."

"No, I did *not*." Thinta-ah backed away from the table but Stilton didn't budge. Instead, he beckoned me over and pulled the 'viewer away from his chest.

Thinta-ah had apparently been either the consummate diplomat or completely undecided. His true face was a grotesque mixture of Entwater's and Farber's. What made it grotesque was not that it had a patchwork aspect but that it was fluid—as if his features had been in the process of melting or flowing from one face to the other and somehow frozen in mid-change.

"I punched to create a control file and the 'viewer informed me that one already existed," Stilton said as I studied the screen. "So I called it up and *olé*."

"*Voilá*," I corrected him.

"In this case, I'd say it rates an olé. But I should have realized it would be here. It was how Entwater created the program, by using Thinta-ah as a control. He must have been teacher's pet. Diplomat's pet. Whatever."

"Freeze it and let's hear the audio," I said. "Unfreeze it when the video and audio are in synch."

A voice that had to be Entwater's came out of the small speaker. "What is your name?"

"Thinta-ah."

"Are you from another planet?"

"Yesss."

The image on the screen came to life. There were a few more questions. Favorite Earth food? Pizza with heavy garlic in the sauce—true. Last eaten yesterday? No—a lie. It was all very disjointed but light stuff, like a dating service application, slightly adapted. But it had served the purpose—the readings were clear. Stilton let it run out, and then put all the readings on the screen together, the seventeen and Thinta-ah's.

"God-*damn*-it," he said and blew out a disgusted breath. "Or maybe we should have known that, too—that if there was a control, then the program stands. They're all telling the truth, or they're the best liars in the universe."

"You're right."

We both jumped and Stilton almost dropped the 'viewer. The Pilot had managed to come right up to us without either one of us knowing. "Right about what?" said Stilton.

She pointed a finger at him, smiling. "You seek the truth. And you—" she swiveled toward me, finger still pointing—"seek the lie."

"What do you seek?" I said, making sure that Thinta-ah wasn't sneaking up on my side.

"Resonance, with all that is. Did you hear the one about the Pilot who went up to the hot-dog-o-mat and said, 'Make me one with everything?' "

"That joke is so old, it's got a long gray beard and a brand-new liver," Stilton said, eyes narrowing. "It's at least half a century since the first time someone told it, and it wasn't a Pilot—"

"It is now."

That wasn't a happy expression, I realized, it was a *serene* one. It was the kind of expression you saw on people who were sure they had all the answers, minus the vacancy of the hard-core cult convert. What was Resonance, anyway? Something about traveling point to point and finding alignment so that two points that seemed to be separated by a great distance actually weren't . . . or something. It didn't make any sense to me, but a Pilot was one more thing I wasn't. If I couldn't figure out how it worked, I sure couldn't figure out why it made her so peaceful.

"The Lazarians taught us Resonance," she said, nodding at me. "And to travel point to point in space, we must travel point to point in here, too." She pointed her finger at her own forehead now. "You don't have the correct alignments in here, so you cannot travel point to point, but point to off-point. Dead end. Wander forty years in the desert and not get out even then."

179

She made us sit down again, while she perched on the edge of the table, placing the 'viewer next to her. "They are all telling the truth, and they are the best liars in the universe that you have ever met, because the truth they tell is *their* truth."

It was one of the few times in my life that I could say I had experienced *satori*. And once I saw it, I felt like a total fool for not seeing it to begin with. Most humans couldn't beat the 'viewer because no matter how much they believed in their own lies, they knew what they believed was at variance with facts that other people knew, and so both couldn't be true. But the Lazarians were aliens, so, of course, their concept of the truth would be alien as well.

Alien truth. True faces. The two concepts were whirling around each other in my head, trying to find a basis for connection.

"So what does that mean?" Stilton said. "Somehow they all killed her, or they're all lying to protect someone?"

The Pilot shook her head. "You don't understand yet. They taught us Resonance with all things. Because *they* Resonate, *always*."

I couldn't tell if this was another *satori* or a continuation. "Entwater liked them. She liked her work." I glanced at Farber. "And she, in turn, was very popular. So popular that—" I broke off, resting one hand casually on the 'viewer. "Tell me, was she popular because she liked them, or did she like them because she was popular?"

"That has Resonated into one thing now. It can no longer be determined because it is no longer distinguishable. All that remains is . . . love. *Not* the trendy brain chemicals," she added to Stilton. "Do you Resonate love?"

"You mean, understand it?" I laughed a little. "Does anyone?"

"What do you do? For love. What does it do to you?"

For once, I was at a loss because I'd never had a long-term relationship or a child. Alone, you can travel faster in a career, but you leave a lot of understanding in the dust that way, too. "Oh, I guess you care about the other person," I said finally, feeling like a sappy greeting card.

"Yeah. And when they stop loving, they stop caring," Stilton said gloomily. "Not responsible, all that shit."

The Pilot's face lit up even more. I hadn't thought it was possible. "Responsible. *Responsible*. Are you always responsible?"

I a-ahm responsible.

It is my fault.

I ha-ahve the blaaaaaa-aimmeh.

Over and over again, sixteen times, from sixteen nearly identical true faces. I almost laughed out loud with the revelation. "They're guilty, all right," I said. "That is, they *feel* guilty, because they felt responsible for her and they didn't prevent her murder!"

All the Lazarians gathered around Entwater's corpse turned their heads to look at me. Except one; the last one, of course.

"Pin a rose on *you*," said the Pilot and patted my hand. "What next?"

"Trouble in Paradise," I said. "There's always trouble in Paradise, you can count on it, on any world. Because nobody can be that popular without someone getting jealous." I got up and walked toward Farber. "Someone got real, *real* jealous. *Killing* jealous."

"No," Farber said, enraged. "Jealous, yes, she had them all eating out of the palm of her hand practically, but I wouldn't—I *couldn't*—"

"And he didn't," said Stilton. "We haven't looked at the readings for his third recording, but I'd bet my life that they say he's as truthful as those from the other two readings."

"I know that," I said, keeping my gaze on Farber. "He's not a good liar. Not *that* good, anyway. And he's not an alien. *And* he didn't have it quite right a minute ago. Entwater didn't have them *all* eating out of her hand, just *almost* all. You made a friend. One out of eighteen, not too popular, but a very, *very* devoted friend. A friend who loves you enough to be responsible for you. For your happiness. For your sadness. And for your anger and jealousy and hate."

Farber's mouth was hanging open. I turned toward Stilton. "Number seventeen's our murderer." I paused. "For a minute there, I was about to tell you to get out the cuffs, but then I remembered. Diplomatic immunity. We have to leave it up to Thinta-ah to administer any justice—poor Thinta-ah, the consummate diplomat of the Lazarian species, torn between both of them."

To my surprise, Thinta-ah didn't seem the least bit embarrassed. On a human, the body language would have screamed *pride*. Aliens; go figure.

Stilton looked from the Lazarians in the group to the Pilot and then to me. "Are you sure?"

"Think about it," I said. "If they were all to blame for not preventing her death, who was really to blame for causing it? A Lazarian in love? Or the one the Lazarian was in love with?" I turned back to Farber.

"I didn't know," he said. "I had no idea." He frowned. "How did you?"

I opened my mouth and then realized I couldn't tell them. "The truth was staring me in the face all along," I said after a long moment. "I just had to recognize it for what it was."

Farber spread his hands helplessly. "I don't understand."

"I know. But one tip before we all get out of here." I pulled him closer by his lapel. "Quit this job. You're not suited for this kind of diplomacy. Really. I *know* this."

"I'm not a diplomat, I'm a secretary. I can get another secretarial job anywhere. But this was . . . exotic, exciting. . . ."

"Give it up, Farber," I said, "or you're going to find that office politics have suddenly turned fatal on you."

That seemed to put the fear of God into him. I went back over to the table where Stilton and the Pilot were still sitting. "I'd say this means we're free to go."

"See for yourself," said the Pilot and gestured at the center of the room. The group of Lazarians around Entwater had broken formation and were moving slowly away from the corpse, clustering in smaller groups of twos and threes. Space density. As if they had to breathe each other's air or something.

"Everyone maaaaaaaaaay leave," said Thinta-ah, bowing to us. "The door is now in service."

"And the truth shall set you free," Stilton murmured, committing everything in the 'viewer to long-term storage formats and then shutting it down.

"Not bad," I said. "In an awful kind of way."

"That's what the truth is supposed to do," he said stubbornly, pulling out the 'viewer strap so he could hang it on his shoulder. "That's what it's *for*. Right?" he added to the Pilot.

The Pilot folded her hands briefly. "What is truth?" She went back to the group of humans, who were all just starting to get warily up from their chairs.

I stared after her.

"What?" said Stilton.

"True faces. Celie Entwater died for human sins. Jesting Pilot."

"What?"

"Nothing, nothing. Let's get out of here."

To say only that Charlotte MacLeod is Canadian is to entirely miss the point of her delightful mysteries. Her stories are often the most cheerful of creations, enlisting the participation of a cast of characters one would, in a moment, invite in for a nice cup of tea. But within her clever constructs there is usually a nasty grain of evil . . . the dark opposite of finding a pearl of great value in a plain, crusted oyster. Here's a lovely mystery to plumb.

The Perplexing Puzzle of the Perfidious Pigeon Poisoner
From the Memoirs of Charlotte MacLeod, Detective

"But damn it all, Charlotte, if you don't take the case, we'll have to go out and *pay* somebody."

I could follow Dolph Kelling's argument easily enough. I had to grant that pigeon poisoning is a despicable practice; poisoning them within the historical purlieus of the Public Gardens amounts, in the eyes of us Bostonians, to something barely short of sacrilege. From a Kelling's viewpoint, having to pay for a service that might, with adequate arm twisting, be got for nothing falls into much the same category.

As a professional private investigator, I knew how to steel myself against blandishments, badgering, and downright bullying. Indeed, I had all too frequently been obliged to do so back when Dolph's Uncle Frederick was alive.

Fred had prided himself on his diplomatic skills, of which in truth he had possessed none whatsoever. Dolph, with his downright foot-in-mouth approach, had often succeeded where Fred would have failed, although he'd never been given any credit for his achievements until Fred at long last had been locked away in the family vault. I had felt in the past, and still retain, a sort of grudging fondness for Dolph. I left the last bite of my crumpet on the plate for Mr. Manners as children of my class and generation had been taught to do, set down my teacup, and groped under the table for my umbrella.

"Very well, Dolph," I told him. "I'll look into the matter."

It would be awkward for me to do so at this time; I was already committed to a potentially more interesting and assuredly more lucrative assignment. This matter was baffling the Boston police and had so far, I confess, also baffled me; although I was confident of ultimate success, since I had never yet failed. I do not boast, I merely state a fact. To fail would result in a waste of time and energy; persons of my ancestry and upbringing deplore waste in any form.

The case I had just accepted involved the recent disappearance of the celebrated Papaver pearls, a long rope of matched India pearls quite improbable in size although in fact quite genuine. The pearls had been handed down to the present owner through a string of ancestresses almost as long as the rope itself. Albernia Papaver (the given name was also hers by inheritance) had worn them to the opera on the previous Friday evening. Somehow or other they had been removed from her person, most probably during that breathless moment when La Tosca was hurling herself from the high parapet to the string mattress below. Mrs. Papaver, a fervent Puccini worshiper, had not noticed the draft around her neck until Baron Scarpia was taking his third curtain call, by which time many seats had been emptied and the thief had evidently made a clean escape. Here indeed was a pretty kettle of fish, and how might so slippery an eel be hauled up from its murky depths?

It had been, I should explain, not Albernia Papaver herself but her daughter and son-in-law who had come three days since to seek my aid. Albernia the Sixth, I believe she was, had been married to Dr. Kenneth Whittler, a brilliant young brain surgeon, some two years previously; it was now apparent to my discerning eye that their union was to be blessed. Mrs. Whittler had come straight to the point.

"I cannot claim any personal disinterest in the matter of the robbery, Miss MacLeod. The pearls would, in the fullness of time, come to me or to my daughter—" she gave her handsome husband a sweet, secret smile "—and would be treasured for their intrinsic worth and beauty but far more for their familial associations. The thought of losing them forever is thus doubly bitter to me. Bitterest of all, however, is having to observe the dreadful effect this shocking event has had on my dear mama. *Our* dear mama, I should have said, since Kenneth dotes upon her as much as I. Do you not, my dearest?"

"How could I not?" cried the rising star of the intracranial correction. "Mother Papaver is the apotheosis of virtuous womanhood: a model of rectitude combined with grace of manner, steadiness of principles, and warmth of heart."

He did not add swiftness of intellect, I noticed. That was understandable. Such standards of decorum as Albernia Papaver exemplified would not leave much room for brilliance. "Does your mother know you are consulting me?" I asked.

"She does not," Mrs. Whittler confessed. "Mama is naturally distressed at the loss of her cherished heirloom, but far more distraught at having become a target for publicity as the victim of so daring a theft. Scrupulous as she is, she cannot help seeing the incident primarily as an appalling breach of etiquette. She won't even let us allude to it in her presence."

"Much as I feel for Mother Papaver," said Dr. Whittler, "my most serious concern is the strain which this grievous situation is putting on my beloved wife. Albernia the Younger is, as you may have divined, in a delicate condition requiring rest and tranquillity above all things. She desires to be her mother's prop and mainstay, but circumstances prevent her remaining long in such an upsetting situation. Mother Papaver is, of course, never neglected; Father Papaver is always close at hand."

"But darling Papa is, like my dear husband, totally caught up in his work," Albernia the Younger all but sobbed.

"And what is it that your father does?" I asked, mainly to divert her mind into a less harrowing channel. "It was my impression that he, a fourth cousin to your esteemed mother and equally an heir to the vast Papaver fortune, lived the life of a country gentleman insofar as one is able to do so in a Beacon Hill town house."

"Oh, Papa is no idle dilettante," the loyal daughter insisted. "He is an expert maker of miniature ship models, which he puts into bottles. He has already succeeded in assembling the *Niña*, the *Pinta*, and the *Santa María* under full sail inside a Haig & Haig Pinch bottle; his next triumph is to be the fight between the *Bonhomme Richard* and the *Guerriere*."

"Father Papaver's is a labor of both aesthetic and historic importance, as we well realize," Dr. Whittler added, "but it does leave Mother Papaver too much to herself, and we cannot but fear the worst. Miss MacLeod, only you can save our dear parent from sinking into melancholy and ultimate decline. Will you help us?"

How could I refuse? Immediately I got down to business.

"Very well, I accept your commission. Now describe to me the precise circumstances of that direful night. Where were you sitting?"

"Row C, left center aisle," Dr. Whittler replied with obvious relief. "We had the first four seats: Father Papaver on the aisle, Mother Papaver next to him, Albernia beside her, and myself farthest in. It would thus have been impossible for anybody else in our row to have reached over and possessed himself on the pearls."

"In fact, we can't see how anyone at all could have removed them without Mama's noticing," said his wife. "Whereas Grandmama always wore them hanging down to her knees, Mama has always preferred to loop them several times around her neck."

"An interesting point," I rejoined. "And who was sitting behind your mother?"

"A man with a beard, I believe."

"I think it was a woman in a mink or sable coat, my dear," the husband objected.

"Might there not have been one of each in adjoining seats?" I ventured, although I do not like to lead a witness.

"That is possible," Mrs. Whittler conceded. "I have only a general impression of furriness."

"And my recollection is, I fear, equally fuzzy," the young doctor added ruefully. "Truth to tell, I always refrain from turning around when I'm out in public, for fear some acquaintance will spot me and start telling me about his symptoms."

"But what of Mr. Papaver?" I asked. "He, it would seem, was best situated to notice those around your party."

Grave as the situation undoubtedly was, Albernia the Younger could not repress a small giggle. "Oh, darling Papa slept through the whole performance. The only parts he likes about going to the opera are the intermissions. His chief recollection is of how long it took him to get served at the champagne bar."

Police interrogation of the ushers and certain members of the audience who had not yet left the auditorium when the loss was discovered had been futile. The furry person or persons, needless to say, had not been found. The only hopeful piece of information my own sources had been able to turn up so far was that the pearls were apparently not yet fenced, either in Boston or elsewhere.

In my mind it was more than likely, indeed quite certain (and, as I mentioned before, I am never wrong) that the priceless strand was still right here in town; hidden until the heat, as we say in the field of detection, should be off. That the rope might have been broken into segments and sold off piecemeal was unthinkable; its great value lay in its being such a truly monumental aggregation of rare pearls all the same size.

I had mulled in vain over the possibilities, and searched not a few likely hiding places without result. Well, the necklace was somewhere, and I would find it. Perhaps turning briefly to a different task, for surely no pigeon poisoner could stay for long concealed from me, would stimulate my keen mind to fresh insights. I crooked my umbrella over my arm, straightened the purple velvet toque which had been an inheritance from my late aunt Elizabeth, and set forth to discover what evildoing columbiphobe had so far successfully dispatched seventeen victims.

How can I pinpoint that number so precisely? First, you must understand that Boston pigeons are not without friends. That is particularly true of those which frequent the Common and, to a somewhat lesser degree, the Public Gardens. While some residents of the Hill and the Back Bay detest the creatures, others are solicitous for their welfare, and the latter are in the moral majority. Moreover, these wily avians know very well how to work the tourists.

I have no statistics as to what percentage of the popcorn and peanuts purveyed by vendors in the area is bought partly, chiefly, or even exclusively for consumption by the local fauna; but it must be considerable. We must also count those dedicated bird lovers who fetch bags of crumbs from home, not to mention the park-bench picnickers who donate portions of their doughnuts and frankfurt rolls either voluntarily or perforce. Common and Garden pigeons can be as aggressively pestiferous as the late Frederick Kelling, which is saying a good deal.

Some of this largess goes to the ducks and the squirrels, I grant you; but the major consumers must surely be the pigeons, because there are so many more of them. Ordinances against feeding the feathered denizens of our cherished inner-city green acres have been passed from time to time but have always failed of their purpose, which is essentially to starve the pigeons into flying off to deposit their unsightly and unsanitary droppings somewhere else. Our pigeons like it where they are, and Bostonians by and large like having them here. Wherefore then the poisonings? And how did Dolph Kelling, my informant, know the precise number of victims to date?

The explanation is only too simple: Dolph knew because Lovella Burdock told him. Lovella Burdock, I suppose I ought to explain, is a Hillite and a longtime embracer of allegedly worthy causes. When I add that for upward of forty years she supported Fred Kelling in each and every one of his loopy undertakings, I believe I have said it all.

Anyway, Lovella had taken it upon herself to be chief mourner for the slain pigeons. Garbed in deepest black, she now spent her days pacing solemnly along the Garden's paths, a black oilcloth bag dangling from her black-gloved hand. When, as too often had happened during the past five or six days, she came upon a feathered corpse, she scooped it up with a trowel she kept somewhere about her person and laid it tenderly in her bag, to be given a decent burial in the tiny garden behind her Beacon Hill brownstone.

These public paradings were innocuous enough, no doubt; but if the silly woman really wanted to do something useful, why didn't she devote her efforts to finding the poisoner and making him—or quite possibly her—stop it? I had asked that question of Dolph Kelling; he'd replied with his usual bluntness, "But then she'd be left without a cause."

So the upshot was that I myself had a new cause to pursue; I might as well get on with it. The afternoon was salubrious enough to have lured forth plenty of strollers, and also, I noticed, a few extra policemen. Some of these were casting suspicious glances at anybody who happened to be carrying a bag of popcorn; others were shooing moppets out of the flower beds, for this was springtime, when the gardens are at their loveliest if one happens to care for tulips en masse.

I am fond of flowers, but those somewhat military-looking blooms are not my favorites, particularly when planted with geometric precision in large beds next to other large beds of clashing colors. The pansy beds are more to my liking; even as a small child I loved their gentle fragrance and little monkey faces, and still do. After having paid my grudging meed of admiration to the gaudy tulips, I paused to visit for a moment with my friends the pansies. It was then I noticed the pigeon.

The bird was in its death throes, and the reason for its impending demise was all too clear. Nothing but strychnine poisoning could cause those agonized back somersaults; the poor thing was rolling like a hoop. The spectacle was heart-wrenching; my sympathies were at once fully enlisted on the side of the preyed-upon. I even began to think less disdainfully of Lovella Burdock.

Or did I? Here she came, just the way Dolph had described her, sooty as a crow from head to foot, with a voluminous mourning veil draped over some sort of black turban affair and billowing out behind her like the exhaust from an uncleaned engine. Thanks to my middle-aged presbyopia, I could make out the expression on her face well enough. Lovella was by no means cast down at the loss of a feathered friend, she was avid for the hunt.

Perhaps it was the ill-concealed glee that repelled me; perhaps it was the tasteless affectation of the antique mourning veil. Whatever it was, I chose not to indulge her whimsy. I opened my umbrella just enough to admit the by now mercifully stilled form at my feet, scooped it inside with one quick motion, closed the trusty bumbershoot, and sauntered on my way, holding the bulgy side concealed against the ample pleats of my well-worn tweed skirt.

Never much of a runner and far too aware of my position to try, I can nevertheless saunter at a surprising rate. In a matter of moments I had left Lovella searching vainly among the tulips, crossed the ornamental bridge over the pond without pausing to gaze down, as was my wont, upon the graceful swan boats and the lines of ducks quacking importunately after them, and made my way to Charles Street.

In my profession, one learns upon occasion, notwithstanding one's innate predilections, to cast economy to the winds. Steeling myself for an exorbitant fee, I hailed a passing taxicab, directing its driver to take me to the office of a veterinary whose name had best not be given for reasons the perspicacious reader either will or will not understand, as the case may be. Suffice it to mention that this was the same vet who had been so viciously—though, thanks to myself, only temporarily—victimized during the lurid affair of the substitute sealyham. He or she (though I might have said she or he, since so many of our outstanding vets are females. The most apposite term in this context would perhaps be bitches, but unfortunately this formerly innocuous word had gradually acquired a pejorative slant)—where was I? Oh yes, the person to whom I refer greeted me as a valued friend and inquired the reason for my visit since I was unaccompanied by an ailing quadruped, as had customarily been the case.

"It is this." I shook my umbrella on the examining table and snapped it open to reveal the pathetic contents. "I require an immediate autopsy on this unfortunate creature, and I intend to watch you perform it."

"You won't like what you see," cautioned the veterinarian.

"It can be no worse than what I have already seen," I retorted. "Only minutes ago, I stood and watched this pigeon die in agony, a victim of the so far invisible fiend who is turning the Public Gardens into a veritable charnel house."

"Good gad! I had not realized the situation was so dire. Just let me finish clipping this savage Doberman pinscher's toenails—now the other paw, Susibelle, that's my good girl—and we'll buckle down to our gruesome task."

My friend was as good as her (or his) word. To my secret relief, the pigeon did not have to be thoroughly dissected; a mere cursory inspection of the opened crop was enough to expose the kernel of popcorn stuck in its throat. Under my direction, a chemical analysis was done forthwith, and my surmise confirmed.

"It's strychnine, all right," said the vet. "A tiny amount, but definitely present."

"A tiny amount?" I queried. "Would so small a dose be sufficient to effect the demise of so large a bird?"

"Oh yes. As a multitalented Harvard faculty member has reminded us, it requires no more than a smidgen to effect the demise of a pigeon. This kernel was the fatal instrument, you may rest assured of that."

As I gazed upon that small, whitish object, a great light dawned. "Then let us," I said, "proceed to dissect the kernel. Carefully, if you please."

"Very well," the vet replied with a shrug, "though I fail to—great Scott! Will you look at that?"

I nodded. "This is no more than I expected. The kernel has been cunningly hollowed out to receive one superb Orient pearl, indubitably taken from the famous rope stolen last Friday night from Mrs. Albernia Papaver during the final scene of *Tosca*."

And I knew where to find seventeen more just like it, but not yet. I must go canny, as some ancestor from the land at which my patronym hints might perhaps have remarked. "I humbly beg that you breathe not even a syllable of this to any living soul, and further that you dispose of this wretched avian's remains forthwith, by whatever means is most expeditious and least detectable."

"It shall be done" was the welcome answer.

I have no doubt that it was, but I did not wait to see. Carrying the pearl with me inside a small envelope of the sort generally used in dispensing worm pills, I made my way back to my modest residence, taking, as always, a quiet pleasure in the aspect of its simple Bulfinch design. Behind the ancestral lavender-hued windows, I exchange my sensible crepe-soled walking shoes for a pair of fuzzy pink house slippers, for even we private investigators have our frivolous moments, rang for my faithful Florence to fetch in the tea, and sat down to brood.

There was much to brood about. Was Lovella Burdock the innocent though rattle-pated do-gooder Dolph Kelling believed her to be, or was she a witting accomplice of the jewel thief? And who was that thief?

The opera box office had been no great help. Those desirable aisle seats behind the Papaver party had indeed been marked off as sold; the middle-aisle ushers had been sure they were occupied on the night, else the gap would have been noticed. The occupants, however, had gone unremarked, as was only natural in so large an assemblage. There was no record of a reservation's having been made in anybody's name; the tickets must have been purchased for cash at the window, or possibly from a scalper, who would certainly never confess to his unethical practice. The police were trying to track down those elusive occupants; good luck to them. It was clear to me now that the thief and the poisoner must be one and the same.

As to the modus operandi (a technical term of the investigative profession), the lone pearl had told me all. Young Mrs. Whittler had expressed puzzlement as to how those multiple strands could have been removed without her mother's noticing. Quite simply, they could not be and had not been.

A rope of pearls, I reflected, is not like, for instance, a diamond necklace wherein each separate jewel is individually mounted on a chain. Pearls are drilled through their centers and strung on strong thread of gut, waxed linen, or in this day and age, more usually nylon, with a knot tied after each bead to guard against loss should the strand be broken. Careful owners, as Albernia Papaver no doubt was, have their pearls restrung from time to time purely as a preventive measure. Why, then, would it in any way impair the value of the rope to take it apart and smuggle the pearls away one by one, to be restrung later in a safer place?

Obviously this was what the thief had reasoned that night at the opera while snipping through the various twists and stealthily pocketing each separate section in its turn. It must have been done with extraordinary deftness by someone almost preternaturally skilled in finicking little operations. A brain surgeon or a bottler of miniature ship models could have done it; an expert pickpocket was far more likely. I thought of alerting my friends on the force to round up the best of the lot. Then I reflected that really expert pickpockets no doubt would be unavailable; they retain their anonymity by never getting caught!

No, this was a task in which I alone had a better chance of succeeding than all the Boston police force put together. I drank my tea, then paid a brief visit to the ancestral attic, where I easily found such things as would best serve my purpose. That done, I ate my dinner with good appetite, read a few chapters of *Sense and Sensibility*, and went early to bed.

Fresh and rested the next morning, I made my ablutions, did a few push-ups, breakfasted as usual on porridge and stewed prunes, and proceeded to array myself in deepest black from head to toe. Great-grandmother's mourning veil was a nuisance but essential to my scheme; I must manage the thing as best I could. Black oilcloth shopping bags must have been all the rage sometime or other; I had been able to duplicate Lovella Burdock's pigeon carrier as closely as made no matter.

One accessory that Lovella seemed not to have thought of was a black umbrella. I resolved not to be parted from mine, since I carry no other weapon and have never needed any. Fully equipped, then, I set forth betimes on my quest. There was no danger of Lovella's showing up to cramp my style; knowing her voracious sweet tooth, I had sent her a box of chocolates heavily laced with a certain patent remedy guaranteed to promote regularity. To lull her into a sense of security, I had enclosed one of Dolph Kelling's visiting cards. Desperate situations require desperate measures.

This was a beautiful morning to be out and about in the Gardens. The trees were all in bloom—those which in fact do bloom, that is; the tulips were rampant in their splendor. The swan boats were bobbing gently at the dock, waiting for their operators to seat themselves inside the carved wooden swans and activate the foot pedals which are these flat, open barges' sole means of locomotion. Many a time from earliest youth had I sat on their slatted benches and been pedaled over these popcorn-sprinkled waters, under the bridge, around the lagoon, past the little island and back again. It would be pleasant to loiter here awhile, but duty called; I must move on.

It was less than a week since the pearls had been stolen. To have killed seventeen pigeons—possibly eighteen by now, since another could have been poisoned while I was at the vet's—was fast work. I was wise to have come early, for the poisoner must even now be abroad. His foul task was not a simple one; he must make sure his quite possibly unwitting confederate was present on the scene, and synchronize his (I have decided to stick with the masculine pronoun, but in its impersonal sense) fell scatterings, as I was about to say, with the chief mourner's peregrinations. It would not do for a pigeon to expire unless Lovella was close enough to pick up the cadaver before one of the park keepers beat her to it.

Strychnine acts quickly; the poisoner need only stay just far enough and not too far ahead of the woman in black. Keeping my pesky mourning veil down over my face and forsaking my customary brisk stride for Lovella's pigeon-toed shamble, I meandered along the more secluded paths, every sense alert for clandestine popcorn tossers.

Anybody feeding a feathered flock that contained even one duck had to be eliminated, of course. Boston ducks are so pushy that they easily beat out even the boldest pigeon to the popcorn; and surely my quarry would not risk poisoning a duck, for it might take to the water, die there, and become impossible for Lovella to retrieve.

I had a couple of false alarms, then I spotted him. Or her. Baggy flannels and jacket, a shapeless poplin rain hat, hair of indeterminate length, and oversize sunglasses created an effect of androgyneity; the disguise would require closer inspection to penetrate than I dared attempt at this juncture.

I could not have been mistaken; the person had collected only three or four pigeons, not a duck among them, and was doling out the popcorn one kernel at a time, eyeing a certain member of the group with peculiar intensity. Ah, now the first dire symptom was beginning to appear. The person flung the rest of his or her popcorn among the avians to create a concealing flurry, cast one hasty but meaningful glance in my direction, and strode briskly away.

Was he heading for the subway kiosk? No, a meter maid was too close by, tagging cars with the self-satisfied expression of her kind. He swerved back whence he had come, thinking no doubt to cross over to the Common and lose himself there among the loiterers and dog walkers. But the popcorn cart was by the gate, and a policeman beside it, eyeing would-be purchasers so intently that they were all passing up the popcorn and buying pinwheels instead. With an aplomb born, one suspects, of much practice, the poisoner changed course again, hung over the bridge for a few moments, then tripped down the steps to the dock, thrust money at the ticket collector, and hopped aboard a swan boat that was just about to pull away.

So that was the miscreant's little game! Well, two could play. His latest victim safely stowed inside my oilcloth bag, I had naturally contrived to make my way again into his vicinity. His sudden dash for the departing swan boat disconcerted me not a whit; the scoundrel had played straight into my hands. A second swan boat rode idly at the dock, empty of passengers, for business was not brisk so early in the day. I hastened aboard, flashed my private investigator's license at the youth who sat inside the swan, and ordered imperiously, "Follow that swanboat!"

"But I'm not supposed to go till the starter tells me," protested the pedaler.

He was but a rosy-cheeked stripling; I thrust him aside, took his place inside the swan, lashed my mourning veil securely around my neck, and began to pedal for dear life.

The youngster stammered further protests and even attempted to take me by the arm, but I shook him off and kept on pedaling. The gap between the two boats narrowed; unfortunately some of the passengers ahead had noticed what was happening. They were craning their necks in our direction, either cheering me on or urging their own swan-man to greater efforts. The pigeon poisoner panicked, leaped inside the swan, and pressed a pistol to the pedaler's head.

Farsighted as I am, I easily discerned what make of pistol it was. The fool! I do loathe incompetence, even in my adversaries. I beckoned the still dithering youngling back into our swan.

"Here," I ordered, "take my place and pedal your heart out. I must board that boat with all dispatch. Yonder villain with the gun is none other than the infamous pigeon poisoner!"

"But if we keep chasing him, he'll shoot my father, for it is in truth my esteemed parent who propels the craft now fleeing before us," moaned the lad. "How can I take action that may precipitate the demise of a beloved sire?"

"Be of cheer, my boy," I replied. "That's only a water pistol."

"Sheesh! Then hang on to your veil, lady."

Si l'agesse pouvait! I had, I think, performed capably on the pedals, but that youngster had the feet of a Hermes. He sent us flying across the water, sending up great fans of spray, leaving an angry squadron of hopelessly outdistanced mallards quacking anatinian profanities in our tempestuous wake.

I half crouched in the bow, accurately calculated the short gap between the boats, and sprang. As I landed, I raised my ever-dependable gamp and brought it smartly down on the hand that held the pistol, now pointed waveringly in my direction. Except for one brief squirt, I remained unscathed, as I always do.

From then on it was, as we say in the profession, a piece of cake. I dragged the by now totally demoralized and half-collapsing miscreant aboard my commandeered craft, wished those on the full boat bon voyage, shrugged off the grateful protestations of the father, and tipped the son handsomely to take us back to the landing. En route, I set the prisoner down on the front bench and took my place—yes, beside *her!* Exactly as I had anticipated, the stealer of Mrs. Papaver's pearls was none other than Albernia herself. Who else, after all, could have done it so well?

But why? I refrained from pressing the question until I had got the wretched woman into my house and rung for Florence to bring the tea. After a few sips (Albernia took milk but no sugar), the erstwhile model of rectitude was able to falter out an explanation. She, Albernia Papaver, that apotheosis of virtuous womanhood, was being blackmailed!

"In God's name, how?" I am not easy to astonish, but who could have anticipated a revelation like this from such as she? "What could you possibly have done?"

She swallowed the last of her tea, as if to stiffen her resolve. "I—I was caught sniffing a hallucinogenic substance."

"What do you mean by a hallucinogenic substance?" I demanded. "Was it cocaine?"

"Oh no! No, never. It was—I suppose I must reveal the whole sordid story."

She held out her empty cup. Hers was a gesture of supplication; neither etiquette nor compassion could have refused her a refill. I performed the time-hallowed ritual of the pot and the pitcher, and waited.

I had not to wait long; Albernia Papaver was no poltroon. "Without trying to make myself sound less perfidious than I am," she began in a low but now firm voice, "I should explain that I had led an even more sheltered life than other girls of my class and generation. I was simply not aware of the pitfalls."

"That is so often the case," I said by way of encouragement. "Please go on."

"It happened at boarding school." Albernia mentioned the name of a distinguished establishment for young gentlewomen, which I shall not repeat for obvious reasons. "We were in the art room. Our instructress, Miss Braque, was an intensely creative person and an inspiration to us all. On this day she had us experimenting with what she termed collage. We were to cut out interesting shapes and arrange them in unusual ways. Each of us was handed a random assortment of materials to cut from and, what becomes germane to my narrative, an individual portion of adhesive."

On that last word, her voice faltered. I pounced on the clue. "By adhesive, do you by chance mean glue?"

"Pray do not condemn me, Miss MacLeod," she cried. "I thought the stuff was just to stick things down with."

"And you therefore proceeded to stick?"

"I stuck. Being neat-handed though by no means vulgarly artistic, I accomplished my task so featly and expeditiously that I was accorded the privilege of cleaning up after class. One of my appointed tasks was to return the leftover portions of—of substance to their original container."

"I see." Oh yes, I saw! "And this container was . . ."

"A large glass jar with a screw-on lid."

"The adhesive itself being a jellylike substance about the consistency of an overcooked blancmange, having a not unpleasant spicy odor?"

"Great heaven, Miss MacLeod, you astound me! How can you have described the noxious substance so accurately?"

I shrugged off the question. "The adhesive had merely been scooped out of the jar in dollops and handed to you on scraps of paper?"

"On small cardboard plates with decorative floral borders," Albernia replied with a hint of asperity. "Violets, I believe they were."

"I stand corrected." I am always gracious when circumstances do not require me to be otherwise. "So as you scooped the remains from the plates back into the jars, you inhaled the aforementioned spicy fragrance?"

"Had I but known, I could have held my breath," Albernia replied bitterly. "Instead, to crown my folly, before screwing the top back on, I leaned over the jar and took a great, heady whiff."

"Did you feel any hallucinogenic effect?"

"I had not time to feel anything but embarrassed. At that moment, a classmate burst into the room and exploded into derisive laughter at finding me with my nose in the jar. Knowing this rude girl's talent at public ridicule of her classmates and being myself a shy child, I begged her not to tell. That was a terrible mistake; she only taunted me further. Desperate at the prospect of being branded by the whole school as Stickynose, I retaliated in the only way open to me. I told her that if she breathed one word about what I'd done, I should go straight to the headmistress and tell her who poured the molasses on the chapel pews!"

"This classmate herself having been the culprit, no doubt," I deduced. "She would have been punished?"

"Oh, direly," cried Albernia. "I should have been believed, and she knew it. Her mischievous propensities had made her many enemies; they would have corroborated my testimony. Even if she escaped expulsion, she'd have been put in Coventry. To one in love with the limelight, being shunned by the entire student body would have been the greatest blow of all. I had her in my power. Grudgingly she yielded. Little did I suspect her grudge would be carried through the years. Or what foul use she would make of it in the end!"

"Were you in contact with her during the long interval?"

"Yes, in a casual way. I could hardly not have been; we both live here on the Hill and have acquaintances in common. One hates to snub an old classmate, and why should one? I had long ago dismissed that distasteful scene from my mind. I honestly believed I'd been guilty of nothing worse than a moment's silliness, and surely my threat to her had lost its power once we were graduated."

Albernia drew a deep breath. "Three weeks ago, this woman solicited from me a large contribution toward the purchase of an island in the South Pacific, to which all the Boston pigeons were to be humanely transported as a means of ending their pollution of the Common and Gardens. This was a scheme the late Frederick Kelling had once proposed but never implemented, since it was just about then that his nephew Adolphus had him declared mentally incompetent; a step which, in my husband's opinion and, I must say, my own, might well have been taken a good deal sooner. Naturally I refused to support such an addlepated scheme."

My prisoner-guest wet her lips with what must by then have been the cold, bitter dregs of her tea. Cold and bitter was Albernia's voice as she drove herself mercilessly on toward the denouement.

"She pounced on me like a lioness on her prey. That is, of course, a figure of speech; although for a moment I actually did fear a physical attack. She said I must pay, and pay handsomely, or all the world should know that I, who had stood for so long as a model of rectitude, was but a whited sepulcher. She would shout from the housetops, she would whisper to the scandalmongering press, that I, Albernia Papaver, had in my youth been a glue sniffer."

"She would actually have done this?"

"Indeed yes! She recalled every detail of that fateful long-ago encounter. She made it sound as though . . . as though . . . Miss MacLeod, I cannot tell you how degraded, how defiled I felt as she poured out upon me the vials of her long-pent hatred. She reminded me with ghoulish glee how easily glue sticks, how ready people are to hear the bad and make it worse. She dwelt upon the effect her revelation would have on my son-in-law's career. What patient, she demanded theatrically, would entrust his cerebrum, his cerebellum, or especially his medulla oblongata, to the son-in-law of a dope fiend?"

"Those were her exact words?"

"She hurled them in my face. She spoke also of the ignominy that would be heaped upon my daughter, the shock and pain that might complicate my Albernia's delicate condition, the cloud that would hang over the newborn, should my darling succeed in carrying it to term. She even hinted that my dear husband might be dropped from his club! For myself, I could have defied her and borne the brunt. For my loved ones, I saw no recourse but to meet her demands, outrageous as they were."

"Precisely how outrageous, Mrs. Papaver?"

"She wanted five million dollars, in cash. I had a dreadful time trying to make her understand that people in our position do not leave great wads of thousand-dollar bills kicking around the house. When she finally had to face the truth about trust funds and long-term investments, she demanded my pearls."

I nodded. "I thought as much. So, to get to the nub of the matter, Lovella Burdock directed you to fabricate a robbery during the opera, then deliver the pearls to her via the pigeons, secretly, one by one, by means of hollowed-out popcorn kernels which she supplied to you. Lovella cautioned you not to handle them without wearing transparent rubber or plastic gloves, did she not?"

"Oh yes, she cautioned me. She had every incentive to keep me alive until I had delivered all the pearls. This was another twist of the knife; Lovella knew full well that I had always been scrupulous about feeding the pigeons wholesome, nourishing birdseed. Each poisoned kernel I tossed was a fresh dagger in my heart."

"No doubt," I rejoined shortly. "Getting back to the adhesive, did it never once occur to you that no conscientious teacher would ever have exposed her pupils' tender nostrils to a hallucinogenic of any sort? What you sniffed that fateful day could have been nothing more dangerous than ordinary library paste."

"But—but—" The teaspoon fell from her nerveless hand. "Then I have killed nineteen pigeons for nothing."

"You have indeed. Come, let us go and end this senseless massacre once and for all."

"You will not force me back to the Public Gardens? I could not!"

"Trust me, Mrs. Papaver. I, too, attended a school for young gentlewomen."

"Might I not first rid myself of this loathsome disguise?"

"Assuredly. My faithful Florence will assist you. Do you require a change of apparel?"

"Thank you, but I have everything I need hidden in my popcorn bag."

I knew I could trust Florence to keep Mrs. Papaver from doing anything silly; still it was a relief to see her reappear a few minutes later in a properly unsmart two-piece suit and sensible pumps, with a handbag too small to conceal any weapon larger than a popcorn kernel. I myself was still in my ancient black; I remained so as I led the way out of my house and down Beacon Hill.

I had calculated the dosage perfectly; Lovella answered the door in her kimono, pale and drawn but obviously capable of being up and about. Despite her histrionic inclinations, acting was not the miscreant's forte; she recoiled at the sight of my mourning veil and turned pea green when she spied my companion. I barged straight in, urging Mrs. Papaver before me. This was no time for the amenities.

Nor did I mince words. "Lovella Burdock," I cried, "your perfidy is exposed. I have in my possession a pearl taken from the crop of a pigeon poisoned under your brutal coercion by this traduced and deluded woman. You yourself have eighteen more pearls. Get them."

The silly woman stamped her foot like a child in a tantrum. "No! I won't! I want them."

"What you want is a brain scan," I retorted. "You are about to be arrested, Lovella Burdock. Your lawyer will offer a plea of insanity, as well he might. You will then be examined by a team of psychiatrists. If that's the way you're going to act, they'll put you in a straitjacket and squirt cold water at you. Get the pearls, Lovella."

"They're still in the pigeons."

"Humbug!" I retorted. "You may be crazy, but you're not stupid."

She picked up a bowl of popcorn from a nearby table. "Here," she cried with a mad *ha-ha!* "Have some."

I buttoned my lips, located her telephone hidden under a ridiculous French doll with a hoop skirt, and dialed the police station. "Sergeant Imbroglio, could you please send someone over? I have captured the mastermind behind the pigeon poisonings and the Papaver pearl robbery. Oh, not at all, you know I am always happy to do your work for you."

I suggested to Lovella that she get some clothes on before they came to arrest her, but she refused to believe the thing was really going to happen until two stalwart officers in uniforms appeared at the door. Albernia Papaver had evidently not quite believed it, either; she threw me a look of agonized supplication.

"Just tell the truth," I told her gently. "These gentlemen understand human weakness. You will not find them unsympathetic, except to the guilty."

At last it dawned on Lovella that she was really going to be arrested. Wildly screaming, "You'll never take me alive!" she plunged her hand into the popcorn bowl and crammed a handful into her mouth, dropping half the kernels in her frenzy and making a sad mess of the carpet.

I draw the curtain of decency over the appalling scene that ensued. An ambulance was sent for, of course; but there was really nothing we could do except stand around and watch, aghast. As her terrible throes subsided into the ultimate stillness, one of the policemen shook his head.

"All that for a few kernels of popcorn!"

"It only requires a single kernel, dipped in strychnine," I replied sadly. "The missing pearls are almost certainly in the late Mrs. Burdock's right-hand bathrobe pocket. Mrs. Papaver will elucidate."

The pearls were there. Seeing her duty now clear before her, Albernia showed the stuff she was made of. The police were understanding; there would be no scandal. Again I had been right. But then, when was I ever wrong?

Max Allan Collins, known for a variety of mystery and suspense achievements, is teamed here with his talented wife, Barbara Collins, in another tale from *Cat Crimes III,* this one worthy of the kind of high regard one felt at the end of the best of vintage "Alfred Hitchcock Presents" television episodes. Appearances don't always lead to the kind of end one might imagine . . .

Cat Got Your Tongue
BARBARA COLLINS
AND
MAX ALLAN COLLINS

The warm California breeze played with Kelli's long blonde hair, which shimmered in the brilliant sun like threads of finely spun gold. Stretched out in a lounge chair by the pool—its water sparkling like diamonds, blinding her in spite of the Ray-Ban sunglasses—she looked like a goddess: long sleek curvy legs led to an even more curvaceous body that spilled over and out her bathing suit, as if resenting having to be clothed. Next to her, on a wrought-iron table, lay fruit, caviar and champagne. Her pouty-pink lips were fixed in a smug, satisfied smile. She was in heaven!

"Oh, poolboy!" she called out to the muscular, shirtless, sandy-haired man dragging a net across the back end of the swimming pool. "More champagne!" She waved an empty crystal goblet at him.

He ignored her.

So she stretched out even more in the lounge chair, moving seductively, suggestively. "I'll make it worth your while," she said, her tongue lingering on her lips.

Now he came to her, and looked down with mild disgust. Sweat beaded his berry-brown body. "Put the stuff back, Kel. It's time to go."

"Just a little longer, Rick," she pleaded.

"It's *time*, Kel."

She sat up in the chair, swung both legs around, and stomped her feet to the ground. "How am *I* supposed to get a tan?" she whined.

He didn't answer but stood silently until she finally got up and picked up the fruit, caviar and champagne, and shuffled off to the house.

"Hurry it up!" he called after her. "They'll be home soon!"

Rick collected his gear, and after a few minutes Kelli returned, standing before him like a dutiful child.

"Everything put back?" he asked.

"Yes."

"And straightened up?"

"Yes."

"Do I have to check?"

"No."

As he turned away, she made a face and stuck out her tongue.

They left, out the patio's wooden gate, and down a winding cobblestone path that led through the gently sloping garden bursting with flowers.

"Why can't *we* live like this?" she complained.

He grunted, moving along. "Because I work for a pool cleaning company and you're on unemployment."

She sighed. "Life just isn't fair."

"Who said it was?"

They were at the street now, by his truck, a beat-up brown Chevy. He threw his gear into the back, then went around to the passenger side and opened the door for her.

"But this is *America!*" Kelli said, tossing her duffel bag inside. "Don't we have a right to *make* things fair?"

He looked at her funny.

"What?" she asked.

"Are those your sunglasses?"

"Yes, *those* are my sunglasses!" she replied indignantly. Anyway, they were now.

She got in the truck, and, while waiting for him to get in the other side, checked herself out in the visor mirror.

Now her hair looked like a cheap blonde wig, her bathing suit the bargain-basement Blue Light Special it was. She glanced down at her legs; they needed a shave. Cinderella, no longer at the palace, had turned back into a peasant!

"Where to?" she asked sullenly, pushing the mirror away.

Rick started the truck. "Samuel Winston's."

"Who the hell is he?" she exclaimed, scrunching up her face unattractively.

Rick didn't bother answering.

"Oh, why can't you clean Tom Cruise's pool or Johnny Depp's or something?"

"I can take you home."

"No." She pouted.

The rumbled off and rode in silence. Then Rick said, somewhat defensively, as he turned off La Brea onto Santa Monica Boulevard, "He's a retired actor."

She perked up a little. "Really?"

"Lives in Beverly Hills."

She perked up a lot. "Oh!" she said.

They rode some more in silence.

"With his wife?" she asked.

Rick looked at her sideways, suspiciously. "No, with his cat," he said.

Kelli smiled and settled back further in the seat.

"Isn't that nice," she purred. "I just love cats!"

With her looks, with her brains, Kelli knew she deserved better in life.

The only child of a commercial airline pilot and an elementary school teacher, she had it pretty easy as a kid, at least until the divorce. At Hollywood High, her good looks enabled her to run with a fast crowd; but it was hard to keep up, what with all their cars and money. Most of her friends had gone on to college; Kelli's terrible grades ruled that out.

She almost wished she had studied harder in school and paid more attention . . .

But what the hell: girls just want to have fun.

"Slow down, Rick!" Kelli said as the truck turned onto Roxbury Drive. She leaned forward intently, peering through the windshield, studying each mansion, every manicured lawn, as they drove by. She would live in a neighborhood like this someday, she just knew it!

The truck pulled into a circular drive.

"Here?" she asked.

Rick nodded and turned off the engine. They got out.

The mansion before them was a sprawling, pink stucco affair, its front mostly obscured by a jungle of foliage and trees that apparently had been left unattended for years. The main entrance didn't look like anybody used it. Kelli frowned, disappointed.

And yet, she thought, this *was* a house in Beverly Hills.

"This way," Rick said, arms loaded with his pool-cleaning gear. Duffel bag slung over her shoulder, she followed him around the side to an iron-scrolled gate.

"Good," Rick said, swinging the gate open.

"What?"

"He remembered to leave it unlocked. I'd hate to have to holler for him till he came and let us in."

Kelli smiled at what lay stretched before her: an Olympic-size swimming pool with an elaborate stone waterfall, a huge Jacuzzi nearby, and expensive-looking patio furniture poolside. And all around nestled exotic plants and flowers and trees, transforming the area into a tropical paradise. But her smile faded when she noticed the old man slumped in one of the chairs, head bowed, snoring. He had on a white terry-cloth robe. By his sandal-covered feet lay a shaggy black cat.

"That's Mr. Winston?" Kelli whispered to Rick.

He nodded, with just a hint of a smile.

Kelli put her hands on her hips. "Why, he's older than the Hollywood Hills!"

"You just be quiet." Rick approached the old man. "Good afternoon, Mr. Winston," he said loudly.

With a snore the old man jolted awake. He focused on them, momentarily confused.

He was a very old man, Kelli thought—somewhere between sixty and a hundred. His head was bald and pink but for some wisps of white, his eyes narrow-set and an almost pretty blue; his nose was hawklike, his lips thin and delicate.

"I'm here to clean the pool," Rick said and set some of his gear down.

The old man cleared his throat and sat up straighter in his chair. "Needs it," he said.

Rick gestured to Kelli. "Mr. Winston, this is my friend, Kelli. Is it all right if she stays while I work?"

The old man looked at her. "Of course." He pointed with a thin, bony finger to a nearby chair. "Have a seat, my dear."

Kelli sat down, crossing her legs.

"Kel, Mr. Winston worked in show business with a lot of famous people," he explained, "like Jack Benny and Houdini and Abbott and Costello . . ."

"Don't forget Bergen and McCarthy!" the old man said, suddenly irritable. He leaned forward and spat. "Bergen, that fraud—who *couldn't* be a ventriloquist on the radio?"

There was an awkward silence, and Kelli gave Rick a puzzled look.

Then Rick said, "Yes, well . . . I'd better get to work . . ." He gathered his things and left them.

Kelli smiled at the old man. "I didn't know Candice Bergen was on the radio," she said.

The old man laughed. And the laugh turned into a cough and he hacked and wheezed.

"Forgive me, my dear," he said when he had caught his breath. "I was referring to Edgar Bergen—her *father*. We were billed together at the Palace."

"The *Palace!*" Kelli said, wide-eyed.

"Ah, you've heard of it?"

"Yes, indeed," she said. She leaned eagerly toward him. "What was the queen like?"

"Not *Buckingham* Palace," he laughed, and wheezed again. "The Palace Theater in New York. Vaudeville. You're so charming, my dear . . . are you an *actress*, by any chance?"

She leaned back in her chair. "I wish!" she said breathlessly.

"Well, don't," he replied gruffly. "They're a sad, sorry lot." He studied her a moment. "I'm afraid, my dear, you belong on the arm of some wealthy man, or stretched out by a luxurious pool."

"That's what I think!" she said brightly, then clouded. "But I don't have one."

"One what, child? A rich man or pool?"

"Either!"

He smiled, just slightly. He bent down and picked up the cat and settled the creature on his lap. "You're welcome to use my pool anytime, my dear," he said.

"You mean it?"

"Most certainly." He drew the cat's face up to his. "We'd love the company, wouldn't we?" he asked it.

"*Meow.*" Its tail swish, swished.

"How old is your cat?" Kelli asked.

Mr. Winston scratched the animal's ear. "Older than you, my dear," he said.

"You must love it."

"Like a child," he whispered, and kissed its head. "But of course, it's no substitute for the real thing."

"You never had any kids?"

"Never married, my dear. Show business is a harsh mistress."

"What was that word you used? Sounded like a town . . ."

"I don't follow you, child."

"Something-ville."

He smiled; his teeth were white and large and fake.

"Vaudeville! That was a form of theater, my dear. Something like the 'Ed Sullivan Show.'"

"What show?"

He smiled, shook his head. "You *are* a child. The Palace, which you inquired about, was only one of countless theaters in those days . . . the Colonial, the Hippodrome . . . but the Palace was the greatest vaudeville theater in America, if not the whole world!"

Kelli couldn't care less about any of this, but she wanted to seem interested. "What was vaudeville like, Mr. Winston?"

"One long, exciting roller-coaster ride . . . while it lasted. You see, vaudeville died in the late 1930s. A show would open with a minor act like acrobats or jugglers, because the audience was still finding their seats, you see. That's where I began, as an opening act . . . but not for long . . ."

He was lost in a smile of self-satisfaction.

"You were a big hit, huh, Mr. Winston?"

"Brought the house down, if you'll pardon my immodesty. Before long I was a top-billed act."

Gag me with a spoon, she thought. "That's so cool. What did you do in your act, Mr. Winston?"

He laughed and shook his head. "What *didn't* I do!" he said.

The old goat sure was full of himself.

"And that's how you got rich and famous, huh?"

His expression changed; it seemed sad, and something else. Bitter?

"I'm afraid I've not been as well remembered as some of my . . . lesser contemporaries have." His eyes hardened. "Sometimes when a person does *everything* well, he isn't remembered for anything."

"Oh, you shouldn't say that, Mr. Winston. Everybody remembers you!"

That melted the old boy. He leaned forward and patted her hand; his wrinkled flabby flesh gave her the creeps, but she just smiled at him.

"If only I could have had a child like you." He stroked the cat and it purred. "How much richer my life would've been."

"I'm lonely, too. My dad died before I was born."

"Oh . . . my dear. I'm so sorry. . . ."

He seemed genuinely touched by that b.s.

"Can I ask you a favor, Mr. Winston?"

"Anything, child."

"Could I come talk to you again, sometime? You know . . . when Rick comes to clean the pool."

His delicate lips were pressed into a smile; he stroked his cat. "I insist, my dear. I insist."

The sound of Rick clearing his throat announced that he had joined the little group; his body was glistening with sweat. He smiled at Mr. Winston, but his brow was furrowed.

"Almost done," he said.

Mr. Winston nodded and stood up, the animal in his arms; he scratched the cat's neck and it seemed to undulate, liking the attention. "Will you children excuse me? I'm going to put my little girl in the house where it's cooler."

"Certainly," Kelli smiled, watching him go into the house through the glass door off the patio.

"I know what you're up to," Rick snapped in her ear.

She didn't reply.

"He's old enough to be your *great*-grandfather. And if he's interested in anyone, it'd be *me!*"

"What do you mean?"

"What do you *think?*" he smirked. "He's been a bachelor since like forever. Besides, he's no fool—he'd see through you before long."

"And if he didn't, you'd tell him, I suppose?"

"I might. Be satisfied with what you've got."

"You, you mean? A poolboy?"

"I put up with your lying ass, don't I?"

She felt her face flush and tried to think of something to say to that, but before she could, the patio door slid open and the old man stepped out.

Rick and Kelli smiled.

As Mr. Winston approached, Kelli asked, "May I use your bathroom?"

"Certainly, my dear. It's just to the left off the kitchen."

Kelli grabbed her duffel bag and headed for the patio door.

"Don't be long, Kel," said Rick behind her. She could feel his eyes boring into her back.

Inside she hesitated only a moment. She was in a knotty-pine TV room; the knickknacks looked pretty worthless, and the only stuff of value was too big to fit in her bag. She moved on, like a shopper searching bargains out in a department store, moving down a narrow hallway to the kitchen. She stopped and turned back. She plucked a small oil painting of a tiger off the wall and started to drop it into her bag. But she changed her mind and put it back; she wasn't nuts about the frame.

In the kitchen she turned to the right which opened into a large, formal hallway. A wide staircase yawned upward, as she stood in the shadow of an elaborate crystal chandelier. To one side was a closed, heavy, dark wood door. She didn't have time to go upstairs and track down the old man's pants and go through the pockets, so she tried the door. It wasn't locked.

The room had stupid zebra-striped wallpaper like the rec room at her drunken uncle Bob's; but there were also a lot of plants, potted and hanging, only when she brushed against one, she discovered all of them were plastic, and dusty. *Yuucch*, she thought. A rich old guy like Winston ought to spring for a damn housekeeper.

There was a fireplace with a lion's head over it—unlike the plants, the lion seemed real, its fangs looking fierce. Big life-size dolls or statues or something of other animals were standing on little platforms against the walls, here and there: a monkey, a hyena, a coiled snake. *Ick!* The couch had a cover that looked like a leopard's skin, and the zebra walls were cluttered with photos of people who must have been famous, because they had signed their names on themselves—she recognized one as that old unfunny comedian Bob Hope. Others she didn't know: a spangly cowboy named Roy Rogers, a guy with buggy eyes named Eddie Cantor. In some of the pictures Mr. Winston wore a weird hat that looked like something out of a jungle movie.

"Koo-koo!"

The sound made her jump; she turned and saw, among the wall clutter, a cuckoo clock. The little bird sticking its head out said its name a few more times and went back inside.

She sighed with relief; but the relief was quickly replaced with panic. She'd been gone too long! She must find something of value, and soon.

She advanced to a desk almost as cluttered as the walls and switched on the green-shaded lamp and rifled through papers, letters mostly, and a stack of photos of Mr. Winston, younger and in the safari hat. Finding nothing that seemed worth anything, she looked around the room and then she saw it.

The cat!

Sleeping in a dark corner of the room, in a little wicker bed; dead to the world . . .

Quickly she went for it, duffel bag at the ready, hands outstretched.

"Nice kitty-kitty," she smiled. "You're coming with Kelli . . ."

"What the hell are you doing?"

A dark shape filled the doorway.

"Nothing!" she said, and the figure stepped into the light.

Rick.

"Don't scare me like that," Kelli said crossly.

"You have no business being in here . . . this is Mr. Winston's private collection . . . things from his career."

"Sorry," she said, almost defiantly. "Can I help it if I took a wrong turn?"

"And what were you going to do with that cat?"

"What cat?"

"Come with me—*now!*" Rick growled. "Mr. Winston's an important account, and you're not screwing this up for me!"

"Okay," she said. She glanced back at the cat, who hadn't stirred. How *easy* it would have been. . . .

On the way out she waved at Mr. Winston like a little girl and he smiled at her impishly and waved back the same way.

"Get in the truck," Rick ordered.

"Oh! I forgot something—my new sunglasses!"

"Hurry up, then."

She hadn't forgotten them, of course; she wanted to go back to make sure the gate was left unlatched.

Larry Hackett had been in California only two days, but already he wanted to go home. The vacation—his first in L.A.—was a major disappointment, from the scuzzy streets of Hollywood to the expensive dress shops of

Century City, where his wife, Millie, had insisted on going, though she certainly couldn't afford (let alone fit into) the youthful, glamorous clothes.

And their stay in Beverly Hills with his wife's aunt—a live-in housekeeper for some director off on location for the summer—was also a disappointment; not that Beverly Hills wasn't nice, but he felt like a hick putzing along in his Toyota, while Porsches and Jaguars honked and zoomed around him on the palm-lined streets.

He supposed he should just make the best of the trip; sit back and look at all the beautiful women—few of whom looked back, and when they did it was as if to say, "Are you kidding? Lose some weight!"

If truth be told, the thirty-five-year-old Larry was just plain homesick. He longed to be back in his office at the computer.

"Tell us, Aunt Katherine," said Millie, pouring some sugar into her coffee, "what famous people live nearby?" The three were seated in the spacious, sunny kitchen, at a round oak table, having a late-morning cup.

"Well, let's see," Millie's aunt said. She was a big woman with a stern face offset by gentle eyes. "Rosemary Clooney has a house just down the street. And Jimmy Stewart."

Millie clasped her hands together. "How thrilling!" she said. "I'd love to meet them."

"We don't intrude on our famous neighbors out here, dear," Aunt Katherine said patiently. "Besides, I'm just hired help, remember."

Millie frowned like a child denied a cookie.

Larry sipped his coffee.

"Well, who's next door in the Deco place?" Millie persisted.

"An Arab sheik."

"No kidding!" Millie exclaimed. "I'll bet some wild parties go on over there, don't you, Larry?" She elbowed her husband, trying to draw him into the conversation.

He smiled politely.

"Actually," Aunt Katherine replied, "the sheik is very reserved."

"And who lives on the other side of you, in the pink stucco house?" Millie persisted in her questioning.

Larry rolled his eyes.

"Oh, you probably wouldn't know him," her aunt said. "His name is Samuel Winston."

Now Millie smiled politely, but Larry sat up straight in his chair. "Who did you say?" he asked.

"Samuel Winston," Aunt Katherine repeated.

Larry, eyes wide, turned to his wife. "Do you know who that *is*?" he asked excitedly.

Millie shook her head.

"*You* know! From when we were kids!"

She looked at him blankly.

"Safari Sam!"

Millie continued her vacant stare.

Larry sighed in irritation. "Didn't you ever watch the 'Safari Sam and Pooky Show'?"

"Ohhh . . ." Millie said slowly, nodding her head, ". . . now I remember. I didn't like that show. I could never tell which animals were real and which weren't. And that Pooky scared me."

"Why would a puppet scare you?"

"It wasn't a puppet, it was a *real* cat!"

Larry leaned toward her. "How can a *real* cat play the violin?" he asked, then added dramatically, "remember its eyes? You can always tell by the eyes."

Millie glared at him—she didn't like to be corrected—then asked innocently, "Didn't Safari Sam get his show cancelled because of cruelty to animals?"

Larry's face flushed. "That was just a vicious rumor!" he said. "Safari Sam loved those animals!"

"I know," Millie laughed. "Maybe he *tortured* that cat until it played the violin!"

"Very funny . . ."

"After all," she said, continuing her verbal assault, "I heard he cut out that cat's voice box so he could pretend to talk for it!"

"He did not!" Larry shouted.

"Did too!" Millie shouted.

Aunt Katherine stood up from the table. "Larry! Millie!" she said. "Children, *please!*"

They stopped their bickering.

"Aunt Katherine," Larry said, "could you please introduce me to Mr. Winston? I'm his biggest fan."

"Well . . ."

"I know all about him . . . his career as a comedian, a magician, a ventriloquist . . ." Larry paused and stared out the window at the pink stucco house. ". . . Samuel Winston was a genius, a great man! He just never got his due. . . ."

Aunt Katherine smiled, but raised a lecturing finger. "Samuel Winston *is* a great man. He deserves respect—*and* to be allowed his privacy."

Reluctantly, Larry nodded. Millie looked sheepish.

Then Larry said, "You're right, Aunt Katherine. I'm sorry I asked."

But Larry knew he'd be asking again; they were staying all week, and he had time to work on her.

The gate creaked as Kelli swung it open; behind her Rick was shaking. The big chicken.

"I can't believe I let you talk me into this," he whispered.

It *had* taken some doing, particularly after he'd bawled her out about it in the truck when they left Winston's earlier that day.

"Jeez, Kel," he had said, the breeze riffling his hair, "if you want a goddamn cat, I'll buy you a goddamn cat!"

"But I want *that* cat!"

"Why?" he said, exasperated. "It's old, it's mangy . . ."

"It's worth a lot of money," she cut in.

She had explained on the waterbed in their tiny apartment off Melrose. He'd stared at her, shook his head. "You want to *kidnap* that cat and hold it for ransom?"

"I wouldn't do that!" she exclaimed, offended, covering her breasts modestly with the sheet.

"Then what? I can't wait to hear."

"I want to kidnap the cat and collect a *reward*."

"Oh, well," Rick jeered, "well, that's different. A reward as in somehow the cat got out and we found it and took it home, then saw the ad in the paper?"

"Exactly."

He had looked at her dazed, as if struck by a stick; but then his eyes had tightened.

"The old man *is* worth a lot of money . . . and it's just a cat."

"Just a cat," she said, stroking him, "just a silly old cat."

The full moon reflected on the shimmering surface of the pool; it was the only light on the patio. The lights in the big pink house were off.

"You got that screwdriver?" she whispered.

Rick, dressed all in black as she was, swallowed and nodded.

But they didn't have to pry the patio door open; it, too, was unlocked. They moved through the house slowly, quietly, and the sound of their footsteps was something even they couldn't detect, let alone some deaf old man.

Soon they stood in the safari room; Kelli turned on the green-shaded desk lamp. The mounted lion's head and the animal shapes and the plastic plants threw distorted shadows.

"It's in the corner," Kelli said.

"You get it. You wanted it."

"It might *scratch* me!"

"It might scratch *me*!"

"Children, don't fight," said Samuel Winston, his voice kindly; but an elephant gun in his hands was pointed right at them. He had plucked it from the gun rack just inside the door.

Kelli jumped behind Rick, who put both hands out in a "stop" motion. "Whoa, Mr. Winston," he said, "don't do anything rash . . ."

The old man moved closer. "Aren't you children the ones behaving rashly? Trying to steal my little girl away from me? If you needed money, all you had to do was ask!"

"Please, Mr. Winston," Rick pleaded. "Don't call the cops. We were going to break in . . ."

"Very wrong, Rick. I'm disappointed. I thought you were a nice young man . . . and you, Kelli. How very sad."

Kelli didn't know what to say; she'd only been caught stealing twice in her life, and both times she'd wormed her way out—once by crying, and once with sex. Neither seemed applicable here.

"Rick can give you free pool service for a year!" she blurted. "Please don't call the police, Mr. Winston!"

"I have no intention of calling the police," the old man said.

Rick backed up with Kelli clinging to him. Seconds seemed like minutes.

Then the old man lowered the gun. "Don't worry," he said, almost wearily. "I'm not going to shoot you, either."

Rick sighed; Kelli relaxed her grip on him.

The old man turned away from them and put the gun back in its rack. "I know what it's like to live in a town where everyone else seems to have everything."

He faced them.

"The only thing worse is to finally *have* everything, and no one to share it with."

Something in the old man's voice told Kelli she was out of danger; smiling a little, she stepped out from behind Rick.

"That is sad, Mr. Winston. I wish we could make this up to you somehow . . ."

His pretty blue eyes brightened. "Perhaps you could! How would you like to live here and share in my wealth? To be my son and daughter?"

Rick was stunned. Kelli's smile froze.

"What's the matter?" the old man chuckled. "Cat got your tongue?"

Rick stuttered, "Well, I . . . we . . ."

But Kelli rushed forward, arms outstretched.

"Daddy!" she cried.

"Koo-koo! Koo-koo!" went the clock, high on the cluttered wall.

"Ah, two o'clock," the old man said. "Shall we discuss this further over a hot cup of cocoa? Perhaps you could heat some milk for Pooky, my dear."

"Pooky?" Kelli asked.

"That's my little girl's name. My cat you were so interested in. . . ."

And with Kelli on his arm, Winston walked out of the den, patting the girl's hand soothingly, a bewildered Rick trailing behind. Kelli glanced over her shoulder and grinned at him like the cat that ate the canary.

* * *

The warm California breeze played with Kelli's long blonde hair, which shimmered in the brilliant sun like threads of finely spun gold. Stretched out in a lounge chair by the pool, she looked like a goddess in her white bathing suit and Ray-Ban sunglasses. Next to her on a wrought-iron table lay fruit, caviar and champagne. Her pouty-pink lips were fixed in a smug, satisfied smile. She was in heaven.

"More champagne, my dear?" asked Samuel Winston, who stood next to her in a terry-cloth robe worn loosely over swimming trunks.

"Yes, please!"

He filled the empty goblet she held in one hand.

"Another beer, Rick?" Samuel called out.

Rick, in a purple polo shirt, white Bermuda shorts and wrap-around sunglasses, sat a few yards away, beneath the umbrella, a can of Bud Lite by his feet.

"No thanks, Sam . . . haven't finished this one."

Samuel returned to his chair, next to Kelli. He looked at her, studying her, and frowned. "You'd better put on more sunscreen, my dear," he advised.

"Am I red?"

Samuel nodded.

"Well, I don't feel it . . . Rick! Do I look red?"

"Not that I can see."

Samuel stood up. "Let me get your back for you," he said.

"Would you? I can't do it myself."

Samuel took the tube of sunscreen off her towel and squeezed some out on his hands. He spread it gently on her back. "Does that hurt?" he asked.

"Not a bit."

When Samuel had finished, he wiped his hands on the towel, then he went over to the cat, which lay on the patio in the shade of the umbrella, and picked it up. He went back to his chair, sat and stroked the animal's fur.

"Are you happy?" he asked it.

"*Meow*." Its tail swish, swished.

"Me, too, Pooky," Samuel said. He peered skyward. "Such a beautiful day. Don't you think?"

"I'll say!" the cat said.

"Oh, *yoo-hoo!*" came a grating voice from the gate.

Samuel looked sharply toward it. "Hell and damnation!" he said. "It's that woman next door. That housekeeper. And who's that with her?" He squinted to make out the forms. "Tweedledee and Tweedledum. Don't worry, my pets, I'll get rid of them."

He waved one hand half-heartedly.

The trio pushed through the gate, the housekeeper marching in the lead, the man and woman trailing timidly behind.

Samuel groaned behind his grin. He put down the cat and stood to greet them.

"Ah, madam," he said, "it's so nice to see you."

"I hope we're not interrupting anything," the housekeeper said with a silly little laugh.

"Not at all."

"I don't make a habit out of intruding . . ."

"Think nothing of it."

"But I'd like to introduce you to my niece Millie, and nephew Larry— Larry is your biggest fan."

Samuel smiled politely at the two. "It's a pleasure to meet you," he said.

The niece had a blank expression, but the nephew looked like an eager puppy-dog, beads of sweat forming on his brow. The boy rushed forward and grabbed one of Samuel's hands, pumping it vigorously.

"Mr. Winston," he gushed, "you don't know how much the 'Safari Sam and Pooky Show' meant to a little kid with asthma in Akron, Ohio!"

Now Samuel smiled genuinely. "Why, thank you," he said. "That's very gratifying."

Suddenly Larry clutched his heart, mouth gasping, eyes bugging.

"Is anything wrong?" Samuel asked, alarmed.

"*Pooky!*" Larry cried, pointing a wavering finger at the cat that lay a few yards away on the ground. "It's Pooky!"

The pudgy boy-man ran to it, and fell on his knees, palms outspread as if worshiping.

Reverently, he looked up at Samuel. "May I?" he asked.

Samuel nodded.

Gingerly, tenderly, Larry picked up the cat. It lay limp in his hands. "It's so well preserved," he said in awe.

"I did it myself."

"Really!"

"Taxidermy has long been an avocation of mine. Have you ever been out to the Roy Rogers Museum?"

"You didn't do . . . *Trigger!*" Larry gasped.

Samuel merely smiled.

Larry seemed spellbound by Pooky. "There's a place for your hand . . . he's real *and* a puppet! So that's your secret!"

"One of them."

Larry gave his wife a withering look. "I told you he was a genius!"

The plump little wife, however, only looked sickened.

Larry handed the cat back to Samuel. "Could you have Pooky sing the 'Pooky Song'?" he asked.

"I'd rather not," the old man answered.

"Oh, please!" Larry pleaded, his chubby hands pressed together, prayer-like.

Samuel sighed. "Well, all right," he said, but irritated.

"And do the Pooky dance . . . ?"

Samuel glared, then nodded, grudgingly.

". . . while you drink a glass of water?"

"I don't *have* a glass of water!"

"I could get you one," Larry offered.

"No!" Samuel snapped. "Never mind. Just hand me that champagne."

Samuel stuck his hand inside the cat, slung the bottle to his lips and drank it, while Pooky, his legs and tail flapping in the crazy jig, sang in a high-pitched voice.

"I'm Pooky, a little kooky, it's kind of spooky . . ."

Larry, with joy on his face and tears in his eyes, applauded wildly. So did the housekeeper. But the niece stood frozen, horrified.

"That was just like the show!" Larry exclaimed.

"Thank you," Samuel said tersely. "Now, if you don't mind, you must go . . . I need my rest."

The housekeeper stepped toward him. "We were just wondering," she said, "if you could join us for lunch."

"I've just had brunch, thank you."

"Well, what about your guests?" the housekeeper pressed.

"My guests?" Samuel asked, annoyed, frowning. He turned and looked at the lounging Kelli and Rick nearby; the two had their backs to Samuel's unwanted company.

"Oh, I've been rude," Samuel said. "I didn't introduce my son and daughter . . . they're on an extended visit . . ."

"We'd love to have all three of you for lunch," the stupid woman persisted.

"Well, I'll have to decline," he said, then added with a wicked little smile, "but of course, I shouldn't speak for Kelli and Rick . . ."

"Oh, I'm not hungry," Rick said.

Though the trio of intruders didn't notice, the lips of Samuel's children didn't move when they spoke, nor did Samuel's—for he was no radio ventriloquist.

"Me neither," Kelli said. "We couldn't possibly eat. We're just stuffed!"

Joan Hess, author of the popular and accomplished Maggody books, has won the Agatha and the Macavity, and will no doubt win more awards before she's done. The following devious tale, from *Malice Domestic*, is full of murder and investigation regarding the identity of the killer or killers.

The Last to Know
JOAN HESS

"Bambi's father was murdered last night," Caron announced as she sailed through the door of the Book Depot, tossed her bulky backpack on the counter, and continued toward my office, no doubt in hopes I had squirreled away a diet soda for what passed for high tea these days, in that scones were out of the question, and clotted cream merely a fantasy.

"Wait a minute," I said to her back. Although her birth certificate claimed we had an irrevocable biological tie, I'd wondered on more than one occasion if the gypsies hadn't pulled a fast one in the nursery. We both had red hair, freckles, green eyes, and a certain determination—in my case, mild and thoughtful; in hers, more like that of a bronco displeased with the unfamiliar and unwelcome weight of a cowboy with spurs.

She stopped and looked back, her nostrils flaring. "I am about to Die of Thirst, Mother. We have a substitute in gym class, and she's nothing but a petty tyrant, totally oblivious to pains and suffering. We had to play volleyball all period without so much as—"

"What did you say about Bambi's father? Was it some sort of obscure Disneyesque reference? Thumper developed rabies? Flower found an assault weapon amidst the buttercups?"

"I am drenched in sweat."

I told her where I'd hidden the soda, then sat on the stool behind the counter and gloomily gazed at the paperwork necessary to return several boxes of unsold books. The sales departments of publishing houses are more adept than the IRS at concocting a miasmatic labyrinth of figures, columns, and sly demands that can delay the process for months, if not years.

Caron returned with my soda and the insufferable smugness of a fifteen-year-old who knows she can seize center stage, if only for a few minutes. The reality that the center stage was in a dusty old bookstore patronized only by the few quasi-literates in Farberville did not deter her. "Not Bambi the geeky deer," she said with a pitying smile for her witless mother. "Bambi McQueen, the senior who's editor of the school newspaper. Don't you remember her from when you substituted in the journalism department?"

It was not the moment to admit all high school students had a remarkably uninteresting sameness, from their clothes to their sulky expressions. "I think so," I said mendaciously. "What happened to her father?"

"It's so melodramatic." Caron paused to pop the top of the can, still relishing her ephemeral power. "It seems he was having an affair with Bambi's mother's best friend. The friend showed up at their house, tanked to the gills and screaming at him for dumping her, then said she was going to go home and kill herself." She paused again to slurp the soda and assess how much longer she could drag out the story. "Pretty dumb, if you ask me. I met him when Bambi had a Christmas party for the staff, and I was not impressed. He's okay-looking, but he's got—had—this prissy little mouth, and he was forever peering at us over the top of his glasses like we were nothing but a bunch of botched lobotomies swilling his expensive eggnog."

"What happened after the friend said she was going to kill herself?" I persisted.

"This is where it gets Utterly Gruesome. Mr. McQueen was really alarmed and followed her outside. She got in her car, but instead of leaving, she ran over him in the driveway and smashed him into the family station wagon like a bug on the windshield. She claimed her foot slipped, but the police aren't so sure." Caron dropped the empty can on the counter and made a grab for her backpack.

I caught her wrist. "That's a tragic story. Where'd you learn the details?"

"It's all over school. Bambi wasn't there today, naturally, but she called Emily at midnight, and Emily told practically everybody in the entire school. Emily's mouth should be in the Smithsonian—in a display case of its own." She removed my hand. "I have tons of homework, Mother. Unless you want me to like flunk out and do menial housework for the rest of my life, you'd better let me go to the library and look up stuff about boring dead presidents."

"I find it difficult to imagine your success as a cleaning woman, considering the sorry state of your closet and the collection of dirty dishes under your bed. By all means, run along to the library and do your homework. Afterwards, you may explore this new career option by cleaning up your room." Her snort was predictable, but I realized there was something that was not. "Where's Inez? Is she sick today?"

"I really couldn't say," Caron said coldly as she headed for the door. "I don't keep track of treacherous bitches."

I was blinking as the bell above the door jangled and the rigid silhouette of my daughter passed in front of the window. Inez Thornton was Caron's shadow, in every sense of the word. Not only did she trail after Caron like an indentured handservant, she did so in a drab, almost inanimate fashion that served as a perfect counterpart to Caron's general air of impending hysteria. Inez was burdened with the lingering softness of baby fat, thick-lensed glasses that gave her an owlish look, and a voice that rarely rose above a whisper, much less rattled the china. On days when Caron was a definitive raging blizzard, Inez was but a foggy spring morning.

And also, from this parting pronouncement, a treacherous bitch. "This, too, will pass," I murmured to myself as I bent down over the devil's own paperwork, determined to banish images of a splattered windshield until I could devise a way to convince a heartless sales department to restore my credit, however fleetingly.

That evening when I arrived in the upstairs duplex across from the lawn of Farber College, Caron's room was uninhabited by any life form more complex than the fuzzy blue mold on the plates under her bed. At the rate they were accumulating, full service for twelve would be available on her wedding day, saving her the tedium of bridal registration.

I closed the door, made myself a drink, and sank down on the sofa to peruse the local newspaper for the article concerning Bambi's father. On the second page I found a few paragraphs, thick with "allegedly" and "purportedly," that related how Charlene "Charlie" Kirkpatrick, longtime friend of Michelle McQueen, had contributed to the untimely demise of Ethan McQueen. Ms. Kirkpatrick would be arraigned as soon as she was released from the detoxification ward of the hospital, and Ms. McQueen was refusing to be interviewed. Mr. McQueen was survived by his wife and daughter of the home, his mother in a nearby town, and a sister in California. The funeral would be held Monday at two o'clock in the yuppiest Episcopal church, followed by a graveside service at the old cemetery only a few blocks from the Book Depot.

I put down the newspaper and tried to envision Bambi. It was too much like seeking to pinpoint one buffalo in a stampeding herd, which was how I'd described the denizens of the hallways of Farberville High School when I'd been coerced into substituting for doddery Miss Parchester, who'd been accused of embezzlement and murder.

I gave up on Bambi's face and turned on the six-o'clock news. The death, accidental or intention, was the lead story, of course, since Farberville was generally a dull place, its criminal activity limited to brawls among the students, armed robberies at the convenience stores, and mundane burglaries. Although the story struck me as nothing more lurid than domestic violence of the worst sort, the anchorman had a jolly time droning on while we were treated to footage of a bloodstained driveway and the battered hood of a station wagon.

Footsteps pounded up the stairs, interspersed with strident voices and bitterly sardonic laughter. Odds were good that it wasn't Peter Rosen, the police lieutenant with whom I'd become embroiled after a distasteful investigation involving the murder of a local romance writer. He was unnervingly handsome, in a hawkish way, and invariably maddening when he scolded me for my brilliant insights into subsequent cases. We were both consenting adults, and indeed consented in ways that left me idly considering the possibility of a permanent liaison. Dawn would break, however, and so would my resolve to give up my reservations about marriage, about dividing the closet, about facing him at breakfast every morning, about assigning him a pillow, and about relinquishing my life as a competent, marginally self-supporting single woman.

Caron stomped into my reverie, her eyes flashing and her mouth curled into a smirk. On her heels was a girl who was briskly introduced as Melissa-from-biology, who bobbled her head indifferently and allowed herself to be led to Caron's room.

"Can you believe Inez is actually spending the night at Rhonda's tomorrow?" Caron said, slathering the sentence with condemnation. "I suspected all along that she was using me so she could cozy up with the cheerleaders. I felt sorry for her because she's so nerdy, but that doesn't like give her the right to—"

Caron's bedroom door closed on whatever right Inez had dared to exercise.

Hoping that Melissa-from-biology was up on her tetanus shots, I made myself another drink, watched the rest of the news and the weather report, and was settled in with a mystery novel when I heard more decorous steps outside the door. I admitted Peter, who greeted me with great style and asked with the quivery optimism of Oliver Twist for a beer. His face was stubbly, and there were darkish crescents under his molasses brown eyes. His usually impeccable three-piece suit was wrinkled, and a coffee stain marred the silk tie I'd given him for his birthday.

Once I'd complied with a beer, I curled up next to him and said, "You look like hell, darling. Were you up all night with this tragedy in the McQueen driveway?"

He glowered briefly at the newspaper I'd inadvertently left folded to the pertinent page. "All night, and most of today," he admitted with a sigh. "Not that we're dealing with something bizarre enough to warrant a true crime novel and a three-part miniseries. The victim's midlife crisis resulted in his death, the destruction of the lives of two women who have been best friends since college, and who knows what kind of psychological problems in the future for the daughter. Married men really shouldn't have affairs." One hand slid around my waist, and the other in a more intimate direction as he nuzzled my neck. "Neither should single men. They should get married and settle down in domestic tranquillity with someone who's undeniably attractive, well-educated, intelligent, meddlesome, and incredibly delightful and innovative in bed."

I removed my neck from his nuzzle. "If you tell me about the case, I'll heat up last night's pizza."

"Are you bribing a police officer?"

"I think there are at least three slices, presuming Caron didn't detour through the kitchen on her way to the library," I countered with said child's smugness, aware that the way to a cop's investigation was through his stomach.

He fell for it, and once I'd carried out my half of the bargain, he gulped down a piece with an apologetic look, wiped tomato sauce off his chin, and said, "Charlie Kirkpatrick and Michelle McQueen met in college, where they were roommates for four years. Both eventually married. Michelle stayed here, and Charlie lived in various other places for the next fifteen or so years. They kept in touch with calls and letters, however, and when Charlie divorced her husband five years ago, she moved back here and bought a house around the corner from the McQueens. Her son's away at college, and her daughter's married and lives in Chicago."

"And?" I said encouragingly.

"She and Michelle resumed their friendship—to the point that Ethan McQueen began to object, according to the daughter. Charlie worked at a travel agency, and was always inviting Michelle to come with her on inexpensive or even free trips. They went to the movies, had lunch several times a week, played golf on Wednesday mornings, and worked on the same charity fund-raisers. Charlie ate dinner with them often, and brunch every Sunday."

"What was the husband like? Caron met him and dismissed him as prissy-mouthed judge, but she's of an age that anyone who doesn't fawn all over her is obviously demented."

"He was a moderately successful lawyer," Peter said. "He was past president of the county bar, involved in local politics, possibly in line for a judgeship in a few years. He played poker with the guys, drove a damned expensive sports car, patted his secretary on the fanny, seduced female clients, all that sort of lawyer thing."

"Including having an affair with his wife's best friend? Have I been underestimating the profession?"

"Michelle says she began to suspect as much about six months ago. She couldn't bring herself to openly confront either of them, although she did break off her relationship with Charlie. Said she couldn't bear to pretend to chatter over lunch when she was envisioning the two of them in a seedy motel room. Last night her suspicions were confirmed."

"What will happen to Charlie?"

"She'll be arraigned in the morning. The prosecuting attorney's talking second-degree murder at the moment, maybe thinking he can get a jury to go for manslaughter. There's no question that Charlie Kirkpatrick was in a state of extreme emotional disturbance; the wife was able to give us a detailed picture of what happened."

Peter put down his plate and tried a diversionary tactic involving my earlobe, but I made it clear I wasn't yet ready for such nonsense. Retrieving his plate, he added, "If the wife repeats her story on the witness stand, the prosecutor knows damn well he'll lose. We already know Charlie had more than enough alcohol in her blood to stop a much larger man in his tracks, and she was incoherent. We're subpoenaing records from her psychiatrist. What's likely to happen is that Charlie will plead guilty to negligent homicide, a class A misdemeanor. She'll receive a fine and no more than a year in the county jail, and be out within three months. If her lawyer's really sharp, she may end up with nothing more annoying than a suspended sentence and a couple of hundred hours of community service."

"Not exactly hard labor in the state's gulag," I said, shaking my head. "If she and Michelle were so close for twenty years, why would she have an affair with her best friend's husband? Unless she's completely devoid of morals, it seems like he'd be her last choice."

"The ways of lust are as mysterious as that charming little freckle just below your left ear," he said. In that I'd gotten as much as I could from him, I allowed him to investigate at his leisure.

Nothing of interest happened over the weekend. Caron continued to hang around with Melissa-from-biology, carping and complaining about Inez's defection to the enemy camp. The general of that camp was Rhonda Maguire, who'd committed the unspeakable sin of snagging Louis Wilderberry, junior varsity quarterback and obviously so bewildered by Rhonda's slutty advances that he was unable to appreciate Caron's more delicate charm and vastly superior intellect.

The extent of Inez's treachery spread like an oil slick on what previously had been a pristine bay: spending Friday night with Rhonda, shopping at the mall the following day, being the first to hear the details of Rhonda's Saturday night date, and actually having the nerve to tell Emily that she felt sorry for Caron for being a moonstruck cow over Louis.

As for the tragedy at the McQueen house, less and less was found worthy to be aired on the evening news or reported in the newspaper. The station wagon was impounded and the driveway hosed down. The arraignment was delayed until Monday, while the doctors monitored Charlie Kirkpatrick's condition, and the prosecuting attorney pondered his alternative. Michelle Mc-Queen and her daughter remained inside the house, admitting only family members and a casserole-bearing group of Episcopalian women.

Sunday afternoon I called my best friend, Luanne Bradshaw, and we talked for a long time about the McQueen case. Our relationship lacked a parallel, in that I was widowed and she divorced; but we did agree that it was perplexing to imagine being so enamored of a mere man that one was willing to throw away a perfectly decent friendship.

Monday morning took an ugly turn. Caron stomped into the kitchen, jerked open the refrigerator to glare at an innocent pitcher of orange juice, and said, "I want to go to the funeral this afternoon. You'll have to check me out at noon so I can come home and change for it."

"Why do you want to go to the funeral? Bambi's hardly a close friend of yours, and it didn't sound as if you were fond of her father."

"Bambi is the editor of the school paper, Mother. Everybody else on the staff will be there. Do you want me to be the only one who Can't Bother to be there for Bambi?"

"Does this have anything to do with gym class?"

She slammed the refrigerator door. "I am trying to show some compassion, for pity's sake! After all, I do happen to know what it feels like when your father's accused of having an affair and then dies. Everyone gossips about it. Poor Bambi's going to have to come back to school and pretend she doesn't hear it, but she'll know when all of a sudden people clam up when she joins them, and she'll know they're staring at her when she walked down the hall."

It was a cheap shot, but a piercing one, and I acknowledged as much by arranging to meet her in the high school office at noon. I was by no means convinced the tyrannical gym teacher was not the primary motive for this untypical display of compassion and empathy, but it wouldn't hurt Caron to suffer through a funeral service in lieu of fifty relentless minutes of volleyball.

Peter called me at the Book Depot later in the morning to ask if I might be interested in a movie that evening. After I'd forced him to tell me that Charlie Kirkpatrick had been arraigned on charges of second-degree murder and then released on her own recognizance, I granted that I might enjoy a movie, and we settled on a time. I may not have mentioned that Caron and I were planning to go to Ethan McQueen's funeral, but it was nothing more than a minor omission, an excusable lapse of memory on the part of a nearly forty-year-old mind. I was attending it only because Caron was not yet old enough drive, and I was unwilling to sit in the car outside the church, I assured myself. And perhaps I was just a bit curious to see the woman whose best friend had killed her husband. Prurient, but true, and a helluva lot more interesting than the stack of muddled invoices and overdue bills on the counter.

Nevertheless, I righteously waded through them until it was time to fetch Caron and go by the apartment to change into our funeral attire. After a spirited debate about which of us was to drive, the individual with the learner's permit flounced around to the passenger's side and flung herself into the seat with all the attractiveness of a thwarted toddler.

"Are things any better between you and Inez?" I asked as I hunted for a parking place in the lot behind the church. There were so many shiny new Mercedes and Beamers that it resembled a dealer's lot, but my crotchety old hatchback slid nicely into a niche by the dumpster.

"Hardly," Caron said, her voice as tight as my panty hose. "If she wants to spend all her time with Rhonda Maguire, I really don't see that it concerns me. Melissa may be dim, but at least she's loyal."

"Would it help if I spoke to her?"

"That'd be swell, Mother. She'll tell Rhonda and her catty friends, and I'll Absolutely Die. There's no way I could show my face at school ever again, and you can't afford one of those snooty, genderless boarding schools for the socially inept."

On that note, we went into the church and found seats for the requiem mass for Ethan McQueen, who was, according to the obituary within a pamphlet, a beloved son, brother, father, and husband. The church was crowded, and the only view I had of the grieving widow was that of soft brown hair and a taut neck. There were a lot of high school students present, and I caught myself wondering how many of them had gym class in the afternoon. It was not a charitable thought, but the mass was impersonal and interminable, and my curiosity unrequited.

"I can't wait to get out of these shoes," I said as Caron and I started for my car.

Her lower lip shot out. "We have to go to the cemetery. Everybody else is going, including the creepy little freshmen with acne for brains, and I don't want to be the only person on the entire staff of the *Falcon Crier* who's so mean-spirited that—"

I cut her off with an admission of defeat. We waited until the hearse and limousines were ready, and joined in the turtlish procession along Thurber Street to the cemetery. Parking was more difficult, and we ended up nearly two blocks from the canvas roof shielding the family from the incongruously bright sunshine.

"Over there," Caron muttered as she nudged me along like a petulent Bo Peep.

I looked at the family seated in chairs alongside the grave. Bambi was familiar; I had an indistinct memory of a simpery voice and well-developed deviousness. Her mother was rather ordinary, with an attractive face and an aura of composure despite an occasional dab with a tissue or a whispered word to Bambi and the white-haired matron on her other side.

We took our position at the back of a crowd of students, most of them shuffling nervously, the boys uncomfortable in suits and ties, the girls covertly appraising one another's dresses and jewelry. I was trying to peer over them to determine when the show would start when a hand tapped my shoulder.

"Hi, Mrs. Malloy," Inez whispered.

"Inez, how nice to see you," I said, then waited to see how Caron would react. She did not so much as quiver.

"This is Emily Cartigan," Inez continued with her typical timidity, blinking as if anticipating a slap. Emily nodded at me, arched her eyebrows at Caron's steely back, and drew Inez toward the perfidious Rhonda Maguire and a neckless boy wearing a letter jacket over his white shirt and dark tie.

I stole a peek at Caron, fully prepared to see steam coming from not only her ears, but also her nostrils and whatever other orifices were available. To my surprise, she had a vaguely triumphant smile as she gazed steadily at the dandruff-dotted shoulders of the boy in front of us.

The graveside service was brief, its major virtue. Very few people seemed inclined to approach the family, and those who did spoke only a word or two before fleeing. I could not imagine myself murmuring how sorry I was that the deceased had been killed by his mistress, and suggested to Caron that we forgo the ritual and go home to change clothes.

"I'll be there later," she said with a guileless look. "I want to stop by my father's grave for a few minutes and see how the plastic flowers are holding up."

"You do?" I had to take a breath to steady myself. "That's a lovely idea, dear. Would you like me to go with you, or wait in the car?"

"No, it may take a long time. I'll be home later, and then I've got to go to Melissa's house so we can work on this really mindless algebra assignment."

She took off on a gravel path that wound among the solitary stones and cozy family plots enclosed by low fences, her walk rather bouncy for someone on what some of us felt was a depressing mission. As she reached a bend, she looked over her shoulder, although not at me, and disappeared behind a row of trees.

Car doors slammed as the mourners began to depart. Bambi sat talking to her mother, who shook her head vehemently. After a moment, Bambi shrugged and stood up, and escorted her grandmother to the baby blue limousine. The preacher handed Michelle a Bible, held her hand for a moment, and walked toward his car with the obligatory introverted expression of the professionally bereaved. Michelle remained in the chair, her hands folded in her lap and her head lowered.

I walked toward my car, wishing I'd tucked more sensible shoes in my purse in anticipation of the distance. The gravel was not conducive to steady progress in even moderately sensible low heels, and I was lamenting the emergence of at least one blister when I saw a figure partially shielded by an unkempt hedge. Despite her sunglasses and a scarf, I recognized her from an earlier newscast when she'd been transferred from the hospital to the county jail. I had no doubt I could confirm the identification when the evening news covered her arraignment in a few hours.

It was curious, but so was my accountant when I tried to report financial quarterly estimates. I reopened the Book Depot, sold a paperback to my pet science fiction weirdo, and tried to reimmerse myself in paperwork, but I was distracted as much by the idea of Caron visiting her father's grave as I was by the image of Charlie Kirkpatrick observing the graveside service from behind the hedge. I finally pushed aside the ledger, propped my elbows on the counter, and, cradling my face in the classic pose of despondency, thought long and hard about the nature of friendship . . . not only between Michelle and Charlie, but also between Caron and Inez.

A theory began to emerge, and I called Luanne. "Would you have had an affair with Carlton?" I asked abruptly, bypassing pleasantries when thinking of my former husband.

"Not on a bet. From what you've said about him, he was a pompous pseudointellectual with an anal-retentive attitude about everything from meat loaf to movies."

"Did I say all that?"

"I am astute."

"I am impressed with your astutity—if that's a word."

"Not in my dictionary. If that's all, I just received a consignment from Dallas, some really nifty beaded dresses. I need to inventory the lot."

I rubbed my face. "Hold on a minute, Luanne. What if Carlton had been more like . . . say, Robert Redford. Would you have had an affair in spite of our friendship?"

"And when he dumped me, drive to your house and run him down in the driveway? Is that your point?" I made a noise indicating that it was, and after a moment of thought, she said, "No, but I'd be seriously tempted. You know how I feel about blue eyes and shaggy blond hair."

"Even sprinkled with gray?"

"I assume you're making rude remarks about his hair, but I wouldn't mind if his eyes were sprinkled with gray. I must count beads. Talk to you later."

I replaced the receiver and resumed staring blankly at the cracked plaster above the self-help rack. Luanne had answered honestly. She wouldn't have betrayed me, although the leap from Carlton to Robert required the imagination of a flimflam artist and the thighs of an aerobics instructor. Ethan to Robert was equally challenging.

Some women would, and had done so since the monosyllabic hunter had run into his distaff chum posing coyly in a scanty mastodon stole. But those weren't the women who had deep and long-lasting friendships with other women. They lacked the essential mechanism to bond, and most of us had learned to spot them quickly and clutch our men's arms possessively when they approached to poach.

I hung the fly-splattered Closed sign on the door, locked up, and let myself out the back door. I then unlocked the door and went inside to find the McQueens' address in the telephone directory. I was still clad in funerary finery, and I hoped I would be inconspicuous in the crowd of lawyers, their spouses, and whoever else was there.

Nobody was there. There was not one blessed car parked out front, not one mourner visible in the living room window, with a cocktail in hand and misty stories about good ol' Ethan. Wishing Luanne were beside me to dissuade me, I forced myself to go onto the porch and ring the doorbell.

Bambi opened the door and gave me a puzzled look through red, puffy eyes. "You're Caron Malloy's mother, right? You subbed for Miss Parchester for a few days when she was trying to poison everybody in the teacher's lounge."

"Something like that," I murmured. "I came by to offer you and your mother my condolences. This has been such a terrible time for you, and all I can say is that I'm really sorry. If there's anything Caron can do for you . . . ?"

"She's like a sophomore," said Bambi, clearly appalled at the concept. "Thanks, but no thanks. Listen, it was nice of you to come by, and I'll pass along the message to my mother when she gets back."

"From the cemetery?"

"Yeah, she was afraid those howling reporters would be here, and she said she wanted to be alone while she tried to understand how . . . Charlie could have done what she did."

"They were really close friends, weren't they?"

"That's what's killing her, she says. They've stayed in touch since college. When Charlie was married, she and my mother didn't talk on the phone every week, but they called at holidays and wrote a lot and sent funny cards and stuff like that. We visited them when they rented a beach house."

"She must have been thrilled when Charlie moved to Farberville and they could see more of each other," I said encouragingly, telling myself I was allowing Bambi to express her grief and confusion—rather than interrogating her four hours after her father's funeral.

"I suppose so." Bambi stepped back as if to close the door, but I opted to interpret it as a gesture of welcome and came into the entry hall. "Like I said, Mrs. Malloy, I'll tell my mother you came by," she said with an uneasy smile, "but it's about time for me to pick her up and—"

I radiated warmth like a veritable space heater. "Of course it is, dear, and I know you're not in the mood for visitors. I'll be off in a minute or two. From what I've heard, your mother began to suspect the two were having an affair about six months ago." I clucked my tongue disapprovingly.

Bambi conceded with a sigh, unable to withstand the persistence of a dedicated meddler. "Right after they came back from a weekend at some bed-and-breakfast in Eureka Springs, they stopped seeing each other. My mother just said she'd learned disturbing things about Charlie and didn't want to be around her anymore. I think my father was secretly pleased that she didn't call all the time or show up Sunday mornings with cinnamon rolls and the newspapers. He seemed happier, but maybe it was because he and Charlie were— you know. Everybody in town knows, so why wouldn't you?" Her eyes brimmed with tears and her hands curled into fists. "Everybody at school knows, along with everybody at church and everybody at the goddamn grocery store! They probably knew the entire time." The tears spilled down her cheeks, but she ignored them with fierceness well beyond her years. "I guess that stupid saying is true—my mother was the last to know."

"One final question," I said despite the guilt that was gushing inside me and threatening to choke my despicable throat. "Were you here the night of the . . . accident?"

"No, I was over at Emily's house cramming for history. My mother usually won't let me go out on school nights, but this time she did on account of how it was the midterm exam. She was supposed to pick me up at ten, but Emily's father had to tell me what happened and drive me home."

"Why don't you rest, Bambi? I'll drive over to the cemetery and bring your mother back." I patted her on the arm and left before she could protest, if she intended to do so. She was more likely to be so relieved at my departure that she was unable to get out a single word.

I parked beside the stone wall girding the cemetery, stuck my fists in my pockets, and walked up a path tangential to the canvas tent. I made an effort to keep my face lowered, although I doubted Michelle would recognize me— since we'd never met. I was not surprised to see two women seated on the grass, legs crossed, hands flickering as they talked. Nor was I surprised to hear laughter. After all, these were two old friends with a history that spanned twenty years. They'd shared stories of married life, of children, of financial woes, of vacations, of triumphs and disasters.

They froze when I veered at the last minute and stopped in front of them. "Charlie Kirkpatrick and Michelle McQueen?" I inquired politely, if rhetorically. "I'm Claire Malloy. I own the Book Depot, and my daughter, Caron, works on the school newspaper with Bambi."

I studied their faces; neither had the glint of a predatory woman incapable of female friendship. Michelle was pretty, if not beautiful, and there was a gap between her front teeth that indicated she was not obsessed with perfection. Charlie had cropped dark hair, a wide mouth, and a longish chin that reminded me of Luanne, especially when she was tired.

These women were tired, but I would be, too, if I'd been propping up a facade for six months, culminating in what amounted to premeditated murder.

"Why are you here?" asked Michelle.

"A better question," I said, gesturing at Charlie, "is why is she here? Isn't she the woman that took advantage of your friendship to have an affair with your husband and then run him down in the driveway?"

Charlie winced. "I came by after the funeral to try to explain what happened to Michelle. Having an affair with Ethan was the lowest, vilest thing I've ever done in my life. I'd been deeply depressed all winter, drinking too much and thinking too hard about how empty my life was. It's taken five years for the divorce to sink in, and once my son left for college and I had the house all to myself, I fell apart."

Michelle squeezed her friend's hand and said, "I knew you were unhappy when Chad left, but I had no idea how bad it was. Ethan must have sensed your vulnerability and moved in like a vulture, just like he did with his clients, such as that woman who was brutalized by her husband and the poor girl last year whose husband and baby were killed in a car wreck." She grimaced. "I'm sure there were others, but I was naive, and he was adept at lying."

"And you were always the last to know," I said as I looked down at her watery eyes and white face. "I wish I believed it, but in this case, Ethan was the last to know, wasn't he?"

"To know what?" Charlie said, then exchanged a quick look with Michelle.

"To know he was having an affair with you," I said. "The plan is very good, by the way. Two old friends stop seeing each other when one suspects the other of the affair. The husband purportedly breaks it off, and the mistress storms the house in a drunken rage and manages to kill him in the ensuing scene. Why, with the wife to testify, the mistress might get off with only a few months in the county jail—or even working weekends in a crisis center or a nursing home. In the meantime, the grieving widow collects the insurance money and bravely faces the future with a daughter who'll be away at college in a year. What were you two planning to do?"

"Buy a bed-and-breakfast," Charlie admitted in a low voice. "The one we stayed at in Eureka Springs is on the market."

"And travel during the off season," added Michelle. "Ethan refused to go anywhere that didn't have at least one championship golf course, which ruled out most of the planet. Charlie found a great deal on a two-week trip to France, but Ethan wouldn't even open the brochure. I was so excited about bicycling and hot-air ballooning through the chateau country, and all he did was shake his head and mention that damned resort on Hilo we've been to every year for the last decade."

I sighed. "I don't know what will happen now. I'll have to tell the police what I know, but it's up to them to prove it."

Michelle smiled serenely. "There's a paper trail of motel receipts, dinners for two on nights when I was visiting his mother, long-distance calls to Charlie, credit card invoices for expensive gifts that never made it home."

"I've been seeing a psychiatrist," Charlie contributed, "and I was so overwhelmed with guilt that I had to tell him about the affair. He's been very worried about my rages and occasional suicide attempts. In the last few months, his service has logged quite a few hysterical midnight calls."

Michelle rolled her eyes. "You'll never get those bloodstains out of the bedspread, dummy. You're dying to get the sofa recovered, but you have to slit your wrists in bed."

"I am so confused," Charlie said, then started to laugh.

Michelle leaned against her, her laughter lilting despite the proximity of her freshly planted husband, and looked up at me with a grin. "Please forgive me—it must be the shock. But if you could see this hideous mauve sofa . . ."

I turned away and took several steps, then looked back at them. "A friend in need, huh?"

They were already lost in a conversation of bicycles and passports. I walked back to my car and drove home, imagining a scenario in which Luanne would risk a jail sentence, albeit a short one, to murder an inconvenient husband in exchange for a trip to France. It was easier than I'd anticipated. I refused to allow myself to ponder the inverse position.

When I arrived home, I went to Caron's door and was about to knock when I heard her say, "I can't tell you my source, Louis, but I swear on last year's Falconnaire that Rhonda has a date with Bruce this Friday while you're at the Southside game. All you have to do is call her the next morning and ask her why she was seen at the drive-in movie with him, and why the car windows were steamier than a sauna." There was a pause. "I can't tell you, but my source is very, very good. We just thought you'd be interested, that's all. I've got to work on this really mindless algebra assignment, so 'bye!"

As I lowered my hand, I heard Inez's muted laugh. It was nearly drowned out by Caron's cackles of victory. Shrugging, I went to the kitchen to fix a drink, then got comfortable on the sofa and reached for the telephone. I should have called Peter to tell him what I'd learned, but I found myself automatically dialing Luanne's number. After all, a good friend deserves to be the first to know.

Loren D. Estleman is a master of many things literary. He's written fine Westerns, strong Sherlock Holmes pastiches, and in the suspense mode he's written the powerful, stylish Amos Walker novels. Here he takes on the challenge of the title, which might daunt a lesser man, and comes through with a crackling tale of anger and greed.

The Man Who Loved *Noir*
LOREN D. ESTLEMAN

The address I'd written down belonged to a house in Lathrup Village three miles north of Detroit, the only one in a cul-de-sac that ended in a berry thicket and a cyclone fence. It was a cool, sprawling ranch-style of brick and frame with four great oaks in the yard arranged in such a way that the house would always be in shade. I felt the sweat drying on my body during the short walk from my car to the front door.

A woman in a gray dress and white apron with her hair caught up by combs led me into a sunken living room and went away. They aren't called maids anymore, but they still can't speak English.

"Thank you for coming on such short notice, Mr. Walker. I'm Gay Cully."

She'd come in through an open sliding glass door from a patio in back when I was looking in another direction, a small compact redhaired woman with the sun behind her. Assuming she'd planned her entrance, that put her over forty. She had large eyes mascaraed all around, a pixie mouth, and a fly waist in a pale yellow dress tailored to show it off.

"I like your home." I borrowed a warm, slightly moist hand with light calluses and returned it. "They don't design them this way since air conditioning."

"Neil has an eye for that kind of thing. He's a building contractor."

"Neil's your husband?"

"Yes. Can I get you something? I'm afraid Netta has narrow ideas about her housekeeping duties."

"Just water. Anything stronger's wasted on a day like this."

She agreed that it was hot and came back after a few minutes with two glasses and a bowl of crushed ice on a tray. When we were seated on either side of a glass occasional table she said, "Neil's officially missing. Twenty-six hours. I trust the police, but they're outnumbered by their cases. That's why I called you."

"This puts me even up. I take it he isn't in the vanishing habit."

"No. He's never been gone without an explanation except for the time he was in the hospital."

"Accident?"

She drank and set down her glass. "He checked himself into a sanitarium. That was eighteen months ago, when the construction business was in a slump. Our lawyer advised him to declare bankruptcy, but Neil insisted on paying back every creditor in full. It was too much for him, the worrying, the long hours. One day he left for work and never showed up. The police traced him to the hospital after three days."

"I guess you checked there this time."

"I called every hospital in the area, public and private. No one answering his description has been seen in any of them."

"How's he been lately?"

"A little keyed up. We're just now getting back on our feet. I didn't think it was anything serious until his partner called yesterday to ask where he was."

I had some water. I wasn't thirsty any more, I just never liked asking the question. "Any reason to suspect he's involved with another woman?"

"Yes, but I called her and she swears she hasn't seen him in months."

"You know her?" I stroked my Adam's apple. A piece of ice had stalled in my throat during her answer.

"Vesta is her name. Vesta Mainwaring. She was the bookkeeper at the office until I made Neil fire her." She leaned over and touched my wrist. The light found hairline creases in her face. "I should explain something before we go any further. My husband is an obsessive personality, Mr. Walker. He's subject to binges."

"Alcohol?"

"No, but just as intoxicating. Come with me to the basement." She rose.

We went through a stainless steel kitchen and down a flight of clean sawdust-smelling steps into a cellar that had been turned into a den, mahogany paneling and tweed wall to wall. It contained a wet bar, Naugahyde chairs and a sofa, and a television set whose forty-eight-inch screen dwarfed the videocassette recorder perched on top. A set of built-in shelves that looked at first as if they held books was packed with videotapes instead.

"My husband's favorite room," said Mrs. Cully. "He spends most of his time here when he's not working."

I read the labels on the tapes. They were all movies: *The Dark Corner, Night and the City, Criss Cross, Double Indemnity*—not a Technicolor title in the bunch, and none of them made after about 1955. "He likes murder mysteries, I see."

"Not just murder mysteries. Dark films with warped gangsters and troubled heroes and fallen women. There's a name for them; my French isn't very good—"

"*Cinema noir*," I said. "Black films. I like old movies myself. So far it hasn't landed me in psychiatric."

"You just like them. Neil sucks on them. In the beginning I watched with him. They were interesting, but not as a steady diet. I don't think he even noticed when I stopped watching. Lately he's been spending every spare minute in front of this set, exposing himself to I don't know how many murders, deceits, and depressing situations. It's not healthy."

An empty cassette sleeve lay on an end table. *Pitfall*, starring Dick Powell, Raymond Burr, and Lizabeth Scott. I went to the VCR and punched *Eject*. A tape licked out. *Pitfall*. It hadn't been rewound. "He was watching this one when?"

"Night before last. He disappeared the next day."

"When was the last time he got on this kick?"

"Just before he entered the hospital. About the time I found out he was having an affair with Vesta Mainwaring."

"How'd you find out?"

"The police told me. The little slut caved in pretty quickly when they started asking questions about his disappearance."

I slid the tape into its sleeve. "Where can I find Miss Mainwaring?"

"She's listed. But as I told you, she doesn't know where he is."

"I'd like to hear her say it. What's the name of your husband's firm?"

She'd anticipated that and gave me a business card from the pocket of her dress. CULLY AND WEBB, it read. "Webb is the partner?"

"His first name's Leo. They've been together longer than Neil and I."

"Can I take this with me?" I held up the videotape.

"Of course. You'll need a picture of Neil, too."

Upstairs she took a five by seven out of its frame and handed it to me. Cully was a craggy-looking party in his late forties with sad eyes and dark hair thinning in front. "Any ideas on what he might be up to?" I asked his wife.

She hesitated. "It might sound crazy."

"Try me."

"You have to understand that he might be unbalanced," she said. "I didn't put it together the first time, but I've seen enough of these things now

231

to recognize the plot. I think Neil wants to be one of these *noir* heroes, Mr. Walker. I think he thinks he's in a film."

Cully and Webb had a small suite on the seventeenth floor of the Michigan Consolidated Gas Company Building on Woodward, a furnace-shaped skyscraper with a lobby out of Cecil B. DeMille, complete with sparkling blue lights mounted under the thirty foot ceiling and a bronze ballerina pirouetting among exterior pools. The offices themselves were just offices. A gray-haired woman with reading glasses suspended from a chain around her neck spoke my name into a telephone, and Leo Webb came out to shake my hand. He was a short wiry sixty with white hair slicked back, a power nose, and eyes like glass shards. His suit was tailored snugly, and there was something about the knot of his silk tie that said he'd given it a jerk and a lift just before his entrance.

When I told him my business, he steered me into his office, a square room full of antiques and statuary trembling on the rim of bad taste. I admired the view of downtown Detroit through his window and managed to sit down without upsetting a plaster cupid notching an arrow into its bow on a pedestal next to the chair.

"Gay's overreacting," Webb said, settling himself behind a French Empire desk crusted all over with gold inlay. "Cully's just off on a toot. He's that age. He'll be back when he's had enough."

"Vesta Mainwaring told her she hasn't seen him in months."

"This town's full of squirming women. I know. That's why I never bothered to get married."

"How's he been acting lately?"

"Same as anyone in this goddamn business, jumpy. Every time it rains on Wall Street, mortgage rates go up and people stop building houses. If you're looking for security, keep going."

"You wouldn't know that to see this office."

He smiled and ran a finger down the side of a Dresden Marie Antoinette on the desk. "I'm a sucker for nice things. We're into developing in a small way. You get a sixth sense for dying old widows looking to unload their property in order to have something to leave their grandchildren. The bargains would surprise you."

Bet they wouldn't. "Do you know where Miss Mainwaring is working? I can't get an answer from her home phone."

"Her new employer called us for a reference." He slid the pointer down the side of one of those nifty message caddies and punched up the cover. "Ziggy's Chop House on Livernois." He gave me a telephone number.

I wrote it down in my old-fashioned notebook. "Do you always hang on to the new numbers of former employees?"

"Everybody has their own records system, and they take it with them when they go. Calling them saves a lot of decoding time."

"Can I see Cully's office?"

"I'll have Frances show you." He picked up his telephone.

"Partners sometimes take out insurance policies on each other," I said when he was through. "Anything like that here?"

"The premiums are too dear for the shoestring we operate on most of the time. His half of the business goes to his wife. Are you suggesting I did something nasty?" A pair of shardlike eyes glittered.

"Just sweeping out all the corners." Someone knocked and the woman I'd spoken to outside stuck her gray head into the office. I stood. "Thanks, Mr. Webb. I'll let you know if he turns up."

He remained seated. "Just tell him to wash off the powder and perfume before he reports to work."

Neil Cully's office was a poor working cousin of his partner's, containing a plain desk and file cabinet and an easel holding a pastel sketch of an embryonic building. The only personal items were a picture of Gay Cully on the desk and a framed movie poster on one wall for *This Gun for Hire*, with Alan Ladd looking sinister in four colors under a fedora. Frances stood in the doorway while I went through the file cabinet and desk. I found files and desk stuff. The message pad by the telephone was blank, but there were indentations in the top page.

"The police called this morning," Frances said. "They said not to disturb anything in the office."

I looked at my watch. "Okay if I call my answering service?"

When she said yes, I lifted the receiver and dialed the number for Cully and Webb. The telephone rang in the reception area. Frances excused herself and withdrew. I laid the receiver on the blotter and tried the trick with the edge of a pencil on the message pad. It made the indentations clearer but not legible. I smoothed out some unedifying crumples in Cully's wastebasket, found a sheet that had been torn off the pad, and got it into my pocket just as Frances returned. I cradled the receiver.

"Odd, there was no one on the other end,' she said.

"Kids." I thanked her and left before she could work it out.

In the elevator I looked at the sheet. An unidentified telephone number. I tried it in a booth on the street.

"Musuraca Investigations," wheezed a voice in my ear.

I hung up without saying anything. I knew Phil Musuraca; not personally or even by sight, but the way a hardworking gardener knew a destructive species of beetle. Where he had gone, no honest investigator could follow without risking having a safe drop on him with Musuraca's name on it. What his number was doing in Neil Cully's wastebasket was one for Ellery Queen.

* * *

"Hello?"

A low voice for a woman, with fine grit in it, like a cat's lick. Conversations collided in the background with the snarling and cracking of a busy griddle. I could almost smell the carcinogens frying at Ziggy's Chop House. "Vesta Mainwaring?"

"Speaking. Listen, I'm busy, so if this is another obscene call, get to the dirty part quick."

I introduced myself and stated my business. I was looking across my little office at Miss August, kneeling in yellow shorts, high heels, and nothing else behind some convenient shrubbery on the calendar. I wondered if Miss Mainwaring ever trimmed hedges.

"Like I told Mrs. Cully and like I told the police, I haven't seen Neil since last fall."

"Not seeing him doesn't cover telephone calls and letters."

"You forgot telegrams, which I didn't get either. I lost one good job over that crumb, you want me to lose a lousy one, too?"

There was no reason to play the card, just the fact I hadn't any other leads. "What about Fat Phil, heard from him?"

The little silence that followed was like tumblers dropping into place. When she spoke again the background noise was muffled, as if she had inserted her body between it and the telephone. "What do you know about him?"

"Meet me and we'll swap stories."

"Not here," she said quickly. "Do you know the Castinet Lounge on Grand River? I get off at ten."

"I'll find it." I hung up and checked my watch. Quitting time. Five hours to kill. I had dinner at a steak place on Chene and stopped at a video store on the way home to rent a VCR from a kid I wouldn't have let follow me into an arcade after sunset.

At the ranch I fixed a drink, hooked up the recorder to my TV set with the help of the instructions and a number of venerable Anglo-Saxon words, and fed the tape of *Pitfall* I had borrowed from Gay Cully into the slot. It was a tight black and white crimer the way they made them in 1948, starring Dick Powell as an insurance agent who has an extramarital affair with sultry Lizabeth Scott, only to run afoul of her embezzler boyfriend and a sex-driven insurance investigator played by Raymond Burr at his pre-Perry Mason heaviest. Powell kills the boyfriend, and Scott kills Burr, but not before Powell's marriage to Jane Wyatt is threatened, leaving their lives considerably darker than they were when first encountered. There were plenty of tricky camera angles and contrasty lighting and one clever scene involving Powell and Burr with guns in a room full of shadows and reflections.

It was a good movie. It wasn't worth going off the deep end over, but then neither are most of the reasons men and women choose to walk away from a perfectly good relationship. When it was over I caught a rerun of *Green Acres*, which made more sense.

The Castinet Lounge was the latest in a series of attempts to perform shock therapy on Detroit's catatonic night life. A foyer paved with blue and white Mexican tiles opened into a big room covered in fake adobe with a bar and tables, a dance floor, and a mariachi band in sombreros and pink ruffled shirts. At a corner table I ordered scotch and soda from a waitress dressed like Carmen Miranda who wouldn't remember Sonny and Cher.

Ten o'clock came and went, followed by ten thirty. A few couples danced, the band finished its set, rested, and started another. They were playing requests, but everything sounded like the little Spanish flea. I nursed the first drink. What I did with the second and third was more like CPR. I was sure I'd been stood up.

Just before eleven she came in. I knew it was she, although I'd never seen a picture or been given a description, and my opinion of Neil Cully went up a notch. Coming in from the floodlit parking lot she was just a silhouette, square shoulders and a narrow waist and long legs in a blue dress and a bonnetlike hat tied under her chin with a ribbon, but as she stopped under the inside lights to look around, I saw eyes slanted just shy of Oriental, soft, untanned cheeks flushed a little from the last of the day's heat, red lips, a strong round chin. If you were going to kick over the traces, you could wait years for a better reason. When her gaze got to me I rose. She came over.

Seated, she took off her heat, shook loose a fall of glistening blueblack hair, and traded the hat to Carmen Miranda for a whisky sour. When we were alone she said, "You don't look like someone who'd be working with Phil Musuraca."

"Never met him."

"Did Neil tell you he was following me?"

"Who hired him?"

She seemed to realize she'd tipped something. She took a cigarette from her purse and fumbled for a light. I struck a match and leaned over. I didn't smell onions. Whatever she had on made me think of blossoms under a full moon. She blew a plume at the ceiling. "You haven't talked to Neil."

"Me and the rest of the human race," I said. "That part I've been spending time with, anyway. Tell me about Fat Phil."

"First tell me why you're asking."

"I found his number in Cully's wastebasket. Did Cully hire him?"

"I suppose you could find out anyway. Musuraca's working for my ex-husband. His name's Ted Silvera."

"Where did I hear that name?"

"He pushed over a bunch of video stores downriver two years ago. They called him the shotgun bandit."

"I remember the trial," I said. "The prosecution offered him a deal if he agreed to tell them where he'd stashed the money."

"Eighty thousand dollars, can you believe it? I keep telling Ziggy he should sell the griddle and rent out tapes. Anyway, Ted spit in their face and he's doing eight to twelve in Jackson. The police followed me around for a while, but when they got the idea I didn't know what Ted did with the money they laid off."

"But not Musuraca."

"Ted's jealous," she said. "He got wind about Neil somehow and had his lawyer retain Musuraca to tail me. Then Neil's wife found out, and I got fired. Musuraca gave up after that. But a week ago I turned from the counter at Ziggy's, and there he was, looking at me through the front window. He tried to duck, but he wasn't fast enough. I'd know that fat slob in the dark."

"Sure he's working for Silvera?"

"I went to Ted's lawyer and he said no. But you can't trust lawyers. Who else would care what I do and who I see?"

"Dicks like Fat Phil are simple organisms. They don't give up as easily as the police. Maybe he thinks you'll lead him to that eighty grand."

"If I knew where it was, would I be flipping burgers?"

I lit a cigarette for myself. "It's only been two years. Inflation isn't so bad you couldn't wait a little longer for the coast to clear."

"Thanks for the drink, mister." She stood.

"Sit," I said. "I don't care if you've got the money sewed inside your brassiere. I'm looking for Neil Cully."

"I don't know where he is."

"What was he doing with Musuraca's number?"

She sat. Carmen drifted over and I ordered another round. Our glasses were less than half empty, but it was that kind of night. Vesta said, "I don't know why he'd still have it. I told Neil about Ted and Musuraca—well, before. After that I couldn't get rid of him. He thought he was protecting me."

"Did you know he had mental problems?"

"What makes him special? My father died when I was little, and if I didn't marry Ted when I was sixteen to get out of the house, my stepfather would've hung me on his belt with every tramp in Detroit. When Ted got sent up, I saved everything I made waiting tables to pay for my bookkeeping classes. Cully and Webb was my ticket out of places like Ziggy's. Some protection job. Neil cracks up and goes to a cushy sanitarium, and I'm back behind a counter."

"He's got a movie complex, his wife says. Your situation comes right off a Hollywood B lot. If he's gone bugs again, he might look up you or Musuraca to write himself in as the hero."

"I haven't seen him. I haven't heard from him. I don't know how to say it so you'll believe it."

"I believe it. Were you followed here tonight?"

"I wouldn't be surprised. Musuraca doesn't make a lot of mistakes."

"Okay, go home."

"What are you going to do?"

"Get a look at Fat Phil."

"You'll be the first who ever wanted it." She got up. "You know, I usually get taken home from this place."

I held up a fifty dollar bill. "That ought to cover gas."

She didn't take it. "I'm not a whore."

"You're a bookkeeper who waits tables. Put this in your ledger."

She smiled briefly, took the bill, and left, carrying her hat. I crushed out my cigarette, put down money for the drinks, and went out after her. Out front the parking lot attendant held the door of a four-year-old green Fiat for her, and she gave him a dollar and drove away. A moment later a pair of headlamps came on, and a black Olds 98 covered with dings pulled out on the first row in the lot and burbled after her. By that time I was sliding under the wheel of my Mercury eight spaces over. I waited until the Olds turned left on Grand River, then swung out into the aisle behind it. Fat Phil and I had one thing in common: We never used valet parking.

Vesta Mainwaring lived in a house that had been converted to apartments in Harper Woods. She parked in a little lot behind the house and let herself in the back door. After a minute a light went on upstairs. The big Olds coasted to a stop.

I parked around the corner and walked back. The car was still there with its light off. I got in the passenger's side.

Fat men are often fast. He sprang the gun from its underarm clip with an economy that would have impressed Hickok. But I showed him my Smith & Wesson while he was still drawing and he let his hand fall to his lap with the gun in it.

"You should lock your doors this time of night," I said.

"Who the hell are you?" It was a light voice for so much man. In the glow from the corner he had on a dark suit that could have been used for a dropcloth and a porkpie hat whose small brim made his face seem bloated. Actually it was in proportion with the rest of him. He would run three hundred stripped, a picture I got out of my mind as quickly as it came in. He had one eyebrow straight across and a blue jaw. I smelled peppermint in the car.

"Trade you my name for the cannon." When I had it—one of those Sig-Sauer automatics the cops are so hot on—I put it on the dash out of his reach and lowered the Smittie. "So much gun for such a little girl. The name's Walker. You wouldn't know it."

"Don't count on it. The town ain't that big, and the racket's smaller. What's the play?"

"Who's paying you to tail the Mainwaring woman?"

"Never heard of her. I was getting set to take a leak when you busted in."

"They arrest you for that here. How about Neil Cully, ever hear of him?"

"Uh-uh."

"He had your number written down in his office."

"So what? I ain't so busy I'm unlisted. Listen, I got a sour gut. There's a bag of peppermints in the glove compartment."

I opened it. The second my eyes flicked away his hand went up to his sun visor. I swung the Smith, cracking the barrel against his elbow. He yelped and brought down the arm. With my free hand I reached up and slid a two-shot .22 off the top of the visor. "For a guy that knows nothing from nothing you've got plenty of ordnance," I said. "What's Vesta Mainwaring to you?"

"Eighty grand." He rubbed his elbow. "She's got that dough stashed somewhere. She can't stay away from it forever."

"You gave up on that once. What makes you think she knows where it is now?"

"Just a hunch I got."

"Save it, Phil. There's too much divorce work in this town for you to give up any of it on a hunch. What's your source?"

"I got a note in my inside coat pocket." He didn't move.

"Fish it out. If it's more iron, I'll shoot you in the head. It's not much of a head, but it'd be a shame to spoil that hat."

He took the note out slowly. I pocketed the .22 and took it, a square of coarse Big Chief notepaper with two words printed on it in block ballpoint capitals: VESTA KNOWS. "Who sent it?"

He shook his head. "Came in the mail. No return address and a USPS postmark. Same printing on the envelope."

"You'd drop everything and take off after her on an anonymous note?"

"I'd do it on less than that for eighty thousand."

I put the note in my pocket and showed him Neil Cully's picture. His eyebrow rippled. "Sure, he was sniffing around the Mainwaring broad last year. I ran his license plate through the Secretary of State's office, but he wasn't nobody. I guess Cully could of been the name. I ain't seen him lately."

"Maybe you did and forgot. Like you forgot his name."

"Hey, I hear a lot of names."

I opened the door. "If I find out there's more to it, I'll be back and you and I will go a round."

"What about my guns?"

"Go straight home from here and I'll mail them to your office. Tell anybody you feel like shooting to take a number till then." I left him.

* * *

I caught six hours' sleep and was standing in front of the Detroit Public Library when they unlocked the doors. The film section had several picture books on *cinema noir* and one scholarly tract, *Dark Dreams: Psychosexual Manifestations of Hollywood Crime Movies Circa 1945–1955*, by Ellis Portman, Ph.D. It had been published that year by Wayne State University Press. I lugged the thick volume over to a reading table and waded through a grand's worth of four-dollar words, then turned to the author's biography at the back. Ellis Portman, it said, taught psychology and film courses at Wayne State.

I also found a withdrawal card at the back bearing signatures of those who had checked the book out recently. I took it.

A public telephone on the main floor put me in touch with Dr. Portman and an acquaintance in the Detroit bureau of the FBI who owed me a favor. I made an appointment with Portman and stopped at the Federal Building on the way to give my acquaintance the note Phil Musuraca had given me.

The room number I'd gotten from Portman belonged to a small auditorium lit by only the black and silver images fluttering on a square screen at the far end. I found a seat in time to watch Robert Mitchum and Jane Greer careening down a country road in a big car with bug-eye headlamps toward a roadblock. Spotting the armed men in uniform, Jane Greer said, "Dirty double-crossing—" and shot Mitchum, who sent the car into a spin while the woman traded fire with the officers. After she was killed and the car came to a stop, a cop opened the driver's door and Mitchum flipped out, dead.

The lights came up and a small man with a big head, half the age I associated with a college professor, dismissed the students with a reminder that their papers were due Monday. As they filed out, discussing the movie, I introduced myself and shook Portman's hand. Up close he was older than he looked from the back of the room. I sketched out the case on the way to the projector.

"Just another manifestation of the Don Quixote complex," he said when I'd finished. "How can I help?"

"Most books on *noir* are for buffs. Yours takes on its psychology. I thought you might translate the Latin."

He switched off the projector and removed the take-up reel. "We've always identified with gods and heroes. The appeal of the *noir* protagonist is he's more approachable than Beowulf or Sherlock Holmes. He's an ordinary guy with tall troubles, but he usually comes out on top, even if it does kill him sometimes."

"Kind of a complex world to want to be part of."

"Actually, it's simplistic. You've got your good guy, your heavy, your good girl, and your tramp. Upon examination, the *noir* landscape makes more sense than our world. I don't wonder that an obsessive like your client's husband would prefer it to his own tangled affairs. His wife, whom he perceives as the good girl, represents the crushing responsibilities that landed him in therapy the first time. The girlfriend, whose situation might have come out of any crime movie of the forties, promises adventure and uninhibited sex and a respite from his oppressive routine. The whole thing might have been made to order for a man with his fixation."

I watched him place the reel in a flat can labeled OUT OF THE PAST and seal the lid. "What would shake him out of it?"

"Nothing, if he's too far gone. If not, the shock of reality might do it. Our world has more twists than any screenplay. Villains turn out to be just guys trying to get along. Bad girls are just good girls in trouble. Angels become whores in front of your eyes. If that doesn't bring him back, electrodes won't."

Later, in my office transcribing the notes I'd taken in Dr. Portman's classroom to my typewritten report, I took a call from my FBI acquaintance. We spoke for five minutes, after which I hung up and placed two calls. The first was to Gay Cully, who agreed to see me at her place that night.

It was just past dark when Netta, the Cullys' maid, answered the bell and told me her mistress would be with me in a few minutes. I asked her to send Mrs. Cully to the basement when she was ready and went down there.

I slid the videotape I'd brought into Neil Cully's VCR and turned on the giant-screen TV set. As the black and white credits for *Pitfall* came on, I turned down the sound and switched off the lights in the room. Now the only illumination came from the screen. Shadows crawled in the silver glow on the tapes perched on their shelves.

"Mr. Walker, is that you?"

I hadn't heard her coming down the stairs. She was standing on the second step from the bottom, a small trim figure in a fresh-looking pale tailored dress like the one she'd had on when we met. One hand rested at her throat.

"It's not Neil," I said. "Is that what you thought, Mrs. Cully?"

"I—well, yes, for a moment. He used to sit down here with no lights on and a movie on the—"

"Couldn't be him, though. You know that better than anyone."

"I don't—do you have news? Where is he?"

I was standing in shadow beside the TV set. The full light of the screen fell on her, as I'd planned. I said, "You were okay for a novice. You only made two mistakes. One was natural: Who'd expect Phil Musuraca to show me the note or that it would find its way to the FBI? The other was just plain stupid.

"Printing *Vesta Knows* was good," I went on. "No handwriting expert could pin that small a sample on you. But that coarse paper holds prints like soft wax. When I had a Fed friend check them against yours on file from an old job, it didn't take long."

"What are you implying?"

"Nuts. You've seen enough of these films to recognize the obligatory explanation scene. The note was smart, all right. It got Musuraca back on Vesta Mainwaring's case and made him a prime suspect: Poor crazy Neil got himself involved all over again in Vesta's troubles and stubbed his toe, permanently. Just in case the cops missed it, you hired me, knowing I'd turn Musuraca eventually. The law couldn't convict him without a body, but his interest in eighty thousand dollars stolen by Vesta's ex would divert suspicion from you. You even read up on *cinema noir* to make sure your story about Neil's obsession would hold water. But that was where you made your other mistake, the bonehead one." I took the card out of my pocket and held it up to the light.

"What's that?"

"A withdrawal card from the Detroit Public Library with your name on it, dated a week before you reported your husband missing. You shouldn't have checked out Dr. Portman's book. That was like signing your own name to a murder contract." I put it away. "How much is Neil's half of the contracting firm worth?"

Shadows and light played over her face. "Fifty thousand. More if I liquidate the real property. But that's not evidence. A note, a card with my signature. They won't convict."

"No, but they're enough to obtain a warrant to dig up that berry patch at the end of this street. Before I rang the bell tonight, I poked around with a flashlight. I found a lot of turned earth. With Neil's corpse, the note and the card will convict."

"You don't know what it's like."

I said nothing.

"Listening to him babble about those stupid films," she said. "Even when he had his affair it wasn't with a woman, just a character in a movie. I'd have killed him for that alone; the half-partnership will just be compensation for the past two years I spent living with a zombie."

"How'd you kill him?"

"Guess." She raised a gun in the hand she'd had resting on the banister. I hadn't seen it in the shadows. "I sent Netta out just now," she said. "Call it a feeling I had."

"Drop it, sister."

I almost laughed. It was the one cliche the scene needed, and you could count on Phil Musuraca to deliver it. His bulk filled the upper stairwell. The Sig-Sauer automatic I'd sent to him by messenger after calling him was in his hand. I took advantage of Gay Cully's confusion to remove the Smith & Wesson from my pocket.

"Make that three mistakes," I said. "You're as much a sucker for that *noir* schtick as Neil. Just because a P.I. is greasy enough to hound a woman for eighty grand doesn't mean I can't call on him for help. You've seen the pictures, Mrs. Cully. A staircase is no place to make a successful play."

Her gun dropped, bounced down two steps, and landed on the carpet. Just then Dick Powell shot Byron Barr onscreen.

Fat Phil said, "I didn't care for that *greasy* crack."

I got away from the Lathrup Village cops around midnight. On the way home I stopped at the video store, rented some tapes, and watched Doris Day movies until I fell asleep.

Norman Partridge is, as Ed Bryant said in his introduction to Partridge's short story collection, *Mr. Fox and Other Feral Tales*, everywhere. Well, he may not be everywhere, but his suspense and horror fiction are becoming a flood of fine work—dark, right, and, maturing with every story. This is clearly evident in this sad, violent tale of betrayals and lost hopes, originally published in *Cemetery Dance*.

Johnny Halloween
NORMAN PARTRIDGE

I should have never been there.

Number one: I was off duty. Number two: even though I'm the sheriff, I believe in letting my people earn their pay. In other words, I don't follow them around with a big roll of toilet paper waiting to wipe their asses for them, even when it comes to murder cases. And number three: I'm a very sound sleeper—generally speaking, you've got a better chance of finding Elvis Presley alive than you've got of waking me between midnight and six.

But it was Halloween, and the kids next door were having a loud party, and I couldn't sleep. Sure, I could have broken up the party, but I didn't. I'm a good neighbor. I like to hear the sound of kids having fun, even if I think the music we listened to back in the fifties was a lot easier on the ears. So I'm not sour on teenagers, like some cops. Probably has something to do with the fact that Helen and I never had any kids of our own.

It just didn't work out for us, is all. When Helen had the abortion, we were young and stupid and we figured we'd have plenty of chances later on. That wasn't the way it worked out, though. I guess timing is everything. The moment passes, things change, and the life you thought you'd have isn't there when you catch up to it.

What it is, is you get older. You change and you don't even notice it. You think you're making the decisions, but mostly life is making them for you.

243

You're just along for the ride. Reacting, not acting. Most of the time you're just trying to make it through another day.

That's how most cops see it. Like my deputies say: shit happens. And then we come along and clean up the mess.

I guess maybe I do carry around that big roll of toilet paper, after all.

So, anyway, Helen had asked me to get another six-pack and some chips. She does like her Doritos. It was hot, especially for late October, and a few more beers sounded like a good idea. I worry about Helen drinking so much, but it's like the kid thing. We just don't talk about it anymore. What I usually do is drink right along with her, and then I don't feel so bad.

So I was headed up Canyon, fully intending to go to Ralph's Supermarket on Arroyo, when I observed some suspicious activity at the old liquor store on the corner of Orchard and Canyon (if you want it in *cop-ese*).

Suspicious isn't the word for it. A couple of Mexican girls were coming out of the place. One was balancing a stack of cigarette cartons that was so high she couldn't see over it. The other had a couple of plastic sacks that looked to be filled with liquor bottles.

I pulled into the lot, tires squealing. The girl with the liquor bottles had pretty good instincts, because she dropped them and rabbited. The strong smell of tequila and rum hit me as I jumped out of the truck—a less sober-hearted man would have thought he'd died and gone to heaven. Me, I had other things on my mind. The girl with the cigarettes hadn't gotten too far. She didn't want to give up her booty. Cartons were slipping and sliding and she looked like a drunken trapeze artist about to take the big dive, but she was holding tough.

Tackling her didn't seem like the best idea, but I sure didn't want to let her work up any steam. I'm not as fast as I used to be. So what I did was I grabbed for her hair, which was long enough to brush her ass when she wasn't running and it wasn't streaming out behind her. I got a good grip first try; her feet went out from under her, she shrieked like a starlet in a horror movie who's about to taste chain saw, the smokes went flying every which way, and it was just damn lucky for me that she wasn't wearing a wig.

"It wasn't me!" she said, trying to fight. "I didn't do it! It was some guy wearing a mask!"

"Yeah, right. And you've got a receipt for these cigarettes in your back pocket. Sorry . . . got you red-handed, little miss."

I hustled her across the lot, stomping cigarette cartons as I went. That gave me a kick. God, I hate smokers. We went inside the store, and that's when I saw what she'd meant when she said she hadn't done anything.

The kid was no more than twenty, and—like the old saying goes—he'd never see twenty-one. He lay on the floor, a pool of dark blood around the hole in his head.

"We saw the guy who did it," the girl said, eager to please, *real* eager to get my fingers out of her hair. "He cleaned out the register. He was wearing a mask. . . ."

Dead eyes stared up at me. My right boot toed the shore of a sea of blood. Already dying, going from red to a hard black on the yellow linoleum. Going down, the clerk had tripped over a stack of newspapers, and they were scattered everywhere. My face was on the front page of every one, ten or twenty little faces, most of them splattered with blood.

". . . a Halloween mask," she continued. "A pumpkin with a big black grin. We weren't with him. We pulled in after it was over, but we saw him leaving. I think he was driving an El Camino. It was silver, and it had those tires that have the chrome spokes. We were gonna call you before we left, honest. We figured the clerk was already dead, and that we'd just take what we wanted and—"

"Let it lay." I finished it for her, and she had the common decency to keep her mouth shut.

I just stood there for a minute, looking at the dead kid. It was like looking at myself thirty years ago. Like that poem about roads not taken. I almost envied him. Then I couldn't see him anymore—I saw myself at eighteen, so I looked away.

At the papers, at my smiling face.

At the headline: HERO RESCUES BABY FROM WELL.

Some hero. A grinning idiot with blood on his face.

The Mexican girl couldn't wait anymore. She'd run out of common decency and was starting to worry about herself again.

She opened her mouth.

I slapped her before she could say anything stupid.

My fingers striking hard against her tattooed tears.

"The other girl got away," I said. "I'll bet she had the gun. Long black hair, about five-six, maybe a hundred pounds. Maybe a little more . . . it's hard to tell with those baggy jackets they wear. Anyway, she probably tossed the weapon. We'll beat the bushes on Orchard. That can wait until tomorrow, though."

Kat Gonzalez nodded, scribbling furiously. She was one of ten deputies who worked under me, and she was the best of the lot.

"I'm leaving this in your hands, Kat. I mean to tell you, I'm all out." I wanted to take a six-pack from the cooler, but I resisted the temptation. "I'm going home."

Kat stopped me with a hand on my shoulder. "Sheriff . . . Hell, Dutch, I know what happened here when you were a kid. This must feel pretty weird. But don't let it eat at you. Don't—"

I waved her off before she could get started. "I know."

"If you need to talk—"

"Thanks." I said it with my back to her, and the only reason it came out okay was that I was already out the door.

I stomped a few more cigarette cartons getting to my truck, but it didn't make me feel any better. The night air was still heavy with the aroma of tequila and rum, only now it was mixed with other less appealing parking lot odors.

Burnt motor oil. Dirt. Piss.

Even so, it didn't smell bad, and that didn't do me any good.

Because it made me want something a hell of a lot stronger than beer.

I drove to Ralph's and bought the biggest bottle of tequila they had.

I was eighteen years old when I shot my first man.

Well, he wasn't a man, exactly. He was seventeen. And he was my brother.

Willie died on Halloween night in 1959. He was wearing a rubber skull mask that glowed in the dark, and "Endless Sleep" was playing on the radio when I shot him. He'd shown up at the store on the corner of Canyon and Orchard—it was a little mom-and-pop joint back them. With him was another boy, Johnny Halowenski, also wearing a mask.

A pumpkin face with a big black grin.

They showed up on that warm night in 1959 wanting money. The store had been robbed three times in the last two months, each time during my shift. The boss had said I'd lose my job if it happened again. I'd hidden my dad's .38 under the counter, and the two bandits didn't know about it.

Skullface asked for the money. I shot him instead. I didn't kill him, though. Not at first. He had enough spit left in him to come over the counter after me. I had to shoot him two more times before he dropped.

By then Pumpkinface had gotten away. I came out of the store just in time to see his Chevy burning rubber down Orchard, heading for the outskirts of town. There wasn't any question about who he was. No question at all. I got off a couple more shots, but none of them were lucky.

I went inside and peeled off the dead bandit's skull mask. I sat there stroking my brother's hair, hating myself, crying.

Then I got myself together and called the sheriff's office.

When the deputies arrived, I told them about Johnny Halowenski. I didn't know what else to do. They recognized the name. L.A. juvie had warned them about him. Johnny had steered clear of trouble since moving to our town, and the deputies had been willing to go along with that and give him a break.

But trouble had caught up with Johnny Halowenski in a big way.

I knew that, and I laid it on. My dad had been a deputy before he got too friendly with the whiskey bottle, and I knew it was important to get things right, to make sure that Halowenski wouldn't be able to get away with anything if the cops caught up to him.

I told the deputies that Halowenski was armed and dangerous.

I told the deputies that Halowenski took off his mask when he got in the Chevy, that there could be no mistake about his identity.

Everything I said ended up in the papers. There were headlines from Los Angeles to San Francisco about the Halloween murder/robbery at a liquor store near the border and the ensuing manhunt.

One paper mentioned that the suspect's nickname was Johnny Halloween. After that I never saw it any other way. Almost every year I'd see it a few times. On FBI wanted posters. In cheap magazines that ran stories about unsolved crimes. And, on Halloween, I could always count on it turning up in the local papers.

Johnny Halloween. I leaned back against my brother's granite tombstone and stared up at the night sky, trying to pick out the name in the bright stars above.

Drinking tequila, thinking how I'd never seen that name where I wanted to.

On a tombstone.

I knew he'd show up sooner or later, because we always met in the cemetery after the robberies.

Johnny came across the grass slow and easy, his pistol tucked under his belt, like the last thing in the world he wanted to do was startle me. I tossed him the bottle when he got near enough. "Let's drink it down to the worm," I said.

He didn't take a drink, though. He would have had to lift his mask, and he didn't seem to want to do that, either.

"Miss me?" he asked, laughing, and his laughter was bottled up inside the mask, like it couldn't quite find its way out of him.

"It's been a while," I said. "But not long enough to suit me."

He tossed me a thin bundle of bills. "Here's your cut. It's the usual third. I don't figure you've still got my dough from the last job. If I could collect interest on it, it might amount to something."

I didn't say anything to that. I didn't want to rise to the bait.

"Well, hell . . . it good to see you too, Dutch. The old town hasn't changed all that much in thirty years. I went by my daddy's house, and damned if he isn't still driving that same old truck. Babyshit brown Ford with tires just as bald as he is. Seventy-five years old and still drives like a bat out of hell, I'll bet. How about your daddy? He still alive?"

I pointed two graves over.

"Yeah, well . . . I bet you didn't shed too many tears. The way he used to beat hell out of you and Willie, I'm here to tell you. Man could have earned money, throwin' punches like those—"

That hit a nerve. "Just why are you here, Johnny?"

Again, the bottled-up laugh. "Johnny? Hell, that's a kid's name, Dutch. Nobody's called me that in twenty-five years. These days I go by Jack."

"Okay, Jack. I'll stick with the same question, though."

"Man, you're still one cold-hearted son of a bitch. And I thought you'd gone and mellowed. Become a humanitarian. Do you know that your picture made the Mexico City dailies? Sheriff rescues baby from well. That took some kind of big brass *cojones*, I bet."

My face had gone red, and I didn't like it. "There wasn't anything to it," I said. "I found the baby. I'm the sheriff. What was I supposed to do?"

We were both quiet for a moment.

"Look, Johnny—Jack—I'm tired. I don't mind telling you that the years have worn on me, and I don't have much patience anymore. Why don't you start by giving me your gun. I'm going to need it for evidence. I've already got one suspect in custody—nobody will ever connect what happened tonight to you. So you can figure you got your revenge, and you can tell me how much money you want, and we can get on with our lives."

"You know," he said, "I hadn't thought about you for years and years. And then I saw that picture in the paper, and damned if I wasn't surprised that you'd actually gone and become a cop. Man oh man, that idea took some getting used to. So I said to myself, *Jack, now you've just got to go see old Dutch before you die, don't you?*"

He knelt before me, his blue eyes floating in the black triangles of that orange mask. "See, I wanted to thank you," he said. "Going to Mexico was the best thing that ever happened to me. I made some money down there. Had a ball. They got lots of pretty boys down there, and I like 'em young and dark. Slim, too—you know, before all those frijoles and tortillas catch up to 'em. You never knew about me, did you, Dutch? Your brother did, you know. I had a real hard-on for his young ass, but he only liked pussy. You remember how he liked his pussy? Man, how he used to talk about it. Non-fucking-stop! Truth be told, I think he maybe liked the talkin' better than the doin'. And you so shy and all. Now that was funny. You two takin' your squirts under the same skirt."

"You got a point in here somewhere, or are you just trying to piss me off?"

"Yeah. I got a point, Dutch."

Johnny Halloween took off the pumpkin mask, and suddenly I had the crazy idea that he was wearing Willie's skull mask beneath it. His blue eyes were the same and his wild grin was the same, but the rest of his face was stripped down, as if someone had sucked all the juice out of him.

"It's what you get when you play rough with pretty boys and don't bother to wear a raincoat," he said. "AIDS. The doctors say it ain't even bad yet. I don't want it to get bad, y'see."

I stared at him. I couldn't even blink.

He gave me the gun. "You ready to use it now?"

I shook my head. "I'm sorry," I said, and I was surprised to find that I really meant it.

"Let me help you out, Dutch." That wild grin welded on Death's own face. "See, there's a reason it took me so long to get here. I had to swing past your place and talk to Helen. Did a little trick-or-treating and got me some Snickers. Nothing more, nothing less. And when I'd had my fill, I told her everything."

There was nothing I could say . . .

"Now, I want you to do it right the first time, Dutch. Don't drag it out."

. . . so I obliged him.

It took two hours to get things done. First I heaved up as much tequila as I could. Then I drove ten miles into the desert and dumped Johnny Halloween's corpse. Next I headed back to the cemetery, got in Johnny's El Camino, and drove two miles north to a highway rest stop. There were four or five illegals standing around who looked like they had no place to go and no way to get there. I left the windows down and the keys in the ignition and I walked back to the cemetery, hoping for the best.

On the way home, I swung down Orchard and tossed Johnny's pistol into some oleander bushes three houses up from the liquor store.

My house was quiet. The lights were out. That was fine with me. I found Helen in the kitchen and untied her. I left the tape over her mouth until I said my piece.

I didn't get through the whole thing, though. Toward the end I ran out of steam. I told her that Johnny and Willie and me had pulled the robberies because we hated being so damn poor. That it seemed easier to take the money than not to take it, with me being the clerk and such a good liar besides. I explained that the Halloween job was going to be my last. That I'd been saving those little scraps of money so we could elope, so our baby wouldn't have to come into the world a bastard.

It hurt me, saying that word. I never have liked it. Just saying it in front of Helen is what made me start to crack.

My voice trembled with rage and I couldn't control it anymore. "Johnny took me over to his house that day," I said. "All the time laughing through that wild grin. He had me peek in the window . . . and I saw Willie on top of you . . . and I saw you smiling . . ."

I slapped Helen then, just the way I'd slapped the Mexican girl at the liquor store, like she didn't mean anything to me at all.

"I was crazy." I clenched my fists, fighting for control. "You know how I get . . . Everything happened too damn fast. They came to the store that night, and I was still boiling. I planned to kill them both and say I hadn't know it was them because of the masks, but it didn't work out that way. Sure, I shot Willie. But I had to shoot him three times before he died. I wanted to kill Johnny, too, but he got away. So I changed the story I'd planned. I hid Willie's skull mask, and I hid the gun and the money, and I said that Willie had been visiting me at the store when a lone bandit came in. That bandit was Johnny Halloween, and he'd done the shooting. And all the time that I was lying, I was praying that the cops wouldn't catch him."

I blew my nose, got control of myself. Helen's eyes were wide in the dark, and there was a welt on her cheek, and she wasn't moving. "I was young, Helen," I told her. "I didn't know what to do. It didn't seem right—getting married, bringing a baby into the world when I couldn't be sure that I was the father. I wanted everything to be just right, you know? It seemed like a good idea to use the money for an abortion instead of a wedding. I figured we'd just go down to Mexico, get things taken care of. I figured we'd have plenty of time for kids later on."

That's when I ran out of words. I took the tape off of Helen's mouth, but she didn't say anything. She just sat there.

I hadn't said so much to Helen in years.

I handed her the tequila bottle. There was a lot left in it.

Her hands shook as she took it. The clear, clean liquor swirled. The worm did a little dance. I turned away and quit the room, but not fast enough to miss the gentle slosh as she tipped back the bottle.

I knew that worm didn't stand a chance.

I don't know why I went out to the garage. I had to go somewhere, and I guess that's where a lot of men go when they want to be alone.

I shuffled some stuff around in my toolbox. Cleaned up the workbench. Changes the oil in the truck. Knowing that I should get rid of the pumpkin mask, but just puttering around instead.

All the time thinking. Questions spinning around in my head.

Wondering if Helen would talk.

Wondering if I'd really be able to pin the clerk's murder on the Mexican girls. Not only if the charges would stick, but if I had enough left in me to go through with it.

Wondering if my deputies would find Johnny's corpse, or his El Camino, or if he'd left any other surprises for me that I didn't know about.

They were the kind of questions that had been eating at me for thirty years, and I was full up with them.

My breaths were coming hard and fast. I leaned against the workbench, staring down at the pumpkin mask. Didn't even know I was crying until my tears fell on oily rubber.

It took me a while to settle down.

I got a .45 out of my toolchest. The silencer was in another drawer. I cleaned the gun, loaded it, and attached the silencer.

I stared at the door that led to the kitchen, and Helen. Those same old questions started spinning again. I closed my eyes and shut them out.

And suddenly I pictured Johnny Halloween down in Mexico, imagined all the fun he'd had over the years with his pretty boys and his money. Not my kind of fun, sure. But it must have been something.

I guess the other guy's life always seems easier.

Sometimes I think even Willie's life was easier.

I didn't want to start thinking that way with a gun in my hands.

I opened my eyes.

I unwrapped a Snickers bar, opened the garage door. The air held the sweet night like a sponge. The sky was going from black to purple, and soon it would be blue. The world smelled clean and the streets were empty. The chocolate tasted good.

I unscrewed the silencer. Put it and the gun in the glove compartment along with the three hundred and fifteen bucks Johnny Halloween had stolen from the liquor store.

Covered all of it with the pumpkin mask.

I felt a little better, a little safer, just knowing it was there.

When Carole Nelson Douglas burst upon the fantasy and science fiction field like a bright burning nova, people asked, "Who *is* this person!" It was clear that she was a bright, clear storyteller with a terrific imagination. That was years ago. Then, when she burst upon the mystery and suspense field with her Irene Adler pastiches, people in her new arena asked the same sorts of questions. Now we have her Midnight Louie books, and anyone who hasn't already become a fan should rethink his or her criteria. "The Maltese Double Cross," first published in *Cat Crimes II,* is a Midnight Louie story, but more than that, it's a delightful pastiche of a famous novel and film with a similar title. We think this is just . . . the cat's meow, not to put too fine a point on it.

The Maltese Double Cross
CAROLE NELSON DOUGLAS

"You are good," I tell her in my best Bogart growl. "You are very good."

Sassafras brushes against my shoulder and purrs like a puma on catnip.

She is a long, lean lady in a two-tone autumn haze coat with carmel-colored eyes. She is also my secretary, occasional nurse and gal Friday. And sometimes more than that.

Right now she has just given me the rundown on a new client: sleek number in foreign furs. Might be money in it. Said she was a Miss Wonder Leigh.

I am the unofficial dick at the Crystal Phoenix Hotel and Casino, the most tasteful joint in Las Vegas. Tasty, too. I keep a private office under the calla lilies out back by the carp pond. The fish add a touch of class to my waiting room, and divert clients while Sassy and I confer. Watching fish can be fascinating, although I prefer catching them. I always was an outdoor dude, when I am not acting as an inside man.

In a moment the lady in question struts in. She is a wonder, all right.

253

Sleek smoke gray fur from head to toe. Legs that do not know the meaning of the word "stop." Limpid eyes as hot blue as Lake Mead at high noon in July. Lake Mead is also quite a haven for carp, did I mention that? I am very fond of carp.

"Oh, Mr. Midnight," this little doll begins in a nervous, high trill, "I do so hope you can help me."

"Have a seat and we will see," say I.

She settles herself delicately upon the base of a nearby birdbath—I like a room with a view—and pats at her little ears and her little mouth. This doll has a case of nerves laudanum could not cure.

"Mr. Midnight, I am so worried about my sister. She is from the East Coast, where she met this most unsuitable gentleman. Now they have come to Las Vegas, and I have not heard from Whimsy for weeks. I fear that this cad might hurt her."

"Description?"

"My sister's or that of her gentleman friend?"

I eye her sleek, languid length. Inside she might be a nervous Nellie, but outside she is a long velvet glove. I am your ordinary American domestic of immigrant stock, but I recognize breeding when I see it.

"Your sister would of course be your twin," I point out. "It is the looks of the dude in question that are a mystery."

She stretched her lovely neck and tilts her head. "Why, Mr. Midnight, however did you know that my sister and I were twins?"

"Easy. I could see right off that you were not from these parts. Where do you hail from?"

She simpers happily. Every dame likes to think that she is exotic, although this babe definitely proves to have a claim to fame in that department. "Malta."

"Malta? Heard of it. That would make you Maltese, then?"

She shrugs with exquisite indifference, the silver-tipped blue gray fur casually draped over her shoulders shifting as subtly as sand in a dune. I had always thought a Maltese was a breed of dog, but no one in his right mind would apply such a noun to this lady. It crosses my mind to wonder whether Miss Wonder's affections are otherwise engaged.

"Now what does this bad-boyfriend of your sister's look like?" I ask instead.

"He goes by the name of Thursday. I have only seen him once since I arrived. A rude-looking bounder who dressed cheaply. Three colors," she sniffs, "and his shirts are none too white. He frequents the Araby Motel."

I wrinkle my nose at the address, a dive a dog would not touch for sanitary purposes. Things look bad for lost Little Miss Malta.

"Thursday, huh?" An odd name for a lowbrow Romeo, but I cannot fault it. Once in my dimmest youth I was called Friday in honor of my antecedents and my black hair by a little doll in anklets interested in keeping me, but I ran out on that dame. She was more than somewhat underage. Now they call me what I tell them. Usually my friends call me Midnight Louie, though I admit I require a professional pseudonym now and then.

"And where do you hang your collar?" I ask, purely for professional reasons.

"The Cattnipp Inn."

"All right, Miss Leigh." I rise and yawn to indicate the interview is over. "I will have my leg man look into it."

On cue Manny slinks from around a palm tree. He is a cobby tailless dude with an untidy set of whiskers, and his interest in legs is close up and personal. While he is eyeballing Miss Leigh's silken gray hose and generally cozying up to my client, I maintain a businesslike distance. She finally tumbles to my fixed stare and offers me a fistful of legal tender—Tender Vittles coupons.

After she leaves, Manny drools over the cash as well. I tell him to tail this Thursday dude and find out where the sister is. Simple enough. Even a Manx could handle it. Then I go home.

I room with a classy redhead named Miss Temple Barr at the Circle Ritz condominium, a fifties establishment long on vintage charm and short on residents of my particular persuasion. I like to stand out, except when I do not wish to be seen while working, and then I am virtually invisible, especially at night.

Miss Temple Barr and I have a very modern arrangement: she provides room and board, I am free to come and go and see whom I will. At two A.M. a scratching on the French door to the patio wakes me from visions of sugarpusses kicking in a chorus.

When I pry open the door, I am hit with a blast of hot air and the news from a snitch of mine that Manny has bought a one-way ticket to Cat Heaven, found dead as a dormouse outside the Araby Motel. Hit and run. I tell my informant to find Sassy and have her look in on the unfortunate widow. Then I got to the scene of the crime. An acquaintance of mine, Detective Sergeant Doghouse, is on the case. Below the embankment I see Manny sprawled on his side, legs askew. I do not hang around.

I am in not too good a mood at the office the next day (sure, I can always grab a catnap, but I need my beauty sleep). Then Mrs. Manx trots in, sides heaving and blue eyes large and limpid. She is a white-hot platinum blonde, but a bit on the neurotic side.

That happens to be the side that is all over me before Sassy can make a discreet exit. The widow's long nails clutch my shoulders, putting a crimp in my tailoring.

"Oh, Louie," says she. "You have heard?"

I discourage the Saran Wrap act, peeling free before she can cause any permanent damage. The scene is delicate. Iva Manx and I have been known to share a midnight rendezvous in more ways than one, both before and after she linked up with Manny.

"Be kind to me, Louie," she whimpers, wriggling her rear.

I disengage as gently as possible and tell her to go home until the murderer is caught. She seems less interested in my investigative schedule than in my off-hours plans. I give her a lick and a promise and escort her to the reception room.

After her exit, Sassy looks up with one amber peeper half-cocked and says, "Wherever she has been, it was not at home. They lived under a desert bungalow, and the cupboard was bare—not even a mouse, much less the lady of the house—when I got there at three A.M."

Sassy has never liked Iva, but then Sassy has a distaste for flashy blondes from exotic climes like Turkey. And maybe Malta, too.

This is troubling news. Iva would not be the first dame to hurry hubby off the planet under the mistaken impression that some other dude—say a business associate of the same spouse—might take her for a stroll under the orange blossoms were she free. I would not take Iva for better or worse if she were even $2.98.

Next I report to Miss Wonder Leigh. The Cattnipp Inn, however, reports a vacancy at the room number—2001—given me by the lady in question. I look it over anyway, and who should ankle into the landscaping out front but the missing Miss Leigh.

"Oh, Mr. Midnight," says she, widening her azure eyes until her pupils are thin vertical slits and I think I am in blue heaven.

I tell her the news, at which she waxes the usual distraught: much pacing, pausing every now and then to chew her nails. She admits she has taken the room under a false name: Blanche White. Given her coloring, I tell her, Griselda Gray would have been better.

She whines a bit about poor dead Mr. Manx.

I tell her to save the sobs, that Manny had a prepaid plot at Smokerise Farm, no kits, and a wife that would not so much as clean his stockings.

"Oh, be generous, Mr. Midnight," she wheedles, all the while wrapping that soft gray fur around me. "You are so brave, so strong. Help me."

"You are good," I tell her. "You are so good I believe that I can get you a job in the soaps. Especially when you get that little catch in your purr."

"Oh, I deserve that," says she, casting herself away. "I have not been straight with you. My sister is not missing at all."

"Never figured that she was. You cannot hide a Maltese dame in Las Vegas. So are you going to tell me the truth now, Miss White?"

"My name is not White. It is really . . . Blue. Babette Blue."

"And Thursday's your, er, pal?"

"My . . . partner. I met him in Hong Kong. He was escorting a shipment of Siamese back to the States for clandestine breeding purposes. I needed protection—"

"Like Schwarzenegger," I interjected, and she flashes me a pleading look that could wring a filet mignon from a vegetarian.

"It is not what you think. Thursday was big and mean. He had come to Hong Kong as bodyguard for a gambler who had to leave the States. He was always ready for action. He even slept with kitty litter around his bed so no one or nothing could creep up on him. Sometimes he . . . he knocked me around. I was afraid of him, Mr. Midnight, that is all. I thought you and Mr. Manx could scare him off. And now Mr. Manx is dead and—"

"And now we get to the nitty gritty, speaking of kitty litter. Who are you so afraid of, that you would hook up with an ugly customer like Thursday?"

"Oh, Mr. Midnight, I cannot tell you."

I rise to go.

"Please, you must help me. It is a matter of life or death."

"More like death, Miss Blue." I examine the dirt at the base of an oleander bush. This is not an act. I really have to go.

"You are right; I cannot expect a stranger to risk life and limb on my behalf. Go, then. I do not blame you."

I pause to scratch my neck. I do not wish to walk out on a lady at a critical moment, even if it is my own. "Listen. I can look into this without knowing everything, but I need some filthy lucre to fling around if you expect me to keep you out of Thursday's death. How much you got lying around?"

She fluffs her furs and goes huffy, but finally produces a fistful of cash from the kitty. "What will I live on?"

"Got any jewelry?"

"Some . . . genuine faux diamond collars."

"Hock 'em," say I, giving her back a few coupons for snacks. "Now I really got to go."

After I leave, I check out the facilities behind the azaleas, then I check with a business acquaintance. In such instances it is necessary to consort with the sorry dogs who run the law and order game in this town. It turns out that they are looking for me. Doghouse, the sergeant and my sometimes pal, is all right, but Lieutenant Dandy is a typically tight Scotsman. The pair collar me and tell me that Thursday has been found dead. Did I do it in revenge for Manny? Might have, say I, but did not get around to it. I talk them out of hanging the rap on me and go where I was heading when so crudely interrupted, my lawyer's office. At least I know a legal beagle who knows how to keep his tongue rolled up like a red carpet and his nose relatively snot-free.

I spread most of Miss Blue's kitty litter coupons around—there is a black market in this stuff; apparently people find it conducive to growing seedlings. Then I go back to the office at the Crystal Phoenix.

It has not moved, and Sassy is out front straightening the seams on her stripes. I head for the desk and a short snooze, seeing as how my slumber has been as fitful as that of the fairy-tale princess forced to recline on an illegally concealed legume.

Sassy soon rounds the calla lily curtain marking my inner sanctum and poses artfully. "Mr. Puss-in-Boots to see you, boss." Her pet name is no compliment to the forthcoming visitor.

She admits a stranger broadcasting a distinct odor of baby powder, a fussy sort born to give basic black a bad name. He accessorizes his fine black coat with pristine white gloves and spats. A precious little spot of pure white like a pearl stickpin nestles in his black cravat. Not my type, believe it.

He gives his real name as Jewel Thebes. I cannot tell if he is announcing his profession but is lisping, or if he is indeed of Egyptian ancestry. I can certainly picture him mummified.

First he consoles me on Manny's death. Then he announces with the softest of purrs that he is prepared to pay five thousand Fancy Feast coupons with no expiration date for an item, merely ornamental, says he, that he believes I know the whereabouts of: "the black bird."

I cannot quarrel with the quality of the color, nor the amount of the reward: five thousand mackerels is nothing to sniff at. Nor am I normally adverse to a little bird hunting. While I am distracted by the sight of Sassy swaying off to lunch under an archway of calla lily leaves, Thebes pulls a pretty little piece from a discreet pocket and asserts that he is about to search my office.

Go ahead, say I, putting my mitts up. As he is searching me, I pinion his white bootie with my rear foot, pounce, and knock the weapon halfway to the birdbath. One good five-finger exercise on that dainty jaw, and Mr. Thebes is seeing the bluebirds of happiness.

I steel myself and search the dude. A flowered pouch of catnip, a fat wallet and a ticket to *Cats!* is about it. Thebes recovers in time to pout at my inroads upon his person, which also enables him to fork over two hundred clams via my intervention. Clams are not carp, but I remain fond of seafood in all forms. I also choke out of him that the lively Miss Blue is now in Room 635 of the Belle Chat Hotel.

When I get outside the Crystal Phoenix, though, I discover that some alley cat is tailing me, so I hop a ride on a motor scooter and head over to the hotel.

She may no longer be owning up to the name "Wonder," but this gray lady still manages to amaze. When I mention Thursday's death and my visit from Thebes, she goes down on all fours and lifts a dainty paw to her worried brow.

"I have not lived a good life," she confides with a tremor. "I have been bad."

To Midnight Louie this is not necessarily a detriment. I remind her that I find her theatrics good, very good. This is a favorite saying of mine. The ladies like it, yet it leaves me room to be cynical, not to mention mysterious.

"If only," wails she, "I had something to give you. What can I bribe you with?"

I manage a quick pass of the kisser that makes the answer painfully evident. The notion does not seem to dismay her, but then the girl is good. All right, bad.

She also comes clean about the black bird. It will be hers within the week, she says. The late Thursday hid it.

What, I ask, really happened to that late unlamented partner?

"The Fat Cat," says she, employing a thrilling tone.

I am not impressed. I weigh in at eighteen pounds on a good day.

Then who should show up but Thebes, still packing that pretty little piece. We three are at a standoff, when who should arrive but my police pals, Doghouse and Dandy. It is hard to take two guys whose names sound like the title of a television cop show seriously.

They take me into the hall and give me trouble. Now they are thinking I might have killed Manny as well as Thursday. Were Iva and I involved? Nope, say I. I only lie in defense of a lady. And was she trying to divorce Manny, but he was against it? Manny, I say, was not against anything, including fur coats.

A commotion erupts inside. We three burst in and what have we but Jewel Thebes sporting a slash above the right eye and lovely Miss Blue holding the decorative gat on the little Egyptian.

"Please," this Thebes dude whines to the police, "do not leave me or these two will kill me when you go."

Nothing gets the police's goat so much as death threats, and the dogged pair settle in for an inquiry. I turn it all into a joke, for by now both the ex-Miss Wonder and the sniveling Thebes have figured out that the one thing neither of them wants is the police involved in the hunt for this black bird. None of us three is particularly big on sharing with the force.

Things do get ugly, though, and Lieutenant Dandy squeezes up his ugly Scottish mug and wipes my face with a big black-gloved paw.

I hold my temper, mainly because there is a reputed lady present. Doghouse finally herds his inferior superior officer out of the room, along with Thebes.

Babette eyes me with her long mascara-black lashes half-lowered. "You are the most persistent pussycat I have ever known," she coos, stroking an agile extremity over my jaw. "So wild and unpredictable."

I never turn down a compliment, but point out that a little accurate information would soothe my wounded kisser more than this rub-and-tickle game.

So she comes across. Babette, Thursday and Thebes stole the black bird from the dude who owned it because the Fat Cat offered five hundred pounds of prime Venezuelan catnip for it. But Thebes planned to ditch the duo and elope with the black bird on his lonesome, so Babette and Thursday teamed up to do to Thebes what he would have done to them before he could do it. That is what a life of crime will do to your grammar.

Then, she confides, she found Thursday was planning to ditch her and keep the bird all to himself.

"What does this desirable bird look like?" I ask.

Big, she says. So high, and shiny. Has feathers. She only saw it once for a few minutes. I gaze deep into those baby blues and tell her she is a liar.

"I have always been a liar," she purrs.

I suggest that she should find something new to brag about.

"Oh, Louie, I am so tired," she says, leaning listlessly against my shoulder. "I am so tired of lying and not knowing what is a lie and what is true. I wish—"

Well, there is only one way to shut up a lady bent on confessing her sins, and I take it. I could tell you that this is the end of that scene, but you were not born yesterday. Let us just say that talk is cheap after that point.

The Belvedere Hotel, when I get there, is cheesy as usual. I spot several rats on the fringes. I also find Thebes fresh from a long interrogation with Doghouse and Dandy. He looks as if he had been mauled by a rat terrier, but claims he told the cops nothing. He also rags me about my association with Babette, but I tell him I had to throw in with her.

Back at the office, Sassy is full of bad news. A Mr. Spongecake called, says she, and Babette is waiting for me. I am surprised to see her so soon again, but the lady is more ruffled than ever, and it has nothing to do with our private matters.

"Oh, Louie," she says, "my place was mussed up when I returned and I am scared."

I stash her where I always stash disheveled dames, at my gal Sassy's place, which is not too bad. It has a great view on the alley behind Sing Ho's Singapore restaurant. No sooner are the two dames on the way there, but my calla lilies part and Iva Manx pads in. Has a dude no privacy?

She admits that she sent the police to my place.

I reply by asking where she was when Manny was given his fatal shove.

This encourages her to leave in a hurry and brings my first peace of the day, which is interrupted by a call on the blower from this Fat Cat, Spongecake. He is in Room 713 of the Crystal Phoenix and wants the black bird.

There is nothing to say but that I got it and we can talk. Like Miss Blue, I am a liar, too, but purely for professional reasons.

When I arrive I realize that the Fat Cat has great taste. He has taken the ghost suite at the Crystal Phoenix. These rooms feature the same forties decor as when Jersey Joe Jackson lived at the hotel, then known as the Joshua Tree. Some say Jersey Joe still lives there. The rooms are never rented, but we law-bending dudes are not against arranging a private powwow on the premises. As for Jersey Joe, he had proclivities of a criminal nature, to hear tell. If he objects to some larcenous company, he is the last to say so.

The Fat Cat is an oversize bewhiskered gent in a brown striped suit with full sideburns and a stomach pouch that would make the spreading chestnut tree look like a bonsai bush. I have heard this particular breed called a Maine Coon, and he is indeed big enough to pass for a raccoon, or perhaps the state of Maine itself.

An anonymous, almost albino gunsel is hunched in the corner with his eyes hooded. I pay him no mind.

"Are you are here, sir, as Miss Blue's representative," says Spongecake, who tends to talk like a preacher addressing the millionaires' club, "or Mr. Thebes's?"

I pull a pussycat face. "There is me," I say modestly.

The bushy eyebrows frosting Spongecake's fat face lift. "She did not tell you what it is, did she?"

"Thebes offered me ten thousand for it," I return, upping the ante to keep things interesting.

Spongecake arranges himself more comfortably in his chair, which is a green satin upholstered job with wine fringe. There is a lot of Spongecake to rearrange. He offers some coffee for my cup of cream, which I accept. A dash of caffeine adds spice to my day and Spongie is big on formalities.

"Let me tell you about the bird," Spongecake begins, his yellow eyes slit with greed and nostalgia. "It is a songbird of sorts," says he, "but not in the usual sense. It wears a glossy black coat somewhat like your own. I like," he adds, "a gentleman who maintains his grooming. This legendary bird dates from the mid-eighteenth century. Eighteen forty-five, to be precise."

I get the impression that Spongecake is nothing if not precise.

"After a circuitous history beginning in the States, the black bird finally arrived in the possession of a gent of antiquarian nature, a Russian blue, in Istanbul. A general. Then, sir," Spongie adds, "I sent agents to acquire it. They did."

"What can one bird be worth?" I ask.

"That depends upon the buyer. I confess that this globe hosts certain . . . collectors, shall we say? Such individuals would be willing to pay dearly for a rare bird of the proper vintage, much as others would kill for a bottle of Napoleon brandy. Reputedly this bird's craw is crammed with diamonds." Spongie leans back to look down his flowing white cravat. "I can offer you, sir, twenty-five thousand in whatever currency you prefer, or one-quarter of what I realize from the sale, which might be a hundred thousand, or even a quarter of a million."

This is not an insignificant amount of nip. Plans for this pile of affluence are dancing in my head, along with something of a chemical character. It occurs to me that the caffeine I have imbibed is having an effect reminiscent of valium.

The room blurs, which is disturbing. Spongecake blurs, which is an improvement. I rise and spar briefly with the furniture, then conk out on the floor.

I wake to the sound of four-and-twenty blackbirds piping in a pie. They flock away like cobwebs. I find myself alone in the Jersey Joe Jackson suite. Whenever I find myself alone, I make good use of the opportunity, but first I lurch to the nearest mirror, which requires a staggering bound atop a console table covered in snakeskin. Speaking of which, it seems one of the dear recently departed—Spongecake, Thebes or the pale gunsel in the corner—has given my head a parting shot. Four slashes decorate my temple. I clean up by rubbing a wet mitt over them, then search the premises. I find little or nothing, but I feel better.

One of the little nothings I find is yesterday's newspaper listing the schedule of charter flights to Las Vegas. La Paloma Airlines is flying in a raft of eager gamblers from Hong Kong, I read. Those of an Oriental persuasion have a fondness for gaming that is exceeded only by my taste for carp, but I find the name of the charter suggestive. According to a hot-tempered hoofer of my acquaintance, "paloma" means dove in Spanish.

Such irony as a white bird flying in a black bird cannot be merely accidental, but it *is* Occidental: the port of departure is in the right quarter of the globe. I recall that the lovely Babette was definite about needing a week to get her paws on the bird.

By the time I return to the office, the sidewalk has stopped playing spin the bottle. Babette is not there, but Sassy says the lady has called and is now at the Wellington Hotel. That lady changes hotels more frequently than a sheepdog rotates fleas.

So I am sitting at my desk nursing my noggin, which requires me to add a little milk to the Scotch I keep in my drawer, when the calla lily leaves part dramatically. I prepare myself for the entrance of another foxy lady. Instead, a wizened Siamese staggers in, dragging a parcel almost as big as he is wrapped in burlap.

The old dude falls over, and a quick check finds him pumped full of birdshot. Sassy is not amused. She does not do cleanup work.

"Do not blame the poor sap for keeling over on our turf," say I. "He has just come in on a long intercontinental flight."

I pat him down and find his identification tag. "Captain Jack." No doubt his last assignment was the La Paloma.

Sassy agrees to tidy the place.

"You are a good man, sister," I tell her, then take the burlap bundle and scram. I deposit it in one of my favorite stashes, which I am not about to divulge, save that it is under a blackjack table in the Crystal Phoenix. I take a hike to the address of the Wellington, and find a vacant lot. I am not surprised. Napoleon did not do well with Wellington, either. So I return to home, sweet homicide.

Guess who is waiting at my place? It could be the police, but it is Miss Babette, looking, as usual, ravishing.

Unfortunately, she is accompanied by Spongecake and Thebes, neither of whom look ravishing, although Thebes always looks as if he would be amenable to the idea. The nondescript gunsel is in the corner, looking threatening.

Spongie wastes no time.

"You are a most headstrong individual, sir. I see we will have to cut you in on ten thousand for your trouble."

"No trouble," I reply. "I want a much bigger cut than that. What say we feed the gunsel to the police dogs? After all, he did shoot Thursday and Captain Jack."

Here Spongie gets apologetic, which he reveals by twitching his whiskers. "You cannot have Wilmar. Wilmar is a particular pet of mine."

I cannot say much for Miss Babette's associates; they all appear to have unnatural attachments. Well, say I, give them Mr. Thebes then.

The dude in question's pouty little peke-face whitens before my eyes.

Wilmar erupts from the corner to spit in my face, the whites of his eyes forming a neat circle around his putty-colored orbs. As far as whisker-twitching goes, he has Big Daddy Spongecake beat by a hairsbreadth.

Poor Wilmar is so wrought up that the beauteous Babette slinks up and disarms the poor sap with one practiced swipe of her pretty paw.

Wilmar belly-crawls into the corner in a funk.

"So, Mr. Midnight," Sponge demands affably, which does not fool me a bit. The only thing affable about Spongecake is his vocabulary. "Where is the bird?"

"It will be delivered here. Shortly. Meanwhile, we might as well entertain ourselves. Let me see if I have the playbill down pat. You," I tell Spongie, "killed Thursday because he was in cahoots with Babette. What about Captain Jack?"

"Oh," says Sponge, "that was Wilmar's doing, as was Thursday. I do not descend to dirty work. And it all really was Miss Babette's fault. She had given Captain Jack the bird in Hong Kong, to deliver it to her here. Wilmar—whom I had, er, picked up in the East—and I called upon Thursday and Miss Blue in Malta. I was to pay Babette for the bird when they snatched it. While I went to get the payment, she and Thursday got away. Wilmar and I traced them to Hong Kong, then here. After La Paloma landed, we followed Captain Jack to Babette's apartment. Captain Jack ran with the bird. Wilmar shot him on the fire escape, but the captain managed to get away. That is when I . . . persuaded Babette to call you and say she was at the Wellington. I wanted to search your office."

"Find anything I been missing?"

Spongecake glowers, then pats his enormous stomach until he withdraws ten one-dollar Whiskas coupons.

I take the cash, look it over, and say I want fifteen.

Spongecake and I dance around some more on price. When I hand back the ten, he says I kept one coupon. No, say I, you padded it. In fact it is crumpled tighter than a love note between his front fingernails.

"A word of advice, Mr. Midnight." Sponge narrows his bland yellow eyes. "Be careful." He jerks his head in Babette's direction. It takes a crook to predict another crook. "Now, where is the bird?"

I manage to dial Sassy's number on the vintage rotary phone and tell her to withdraw the bundle from my favorite storage facility. Not much later the ever-efficient Sassy drops off the burlap-wrapped object of all our affections.

Spongecake is so pleased he hyperventilates as he claws away the wrappings. What we see is one large, black bird, its scrawny feet tied with some sort of leather anklet. Over its head is a leather hood like you see on fancy hunting birds like falcons.

Spongecake's long nails tremble as they pluck the bag away.

The big bird is somewhat disoriented, which—given its port of departure —is understandable.

"Hawwwk," this creature declares.

Spongecake recoils as if scratched, and indeed the sound is crude enough to scar the most sensitive ear.

"Fraud," Spongecake declares, still incensed at the idea of criminal doings. "Fakery. This is a genuine, live bird!" he snarls at Babette. "I expected a stuffed specimen—stuffed with diamonds. A live bird could not harbor such treasure for long."

Babette shakes her pretty head. "I did not know—"

"You cheated me," Thebes screams at Spongecake, bristling until his hair stands up all over, even on his white-socked feet. "You promised me riches beyond counting!"

I turn to Babette. "You must have known."

"No, Louie, I did not!" She curls sharply filed fingernails into my lapels. "I never saw the bird for more than a few moments—"

"Peacock feathers!"

"I want my ten coupons back." Spongecake pokes me crudely on the shoulder.

I shrug. "Too bad."

Thebes and Spongecake depart, arguing. Spongecake is threatening to find the Russian blue who pulled the switch in Malta. Thebes is threatening to go along for the ride. That is what you call company that loves misery. No one notices Wilmar hunched quietly in the corner.

I turn to Babette, who is looking nervous.

"All right, baby, time to talk turkey. What exactly is this here bird?"

"I do not know, Louie, truly I do not," she says, barely casting the creature a glance.

"What about Manny?"

"What *about* Manny?" She runs light nails up and down my spine.

"You warned Thursday that he was being followed, hoping he would confront Manny and force him to kill Thursday for you. When that did not work, and Manny went up the alley, just doing his job, you pushed him into the path of an oncoming Brinks truck. You knew the Crystal Phoenix transports the casino take at that hour along that route. So did I. You set Manny up. You killed him."

"Why, why, Louie? Why would I do it?"

"Because you are bad, sweetheart; you said it yourself. And you figured that I would go after Thursday to avenge Manny. You were right, only Wilmar got there first. Do not fret, pet; maybe someone will bail you out of stir. You still have your long legs and eyelashes. They say there is a sucker born every minute. You are a pretty swell-looking purebred, after all, both you *and* your sister."

"S-sister?" She swishes past me nervously, twitching her tail in a way that is not a come-on. "I have no sister, I told you. That was a lie."

"Sure you do." I nod at the subdued gunsel everybody has overlooked. "In that corner, we have Wilma Leigh, aka Whimsy. And here, weighing in at seven pounds soaking wet, is her sister Wonder, aka Babette. No wonder you disarmed 'Wilmar' so easily just now. How long did your sister work for the Fat Cat by posing as a pansy?"

"Louie . . . what are you saying?"

"You gave it away yourself. Came from Malta, you said. Could not help bragging about your exotic origins. That was about the only honest thing you said. See, there is this small oddity about certain types of purebreds that gave you away. If you had not snagged the black bird, your sister would have been around to collect it off Spongecake and Thebes when they got it. She was your ace in the hole. Either way, Midnight Louie would have been out in the cold wailing Dixie, and I do not play the patsy for any dame."

Wilma is ankling over, shaking herself out of the nondescript tan trenchcoat that hid her natural coat of creamy blonde fur. Once Wilma doffs her macho demeanor she proves to be a nubile lady with eyelashes as extenuated as the gams on a daddy-longlegs.

"You are both the unacknowledged daughters of the general, the Russian blue from Malta who owned the bird," I tell them. "There is something called the Maltese dilution in cat-breeding circles, in which I am not normally intimate, I admit.

"In the Maltese dilution, a coat that is black dilutes to blue, and one that is yellow dilutes to cream. The Russian blue was already one watered-down dude. You two came from the same litter—twin sisters, only one of you came out cream, and the other gray. It is a Maltese peculiarity. You remember when I met you, angel? I said I had heard of Malta. As it happens, the dilution is the solution."

"Will you turn us in, Louie?" Babette pouts, pressing her warm soft body close to mine.

"I should."

Wilma pressed close to my other side, giving me the eye but no lip.

"Naw," I decide. "The bird is a family heirloom of sorts. But I will never turn my back on you two."

As the evening turns out, such a maneuver is not in the least necessary. I must say that these Maltese dilutions lack for nothing when it comes to nocturnal gymnastics.

As for the bird, the twins insist that it is valuable to their esteemed daddy for reasons relating not to diamonds, but to dinner. Some gourmands, they claim, would kill to consume a rare bird of proper vintage, much as other individuals would sell their souls for the aforementioned bottle of Napoleon brandy. I tell the Maltese sisters that I wish to keep the black bird for a while as a souvenir, and they can hardly object.

The next morning—late—I take it over to a friend of mine who runs a used musical instrument shop off the Strip. This dude can play a riff on a piano that would have a shar-pei tapping its tail, and that particular breed is notoriously tone-deaf. My pal is also something of a feather fancier. His moniker is Earl E. Bird. He shares the same sophisticated coloring I do, only he happens to be short on hair, long on skin and as bald as an eight ball on top of it.

I show him the bird.

He jerks off the hood and smiles until he exposes what look like all fifty-two ivories in his mouth.

"Say, Louie, my man! Where did you get this? This here bird is a genuine mynah, or maybe a raven. Or possibly a crow."

Some expert. "Do these mynahs, ravens and crows live for a long time?"

"Some parrots can reach a hundred."

I would whistle if I could; most dudes I know do not make much more than twelve. "I had in mind about a hundred and fifty years."

Earl E. shrugs. "I do not know how well these black birds age, but I know this one to be a mellow fellow, and an oracle of old. Talks, if you know what to say to it. What is the word, bird? Tell me your name. Where are the seven keys to Baldpate? When will the Cubs win the World Series?"

Earl E. can go on like this indefinitely, but at this interrogation the bird finally perks up, cocks its head, flashes a beady eye about the premises and intones, "Nevermore."

I wish that I could say what this means, since I have a feeling that it expresses the dark, brooding soul of mystery itself. But I am a practical dude, not a poet. At that pivotal moment I find the room spinning as if I had imbibed another shot-glass of Spongecake's spiked Coffeemate.

The bird starts flapping its wings and squawking "Nevermores." Brass instruments glitter past like a carousel. Must have been something Maltese I had for dinner the night before.

As my vision clears, I find myself alone in Miss Temple Barr's comfy condominium, stretched out on her batik pillows with one mitt on the television remote control.

Some black-and-white film of days gone by is reeling off the screen. I breathe a sigh of relief. For a moment, in my mental fog, I thought that this vintage classic had been colorized. As anyone of any taste whatsoever knows, the only classic colors in film and real life are black with a dash of white around the whiskers and the incisors.

I still cannot figure out how the bird lasted almost a hundred and fifty years, or who would pay big dough to consume such a senior citizen. I do know one thing: if Midnight Louie keeps snoozing in front of the television set, the Bogeyman will get him.

Best known for her Sharon McCone novels, Marcia Muller has been writing literate, entertaining fiction for over fifteen years. She's also been an editor, with anthologies in both the suspense and Western fields. And she's collaborated on fiction, as has been previously noted. "Benny's Space," reprinted from *A Woman's Eye*, is a rather deceptive tale. Effortlessly, Muller explicates the *modus operandi* of criminal investigation, showing in brief, effective strokes how the background of a case can tell the whole story of guilt and blame.

In addition, Muller shows here how words like "guilt" and "blame" can cover up vast emotional and social interactions that lie beneath the motivations of criminal acts. Her deft handling of the gang milieu and the world where gangs are a constant, menacing presence is well worth your attention.

Benny's Space
MARCIA MULLER

Amorfina Angeles was terrified, and I could fully empathize with her. Merely living in the neighborhood would have terrified me—all the more so had I been harassed by members of one of its many street gangs.

Hers was a rundown side street in the extreme southeast of San Francisco, only blocks from the drug- and crime-infested Sunnydale public housing projects. There were bars over the windows and grilles on the doors of the small stucco houses; dead and vandalized cars stood at the broken curbs; in the weed-choked yard next door, a mangy guard dog of indeterminate breed paced and snarled. Fear was written on this street as plainly as the graffiti on the walls and fences. Fear and hopelessness and a dull resignation to a life that none of its residents would willingly have opted to lead.

I watched Mrs. Angeles as she crossed her tiny living room to the front window, pulled the edge of the curtain aside a fraction, and peered out at the street. She was no more than five feet tall, with rounded shoulders, sallow skin, and graying black hair that curled in short, unruly ringlets. Her shapeless flower-printed dress did little to conceal a body made soft and fleshy by bad food and too much childbearing. Although she was only forty, she moved like a much older woman.

Her attorney and my colleague, Jack Stuart of All Souls Legal Cooperative, had given me a brief history of his client when he'd asked me to undertake an investigation on her behalf. She was a Filipina who had emigrated to the states with her husband in search of their own piece of the good life that was reputed to be had here. But as with many of their countrymen and -women, things hadn't worked out as the Angeleses had envisioned: first Amorfina's husband had gone into the import-export business with a friend from Manila; the friend absconded two years later with Joe Angeles's life savings. Then, a year after that, Joe was killed in a freak accident at a construction site where he was working. Amorfina and their six children were left with no means of support, and in the years since Joe's death their circumstances had gradually been reduced to this two-bedroom rental cottage in one of the worst areas of the city.

Mrs. Angeles, Jack told me, had done the best she could for her family, keeping them off the welfare rolls with a daytime job at a Mission district sewing factory and nighttime work doing alterations. As they grew older, the children helped with part-time jobs. Now there were only two left at home: sixteen-year-old Alex and fourteen-year-old Isabel. It was typical of their mother, Jack said, that in the current crisis she was more concerned for them than for herself.

She turned from the window now, her face taut with fear, deep lines bracketing her full lips. I asked, "Is someone out there?"

She shook her head and walked wearily to the worn recliner opposite me. I occupied the place of honor on a red brocade sofa encased in the same plastic that doubtless had protected it long ago upon delivery from the store. "I never see anybody," she said. "Not till it's too late."

"Mrs. Angeles, Jack Stuart told me about your problem, but I'd like to hear it in your own words—from the beginning, if you would."

She nodded, smoothing her bright dress over her plump thighs. "It goes back a long time, to when Benny Crespo was . . . they called him the Prince of Omega Street, you know."

Hearing the name of her street spoken made me aware of its ironic appropriateness: the last letter of the Greek alphabet is symbolic of endings, and for most of the people living here, Omega Street was the end of a steady decline into poverty.

Mrs. Angeles went on, "Benny Crespo was Filipino. His gang controlled the drugs here. A lot of people looked up to him; he had power, and that don't happen much with our people. Once I caught Alex and one of my older boys calling him a hero. I let them have it pretty good, you bet, and there wasn't any more of *that* kind of talk around this house. I got no use for the gangs—Filipino or otherwise."

"What was the name of Benny Crespo's gang?"

"The *Kabalyeros*. That's Tagalog for Knights."

"Okay—what happened to Benny?"

"The house next door, the one with the dog—that was where Benny lived. He always parked his fancy Corvette out front, and people knew better than to mess with it. Late one night he was getting out of the car and somebody shot him. A drug burn, they say. After that the *Kabalyeros* decided to make the parking space a shrine to Benny. They roped it off, put flowers there every week. On All Saints Day and the other fiestas, it was something to see."

"And that brings us to last March thirteenth," I said.

Mrs. Angeles bit her lower lip and smoothed her dress again.

When she didn't speak, I prompted her. "You'd just come home from work."

"Yeah. It was late, dark. Isabel wasn't here, and I got worried. I kept looking out the window, like a mother does."

"And you saw . . . ?"

"The guy who moved into the house next door after Benny got shot, Reg Dawson. He was black, one of a gang called the Victors. They say he moved into that house to show the *Kabalyeros* that the Victors were taking over their turf. Anyway, he drives up and stops a little way down the block. Waits there, revving his engine. People start showing up; the word's been out that something's gonna go down. And when there's a big crowd, Reg Dawson guns his car and drives right into Benny's space, over the rope and the flowers.

"Well, that started one hell of a fight—Victors and *Kabalyeros* and folks from the neighborhood. And while it's going on, Reg Dawson just stands there in Benny's space acting macho. That's when it happened, what I saw."

"And what was that?"

She hesitated, wet her lips. "The leader of the *Kabalyeros*, Tommy Dragón—the Dragon, they call him—was over by the fence in front of Reg Dawson's house, where you couldn't see him unless you were really looking. I was, 'cause I was trying to see if Isabel was anyplace out there. And I saw Tommy Dragón point this gun at Reg Dawson and shoot him dead."

"What did you do then?"

"Ran and hid in the bathroom. That's where I was when the cops came to the door. Somebody'd told them I was in the window when it all went down and then ran away when Reg got shot. Well, what was I supposed to do? I got no use for the *Kabalyeros* or the Victors, so I told the truth. And now here I am in this mess."

Mrs. Angeles had been slated to be the chief prosecution witness at

271

Tommy Dragón's trial this week. But a month ago the threats had started: anonymous letters and phone calls warning her against testifying. As the trial date approached, this had escalated into blatant intimidation: a fire was set in her trash can; someone shot out her kitchen window; a dead dog turned up on her doorstep. The previous Friday, Isabel had been accosted on her way home from the bus stop by two masked men with guns. And that had finally made Mrs. Angeles capitulate; in court yesterday, she'd refused to take the stand against Dragón.

The state needed her testimony; there were no other witnesses, Dragón insisted on his innocence, and the murder gun had not been found. The judge had tried to reason with Mrs. Angeles, then cited her for contempt—reluctantly, he said. "The court is aware that there have been threats made against you and your family," he told her, "but it is unable to guarantee your protection." Then he gave her forty-eight hours to reconsider her decision.

As it turned out, Mrs. Angeles had a champion in her employer. The owner of the sewing factory was unwilling to allow one of his long-term workers to go to jail or to risk her own and her family's safety. He brought her to All Souls, where he held a membership in our legal-services plan, and this morning Jack Stuart had asked me to do something for her.

What? I'd asked. What could I do that the SFPD couldn't to stop vicious harassment by a street gang?

Well, he said, get proof against whoever was threatening her so they could be arrested and she'd feel free to testify.

Sure, Jack, I said. And exactly why *hadn't* the police been able to do anything about the situation?

His answer was not surprising: lack of funds. Intimidation of prosecution witnesses in cases relating to gang violence was becoming more and more prevalent and open in San Francisco, but the city did not have the resources to protect them. An old story nowadays—not enough money to go around.

Mrs. Angeles was watching my face, her eyes tentative. As I looked back at her, her gaze began to waver. She'd experienced too much disappointment in her life to expect much in the way of help from me.

I said, "Yes, you certainly are in a mess. Let's see if we can get you out of it."

We talked for a while longer, and I soon realized that Amor—as she asked me to call her—held the misconception that there was some way I could get the contempt citation dropped. I asked her if she'd known beforehand that a balky witness could be sent to jail. She shook her head. A person had a right to change her mind, didn't she? When I set her straight on that, she seemed to lose interest in the conversation; it was difficult to get her to focus long enough to compile a list of people I should talk with. I settled for enough names to keep me occupied for the rest of the afternoon.

I was ready to leave when angry voices came from the front steps. A young man and woman entered. They stopped speaking when they saw the room was occupied, but their faces remained set in lines of contention. Amor hastened to introduce them as her son and daughter, Alex and Isabel. To them she explained that I was a detective "helping with the trouble with the judge."

Alex, a stocky youth with a tracery of mustache on his upper lip, seemed disinterested. He shrugged out of his high school letter jacket and vanished through a door to the rear of the house. Isabel studied me with frank curiosity. She was a slender beauty, with black hair that fell in soft curls to her shoulders; her features had a delicacy lacking in those of her mother and brother. Unfortunately, bright blue eyeshadow and garish orange lipstick detracted from her natural good looks, and she wore an imitation leather outfit in a particularly gaudy shade of purple. However, she was polite and well-spoken as she questioned me about what I could do to help her mother. Then, after a comment to Amor about an assignment that was due the next day, she left through the door her brother had used.

I turned to Amor, who was fingering the leaves of a philodendron plant that stood on a stand near the front window. Her posture was stiff, and when I spoke to her she didn't meet my eyes. Now I was aware of a tension in her that hadn't been there before her children returned home. Anxiety, because of the danger her witnessing the shooting had placed them in? Or something else? It might have had to do with the quarrel they'd been having, but weren't arguments between siblings fairly common? They certainly had been in my childhood home in San Diego.

I told Amor I'd be back to check on her in a couple of hours. Then, after a few precautionary and probably unnecessary reminders about locking doors and staying clear of windows, I went out into the chill November afternoon.

The first name on my list was Madeline Dawson, the slain gang leader's widow. I glanced at the house next door and saw with some relief that the guard dog no longer paced in its yard. When I pushed through the gate in the chain link fence, the creature's whereabouts quickly became apparent: a bellowing emanated from the small, shabby cottage. I went up a broken walk bordered by weeds, climbed the sagging front steps, and pressed the bell. A woman's voice yelled for the dog to shut up, then a door slammed somewhere within, muffling the barking. Footsteps approached, and the woman called, "Yes, who is it?"

"My name's Sharon McCone, from All Souls Legal Cooperative. I'm investigating the threats your neighbor, Mrs. Angeles, has been receiving."

A couple of locks turned and the door opened on its chain. The face that peered out at me was very thin and pale, with wisps of red hair straggling over the high forehead; the Dawson marriage had been an interracial one, then. The woman stared at me for a moment before she asked, "What threats?"

"You don't know that Mrs. Angeles and her children have been threatened because she's to testify against the man who shot your husband?"

She shook her head and stepped back, shivering slightly—whether from the cold outside or the memory of the murder, I couldn't tell. "I . . . don't get out much these days."

"May I come in, talk with you about the shooting?"

She shrugged, unhooked the chain, and opened the door. "I don't know what good it will do. Amor's a damned fool for saying she'd testify in the first place."

"Aren't you glad she did? The man killed your husband."

She shrugged again and motioned me into a living room the same size as that in the Angeles home. All resemblance stopped there, however. Dirty glasses and dishes, full ashtrays, piles of newspapers and magazines covered every surface; dust balls the size of rats lurked under the shabby Danish modern furniture. Madeline Dawson picked up a heap of tabloids from the couch and dumped it on the floor, then indicated I should sit there and took a hassock for herself.

I said, "You *are* glad that Mrs. Angeles was willing to testify, aren't you?"

"Not particularly."

"You don't care if your husband's killer is convicted or not?"

"Reg was asking to be killed. Not that I wouldn't mind seeing the Dragon get the gas chamber—he may not have killed Reg, but he killed plenty of other people—"

"What did you say?" I spoke sharply, and Madeline Dawson blinked in surprise. It made me pay closer attention to her eyes; they were glassy, their pupils dilated. The woman, I realized, was high.

"I said the Dragon killed plenty of other people."

"No, about him not killing Reg."

"Did I say that?"

"Yes."

"I can't imagine why. I mean, Amor must know. She was up there in the window watching for sweet Isabel like always."

"You don't sound as if you like Isabel Angeles."

"I'm not fond of flips in general. Look at the way they're taking over this area. Daly City's turning into another Manila. All they do is buy, buy, buy—houses, cars, stuff by the truckload. You know, there's a joke that the first three words their babies learn are 'Mama, Papa, and Serramonte.'" Serramonte was a large shopping mall south of San Francisco.

The roots of the resentment she voiced were clear to me. One of our largest immigrant groups today, the Filipinos are highly westernized and by and large better educated and more affluent than other recent arrived Asians —or many of their neighbors, black or white. Isabel Angeles, for all her bright, cheap clothing and excessive makeup, had behind her a tradition of industriousness and upward mobility that might help her to secure a better place in the world than Madeline Dawson could aspire to.

I wasn't going to allow Madeline's biases to interfere with my line of questioning. I said, "About Dragón not having shot your husband—"

"Hey, who knows? Or cares? The bastard's dead, and good riddance."

"Why good riddance?"

"The man was a pig. A pusher who cheated and gouged people—people like me who need the stuff to get through. You think I was always like this, lady? No way. I was a nice Irish Catholic girl from the Avenues when Reg got his hands on me. Turned me on to coke and a lot of other things when I was only thirteen. Liked his pussy young, Reg did. But then I got old—I'm all of nineteen now—and I needed more and more stuff just to keep going, and all of a sudden Reg didn't even *see* me anymore. Yeah, the man was a pig, and I'm glad he's dead."

"But you don't think Dragón killed him."

She sighed in exasperation. "I don't know what I think. It's just that I always supposed that when Reg got it it would be for something more personal than driving his car into a stupid shrine in a parking space. You know what I mean? But what does it matter who killed him, anyway?"

"It matters to Tommy Dragón, for one."

She dismissed the accused man's life with a flick of her hand. "Like I said, the Dragon's a killer. He might as well die for Reg's murder as for any of the others. In a way it'd be the one good thing Reg did for the world."

Perhaps in a certain primitive sense she was right, but her offhandedness made me uncomfortable. I changed the subject. "About the threats to Mrs. Angeles—which of the *Kabalyeros* would be behind them?"

"All of them. The guys in the gangs, they work together."

But I knew enough about the structure of street gangs—my degree in sociology from UC Berkeley hadn't been totally worthless—to be reasonably sure that wasn't so. There is usually one dominant personality, supported by two or three lieutenants; take away these leaders, and the followers become ineffectual, purposeless. If I could turn up enough evidence against the leaders of the *Kabalyeros* to have them arrested, the harassment would stop.

I asked, "Who took over the *Kabalyeros* after Dragón went to jail?"

"Hector Bulis."

It was a name that didn't appear on my list; Amor had claimed not to know who was the current head of the Filipino gang. "Where can I find him?"

"There's a fast-food joint over on Geneva, near the Cow Palace. Fat Robbie's. That's where the *Kabalyeros* hang out."

The second person I'd intended to talk with was the young man who had reportedly taken over the leadership of the Victors after Dawson's death, Jimmy Willis. Willis could generally be found at a bowling alley, also on

Geneva Avenue near the Cow Palace. I thanked Madeline for taking the time to talk with me and headed for the Daly City line.

The first of the two establishments that I spotted was Fat Robbie's, a cinderblock-and-glass relic of the early sixties whose specialties appeared to be burgers and chicken-in-a-basket. I turned into a parking lot that was half-full of mostly shabby cars and left my MG beside one of the defunct drive-in speaker poles.

The interior of the restaurant took me back to my high school days: orange leatherette booths beside the plate glass windows; a long Formica counter with stools; laminated color pictures of disgusting-looking food on the wall above the pass-through counter from the kitchen. Instead of a juke-box there was a bank of video games along one wall. Three Filipino youths in jeans and denim jackets gathered around one called "Invader!" The *Kabalyeros*, I assumed.

I crossed to the counter with only a cursory glance at the trio, sat, and ordered coffee from a young waitress who looked to be Eurasian. The *Kabalyeros* didn't conceal their interest in me; they stared openly, and after a moment one of them said something that sounded like "tick-tick," and they all laughed nastily. Some sort of Tagalog obscenity, I supposed. I ignored them, sipping the dishwater-weak coffee, and after a bit they went back to their game.

I took out a paperback that I keep in my bag for protective coloration and pretended to read, listening to the few snatches of conversation that drifted over from the three. I caught the names of two: Sal and Hector—the latter presumably Bulis, the gang's leader. When I glanced covertly at him, I saw he was tallish and thin, with long hair caught back in a ponytail; his features were razor-sharp and slightly skewed, creating the impression of a perpetual sneer. The trio kept their voices low, and although I strained to hear, I could make out nothing of what they were saying. After about five minutes Hector turned away from the video machine. With a final glance at me he motioned to his companions, and they all left the restaurant.

I waited until they'd driven away in an old green Pontiac before I called the waitress over and showed her my identification. "The three men who just left," I said. "Is the tall one Hector Bulis?"

Her lips formed a little "O" as she stared at the ID. Finally she nodded.

"May I talk with you about them?"

She glanced toward the pass-through to the kitchen. "My boss, he don't like me talking with the customers when I'm supposed to be working."

"Take a break. Just five minutes."

Now she looked nervously around the restaurant. "I shouldn't—"

I slipped a twenty-dollar bill from my wallet and showed it to her. "Just five minutes."

She still seemed edgy, but fear lost out to greed. "Okay, but I don't want anybody to see me talking to you. Go back to the restroom—it's through that door by the video games. I'll meet you there as soon as I can."

I got up and found the ladies' room. It was tiny, dimly lit, with a badly cracked mirror. The walls were covered with a mass of graffiti; some of it looked as if it had been painted over and had later worked its way back into view through the fading layers of enamel. The air in there was redolent of grease, cheap perfume, and stale cigarette and marijuana smoke. I leaned against the sink as I waited.

The young Eurasian woman appeared a few minutes later. "Bastard gave me a hard time," she said. "Tried to tell me I'd already taken my break."

"What's your name?"

"Anna Smith."

"Anna, the three men who just left—do they come in here often?"

"Uh-huh."

"Keep pretty much to themselves, don't they?"

"It's more like other people stay away from them." She hesitated. "They're from one of the gangs; you don't mess with them. That's why I wanted to talk with you back here."

"Have you ever heard them say anything about Tommy Dragón?"

"The Dragon? Sure. He's in jail; they say he was framed."

Of course they would claim that. "What about a Mrs. Angeles— Amorfina Angeles?"

". . . Not that one, no."

"What about trying to intimidate someone? Setting fires, going after someone with a gun?"

"Uh-uh. That's gang business; they keep it pretty close. But it wouldn't surprise me. Filipinos—I'm part Filipina myself, my mom met my dad when he was stationed at Subic Bay—they've got this saying, *kumukuló ang dugó*. It means 'the blood is boiling.' They can get pretty damn mad, 'specially the men. So stuff like what you said—sure they do it."

"Do you work on Fridays?"

"Yeah, two to ten."

"Did you see any of the *Kabalyeros* in here last Friday around six?" That was the time when Isabel had been accosted.

Anna Smith scrunched up her face in concentration. "Last Friday . . . oh, yeah, sure. That was when they had the big meeting, all of them."

"*All* of them?"

"Uh-huh. Started around five thirty, went on a couple of hours. My boss, he was worried something heavy was gonna go down, but the way it turned out, all he did was sell a lot of food."

"What was this meeting about?"

"Had to do with the Dragon, who was gonna be character witnesses at the trial, what they'd say."

The image of the three I'd seen earlier—or any of their ilk—as character witnesses was somewhat ludicrous, but I supposed in Tommy Dragón's position you took what you could get. "Are you sure they were all there?"

"Uh-huh."

"And no one at the meeting said anything about trying to keep Mrs. Angeles from testifying?"

"No. That lawyer the Dragon's got, he was there too."

Now that was odd. Why had Dragón's public defender chosen to meet with his witnesses in a public place? I could think of one good reason: he was afraid of them, didn't want them in his office. But what if the *Kabalyeros* had set the time and place—as an alibi for when Isabel was to be assaulted?

"I better get back to work," Anna Smith said. "Before the boss comes looking for me."

I gave her the twenty dollars. "Thanks for your time."

"Sure." Halfway out the door she paused, frowning. "I hope I didn't get any of the *Kabalyeros* in trouble."

"You didn't."

"Good. I kind of like them. I mean, they push dope and all, but these days, who doesn't?"

These days, who doesn't? I thought. *Good Lord. . . .*

The Starlight Lanes was an old-fashioned bowling alley girded by a rough cliff face and an auto dismantler's yard. The parking lot was crowded, so I left the MG around back by the garbage cans. Inside, the lanes were brightly lit and noisy with the sound of crashing pins, rumbling balls, shouts, and groans. I paused by the front counter and asked where I might find Jimmy Willis. The woman behind it directed me to a lane at the far left.

Bowling alleys—or lanes, as the new upscale bowler prefers to call them —are familiar territory to me. Up until a few years ago my favorite uncle Jim was a top player on the pro tour. The Starlight Lanes reminded me of the ones where Jim used to practice in San Diego—from the racks full of tired-looking rental shoes to the greasy-spoon coffeeshop smells to the molded plastic chairs and cigarette-burned scorekeeping consoles. I walked along, soaking up the ambience—some people would say the lack of it—until I came to lane 32 and spotted an agile young black man bowling alone. Jimmy Willis was a left-hander, and his ball hooked out until it hung on the edge of the channel, then hooked back with deadly precision. I waited in the spectator area, admiring his accuracy and graceful form. His concentration was go great that he didn't notice me until he'd finished the last frame and retrieved his ball.

"You're quite a bowler," I said. "What's your average?"

He gave me a long look before he replied, "Two hundred."

"Almost good enough to turn pro."

"That's what I'm looking to do."

Odd, for the head of a street gang that dealt in drugs and death. "You ever hear of Jim McCone?" I asked.

"Sure. Damned good in his day."

"He's my uncle."

"No kidding." Willis studied me again, now as if looking for a resemblance.

Rapport established, I showed him my ID and explained that I wanted to talk about Reg Dawson's murder. He frowned, hesitated, then nodded. "Okay, since you're Jim McCone's niece, but you'll have to buy me a beer."

"Deal."

Willis toweled off his ball, stowed it and his shoes in their bag, and led me to a typical smoke-filled, murkily lighted bowling alley bar. He took one of the booths while I fetched us a pair of Buds.

As I slid into the booth I said, "What can you tell me about the murder?"

"The way I see it, Dawson was asking for it."

So he and Dawson's wife were of a mind about that. "I can understand what you mean, but it seems strange, coming from you. I hear you were his friend, that you took over the Victors after his death."

"You heard wrong on both counts. Yeah, I was in the Victors, and when Dawson bought it, they tried to get me to take over. But by then I'd figured out—never mind how, doesn't matter—that I wanted out of that life. Ain't nothing in it but what happened to Benny Crespo and Dawson—or what's gonna happen to the Dragon. So I decided to put my hand to something with a future." He patted the bowling bag that sat on the banquette beside him. "Got a job here now—not much, but my bowling's free and I'm on my way."

"Good for you. What about Dragón—do you think he's guilty?"

Willis hesitated, looking thoughtful. "Why you ask?"

"Just wondering."

". . . Well, to tell you the truth, I never did believe the Dragon shot Reg."

"Who did, then?"

He shrugged.

I asked him if he'd heard about the *Kabalyeros* trying to intimidate the chief prosecution witness. When he nodded, I said, "They also threatened the life of her daughter last Friday."

He laughed mirthlessly. "Wish I could of seen that. Kind of surprises me, though. That lawyer of Dragón's, he found out what the *Kabalyeros* were up to, read them the riot act. Said they'd put Dragón in the gas chamber for sure. So they called it off."

"When was this?"

"Week, ten days ago."

Long before Isabel had been accosted. Before the dead dog and shooting incidents, too. "Are you sure?"

"It's what I hear. You know, in a way I'm surprised that they'd go after Mrs. Angeles at all."

"Why?"

"The Filipinos have this macho tradition. 'Specially when it comes to their women. They don't like them messed with, 'specially by non-Filipinos. So how come they'd turn around and mess with one of their own?"

"Well, her testimony *would* jeopardize the life of one of their fellow gang members. It's an extreme situation."

"Can't argue with that."

Jimmy Willis and I talked a bit more, but he couldn't—or wouldn't—offer any further information. I bought him a second beer, then went out to where I'd left my car.

And came face-to-face with Hector Bulis and the man called Sal.

Sal grabbed me by the arm, twisted it behind me, and forced me up against the latticework fence surrounding the garbage cans. The stench from them filled my nostrils; Sal's breath rivaled it in foulness. I struggled, but he got hold of my other arm and pinned me tighter. I looked around, saw no one, nothing but the cliff face and the high board fence of the auto dismantler's yard. Bulis approached, flicking open a switchblade, his twisty face intense. I stiffened, went very still, eyes on the knife.

Bulis placed the tip of the knife against my jawbone, then traced a line across my cheek. "Don't want to hurt you, bitch," he said. "You do what I say, I won't have to mess you up."

The Tagalog phrase that Anna Smith had translated for me—*kumukuló ang dugó*— flashed through my mind. *The blood is boiling.* I sensed Bulis's was —and dangerously high.

I wet my dry lips, tried to keep my voice from shaking as I said, "What do you want me to do?"

"We hear you're asking around about Dawson's murder, trying to prove the Dragon did it."

"That's not—"

"We want you to quit. Go back to your own part of town and leave our business alone."

"Whoever told you that is lying. I'm only trying to help the Angeles family."

"They wouldn't lie." He moved the knife's tip to the hollow at the base of my throat. I felt it pierce my skin—a mere pinprick, but frightening enough.

When I could speak, I did so slowly, phrasing my words carefully. "What

I hear is that Dragón is innocent. And that the *Kabalyeros* aren't behind the harassment of the Angeleses—at least not for a week or ten days."

Bulis exchanged a look with his companion—quick, unreadable.

"Someone's trying to frame you," I added. "Just like they did Dragón."

Bulis continued to hold the knife to my throat, his hand firm. His gaze wavered, however, as if he was considering what I'd said. After a moment he asked, "All right—who?"

"I'm not sure, but I think I can find out."

He thought a bit longer, then let his arm drop and snapped the knife shut. "I'll give you till this time tomorrow," he said. Then he stuffed the knife into his pocket, motioned for Sal to let go of me, and the two quickly walked away.

I sagged against the latticework fence, feeling my throat where the knife had pricked it. It had bled a little, but the flow already was clotting. My knees were weak and my breath came fast, but I was too caught up in the possibilities to panic. There were plenty of them—and the most likely was the most unpleasant.

Kumukuló ang dugó. The blood is boiling. . . .

Two hours later I was back at the Angeles house on Omega Street. When Amor admitted me, the tension I'd felt in her earlier had drained. Her body sagged, as if the extra weight she carried had finally proved to be too much for her frail bones; the skin of her face looked flaccid, like melting putty; her eyes were sunken and vague. After she shut the door and motioned for me to sit, she sank into the recliner, expelling a sigh. The house was quiet—too quiet.

"I have a question for you," I said. "What does 'tick-tick' mean in Tagalog?"

Her eyes flickered with dull interest. *"Tiktík."* She corrected my pronunciation. "It's a word for detective."

Ever since Hector Bulis and Sal had accosted me I'd suspected as much.

"Where did you hear that?" Amor asked.

"One of the *Kabalyeros* said it when I went to Fat Robbie's earlier. Someone had told them I was a detective, probably described me. Whoever it was said I was trying to prove Tommy Dragón killed Reg Dawson."

"Why would—"

"More to the point, *who* would? At the time, only four people knew that I'm a detective."

She wet her lips, but remained silent.

"Amor, the night of the shooting, you were standing in your front window, watching for Isabel."

"Yes."

"Do you do that often?"

". . . Yes."

"Because Isabel is often late coming home. Because you're afraid she may have gotten into trouble."

"A mother worries—"

"Especially when she's given a good cause. Isabel is running out of control, isn't she?"

"No, she—"

"Amor, when I spoke with Madeline Dawson, she said you were standing in the window watching for 'sweet Isabel, like always.' She didn't say 'sweet' in a pleasant way. Later, Jimmy Willis implied that your daughter is not . . . exactly a vulnerable young girl."

Amor's eyes sparked. "The Dawson woman is jealous."

"Of course she is. There's something else: when I asked the waitress at Fat Robbie's if she'd ever overheard the *Kabalyeros* discussing you, she said, 'No, not that one.' It didn't register at the time, but when I talked to her again a little while ago, she told me Isabel is the member of your family they discuss. They say she's wild, runs around with the men in the gangs. You know that, so does Alex. And so does Madeline Dawson. She just told me the first man Isabel became involved with was her husband."

Amor seemed to shrivel. She gripped the arm of the chair, white-knuckled.

"It's true, isn't it?" I asked more gently.

She lowered her eyes, nodding. When she spoke her voice was ragged. "I don't know what to do with her anymore. Ever since that Reg Dawson got to her, she's been different, not my girl at all."

"Is she on drugs?"

"Alex says no, but I'm not so sure."

I let it go; it didn't really matter. "When she came home earlier," I said, "Isabel seemed very interested in me. She asked questions, looked me over carefully enough to be able to describe me to the *Kabalyeros*. She was afraid of what I might find out. For instance, that she wasn't accosted by any men with guns last Friday."

"She was!"

"No, Amor. That was just a story, to make it look as if your life—and your children's—were in danger if you testified. In spite of what you said early on, you haven't wanted to testify against Tommy Dragón from the very beginning.

"When the *Kabalyeros* began harassing you a month ago, you saw that as the perfect excuse not to take the stand. But you didn't foresee that Dragón's lawyer would convince the gang to stop the harassment. When that happened, you and Isabel, and probably Alex, too, manufactured incidents—the shot-out window, the dead dog on the doorstep, the men with the guns—to make it look as if the harassment was still going on."

"Why would I? They're going to put me in jail."

"But at the time you didn't know they could do that—or that your employer would hire me. My investigating poses yet another danger to you and your family."

"This is . . . why would I do all that?"

"Because basically you're an honest woman, a good woman. You didn't want to testify because you knew Dragón didn't shoot Dawson. It's my guess you gave the police his name because it was the first one that came to mind."

"I had no reason to—"

"You had the best reason in the world: a mother's desire to protect her child."

She was silent, sunken eyes registering despair and defeat.

I kept on, even though I hated to inflict further pain on her. "The day he died, Dawson had let the word out that he was going to desecrate Benny's space. The person who shot him knew there would be fighting and confusion, counted on that as a cover. The killer hated Dawson—"

"Lots of people did."

"But only one person you'd want to protect so badly that you'd accuse an innocent man."

"Leave my mother alone. She's suffered enough on account of what I did."

I turned. Alex had come into the room so quietly I hadn't noticed. Now he moved midway between Amor and me, a Saturday night special clutched in his right hand.

The missing murder weapon.

I tensed, but one look at his face told me he didn't intend to use it. Instead he raised his arm and extended the gun, grip first.

"Take this," he said. "I never should have bought it. Never should of used it. I hated Dawson on account of what he did to my sister. But killing him wasn't worth what we've all gone through since."

I glanced at Amor; tears were trickling down her face.

Alex said, "Mama, don't cry. I'm not worth it."

When she spoke, it was to me. "What will happen to him?"

"Nothing like what might have happened to Dragón; Alex is a juvenile. You, however—"

"I don't care about myself, only my children."

Maybe that was the trouble. She was the archetypal selfless mother: living only for her children, sheltering them from the consequences of their actions—and in the end doing them irreparable harm.

There were times when I felt thankful that I had no children. And there were times when I was thankful that Jack Stuart was a very good criminal lawyer. This was a time when I was thankful on both counts. I went to the phone, called Jack, and asked him to come over here. At least I could leave the Angeles family in good legal hands.

After he arrived, I went out into the gathering dusk. An old yellow VW was pulling out of Benny's space. I walked down there and stood on the curb. Nothing remained of the shrine to Benny Crespo. Nothing remained to show that blood had boiled and been shed there. It was merely a stretch of cracked asphalt, splotched with oil drippings, littered with the detritus of urban life. I stared at it for close to a minute, then turned away from the bleak landscape of Omega Street.

Sara Paretsky's V.I. Warshawski has appeared in novels and short fiction; in "Settled Score," reprinted from *A Woman's Eye*, the author of such novels as *Burn Marks, Bloodshot,* and *Killing Orders* does something she does better than most. Vic takes us once again into her world and introduces us to her wide and wonderfully diverse circle of acquaintances. Using music as her metaphor she shows, in a gently horrific way, that the rich, famous, or very talented are like the rest of us, with emotions that can drive usually rational people to committing criminal acts of violence.

Settled Score

A V. I. WARSHAWSKI STORY

SARA PARETSKY

For Bob Kirschner, who helped make it work

I

"It's such a difficult concept to deal with. I just don't like to use that word." Paul Servino turned to me, his mobile mouth pursed consideringly. "I put it to you, Victoria: you're a lawyer. Would you not agree?"

"I agree that the law defines responsibility differently than we do when we're talking about social or moral relations," I said carefully. "No state's attorney is going to try to get Mrs. Hampton arrested, but does that—"

"You see," Servino interrupted. "That's just my point."

"But it's not mine," Lotty said fiercely, her thick dark brows forming a forbidding line across her forehead. "And if you had seen Claudia with her guts torn out by lye, perhaps you would think a little differently."

The table was silenced for a moment: we were surprised by the violent edge to Lotty's anger. Penelope Herschel shook her head slightly at Servino.

He caught her eye and nodded. "Sorry, Lotty. I didn't mean to upset you so much."

Lotty forced herself to smile. "Paul, you think you develop a veneer after thirty years as a doctor. You think you see people in all their pain and that your professionalism protects you from too much feeling. But that girl was fifteen. She had her life in front of her. She didn't want to have a baby. And her mother wanted her to. Not for religious reasons, even—she's English with all their contempt for Catholicism. But because she hoped to continue to control her daughter's life. Claudia felt overwhelmed by her mother's pressure and swallowed a jar of oven cleaner. Now don't tell me the mother is not responsible. I do not give one damn if no court would try her: to me, she caused her daughter's death as surely as if she had poured the poison into her."

Servino ignored another slight headshake from Lotty's niece. "It is a tragedy. But a tragedy for the mother, too. You don't think she meant her daughter to kill herself, do you, Lotty?"

Lotty gave a tense smile. "What goes on in the unconscious is surely your department, Paul. But perhaps that was Mrs. Hampton's wish. Of course, if she didn't *intend* for Claudia to die, the courts would find her responsibility diminished. Am I not right, Vic?"

I moved uneasily in my chair. I didn't want to referee this argument: it had all the earmarks of the kind of domestic fight where both contestants attack the police. Besides, while the rest of the dinner party was interested in the case and sympathetic to Lotty's feelings, none of them cared about the question of legal versus moral responsibility.

The dinner was in honor of Lotty Herschel's niece Penelope, making one of her periodic scouting forays into Chicago's fashion scene. Her father—Lotty's only brother—owned a chain of high-priced women's dress shops in Montreal, Quebec, and Toronto. He was thinking of making Chicago his US beachhead, and Penelope was out looking at locations as well as previewing the Chicago designers' spring ideas.

Lotty usually gave a dinner for Penelope when she was in town. Servino was always invited. An analyst friend of Lotty's, he and Penelope had met on one of her first buying trips to Chicago. Since then, they'd seen as much of each other as two busy professionals half a continent apart could manage. Although their affair now had five years of history to it, Penelope continued to stay with Lotty when she was in town.

The rest of the small party included Max Loewenthal, the executive director of Beth Israel, where Lotty treated perinatal patients, and Chaim Lemke, a clarinetist with the Aeolus Woodwind Quintet. A slight, melancholy man, he had met Lotty and Max in London, where they'd all been refugees. Chaim's wife, Greta, who played harpsichord and piano for an early music group, didn't come along. Lotty said not to invite her because she was seeing

Paul professionally, but anyway, since she was currently living with Aeolus oboist Rudolph Strayarn, she probably wouldn't have accepted.

We were eating at my apartment. Lotty had called earlier in the day, rattled by the young girl's death and needing help putting the evening together. She was so clearly beside herself that I'd felt compelled to offer my own place. With cheese and fruit after dinner Lotty had begun discussing the case with the whole group, chiefly expressing her outrage with a legal system that let Mrs. Hampton off without so much as a warning.

For some reason Servino continued to argue the point despite Penelope's warning frowns. Perhaps the fact that we were on our third bottle of Barolo explained the lapse from Paul's usual sensitive courtesy.

"Mrs. Hampton did not point a gun at the girl's head and force her to become pregnant," he said. "The daughter was responsible, too, if you want to use that word. And the boy—the father, whoever that was."

Lotty, normally abstemious, had drunk her share of the wine. Her black eyes glittered and her Viennese accent became pronounced.

"I know the argument, believe you me, Paul: it's the old 'who pulled the trigger?'—the person who fired the gun, the person who manufactured it, the person who created the situation, the parents who created the shooter. To me, that is Scholastic hairsplitting—you know, all that crap they used to teach us a thousand years ago in Europe. Who is the ultimate cause, the immediate cause, the sufficient cause and on and on.

"It's dry theory, not life. It takes people off the hook for their own actions. You can quote Heinz Kohut and the rest of the self-psychologists to me all night, but you will never convince me that people are unable to make conscious choices for their actions or that parents are not responsible for how they treat their children. It's the same thing as saying the Nazis were not responsible for how they treated Europe."

Penelope gave a strained smile. She loved both Lotty and Servino and didn't want either of them to make fools of themselves. Max, on the other hand, watched Lotty affectionately—he liked to see her passionate. Chaim was staring into space, his lips moving. I assumed he was reading a score in his head.

"I would say that," Servino snapped, his own Italian accent strong. "And don't look at me as though I were Joseph Goebbels. Chaim and I are ten years younger than you and Max, but we share your story in great extent. I do not condone or excuse the horrors our families suffered, or our own dispossession. But I can look at Himmler, or Mussolini, or even Hitler and say, they behaved in such and such a way because of weaknesses accentuated in them by history, by their parents, by their culture. You could as easily say the French were responsible, the French because their need for—for—*rappresaglia*—what am I trying to say, Victoria?"

"Reprisal," I supplied.

"Now you see, Lotty, now I, too, am angry; I forget my English. . . . But if they and the English had not stretched Germany with reparations, the situation might have been different. So how can you claim responsibility—for one person, or one nation? You just have to do the best you can with what is going on around you."

Lotty's face was set. "Yes, Paul. I know what you are saying. Yes, the French created a situation. And the English wished to accommodate Hitler. And the Americans would not take in the Jews. All these things are true. But the Germans chose, nonetheless. They could have acted differently. I will not take them off the hook just because other people should have acted differently."

I took her hand and squeezed it. "At the risk of being the Neville Chamberlain in the case, could I suggest some appeasement? Chaim brought his clarinet and Max his violin. Paul, if you'll play the piano, Penelope and I will sing."

Chaim smiled, relaxing the sadness in his thin face. He loved making music, whether with friends or professionals. "Gladly, Vic. But only a few songs. It's late and we go to California for a two-week tour tomorrow."

The atmosphere lightened. We went into the living room, where Chaim flipped through my music, pulling out Wolf's *Spanisches Liederbuch*. In the end, he and Max stayed with Lotty, playing and talking until three in the morning, long after Servino and Penelope's departure.

II

The detective business is not as much fun in January as at other times of the year. I spent the next two days forcing my little Chevy through unplowed side streets trying to find a missing witness who was the key to an eighteen-million-dollar fraud case. I finally succeeded Tuesday evening a little before five. By the time I'd convinced the terrified woman, who was hiding with a niece at Sixty-seventh and Honore, that no one would shoot her if she testified, gotten her to the state's attorney, and seen her safely home again, it was close to ten o'clock.

I fumbled with the outer locks on the apartment building with my mind fixed on a hot bath, lots of whiskey, and a toasted cheese sandwich. When the ground-floor door opened and Mr. Contreras popped out to meet me, I ground my teeth. He's a retired machinist with more energy than Navratilova. I didn't have the stamina to deal with him tonight.

I mumbled a greeting and headed for the stairs.

"There you are, doll." The relief in his voice was marked. I stopped wearily. Some crisis with the dog. Something involving lugging a sixty-pound retriever to the vet through snow-packed streets.

"I thought I ought to let her in, you know. I told her there was no saying when you'd be home, sometimes you're gone all night on a case"—a delicate reference to my love life—"but she was all set she had to wait and she'd'a been sitting on the stairs all this time. She won't say what the problem is, but you'd probably better talk to her. You wanna come in here or should I send her up in a few minutes?"

Not the dog, then. "Uh, who is it?"

"Aren't I trying to tell you? That beautiful girl. You know, the doc's niece."

"Penelope?" I echoed foolishly.

She came out into the hall just then, ducking under the old man's gesticulating arms. "Vic! Thank God you're back. I've got to talk to you. Before the police do anything stupid."

She was huddled in an ankle-length silver fur. Ordinarily elegant, with exquisite makeup and jewelry and the most modern of hairstyles, she didn't much resemble her aunt. But shock had stripped the sophistication from her, making her dark eyes the focus of her face; she looked so much like Lotty that I went to her instinctively.

"Come on up with me and tell me what's wrong." I put an arm around her.

Mr. Contreras closed his door in disappointment as we disappeared up the stairs. Penelope waited until we were inside my place before saying anything else. I slung my jacket and down vest on the hooks in the hallway and went into the living room to undo my heavy walking shoes.

Penelope kept her fur wrapped around her. Her highheeled kid boots were not meant for streetwear: they were rimmed with salt stains. She shivered slightly despite the coat.

"Have—have you heard anything?"

I shook my head, rubbing my right foot, stiff from driving all day.

"It's Paul. He's dead."

"But—he's not that old. And I thought he was very healthy." Because of his sedentary job, Servino always ran the two miles from his Loop office to his apartment in the evening.

Penelope gave a little gulp of hysterical laughter. "Oh, he was very fit. But not healthy enough to overcome a blow to the head."

"Could you tell the story from the beginning instead of letting it out in little dramatic bursts?"

As I'd hoped, my rudeness got her angry enough to overcome her incipient hysteria. After flashing me a Lotty-like look of royal disdain, she told me what she knew.

Paul's office was in a building where a number of analysts had their practices. A sign posted on his door this morning baldly announced that he had canceled all his day's appointments because of a personal emergency. When a janitor went in at three to change a light bulb, he'd found the doctor dead on the floor of his consulting room.

Colleagues agreed they'd seen Servino arrive around a quarter of eight, as he usually did. They'd seen the notice and assumed he'd left when everyone else was tied up with appointments. No one thought any more about it.

Penelope had learned of her lover's death from the police, who picked her up as she was leaving a realtor's office where she'd been discussing shop leases. Two of the doctors with offices near Servino's had mentioned seeing a dark-haired woman in a long fur coat near his consulting room.

Penelope's dark eyes were drenched with tears. "It's not enough that Paul is dead, that I learn of it such an unspeakable way. They think I killed him— because I have dark hair and wear a fur coat. They don't know what killed him —some dreary blunt instrument—it sounds stupid and banal, like an old Agatha Christie. They've pawed through my luggage looking for it."

They'd questioned her for three hours while they searched and finally, reluctantly, let her go, with a warning not to leave Chicago. She'd called Lotty at the clinic and then come over to find me.

I went into the dining room for some whiskey. She shook her head at the bottle. I poured myself an extra slug to make up for missing my bath. "And?"

"And I want you to find who killed him. The police aren't looking very hard because they think it's me."

"Do they have a reason for this?"

She blushed unexpectedly. "They think he was refusing to marry me."

"Not much motive in these times, one would have thought. And you with a successful career to boot. Was he refusing?"

"No. It was the other way around, actually. I felt—felt unsettled about what I wanted to do—come to Chicago to stay, you know. I have—friends in Montreal, too, you know. And I've always thought marriage meant monogamy."

"I see." My focus on the affair between Penelope and Paul shifted slightly. "You didn't kill him, did you—perhaps for some other reason?"

She forced a smile. "Because he didn't agree with Lotty about responsibility? No. And for no other reason. Are you going to ask Lotty if she killed him?"

"Lotty would have mangled him Sunday night with whatever was lying on the dining room table—she wouldn't wait to sneak into his office with a club." I eyed her thoughtfully. "Just out of vulgar curiosity, what were you doing around eight this morning?"

Her black eyes scorched me. "I came to you because I thought you would be sympathetic. Not to get the same damned questions I had all afternoon from the police!"

"And what were you doing at eight this morning?"

She swept across the room to the door, then thought better of it and affected to study a Nell Blaine poster on the nearby wall. With her back to me she said curtly, "I was having a second cup of coffee. And no, there are no witnesses. As you know, by that time of day Lotty is long gone. Perhaps someone saw me leave the building at eight thirty—I asked the detectives to question the neighbors, but they didn't seem much interested in doing so."

"Don't sell them short. If you're not under arrest, they're still asking questions."

"But you could ask questions to clear me. They're just trying to implicate me."

I pinched the bridge of my nose, trying to ease the dull ache behind my eyes. "You do realize the likeliest person to have killed him is an angry patient, don't you? Despite your fears the police have probably been questioning them all day."

Nothing I said could convince her that she wasn't in imminent danger of a speedy trial before a kangaroo court, with execution probable by the next morning. She stayed until past midnight, alternating pleas to hide her with commands to join the police in hunting down Paul's killer. She wouldn't call Lotty to tell her she was with me because she was afraid Lotty's home phone had been tapped.

"Look, Penelope," I finally said, exasperated. "I can't hide you. If the police really suspect you, you were tailed here. Even if I could figure out a way to smuggle you out and conceal you someplace, I wouldn't do it—I'd lose my license on obstruction charges and I'd deserve to."

I tried explaining how hard it was to get a court order for a wiretap and finally gave up. I was about ready to start screaming with frustration when Lotty herself called, devastated by Servino's death and worried about Penelope. The police had been by with a search warrant and had taken away an array of household objects, including her umbrella. Such an intrusion would normally have made her spitting mad, but she was too upset to give it her full emotional attention. I turned the phone over to Penelope. Whatever Lotty said to her stained her cheeks red, but did make her agree to let me drive her home.

When I got back to my place, exhausted enough to sleep round the clock, I found John McGonnigal waiting for me in a blue-and-white outside my building. He came up the walk behind me and opened the door with a flourish.

I looked at him sourly. "Thanks, Sergeant. It's been a long day—I'm glad to have a doorman at the end of it."

"It's kind of cold down here for talking, Vic. How about inviting me up for coffee?"

"Because I want to go to bed. If you've got something you want to say, or even ask, spit it out down here."

I was just ventilating and I knew it—if a police sergeant wanted to talk to me at one in the morning, we'd talk. Mr. Contreras's coming out in a magenta bathrobe to see what the trouble was merely speeded my decision to cooperate.

While I assembled cheese sandwiches, McGonnigal asked me what I'd learned from Penelope.

"She didn't throw her arms around me and howl, 'Vic, I killed him, you've got to help me.' " I put the sandwiches in a skillet with a little olive oil. "What've you guys got on her?"

The receptionist and two of the other analysts who'd been in the hall had seen a small, dark-haired woman hovering in the alcove near Servino's office around twenty of eight. Neither of them had paid too much attention to her; when they saw Penelope they agreed it might have been she, but they couldn't be certain. If they'd made a positive ID, she'd already have been arrested, even though they couldn't find the weapon.

"They had a shouting match at the Filigree last night. The maître d' was quite upset. Servino was a regular and he didn't want to offend him, but a number of diners complained. The Herschel girl"—McGonnigal eyed me warily—"woman, I mean, stormed off on her own and spent the night with her aunt. One of the neighbors saw her leave around seven the next morning, not at eight thirty as she says."

I didn't like the sound of that. I asked him about the cause of death.

"Someone gave him a good crack across the side of the neck, close enough to the back to fracture a cervical vertebra and sever one of the main arteries. It would have killed him pretty fast. And as you know, Servino wasn't very tall—the Herschel woman could easily have done it."

"With what?" I demanded.

That was the stumbling block. It could have been anything from a baseball bat to a steel pipe. The forensic pathologist who'd looked at the body favored the latter, since the skin had been broken in places. They'd taken away anything in Lotty's apartment and Penelope's luggage that might have done the job and were having them examined for traces of blood and skin.

I snorted. "If you searched Lotty's place, you must have come away with quite an earful."

McGonnigal grimaced. "She spoke her mind, yes. . . . Any ideas? On what the weapon might have been?"

I shook my head, too nauseated by the thought of Paul's death to muster intellectual curiosity over the choice of weapon. When McGonnigal left around two thirty, I lay in bed staring at the dark, unable to sleep despite my fatigue. I didn't know Penelope all that well. Just because she was Lotty's niece didn't mean she was incapable of murder. To be honest, I hadn't been totally convinced by her histrionics tonight. Who but a lover could get close enough to you to snap your neck? I thrashed around for hours, finally dropping into an uneasy sleep around six.

Lotty woke me at eight to implore me to look for Servino's killer; the police had been back at seven thirty to ask Penelope why she'd forgotten to mention she'd been at Paul's apartment early yesterday morning.

"Why was she there?" I asked reasonably.

"She says she wanted to patch things up after their quarrel, but he'd already left for the office. When the police started questioning her, she was too frightened to tell the truth. Vic, I'm terrified they're going to arrest her."

I mumbled something. It looked to me like they had a pretty good case, but I valued my life too much to say that to Lotty. Even so the conversation deteriorated rapidly.

"I come out in any wind or weather to patch you up. With never a word of complaint." That wasn't exactly true, but I let it pass. "Now, when I beg you for help you turn a deaf ear to me. I shall remember this, Victoria."

Giant black spots formed and re-formed in front of my tired eyes. "Great, Lotty."

Her receiver banged in my ear.

III

I spent the day doggedly going about my own business, turning on WBBM whenever I was in the car to see if any news had come in about Penelope's arrest. Despite all the damaging eyewitness reports, the state's attorney apparently didn't want to move without a weapon.

I trudged up the stairs to my apartment a little after six, my mind fixed on a bath and a rare steak followed immediately by bed. When I got to the top landing, I ground my teeth in futile rage: a fur-coated woman was sitting in front of the door.

When she got to her feet I realized it wasn't Penelope but Greta Schipauer, Chaim Lemke's wife. The dark hallway had swallowed the gold of her hair.

"Vic! Thank God you've come back. I've been here since four and I have a concert in two hours."

I fumbled with the three stiff locks. "I have an office downtown just so that people won't have to sit on the floor outside my home," I said pointedly.

"You do? Oh—it never occurred to me you didn't just work out of your living room."

She followed me in and headed over to the piano, where she picked out a series of fifths. "You really should get this tuned, Vic."

"Is that why you've been here for two hours? To tell me to tune my piano?" I slung my coat onto a hook in the entryway and sat on the couch to pull off my boots.

"No, no." She sat down hastily. "It's because of Paul, of course. I spoke to Lotty today and she says you're refusing to stir yourself to look for his murderer. Why, Vic? We all need you very badly. You can't let us down now. The police were questioning me for two hours yesterday. It utterly destroyed my concentration. I couldn't practice at all; I know the recital tonight will be a disaster. Even Chaim has been affected, and he's out on the West Coast."

I was too tired to be tactful. "How do you know that? I thought you've been living with Rudolph Strayarn."

She looked surprised. "What does that have to do with anything? I'm still interested in Chaim's music. And it's been terrible. Rudolph called this morning to tell me and I bought an L.A. paper downtown."

She thrust a copy of the L.A. *Times* in front of me. It was folded back to the arts section where the headline read AEOLUS JUST BLOWING IN THE WIND. They'd used Chaim's publicity photo as an inset.

I scanned the story:

Chaim Lemke, one of the nation's most brilliant musicians, must have left his own clarinet at home because he played as though he'd never handled the instrument before. Aeolus manager Claudia Laurents says the group was shattered by the murder of a friend in Chicago; the rest of the quintet managed to pull a semblance of a concert together, but the performance by America's top woodwind group was definitely off-key.

I handed the paper back to Greta. "Chaim's reputation is too strong—an adverse review like this will be forgotten in two days. Don't worry about it—go to your concert and concentrate on your own music."

Her slightly protuberant blue eyes stared at me. "I didn't believe Lotty when she told me. I don't believe I'm hearing you now. Vic, we need you. If it's money, name your figure. But put aside this coldness and help us out."

"Greta, the only thing standing between the police and an arrest right now is the fact that they can't find the murder weapon. I'm not going to join them in hunting for it. The best we can hope for is that they never find it.

After a while they'll let Penelope go back to Montreal and your lives will return to normal."

"No, no. You're thinking Penelope committed this crime. Never, Vic, never. I've known her since she was a small child—you know I grew up in Montreal—it's where I met Chaim. Believe me, I know her. She never committed this murder."

She was still arguing stubbornly when she looked at her watch, gave a gasp, and said she had to run or she'd never make the auditorium in time. When I'd locked the door thankfully behind her, I saw she'd dropped her paper. I looked at Chaim's delicate face again, sad as though he knew he would have to portray mourning in it when the picture was taken.

IV

When the police charged Penelope late on Thursday, I finally succumbed to the alternating pleas and commands of her friends to undertake an independent investigation. The police had never found a weapon, but the state's attorney was willing to believe it was in the Chicago River.

I got the names of the two analysts and the receptionist who'd seen Servino's presumed assailant outside his office on Tuesday. They were too used to seeing nervous people shrinking behind partitions to pay much attention to this woman; neither of them was prepared to make a positive ID in court. That would be a help to Freeman Carter, handling Penelope's defense, but it couldn't undo the damage caused by Penelope's original lies about her Tuesday morning activities.

She was free on $100,000 bond. Swinging between depression and a kind of manic rage, she didn't tell a very convincing story. Still, I was committed to proving her innocence; I did my best with her and trusted that Freeman was too savvy to let her take the witness stand herself.

I got a list of Paul's patients, both current and former, from a contact at the police. Lotty, Max, and Greta were bankrolling both Freeman and me to any amount we needed, so I hired the Streeter Brothers to check up on patient alibis.

I talked to all of them myself, trying to ferret out any sense of betrayal or rage urgent enough to drive one of them to murder. With a sense of shameful voyeurism, I even read Paul's notes. I was fascinated by his descriptions of Greta. Her total self-absorption had always rubbed me the wrong way. Paul, while much more empathic, seemed to be debating whether she would ever be willing to participate in her own analysis.

"How did Paul feel about your affair with Rudolph?" I asked Greta one afternoon when she had made one of her frequent stops for a progress report.

"Oh, you know Paul: he had a great respect for the artistic temperament and what someone like me needs to survive in my work. Besides, he convinced me that I didn't have to feel responsible—you know, that my own parents' cold narcissism makes me crave affection. And Rudolph is a much more relaxing lover than poor Chaim, with his endless parade of guilt and self-doubt."

I felt my skin crawl slightly. I didn't know any psychoanalytic theory, but I couldn't believe Paul meant his remarks on personal responsibility to be understood in quite this way.

Meanwhile, Chaim's performance had deteriorated so badly that he decided to cancel the rest of the West Coast tour. The Aeolus found a backup, the second clarinet in the Chicago Symphony, but their concert series got mediocre reviews in Seattle and played to half-full houses in Vancouver and Denver.

Greta rushed to the airport to meet Chaim on his return. I knew because she'd notified the local stations and I found her staring at me on the ten o'clock news, escorting Chaim from the baggage area with a maternal solicitude. She shed the cameras before decamping for Rudolph's—she called me from there at ten thirty to make sure I'd seen her wifely heroics.

I wasn't convinced by Greta's claims that Chaim would recover faster on his own than with someone to look after him. The next day I went to check on him for myself. Even though it was past noon, he was still in his dressing gown. I apologized for waking him, but he gave a sweet sad smile and assured me he'd been up for some time. When I followed him into the living room, a light, bright room facing Lake Michigan, I was shocked to see how ill he looked. His black eyes had become giant holes in his thin face; he apparently hadn't slept in some time.

"Chaim, have you seen a doctor?"

"No, no." He shook his head. "It's just that since Paul's death I can't make music. I try to play and I sound worse than I did at age five. I don't know which is harder—losing Paul or having them arrest Penelope. Such a sweet girl. I've known her since she was born. I'm sure she didn't kill him. Lotty says you're investigating?"

"Yeah, but not too successfully. The evidence against her is very sketchy —it's hard for me to believe they'll get a conviction. If the weapon turns up . . ." I let the sentence trail away. If the weapon turned up, it might provide the final caisson to shore up the state's platform. I was trying hard to work for Penelope, but I kept having disloyal thoughts.

"You yourself are hunting for the weapon? Do you know what it is?"

I shook my head. "The state's attorney gave me photos of the wound. I had enlargements made and I took them to a pathologist I know to see if he could come up with any ideas. Some kind of pipe or stick with spikes or something on it—like a caveman's club—I'm so out of ideas I even went to the Field Museum to see if they could suggest something, or were missing some old-fashioned lethal weapon."

Chaim had turned green. I felt contrite—he had such an active imagination. I should have watched my tongue. Now he'd have nightmares for weeks and would wait even longer to get his music back. I changed the subject and persuaded him to let me cook some lunch from the meager supplies in the kitchen. He didn't eat much, but he was looking less feverish when I left.

V

Chaim's cleaning woman found him close to death the morning Penelope's trial started. Lotty, Max, and I had spent the day in court with Lotty's brother Hugo and his wife. We didn't get any of Greta's frantic messages until Lotty checked in at the clinic before dinner.

Chaim had gone to an Aeolus rehearsal the night before, his first appearance at the group in some weeks. He had bought a new clarinet, thinking perhaps the problem lay with the old one. Wind instruments aren't like violins—they deteriorate over time, and an active clarinetist has to buy a new one every ten years or so. Despite the new instrument, a Buffet he had flown to Toronto to buy, the rehearsal had gone badly.

He left early, going home to turn on the gas in the kitchen stove. He left a note which simply said: "I have destroyed my music." The cleaning woman knew enough about their life to call Greta at Rudolph's apartment. Since Greta had been at the rehearsal—waiting for the oboist—she knew how badly Chaim had played.

"I'm not surprised," she told Lotty over the phone. "His music was all he had after I left him. With both of us gone from his life he must have felt he had no reason to live. Thank God I learned so much from Paul about why we aren't responsible for our actions, or I would feel terribly guilty now."

Lotty called the attending physician at Mitchell Hospital and came away with the news that Chaim would live, but he'd ruined his lungs—he could hardly talk and would probably never be able to play again.

She reported her conversation with Greta with a blazing rage while we waited for dinner in her brother's suite at the Drake. "The wrong person's career is over," she said furiously. "It's the one thing I could never understand about Chaim—why he felt so much passion for that self-centered whore!"

Marcella Herschel gave a grimace of distaste—she didn't deal well with Lotty at the best of times and could barely tolerate her when she was angry. Penelope, pale and drawn from the day's ordeal, summoned a smile and patted Lotty's shoulder soothingly while Max tried to persuade her to drink a little wine.

Freeman Carter stopped by after dinner to discuss strategy for the next day's session. The evening broke up soon after, all of us too tired and depressed to want even a pretense of conversation.

The trial lasted four days. Freeman did a brilliant job with the state's sketchy evidence; the jury was out for only two hours before returning a "not guilty" verdict. Penelope left for Montreal with Hugo and Marcella the next morning. Lotty, much shaken by the winter's events, found a locum for her clinic and took off with Max for two weeks in Portugal.

I went to Michigan for a long weekend with the dog, but didn't have time or money for more vacation than that. Monday night, when I got home, I found Hugo Wolf's *Spanisches Liederbuch* still open on the piano from January's dinner party with Chaim and Paul. Between Paul's murder and preparing for Penelope's trial I hadn't sung since then. I tried picking out *"In dem Schatten meiner Locken,"* but Greta was right: The piano needed tuning badly.

I called Mr. Fortieri the next morning to see if he could come by to look at it. He was an old man who repaired instruments for groups like the Aeolus Quintet and their ilk; he also tuned pianos for them. He only helped me because he'd known my mother and admired her singing.

He arranged to come the next afternoon. I was surprised—usually you had to wait four to six weeks for time on his schedule—but quickly reshuffled my own Tuesday appointments to accommodate him. When he arrived, I realized that he had come so soon because Chaim's suicide attempt had shaken him. I didn't have much stomach for rehashing it, but I could see the old man was troubled and needed someone to talk to.

"What bothers me, Victoria, is what I should do with his clarinet. I've been able to repair it, but they tell me he'll never play again—surely it would be too cruel to return it to him, even if I didn't submit a bill."

"His clarinet?" I asked blankly. "When did he give it to you?"

"After that disastrous West Coast tour. He said he had dropped it in some mud—I still don't understand how that happened, why he was carrying it outside without the case. But he said it was clogged with mud and he'd tried cleaning it, only he'd bent the keys and it didn't play properly. It was a wonderful instrument, only a few years old, and costing perhaps six thousand dollars, so I agreed to work on it. He'd had to use his old one in California and

I always thought that was why the tour went so badly. That and Paul's death weighing on him, of course."

"So you repaired it and got it thoroughly clean," I said foolishly.

"Oh, yes. Of course, the sound will never be as good as it was originally, but it would still be a fine instrument for informal use. Only—I hate having to give him a clarinet he can no longer play."

"Leave it with me," I said gently. "I'll take care of it."

Mr. Fortieri seemed relieved to pass the responsibility on to me. He went to work on the piano and tuned it back to perfection without any of his usual criticisms on my failure to keep to my mother's high musical standard.

As soon as he'd gone, I drove down to the University of Chicago hospital. Chaim was being kept in the psychiatric wing for observation, but he was allowed visitors. I found him sitting in the lounge, staring into space while *People's Court* blared meaninglessly on the screen overhead.

He gave his sad sweet smile when he saw me and croaked out my name in the hoarse parody of a voice.

"Can we go to your room, Chaim? I want to talk to you privately."

He flicked a glance at the vacant faces around us but got up obediently and led me down the hall to a spartan room with bars on the window.

"Mr. Fortieri was by this afternoon to tune my piano. He told me about your clarinet."

Chaim said nothing, but he seemed to relax a little.

"How did you do it, Chaim? I mean, you left for California Monday morning. What did you do—come back on the red-eye?"

"Red-eye?" he croaked hoarsely.

Even in the small space I had to lean forward to hear him. "The night flight."

"Oh. The red-eye. Yes. Yes, I got to O'Hare at six, came to Paul's office on the El, and was back at the airport in time for the ten o'clock flight. No one even knew I'd left L.A.—we had a rehearsal at two and I was there easily."

His voice was so strained it made my throat ache to listen to him.

"I thought I hated Paul. You know, all those remarks of his about responsibility. I thought he'd encouraged Greta to leave me." He stopped to catch his breath. After a few gasping minutes he went on.

"I blamed him for her idea that she didn't have to feel any obligation to our marriage. Then, after I got back, I saw Lotty had been right. Greta was just totally involved in herself. She should have been named Narcissus. She used Paul's words without understanding them."

"But Penelope," I said. "Would you really have let Penelope go to jail for you?"

He gave a twisted smile. "I didn't mean them to arrest Penelope. I just thought—I've always had trouble with cold weather, with Chicago winters. I've worn a long fur for years. Because I'm so small people often think I'm a woman when I'm wrapped up in it. I just thought, if anyone saw me they would think it was a woman. I never meant them to arrest Penelope."

He sat panting for a few minutes. "What are you going to do now, Vic? Send for the police?"

I shook my head sadly. "You'll never play again—you'd have been happier doing life in Joliet than you will now that you can't play. I want you to write it all down, though, the name you used on your night flight and everything. I have the clarinet; even though Mr. Fortieri cleaned it, a good lab might still find blood traces. The clarinet and your statement will go to the papers after you die. Penelope deserves that much—to have the cloud of suspicion taken away from her. And I'll have to tell her and Lotty."

His eyes were shiny. "You don't know how awful it's been, Vic. I was so mad with rage that it was like nothing to break Paul's neck. But then, after that, I couldn't play anymore. So you are wrong: even if I had gone to Joliet I would still never have played."

I couldn't bear the naked anguish in his face. I left without saying anything, but it was weeks before I slept without seeing his black eyes weeping onto me.

Nick Velvet certainly isn't the only character Edward D. Hoch has created. A complete list of his most beloved characters would take up more room than we can devote to it. But whatever character he writes about, Hoch is always enjoyable, professional, and great fun.

The Theft of the Barking Dog

A Nick Velvet Story

EDWARD D. HOCH

Nick Velvet had come to England to steal a dog.

"It's no Hound of the Baskervilles," the woman in blue had told him. "If he didn't have those guards around his place I'd go after it myself. It's just a big Old English sheepdog named Rodney, the friendliest creature in the world."

"This Manuel Curzon is your former husband?" Nick asked, making notes as he spoke with Evita Curzon. She was a dark, Latin type with a slow, seductive smile.

"That's correct. Rodney should really be my dog, but Manuel won't give him up. He's being very unreasonable about the whole thing."

"My fee would be twenty-five thousand dollars plus travel expenses. Is Rodney worth that much to you?"

"That much and more."

Nick's original plan had involved a dog substitution—replacing Rodney with an identical pooch while he made his escape with the original. Using photographs of the sheepdog that Evita had supplied, he was about to purchase a passable substitute to accompany him to England when he learned about that country's rigid pet-quarantine laws. If he wanted to complete his assignment in a reasonable length of time, he would have to obtain a dog in England.

So Nick flew to London alone after kissing Gloria goodbye at the airport and promising to bring her back a gift. His first stop after checking into his Mayfair hotel and renting a car was a big kennel on the outskirts of the city. He asked about large Old English sheepdogs, but the only ones available were either too small or had the wrong coloring.

"He has to be gray and white, like the one in this picture," Nick told the young man in charge.

"Funny, there was someone here a few days ago asking for the same thing. In fact, he had a photo that could have been the same dog. He didn't care about the coloring, though, as long as the size was right. I'm supposed to call him if one turns up."

Nick found this extremely interesting, and possibly more than a coincidence. "Do you have the man's name handy?"

"I put his card in my drawer here. It should be near the top. Yes, here it is —Percy Apjohn. Lives in Wembley."

"Thank you," Nick said with a smile. "I'll contact him. If we're on the same mission we should pool our resources."

He tried phoning Apjohn's number, on the pretense of having a dog available, but there was no answer. Because Wembley was on the way to Manuel Curzon's home near Oxhey, he decided to swing by there first. Apjohn lived in a small detached house across from a neighborhood pub. When no one answered his ring, Nick crossed the street and ordered a pint from the bartender.

"I'm looking for Percy Apjohn," he said quietly. "Seen him around?"

"Not in a couple of days. That's odd for him. Usually stops in every night for his pint."

Nick finished the beer and recrossed the street. The little house seemed far too quiet, and he noticed something he'd missed earlier. There were two newspapers on the front stoop, half hidden by a flowering plant. He walked around to the rear of the house and used a credit card to force the bolt on the back door.

As soon as he stepped into the kitchen he caught the odor. It wasn't pleasant and he knew what it meant. The man's body lay halfway into the living room, in a pool of dried blood. He'd been dead for some time. The cause of death seemed to be a gaping wound in his throat. Nick hoped it had been caused by a weapon of some sort and not by a large, vicious dog. He glanced quickly around the room and noticed a business card on the table, from someplace called Essex Storage Facilities. He stuck it in his pocket, for no special reason.

He went out the way he'd come and cut across the back yards so no one from the pub would see him leaving. Finding a man's body wasn't the best way to start off an assignment, and he could only hope the two things were just coincidental. In any event, he would visit no more kennels for a time. The road to Oxhey lay just ahead.

Manuel Curzon was well known in this suburb of Greater London. He owned several acres of land along London Road and seemed to be well-off, though the people to whom Nick spoke were vague as to the source of his income. Pausing in his rental car along the side of the road, Nick affixed a large circular insignia to each of the two doors. They read: Oxhey Animal Control Unit. From a distance he thought they looked quite convincing.

Nick parked in the driveway of the Curzon home and walked up the stone path to the front door. His approach immediately set off the deep-throated barking of a large dog that was most likely to be Rodney. The door was not opened in response to his arrival. Instead, a broad-shouldered young man in a chauffeur's uniform appeared suddenly behind him. "Can I help you, sir?"

"I'm looking for Manuel Curzon. We've had a complaint about a barking dog." His words seemed to enrage Rodney even more, and the barking from within grew noticeably louder.

"Mr. Curzon doesn't receive visitors."

"I'll have to issue an official warning about the dog," Nick told him. "What's your name?"

"Gilligan, sir."

Nick's British accent was none too good, but he tried to act bureaucratic as he filled out an impressive-looking form and handed it to the man. "Well, Gilligan, here's a warning for your employer. If there are any more complaints I may be forced to confiscate—"

"What's this?" A young woman in jeans and a man's shirt had come around the corner of the house. "What's the trouble, Gilligan?"

"He's from animal control, Miss. There's been a complaint about Rodney's barking."

"I'll handle this."

Gilligan hesitated only a moment and then retreated. Nick faced the young woman and saw at once the familiar features and coloring of Evita Curzon, the woman who'd hired him. This could only be her daughter, and she quickly confirmed the fact. "I'm Mr. Curzon's daughter, Catherine. Can I be of help?"

Nick waved the form at her. "Complaint of a barking dog."

"It couldn't be Rodney. He never disturbs anyone."

"Could I see your father?"

"He's—He's quite ill. He suffered a stroke last month."

"I'm sorry to hear that, Miss."

"He still can't speak, though the doctor thinks he'll improve somewhat." She hesitated and then decided. "You can see the dog if you'd like, though. I'm sure you'll agree that Rodney is a lovable animal."

She opened the front door and led him inside. The large sheepdog came bounding to her at once, his red tongue about the only thing visible through the coat of long white and dark-gray hair. She dropped to her knees and hugged him, then said, "Look, Rodney! Here's a nice man from the town come to see you, Mr.—?"

"Velvet," Nick supplied, taking in the expensive furnishings.

"Mr. Velvet likes big dogs, but he likes them best when they're a little bit quiet."

Rodney's answering bark did indeed seem to be a bit subdued. Nick patted him to show approval. "You behave yourself like a good dog," he cautioned, "and I won't have to give your mistress another warning."

As he straightened up, a framed photograph on the piano caught his eye. It was in among several family pictures and showed five men grouped around a red sports car. He'd never have noticed it except that the second man from the left was clearly Percy Apjohn, whose body he'd found and abandoned earlier that day. "Who are these handsome fellows?" he asked casually.

"Friends of my father's. That's him in the center." She eyed Nick a bit dubiously.

Nick studied the dark, pockmarked face. Even the smile Curzon allowed for the photograph with his friends seemed hasty and forced. Nick could understand why Evita Curzon might have found life difficult with such a man. He turned back to Catherine and said, "One of these men looks familiar. It's Percy Apjohn, isn't it?"

"That's right. He's been a dear through all of this, driving over frequently to visit my father."

"Do the others live around here?"

"Two of them do. The other, Matthew Kane, is out of the country somewhere. I don't even know if he's heard about Daddy's stroke."

"It almost looks as if they're a team of some sort, the way they're posed."

She chuckled at that. "Hardly! Except for a little hunting, Daddy has never been a sportsman. The five of them used to get together to chat and play cards on Saturday nights. A few years ago they started to drift apart."

"Well, you will keep Rodney under control, won't you?"

"Certainly. Thank you for being so understanding, Mr. Velvet."

He went back to his car, aware that Gilligan's eyes were on him all the time. Still, if the chauffeur was the only guard to be overcome, it wasn't such a difficult job. Rodney could be in his hands by the next morning. He took a room at an inn for the night.

Evita Curzon had planned to arrive in London that evening and Nick phoned her hotel after dinner to inform her that Rodney would be delivered the following day. "I scouted out the place today and met your daughter."

"Catherine? How is she?"

"Better than your husband, apparently. Are you aware that he suffered a stroke last month?"

"I heard that, yes."

"But not from your daughter."

"It's not important who told me. Deliver the dog and you'll get your money."

"Do you know a friend of your husband's named Percy Apjohn?"

"I know him. I don't admire him."

"Why is that?"

"Look, Mr. Velvet, I hired you to do a job. You specialize in stealing items of little or no value and I'm paying you to get back my dog. It's all that need concern you."

"Of course. I do have one important question, though. Is Gilligan the only guard at the house?"

"Yes, but don't underestimate him. He says he killed a man once."

Or maybe twice, Nick thought, remembering Apjohn's body. "I'll be careful."

He hung up just as a knock sounded on the door. Thinking it might be the innkeeper, he opened the door without hesitation. A tall man with a vaguely familiar face hit him on the chest with the flat of his hand. "Inside, mister!"

A second man crowded in behind the first and Nick saw that he had little choice. The door was closed and he was alone with them. "Is this a robbery?" he asked, dropping all pretense of an English accent.

"Not yet it isn't," the second man snarled. "And we're here to see it doesn't become one, Mr. Nick Velvet! Catherine Curzon phoned me. She said some animal control person called Velvet was at the house, acting a bit strange. Showed an interest in our picture, among other things."

"I don't know what you're talking about," Nick insisted, but he knew only too well. They were two of the group standing with Manuel Curzon in the photograph on the piano.

The tall one took a folded newspaper from his pocket. "Try to tell me this isn't you."

It was a full page ripped from a London tabloid dated nearly four years earlier. The story dealt with one of Britain's periodic great train robberies, in which a gang of thieves had held up a train in the north country and escaped with a fortune in bank notes. Nick's picture, somewhat fuzzy but still recognizable, was part of a sidebar article on great thieves. In fairness, the story admitted that he'd never been known to steal anything of value.

"That's me, all right," Nick agreed with a smile. "No doubt about it. But you have the advantage on me. Who are you?"

"Phil Banyon," the tall one said. "And this is Roger Green. What are you doing here?"

"I'm on holiday. What about you?"

"We both live in Oxhey. We're friends of Manuel Curzon and we're worried you've been snooping around there."

"Oh, hardly snooping around!"

"What would you call it, with that fake sign on the side of your car?" Green asked. "Oxhey doesn't even have an animal control unit."

"Then they might be willing to let me establish one."

Neither man smiled. Banyon's right fist shot out before Nick realized what was happening. It caught him on the tip of the jaw and sent him reeling backward onto the bed. He started to get up and the other one hit him.

Nick met Evita Curzon in London's Green Park the following morning as scheduled. She walked up to him, trim and proper in a tailored blue suit, and removed her sunglasses. "Where's Rodney?" she asked.

"I don't have him yet."

"Don't have him? Why not? What happened to your face?"

"A couple of gentlemen visited my room last evening. We had a bit of a tussle and I'm afraid they won. I was dozing when they left and by the time I woke up it was too late to go after your dog."

"Who were these men?"

"A couple of your old friends—Banyon and Green."

"They were my husband's friends, not mine. What did they say to you?"

"They accused me of snooping around. Then they just started punching me."

"Yes, that sounds like them."

"Perhaps you should tell me what this is all about."

"I only hired you to steal my dog, Mr. Velvet. You needn't concern yourself with anything else."

"You didn't tell me about your daughter."

"Catherine's not involved in this."

Nick stared up at the trees. "Tell me one thing, Mrs. Curzon—how did you learn about me?"

"How—?"

"You sought me out and hired me. How did you hear about me here in England? Was it through a tabloid newspaper article? They showed me the article before they started punching me. One of those great train robbery things you Brits are so fond of."

She was silent for a moment. Finally she said, "You're right about the tabloid. That's where I first saw your name."

"Your husband and the others were especially interested in that article about the train robbery—interested enough to keep it for nearly four years. Could they be the ones who robbed the train? All five of them?"

"I don't know," she replied. "Certainly the thought has crossed my mind.

The press agreed that the bandits would have to keep their loot hidden for years, until after the statute of limitations ran out. I saw no evidence of anything around the house."

"If your husband was the guardian of this money, his stroke might have made the others nervous." Nick had suddenly remembered something.

"I've no interest in train robberies," she insisted. "I only want to get my dog back."

"All right," he agreed.

"Tonight?"

"Tonight."

But first Nick Velvet had another stop to make. He'd remembered the business card for Essex Storage Facility which he'd found on the table at Percy Apjohn's house. It might mean nothing, but if there was hidden loot a storage facility was certainly a likely hiding place. It was located closer in to London, not far from Apjohn's place in Wembley. When Nick reached the address, he found a long low building with a line of overhead doors, capable of storing motor vehicles if necessary. The painted sign on a side wall read: Essex Storage Facility—Key, Combination, and Voiceprint Locks Available.

Nick found the manager, a robust young man named Jennings. "I am making inquiries regarding the estate of Manuel Curzon," Nick said in his most officious banker's voice.

Jennings seemed surprised. "Has he died?"

"He's clinging to life since his stroke, but the family feels the need to make certain preparations for the inevitable."

"I see."

"We understand he maintains storage space with you."

"That's right. Comes down about every six months to check it over."

"How much can you tell me about what's kept in his space?"

"Nothing. Against the regulations, you see."

"You mean I'd have to have a key?"

"No, no—Curzon rents our top-of-the-line option. He has a voiceprint lock."

"Just what is that?"

"Sort of a computer thing, as I understand it. The client's voiceprint is kept in the memory and compared to a voiceprint of anyone trying to gain access. If they don't match, the door remains locked. We're one of the first facilities in the country to offer it."

"The speaker has to say a certain word or phrase?"

"That's the idea. There's a slight leeway for natural variations, but the voice has to be pretty much the same. Someone imitating the voice wouldn't know the secret phrase, of course."

"Well, that's part of the problem, you see. Curzon's stroke has robbed him of the ability to speak. It's doubtful that he'll ever recover."

"With the voice lock we insist on a second speaker for just that reason. In the event one person dies or is incapacitated, the second person can open the lock."

"Who was Curzon's second person?"

"I have no idea. We only record the name of the primary leaseholder."

Nick sneaked a ten-pound note from his pocket and held it casually between his fingers. "It's important that we find this person."

"No chance, governor. I just don't know."

"What number is his unit?"

"The records will tell me that," he replied, his eyes on the banknote. "Come into the office."

He flipped through the pages of a loose-leaf record book. "Here it is—number sixty-five, around on the other side."

"Does it say what he stored?"

Jennings replied with some reluctance. "A Land Rover."

"That's all?"

"That's all he listed."

Nick nodded and handed over the ten-pound note. "Thank you, Mr. Jennings."

That night, after dark, Nick parked his car some distance from the Curzon estate. He carried a number of items with him, some clipped to a gadget belt around his waist. He was dressed all in black and even his flashlight had a black rubber casing. Crossing the yard toward the house, Nick was careful to avoid the obvious alarm systems. There was no sign of Gilligan patrolling the grounds, and he wanted to keep it that way.

It had been obvious on his earlier visit that Rodney spent the nights indoors. This was no animal to be relegated to a doghouse. Nick found some open ground-floor windows and taped small tubes of chemical scent to the sills. Wherever Rodney was, he would soon be getting whiffs of a female dog in heat.

Nick retreated to the road where he'd left the car. He was barely back to it when he heard the big sheepdog begin to bark. He stuck the animal control signs back on the sides of the vehicle and slipped on a tweed jacket that made him appear more businesslike. After ten minutes Rodney was still barking. He started the car and drove up to the house.

Before the car had come to a full stop, Gilligan was out the front door, a powerful Webley air pistol held at the ready. He was wearing a dressing gown, but it didn't seem to interfere with his aim as he leveled the weapon at the car. "Put that down!" Nick commanded in the most authoritative voice he could muster. "You're interfering with the Oxhey Animal Control Unit!"

"Get off this property!"

"Not until I take that hound with me! He's disturbing the peace and quiet of the entire township."

Gilligan kept the pistol steady. Nick knew that British-made air pistols could be deadly, and he had no desire to test this one's velocity. At that instant, Catherine Curzon appeared in the doorway behind the chauffeur and snapped, "Put that weapon down, Gilligan! What's the meaning of this?"

"The dog—" Nick began, getting out of the car.

"I don't know what's wrong with Rodney," she said, truly distressed. "He's never behaved like this before."

Before they knew it, Rodney himself was on the scene, trailing a broken rope with which he'd been tied. Nick bent down and grabbed the rope, reining him in as he tried to escape out the front door. "I've got him," he announced. "I'll have to take him with me, I'm afraid. You can apply for his release tomorrow morning at the animal control center." By that time the dog would be in London with Evita Curzon and Nick would be counting his fee.

"Mr. Curzon would never let this happen," Gilligan said, anxious to use the weapon he still held.

Catherine walked up to him and placed her hand over the gun. "There'll be none of that. I don't know what your game is, Mr. Velvet, but I can see from your bruised face that you're a hard man to convince. I'll be on the phone to the animal control center first thing in the morning, and you'll be out of a job!"

Nick opened the rear door of his car. He'd left some of the chemical there to induce the dog in, and it offered no resistance. Then Nick got behind the wheel, handed Catherine Curzon an official-looking receipt for the dog, and drove away. Rodney gave a final bark from the back seat and then settled down in frustration.

The following morning, on a cool but sunny spring day, Nick Velvet took Rodney for a romp in Green Park. It was truly a magnificent sheepdog, attracting admiring glances from virtually everyone they passed. He'd expected his client to be there waiting and was mildly surprised when she was nowhere in sight. A smaller dog's approach brought a woof from Rodney, who was ready to give chase until Nick tugged on the leash.

Fifteen minutes later, he began to suspect she wasn't coming. Something had happened. Something Nick didn't know about. He pondered what to do next, saddled with a big friendly dog who liked to bark.

"Mr. Velvet?"

Nick turned and saw a middle-aged man with a round face and thinning hair standing behind him. It was the fifth man from the photo at Curzon's house, the missing Matthew Kane. "Yes?" Nick replied, not showing any recognition.

"Evita couldn't make it. She sent me for the dog."

As if in understanding, Rodney gave a low but distinct growl. "Do you have the money?" Nick asked, tightening his hold on the leash.

"You're to see her for the rest of it. She just sent me for the dog."

"No deal."

The man's eyes hardened. "I have a gun in my pocket, Mr. Velvet. I won't hesitate to use it."

"Take me to her. Take me to Evita Curzon. As soon as I get the money, you get the dog."

"All right. No funny business."

"Which way are we going?"

"She's leasing a flat on St. James's Street. It's only a block away."

Nick fully expected that the flat would yield Evita Curzon's dead body, and he'd be fighting for his life in a matter of minutes. Instead she opened the door when they arrived, smiling and seemingly quite healthy. "I should have known you wouldn't give up the dog without the balance of your money, Mr. Velvet. I was making travel arrangements."

"I was expecting you, not one of your ex-husband's friends."

"Oh? You know each other?"

"I saw his photograph at your old house. Matthew Kane, I expect, back from a long absence."

Kane and Evita exchanged glances. "I told you before that none of this concerned you," she told Nick. "You've delivered the dog and here's your money."

He accepted the envelope and did a quick count of the money. "Thank you," he said with a smile. "It's been a pleasure doing business with you, Mrs. Curzon. With both of you, in fact."

Rodney gave a final bark of farewell as he went out the door.

Nick Velvet should have headed for the airport and forgotten the whole thing. Percy Apjohn was dead, but that meant nothing to him. He hadn't even known the man, and the whole crowd of them might be train robbers for all he knew. It was odd he hadn't seen anything in the papers about Apjohn, but maybe the body hadn't yet been found.

That was one thing he could do before he caught his plane. He'd drive up to Wembley, and if the body was still undiscovered he'd phone the police. Then he'd catch the next plane to New York. He stopped at a store and picked up some Waterford crystal for Gloria, then headed to Apjohn's house. It looked the same as it had two days earlier.

There was a man mowing the grass at the house down the street and Nick asked him, "Has Percy Apjohn been around lately? I have some business with him."

"He was there yesterday," the man replied. "I was talking to him. Did you try the bell?"

"Yesterday?" Nick wondered if his mouth was hanging open. "Are you sure?"

"Of course I'm sure! You think I'm feeble-minded or something? I say yesterday, I mean yesterday."

Nick went up to the door and rang the bell, half fearing that the corpse he'd seen would answer it. But no one came. He glanced back at the neighbor, waited until he pushed the mower around the side of the house, and then circled to the rear of Apjohn's house. He forced the bolt with the credit card as he'd done on his earlier visit.

This time it was different. This time there was no body in the living room doorway.

All traces of dried blood had been removed, and if there was any odor in the air it was the sweet smell of a strong disinfectant.

Nick thought about Percy Apjohn dead and Percy Apjohn back to life. He thought about Rodney and he thought about the photograph of those five men. Then he went back to his car and drove to Curzon's home in Oxhey.

For once he was greeted by someone other than Gilligan. Catherine Curzon herself answered the door and stepped aside to let him enter. "There is no Oxhey Animal Control Unit," she told him angrily. "Suppose you explain yourself!"

"I will, in due course."

"Where's Rodney?"

"First let me see your father."

"What? Are you crazy? My father's a sick man!"

"It's very important that I see him. I don't have to speak to him. I just have to see him. I can stand in the doorway of his room."

But she was firm in blocking his path. "You'd better tell me what this is all about."

"It's about the great train robbery of four years ago. I believe your father and his four friends were involved in it. Your mother knew it, and I think you must have had your suspicions, too."

"Those men in the photograph are no longer close friends of my father's."

"There's a good reason for that. The loot from the train robbery is hidden away and everyone is lying low until the statute of limitations makes prosecution impossible. The conspirators seem to have split into three groups —Banyon and Green are still together, your mother seems to have taken up with Matthew Kane, and Percy Apjohn may or may not have been murdered."

"What?"

"I've seen the photograph and I've seen the people—all except your father, that is. I have only your word that he's still alive."

She bit her lip uncertainly and then turned toward the stairway. "Follow me, Mr. Velvet. Please try to be quiet."

She led him to an enclosed sun porch at the rear of the second floor. There, seated in a wheelchair with a blanket over his legs, was the fifth man in the photograph, Manuel Curzon. His head lifted as they entered and he tried to speak, but only jumbled fragments of sound came out.

"Are you satisfied now?" she asked Nick.

"I'm sorry. I had to be sure."

She led the way back downstairs. "Sure of what?"

"Did you know your father rents space at the Essex Storage Facility?"

"I never heard of it."

"He has a space the size of a small garage where he keeps a Land Rover."

"He used to have one years ago. I thought he sold it."

"The lock is controlled by a voiceprint."

"What's that?"

"A graphic representation of your father's voice, with the frequencies analyzed by a sound spectrograph. His voice, speaking some code word or phrase, was used to unlock the storage compartment."

"But he can't speak!"

"That's why his stroke threw the other four conspirators into a panic. He'd used someone else's voice as a backup, in case he died or was disabled, but none of them knew who it was."

"If what you say is true, he must have told someone."

"He did. He told your mother."

Nick knew they'd be there ahead of him, and common sense kept telling him he was only looking for trouble by returning to the Essex Storage Facility. Still, he needed an ending when he told the story to Gloria back home.

This time he didn't stop at the office but swung his car around to the back of the building, to storage space number 65. Another car was already there, and he spotted Evita Curzon and Matthew Kane at once. They had the big sheepdog with them and Rodney gave a bark of recognition as Nick came forward.

"What are you doing here?" Evita Curzon asked. "You have your money."

"I had to see if this thing would really work," Nick said with a smile. "I never saw the barking of a dog open a voiceprint lock before."

Kane reached under his jacket and brought out a snub-nosed revolver. "I warned you earlier that I had a gun, Velvet. You should have stayed in London."

"Let's hurry," Evita urged. "Banyon and Green might show up any minute."

"I have to correct an earlier misstatement," Nick told the round-faced man. "I called you Matthew Kane, but of course you're really Percy Apjohn. You murdered the real Matthew Kane at your house in Wembley two days ago."

"You seem to know a great deal."

"I jumped to the wrong conclusion when I entered your house and found his body. But today I learned you were very much alive and at home yesterday. The body was gone, so you must have removed it and cleaned up. You must have killed him. It had to be Kane because everyone else in the photograph is accounted for—even Manuel Curzon, whom I saw for the first time today."

"How is he?" Evita asked.

"As advertised. He can't speak. That's why you needed Rodney, the back-up voice." A bark from Rodney, right on cue. "I should have known you two were in this together because what led me to Apjohn's house in the first place was a kennel owner who said I was the second person trying to buy an Old English sheepdog. Mr. Apjohn, he said, didn't care about the dog's coloring so long as the size was right. If the dog wasn't important for its looks, why was it important? I had no idea until I learned of this voiceprint business. It seemed likely that two sheepdogs of the same size might have the same tonal quality to their barks. But you couldn't find a suitable duplicate so I was hired to steal the original. If you both knew of Rodney's importance, I guessed you were working together, except that made it Evita and Apjohn, not Evita and Kane."

"Keep him covered," Evita told Apjohn. She took Rodney from the car and led him to the microphone mounted on the lock of the storage door.

Nick kept on talking. He always figured it was better to talk when a gun was pointed at him. "Matthew Kane heard about Curzon's stroke and came back from overseas. He wanted to make sure of his share of the loot. He confronted you at your house and you killed him, probably with a gardening tool. I don't know what you did with the body."

Apjohn chuckled. "You'll find out soon enough."

With a bit of urging from Evita, Rodney barked twice into the microphone. There was a distinct click as the mechanism unlocked. Evita opened the wide overhead door to reveal a dark-green Land Rover in fairly good condition. She dropped to the ground and pulled herself under the vehicle, starting to tear away pieces of tape from the undercarriage. "It's still here," she told Apjohn.

"Good!"

Bundles of plastic-wrapped currency began to litter the floor of the storage garage. "You're cutting the others out of this?" Nick asked.

"Damn right we are!" Apjohn hefted the gun. "But you're in for the same share as Kane. His body's wrapped in oilskin in the trunk of my car. You're both going in there, in place of the money. They'll find your bodies one of these years."

"A car's coming!" Evita warned.

Percy Apjohn cursed and swung around. Nick couldn't wait for a second chance. He was on the man in an instant, grabbing the gun and wrestling it away as they both toppled to the ground. Nick landed on top and the fight ended just as the car pulled up. It was Gilligan, the Curzon chauffeur.

"I was expecting Banyon and Green," Nick said, holding onto Apjohn.

"They've been delayed," Gilligan said. "They're cooperating with the authorities."

"What's the meaning of this?" Evita Curzon asked. "Are you still my former husband's chauffeur?"

"Scotland Yard Special Branch," Gilligan told her. "We've been waiting four years for this day. We couldn't prove a thing until we found the money. Don't try to run. I'm not alone."

Nick saw the other cars converging on them then, and knew that his return home would be delayed by a few days. No one was likely to prosecute him for stealing a dog, though. He walked over and gave Rodney a friendly hug.

Sharyn McCrumb rocketed into the consciousness of the mystery world with a novel of the unlikely title *Bimbos of the Death Sun.* Until publication of this Edgar Award-winner, such a title would have brought snickers to the lips of mystery afficionados. (Indeed, many did snicker at the time.) But since then McCrumb has brought us Jay Omega's second outing, the equally compelling *Zombies of the Gene Pool* and the quite different but terrific Elizabeth MacPherson mysteries, not to mention the Anthony nominee, *If I Ever Return, Pretty Peggy-O,* was a strongly affecting novel. The following story, reprinted from *Sisters in Crime 4,* is set in England, but its central metaphor, that of serial-killer-as-tabloid-fodder, could just as easily be treated as an American theme. The treatment here is quite powerful; McCrumb captures the precise tenor of tabloid journalism and the insidious appeal of its twisted version of fame. In this short piece, she exposes the sordid secrets of one of the myriad worlds that exist within society, with its own rules, rulers, and its own small but lethal set of vices and perversions. A wonderfully subtle but nasty twist brings the story to a fitting conclusion.

A Predatory Woman
SHARYN McCRUMB

"She looks a proper murderess, doesn't she?" said Ernie Sleaford, tapping the photo of a bleached blonde. His face bore that derisive grin he reserved for the "puir doggies," his term for unattractive women.

With a self-conscious pat at her own more professionally lightened hair, Jackie Duncan nodded. Because she was twenty-seven and petite, she had never been the object of Ernie's derision. When he shouted at her, it was for more professional reasons—a missed photo opportunity or a bit of careless reporting. She picked up the unappealing photograph. "She looks quite tough. One wonders that children would have trusted her in the first place."

"What did they know, poor lambs? We never had a woman like our Erma before, had we?"

Jackie studied the picture, wondering if the face were truly evil, or if their knowledge of its possessor had colored the likeness. Whether or not it was a cruel face, it was certainly a plain one. Erma Bradley had dumpling features with gooseberry eyes, and that look of sullen defensiveness that plain women often have in anticipation of slights to come.

Ernie had marked the photo *Page One*. It was not the sort of female face that usually appeared in the pages of *Stellar*, a tabloid known for its daily photo of Princess Diana, and for its bosomy beauties on page three. A beefy woman with a thatch of badly bleached hair had to earn her way into the tabloids, which Erma Bradley certainly had. Convicted of four child murders in 1966, she was serving a life sentence in Holloway Prison in north London.

Gone, but not forgotten. Because she was Britain's only female serial killer, the tabloids kept her memory green with frequent stories about her, all accompanied by that menacing 1965 photo of the scowling, just-arrested Erma. Most of the recent articles about her didn't even attempt to be plausible: *Erma Bradley: Hitler's Illegitimate Daughter; Children's Ghosts Seen Outside Erma's Cell;* and, the October favorite, *Is Erma Bradley a Vampire?* That last one was perhaps the most apt, because it acknowledged the fact that the public hardly thought of her as a real person anymore; she was just another addition to the pantheon of monsters, taking her place alongside Frankenstein, Dracula, and another overrated criminal, Guy Fawkes. Thinking up new excuses to use the old Erma picture was Ernie Sleaford's specialty. Erma's face was always good for a sales boost.

Jackie Duncan had never done an Erma story. Jackie had been four years old at the time of the infamous trial, and later, with the crimes solved and the killers locked away, the case had never particularly interested her. "I thought it was her boyfriend, Sean Hardie, who actually did the killing," she said, frowning to remember the details of the case.

Stellar's editor sneered at her question. "Hardie? I never thought he had a patch on Erma for toughness. Look at him now. He's completely mental, in a prison hospital, making no more sense than a vegetable marrow. That's how you *ought* to be with the lives of four kids on your conscience. But not our Erma! Got her university degree by telly, didn't she? Learned to talk posh in the cage? And now a bunch of bloody do-gooders have got her out!"

Jackie, who had almost tuned out this tirade as she contemplated her new shade of nail varnish, stared at him with renewed interest. "I hadn't heard that, Sleaford! Are you sure it isn't another of your fairy tales?" She grinned. "*Erma Bradley, Bride of Prince Edward?* That was my favorite."

Ernie had the grace to blush at the reminder of his last Erma headline, but he remained solemn. "S'truth, Jackie. I had it on the quiet from a screw in Holloway. She's getting out next week."

"Go on! It would have been on every news show in Britain by now! Banner headlines in the *Guardian*. Questions asked in the House."

"The prison officials are keeping it dark. They don't want Erma to be pestered by the likes of us upon her release. She wants to be let alone." He smirked. "I had to pay dear for this bit of information, I can tell you."

Jack smiled. "Poor mean Ernie! Where do I come into it, then?"

"Can't you guess?"

"I think so. You want Erma's own story, no matter what."

"Well, we can write that ourselves in any case. I have Paul working on that already. What I really need is a new picture, Jackie. The old cow hasn't let herself be photographed in twenty years. Wants her privacy, does our Erma. I think *Stellar*'s readers would like to take a butcher's at what Erma Bradley looks like today, don't you?"

"So they don't hire her as the nanny." Jackie let him finish laughing before she turned the conversation round to money.

The cell was beginning to look the way it had when she first arrived. Newly swept and curtainless, it was a ten-by-six-foot rectangle containing a bed, a cupboard, a table and a chair, a wooden wash basin, a plastic bowl and jug, and a bucket. Gone were the posters and the photos of home. Her books were stowed away in a Marks & Spencers shopping bag.

Ruthie, whose small, sharp features earned her the nickname Minx, was sitting on the edge of the bed, watching her pack. "Taking the lot, are you?" she asked cheerfully.

The thin dark woman stared at the array of items on the table. "I suppose not," she said, scowling. She held up a tin of green tooth powder. "Here. D'you want this, then?"

The Minx shrugged and reached for it. "Why not? After all, you're getting out, and I've a few years to go. Will you write to me when you're on the outside?"

"You know that isn't permitted."

The younger woman giggled. "As if that ever stopped you." She reached for another of the items on the bed. "How about your Christmas soap? You can get more on the outside, you know."

She handed it over. "I shan't want freesia soap ever again."

"Taking your posters, love? Anyone would think you'd be sick of them by now."

"I am. I've promised them to Senga." She set the rolled-up posters on the bed beside Ruthie, and picked up a small framed photograph. "Do you want this, then, Minx?"

The little blonde's eyes widened at the sight of the grainy snapshot of a scowling man. "Christ! It's Sean, isn't it? Put it away. I'll be glad when you've taken that out of here."

Erma Bradley smiled and tucked the photograph in among her clothes. "I shall keep this."

Jackie Duncan seldom wore her best silk suit when she conducted interviews, but this time she felt that it would help to look both glamorous and prosperous. Her blond hair, shingled into a stylish bob, revealed shell-shaped earrings of real gold, and her calf leather handbag and shoes were an expensive matched set. It wasn't at all the way a working *Stellar* reporter usually dressed, but it lent Jackie an air of authority and professionalism that she needed in order to profit from this interview.

She looked around the shabby conference room, wondering if Erma Bradley had ever been there, and, if so, where she had sat. In preparation for the new assignment, Jackie had read everything she could find on the Bradley case: the melodramatic book by the BBC journalist; the measured prose of the prosecuting attorney; and a host of articles from more reliable newspapers than *Stellar*. She had begun to be interested in Erma Bradley and her deadly lover, Sean Hardie: *the couple who slays together stays together?* The analyses of the case had made much of the evidence and horror at the thought of child murder, but they had been at a loss to provide motive, and they had been reticent about details of the killings themselves. There was a book in that, and it would earn a fortune for whoever could get the material to write it. Jackie intended to find out more than she had uncovered, but first she had to find Erma Bradley.

Her Sloane Ranger outfit had charmed the old cats in the prison office into letting her in to pursue the story in the first place. The story they thought she was after. Jackie glanced at herself in the mirror. Very useful for impressive old sahibs, this posh outfit. Besides, she thought, why not give the prison birds a bit of a fashion show?

The six inmates, dressed in shapeless outfits of polyester, sprawled in their chairs and stared at her with no apparent interest. One of them was reading a Barbara Cartland novel.

"Hello, girls!" said Jackie in her best nursing home voice. She was used to jollying up old ladies for feature stories, and she decided that this couldn't be much different. "Did they tell you what I'm here for?"

More blank stares, until a heavyset redhead asked, "You ever do it with a woman?"

Jackie ignored her. "I'm here to do a story about what it's like in prison. Here's your chance to complain, if there are things you want changed."

Grudgingly then, they began to talk about the food, and the illogical, unbending rules that governed every part of their lives. The tension eased as they talked, and she could tell that they were becoming more willing to confide in her. Jackie scribbled a few cursory notes to keep them talking. Finally one of them said that she missed her children: Jackie's cue.

As if on impulse, she put down her notepad. "Children!" she said breathlessly. "That reminds me! Wasn't Erma Bradley a prisoner here?"

They glanced at each other. "So?" said the dull-eyed woman with unwashed hair.

A ferrety blonde, who seemed more taken by Jackie's glamour than the older ones, answered eagerly, "I knew her! We were best friends!"

"To say the least, Minx," said the frowsy embezzler from Croydon.

Jackie didn't have to feign interest anymore. "Really?" she said to the one called Minx. "I'd be terrified! What was she like?"

They all began to talk about Erma now.

"A bit reserved," said one. "She never knew who she could trust, because of her rep, you know. A lot of us here have kids of our own, so there was feeling against her. In the kitchen, they used to spit in her food before they took it to her. And sometimes, new girls would go at her to prove they were tough."

"That must have taken nerve!" cried Jackie. "I've seen her pictures!"

"Oh, she didn't look like that anymore!" said Minx. "She'd let her hair go back to its natural dark color, and she was much smaller. Not bad, really. She must have lost fifty pounds since the trial days!"

"Do you have a snapshot of her?" asked Jackie, still doing her best impression of breathless and impressed.

The redhead laid a meaty hand on Minx's shoulder. "Just a minute. What are you really here for?"

Jackie took a deep breath. "I need to find Erma Bradley. Can you help me? I'll pay you."

A few minutes later, Jackie was saying a simpering good-bye to the warden, telling her that she'd have to come back in a few days for a follow-up. She had until then to come up with a way to smuggle in two bottles of Glenlivet: the price on Erma Bradley's head. Ernie would probably make her pay for the liquor out of her own pocket. It would serve him right if she got a book deal out of it on the side.

The flat could have used a coat of paint, and some better quality furniture, but that could wait. She was used to shabbiness. What she liked best about it was its high ceiling and the big casement window overlooking the moors. From that window you could see nothing but hills and heather and sky; no roads, no houses, no people. After twenty-four years in the beehive of a women's prison, the solitude was blissful. She spent hours each day just staring out that window, knowing that she could walk on the moors whenever she liked, without guards or passes or physical restraints.

Erma Bradley tried to remember if she had ever been alone before. She had lived in a tiny flat with her mother until she finished O levels, and then, when she'd taken the secretarial job at Hadlands, there had been Sean. She had gone into prison at the age of twenty-three, an end to even the right to privacy. She could remember no time when she could have had solitude, to get to know her own likes and dislikes. She had gone from Mum's shadow to Sean's. She kept his picture, and her mother's, not out of love, but as a reminder of the prisons she had endured before Holloway.

Now she was learning that she liked plants, and the music of Sibelius. She liked things to be clean, too. She wondered if she could paint the flat by herself. It would never look clean until she covered those dingy green walls.

She reminded herself that she could have had a house, *if*. If she had given up some of that solitude. Sell your story to a book publisher; sell the film rights to this movie company. Keith, her long-suffering attorney, dutifully passed along all the offers for her consideration. The world seemed willing to throw money at her, but all she wanted was for it to go away. The dowdy but slender Miss Emily Kay, newborn at forty-seven, would manage on her own, with tinned food and second-hand furniture, while the pack of journalists went baying after Erma Bradley, who didn't exist anymore. She wanted solitude. She never thought about those terrible months with Sean, the things they did together. For twenty-four years she had not let herself remember any of it.

Jackie Duncan looked up at the gracefully ornamented stone building, carved into apartments for working-class people. The builders in that gentler age had worked leaf designs into the stonework framing the windows, and they had set gargoyles at a corner of each roof. Jackie made a mental note of this useful detail; yet another monster has been added to the building.

In the worn but genteel hallway, Jackie checked the names on mailboxes to make sure that her information was correct. There it was: E. Kay. She hurried up the stairs with only a moment's thought to the change in herself these past few weeks. When Ernie first gave her the assignment, she might have been fearful of confronting a murderess, or she might have gone upstairs with the camera poised to take the shot just as Erma Bradley opened her door, and then she would have fled. But now she was as anxious to meet the woman as she would be to interview a famous film star. More so, because this celebrity was hers alone. She had not even told Ernie that she had found Erma. This was her show, not *Stellar*'s. Without another thought about what she would say, Jackie knocked at the lair of the beast.

After a few moments, the door opened partway, and a small dark-haired woman peered nervously out at her. The woman was thin, and dressed in a simple green jumper and skirt. She was no longer the brassy blonde of the 'sixties. But the eyes were the same. The face was still Erma Bradley's.

Jackie was brisk. "May I come in, Miss *Kay?* You wouldn't want me to pound on your door calling out your real name, would you?"

The woman fell back and let her enter. "I suppose it wouldn't help to tell you that you're mistaken?" No trace remained of her Midlands accent. She spoke in quiet, cultured tones.

"Not a hope. I swotted for weeks to find you, dear."

"Couldn't you just leave me alone?"

Jackie sat down on the threadbare brown sofa and smiled up at her hostess. "I suppose I could arrange it. I could, for instance, *not* tell the BBC, the tabloids, and the rest of the world what you look like, and where you are."

The woman looked down at her ringless hands. "I haven't any money," she said.

"Oh, but you're worth a packet all the same, aren't you? In all the years you've been locked up, you never said anything except, *I didn't do it*, which is rubbish, because the world knows you did. You taped the Doyle boy's killing on a bloody tape recorder!"

The woman hung her head for a moment, turning away. "What do you want?" she said at last, sitting in the chair by the sofa.

Jackie Duncan touched the other woman's arm. *"I want you to tell me about it."*

"No. I can't. I've forgotten."

"No, you haven't. Nobody could. And that's the book the world wants to read. Not this mealymouthed rubbish the others have written about you. I want you to tell me every single detail, all the way through. That's the book I want to write." She took a deep breath, and forced a smile. "And in exchange, I'll keep your identity and whereabouts a secret, the way Ursula Bloom did when she interviewed Crippen's mistress in the 'fifties."

Erma Bradley shrugged. "I don't read crime stories," she said.

The light had faded from the big window facing the moors. On the scarred pine table a tape recorder was running, and in the deepening shadows, Erma Bradley's voice rose and fell with weary resignation, punctuated by Jackie's eager questions.

"I don't know," she said again.

"Come on. Think about it. Have a biscuit while you think. Sean didn't have sex with the Allen girl, but did he make love to *you* afterwards? Do you think he got an erection while he was doing the strangling?"

A pause. "I didn't look."

"But you made love after he killed her?"

"Yes."

"On the same bed?"

"But later. A few hours later. After we had taken away the body. It was Sean's bedroom, you see. It's where we always slept."

"Did you picture the child's ghost watching you do it?"

"I was twenty-two. He said—He used to get me drunk—and I—"

"Oh, come on, Erma. There's no bloody jury here. Just tell me if it turned you on to watch Sean throttling kids. When he did it, were both of you naked, or just him?"

"Please, I—Please!"

"All right, Erma. I can have the BBC here in time for the wake-up news."

"Just him."

An hour later. "Do stop sniveling, Erma. You lived through it once, didn't you? What's the harm in talking about it? They can't try you again. Now come on, dear, answer the question."

"Yes. The little boy—Brian Doyle—he was quite brave, really. Kept saying he had to take care of his mum, because she was divorced now, and asking us to let him go. He was only eight, and quite small. He even offered to fight us if we'd untie him. When Sean was getting the masking tape out of the cupboard, I went up to him, and I whispered to him to let the boy go, but he . . ."

"There you go again, Erma. Now I've got to shut the machine off again while you get hold of yourself."

She was alone now. At least, the reporter woman was gone. Just before eleven, she had scooped up her notes and her tape recorder, and the photos of the dead children she had brought from the photo archives, and she'd gone away, promising to return in a few days to "put the finishing touches on the interview." The dates and places and forensic details she could get from the other sources, she'd said.

The reporter had gone, and the room was empty, but Miss Emily Kay wasn't alone anymore. Now Erma Bradley had got in as well.

She knew, though, that no other journalists would come. This one, Jackie, would keep her secret well enough, but only to ensure the exclusivity of her own book. Other than that, Miss Emily Kay would be allowed to enjoy her freedom in the shabby little room overlooking the moors. But it wasn't a pleasant retreat any longer, now that she wasn't alone. Erma had brought the ghosts back with her.

Somehow the events of twenty-five years ago had become more real when she told them than when she lived them. It had been so confused back then. Sean drank a lot, and he liked her to keep him company in that. And it happened so quickly the first time, and then there was no turning back. But she never let herself think about it. It was Sean's doing, she would tell herself, and then that part of her mind would close right down, and she would turn her attention to something else. At the trial, she had thought about the hatred that she could almost touch, flaring at her from nearly everyone in the courtroom. She couldn't think then, for if she broke down, they would win.

They never put her on the stand. She answered no questions, except to say when a microphone was thrust in her face, *I didn't do it.* And then later in prison there were adjustments to make, and bad times with the other inmates to be faced. She didn't need a lot of sentiment dragging her down as well. *I didn't do it* came to have a truth for her: it meant, I am no longer the somebody who did that. I am small, and thin, and well-spoken. The ugly, ungainly monster is gone.

But now she had testified. Her own voice had conjured up the images of Sarah Allen calling out for her mother, and of Brian Doyle, offering to sell his bike to ransom himself, for his mum's sake. The hatchet-faced blonde, who had told them to shut up, who had held them down . . . she was here. And she was going to live here, too, with the sounds of weeping, and the screams. And every tread on the stair would be Sean, bringing home another little lad for a wee visit.

I didn't do it, she whispered. And it had come to have another meaning. *I didn't do it.* Stop Sean Hardie from hurting them. Go to the police. Apologize to the parents during the years in prison. Kill myself from the shame of it. *I didn't do it,* she whispered again. *But I should have.*

Ernie Sleaford was more deferential to her now. When he heard about the new book, and the size of her advance, he realized that she was a player, and he had begun to treat her with a new deference. He had even offered her a raise, in case she was thinking of quitting. But she wasn't going to quit. She quite enjoyed her work. Besides, it was so amusing now to see him stand up for her when she came into his grubby little office.

"We'll need a picture of you for the front page, love," he said in his most civil tones. "Would you mind if Denny took your picture, or is there one you'd rather use?"

Jackie shrugged. "Let him take one. I just had my hair done. So I make the front page as well?"

"Oh yes. We're devoting the whole page to Erma Bradley's suicide, and we want a sidebar of your piece: *I Was the Last to See the Monster Alive.* It will make a nice contrast. Your picture beside pudding-faced Erma."

"I thought she looked all right for forty-seven. Didn't the picture I got turn out all right?"

Ernie looked shocked. "We're not using that one, Jackie. We want to remember her the way she *was.* A vicious ugly beastie in contrast to a pure young thing like yourself. Sort of a moral statement, like."

Michael Z. Lewin, author of the fine Albert Samson novels and the Lt. Leroy Powder procedurals, has been giving readers the benefit of his well-written, satisfying suspense for over twenty years. He shows his considerable panache in "Wedding Bells." Neither the premise nor the resolution are anything like standard, and his cast of memorable characters just don't do things by the book. Don't forget to bring a present for the lovely couple . . . whoever they turn out to be. This gem was originally published in *New Crimes 2*.

Wedding Bells
MICHAEL Z. LEWIN

The case came into the office because of Salvatore, the artist.

One of Sal's models—a real one this time, in that she did actually model for him as well—took Sal home for a meal, to meet her father. The meal was a *disaster*, a real-thing, double-dyed, wave-the-flag disaster, at least for the purpose it was conceived for. Salvatore and "Daddy" did not hit it off.

"I don't know why I agreed to go in the first place," Sal said when he talked about it next afternoon at the Lunghi family's Sunday dinner.

Momma had a theory. "Maybe, just maybe, this girl you thought she was something special, like you were thinking serious."

"We'll whip her with the vermicelli!" David, Angelo's nephew and Momma's grandson, suggested.

There were a few titters around the table.

But not from Momma. Her preoccupation, re Salvatore, was to get him married. To anybody. "We'll whip her into shape once we know what we're dealing with," she had stated in his absence once. It had become family-famous, "the whipping meal," and was what David was referring to.

Nevertheless everyone was impressed to hear that Sal had actually gone to this girl's house. How many he got up to in his studio there weren't records,

325

and Sal did bring quite a few of his "models" home, that is, to the home now headed by his brother Angelo with wife Gina.

But bringing a girl to meet the Lunghi family was different. Knowing the family was part of knowing Salvatore.

"You wouldn't believe," Sal said. "I didn't believe. This guy started cross-examining me as soon as I got through the door. How much do I make in a year? What are my prospects? That whole archaic business, like: 'What are your intentions for my daughter?' "

"He raises two daughters alone after a wife divorces him. I can understand he'd be concerned," the Old Man said. But his mind was on other things. "Hey, Rosetta!" the Old Man called. "My plate's starving to death out here!"

"Some people," Gina said, "they still expect their daughters to keep company with civilized people." But the comment was not being offered to Sal. Gina directed the remark at Marie, her own fourteen-year-old who was hanging around with an earring and a nineteen-year-old earring at that.

"Ollie, Ollie Ollie," David taunted.

Marie blushed, to her great annoyance, but lifted her nose as an act of disdain and self-control. "Oliver is very intelligent," she said.

"I tell you," Sal said. "I told this guy, my intentions for your daughter are to get her to move less when she is posing and to pose less when she is supposed to be moving."

The Old Man—Sal and Angelo and Rosetta's father—laughed. Momma, the Old Man's wife, did not.

"Anyway," Sal said, "so I told this guy about the agency and how I did a bit of private detecting on the side for the family business to supplement my income. I *thought* it would rattle him even more. I can tell you I was fed up from the start, so fed up that I was getting sick to my stomach even before the cook trotted out this weird stuff they said was veal."

"Veal they serve you," Momma said. "What's this girl's name again? Susie?"

"No need to remember it anymore, Momma," Sal said.

"Oh, poor girl!" Momma said.

Rosetta served the chicken and said, "You use it right, Momma, veal doesn't have to cost that much." As well as organizing household domestic functions, Rosetta was the family business's bookkeeper. She knew how much things cost.

Angelo, now head of the Lunghi Private Detective Agency that the Old Man had started, said, "You said there was something coming to us in a business way."

"That's right," Salvatore said. "I thought when I said 'private detective' the guy might take it as the last straw and kick me out then and there and tell me never to darken his daughter again."

"But he didn't?" Gina asked.

"No. Instead he looked at Susie and then he looked back at me and he started crying."

"My brother Salvatore said that you would probably be contacting us, Mr. Notice," Angelo said. "But before we start I want to introduce my wife, Gina."

"Hello," Gina said.

"Hello," Heyward Notice said quietly. He was a small, lugubrious looking man who revealed an extremely expensive suit when the Lunghis finally prevailed on him to take his overcoat off.

"Gina is our receptionist and handles agency correspondence. This is a family business and I like, when I can, to have Gina present at initial interviews. It saves time later on."

"I understand," Notice said.

"Salvatore did not tell us what it was all about," Angelo lied. "Only that you had a problem, that it was a delicate family matter and that you felt in desperate need of help. Desperate was the word he used. I don't know whether that was accurate."

"It was an accurate use of the word," Notice said.

"Perhaps then you would explain the situation. I can assure you that anything you tell us will be kept in complete confidence. My father once went to gaol rather than betray something he was told in confidence in this office."

The exaggerated assurance seemed to have the desired effect. Notice said, "I have a desperate problem with my daughter."

"Would that be Susan?" Angelo asked.

"No. With my younger daughter, Barbara."

"I see."

"She wants to get married. She *insists* on getting married." Heyward Notice was suddenly breathing heavily. He had to pause.

Angelo and Gina exchanged glances. "Uh huh," Angelo said, to invite a continuation.

"A marriage must be prevented. It must not take place. The man she wants to marry is an utter scoundrel and rogue. It is obvious to anybody with an ounce of sense that he is only after what he perceives as her money, that is, her share of my money."

"I see." Angelo said.

"Of course I can always tie the actual cash up so he can't get hold of it, but even more than the money I am convinced that a lasting and legal entanglement with this man will ruin my poor Barbara's youth and possibly her life. It's bad enough that she wishes to see the man, to have do with him. At least, thank God, she is sensible enough to know that she is too young to have children."

"How old is Barbara?" Gina asked.

"Eighteen years of age. She is in art college, like Susie. With her whole life in front of her. A wonderful girl. Well, they both are."

"And the man?" Angelo asked.

"His name is Maurice Franklin. He is a so-called student himself, although he is twenty-six years old and has been enrolled at the college for seven years. Seven years! He has a veneer of maturity that is, no doubt, attractive to a child of Barbara's age. But he is an opportunist and sponger. He is the type to live off older women, but he has latched onto my little Barbara for some reason and I intend to make him let her go."

"I see," Angelo said. His voice was thoughtful.

"I *cannot*, I *will not* let this marriage take place. Legal entanglements have ruined vast tracts of my life and I will not let that happen to my children. I am just about prepared to commit murder, I'm that resolved."

"I see," Angelo said. His voice was calm but his face showed clearly the surprise he felt at hearing such a threat.

For the first time Notice smiled. "I would prefer, of course, to avoid such an extreme. Which is why I have to come to you."

"So this Susie of Salvatore's has real money?" Momma said. "Oh dear, oh dear." Profound regret.

"It wasn't that the father disliked Sal, Momma," Gina said. "He was upset about the younger daughter."

"At least my Salvatore is an established artist. Not some *student* of twenty-six years old."

"What does the father do?" the Old Man asked. "Is he good for the bill?"

"He owns some farms and other property," Angelo said. "He got started with inherited money but he has been quite successful in his own right too." After a dramatic pause Angelo said, "And he said that we should spare no expense." Angelo knew that would impress the Old Man.

"He actually said that?"

"Yes."

"I one time had a guy say that, but what he meant, as it turned out, was that I should spare none of my expense. He never paid up."

"Yes he did," Momma said. "Eventually."

"Not everything. Not everything."

"But most."

"All right. He paid most. But it was a hell of a struggle."

"Heyward Notice gave us a retainer of £1000."

"I like yours better than mine," the Old Man said. "What do you think he's going to be worth to us, Angelo?"

"That's the problem," Angelo said. "I'm not all that sure what we can do for him."

"We can lighten his wallet a little, we can do that."

Gina said, "The girl is of age. There is no way her father can prevent her marrying, if she doesn't care what he thinks."

"Maybe this Maurice Franklin is already married," the Old Man said.

"That's one place to start and I thought you might check that out tomorrow, Poppa."

"Right," the Old Man said.

"Otherwise I think we're looking to turn up information that will show this Franklin in a bad light and will put Barbara off. That could be things about his personal past or it could be other women that he is seeing now. But at the moment we are just fishing around for a real angle."

"Are you going in gang-busters?" the Old Man asked.

"He's been watching television again," Momma said.

"I just mean are you going to work on all the possible directions at once or do you wait till I find out about marital status?"

"The client is very upset," Gina said. "So we need to explore all the possibilities as fast as we can. He even threatened to kill Franklin rather than see him marry the girl."

"We can't have that," the Old Man said with concern.

"No," Gina said.

"If he killed the guy we'd never get paid."

Gang-busters it was. Salvatore was booked to follow Franklin. The Old Man worked on marital status, police record, credit rating, educational history, bank balance and all the other information held on the various computers that long-established Lunghi contacts could get at.

Angelo himself went to the art college to talk to administrators and secretaries and to get what he could generally from college sources.

And Gina decided to have a go at Maurice Franklin himself.

"I'll go as a rich woman thinking about entering the college as a mature student. I'll sound him out to ask if there are any special problems about being older than the other students. I'll flirt outrageously and see if he'll propose to me on the spot."

Angelo was not altogether taken with the idea, but Gina said, "Don't be stupid. There are two good reasons why I should do it."

"Oh yes?" Angelo said.

"First the client said spare no expense. Second I've been dying for an excuse to buy a mini skirt."

After two days the Gang-busters knew a lot about Maurice Franklin. They knew he was twenty-nine and not twenty-six. They knew that his mother was a widow. They knew that he was banned from driving. They knew he had had stereo equipment repossessed, but was not now in debt.

Paid off by Barbara?

They knew that he was five feet seven inches tall and they knew that a number of the girls at the college admired his tight little bum.

They knew that he liked green socks and lived in a bedsit.

They knew his status with the college was ambiguous but since he was "helpful" with the younger students and didn't cost anything, the lecturing staff was happy enough to have him around.

"Huh!" Gina said. "Some kind of 'helpful'!" She had met Franklin easily, but mini skirt and the recent death of her extremely rich husband notwithstanding, he had not shown the slightest interest in her.

A sculpture teacher who dressed like a cowboy, however, had begged to model her legs so Gina did not return dispirited. The cowboy had been steered to talk of Franklin. He was dismissive of "the randy sod," and had referred to him as a womanizer. But pressed, the cowboy had conceded that these days Franklin seemed totally occupied with Barbara Notice.

"Personally I just can't see it," the cowboy had said.

"No?" Gina asked.

"She's a mere child! Pleasantly enough composed, but an empty well, a nothing. Me, I have always felt powerfully attracted to the well-preserved more mature woman. A woman who has seen life, who has suffered despair and known exultation. A woman who—"

"All right, all right, all right!" Angelo said. "I get the picture."

Salvatore, in his turn, reported a particularly boring two days tailing Franklin and confirmed that there was no hint at any time that there was any woman in the target's life but Barbara.

"The mail at his place gets left on a table. But all he gets is junk mail and bills. I talked to the caretaker's wife even."

Momma's eyes narrowed. "Stay away from wives," she said.

Salvatore laughed, but they all knew his pattern. If he ended with one model he was always in a hurry to get into the next.

With all the bits and pieces of information Angelo felt that they knew a fair amount about Maurice Franklin, and that it was unlikely that Franklin was either a very special or a very evil character.

A lecturer Angelo had talked to at the college summed Franklin up as "a man with some talent who had trouble disciplining his talents to develop in one direction to the exclusion of others." The lecturer had also talked of Franklin as, "from a rather difficult background and a man who had trouble sustaining relationships."

It wasn't the kind of language Angelo would use himself but he suspected the drift was fair enough.

"It's not going very well," Angelo said when the Old Man asked at breakfast on the third day of active investigation. "We're having trouble coming up with a strategy. As far as we can tell, the relationship between Franklin and the girl is *likely* to peter out. But, on the other hand, it is possible that Barbara is the right girl for the guy and will be the making of him. It does happen sometimes." He looked at Momma. The Old Man snorted.

Angelo said, "But we've got nothing that looks like being any use to prevent a marriage."

"When is the client coming?"

"Day after tomorrow, in the morning, unless we call him."

"So, you got two days. What you doing?"

"Sal's still following him. And we've hired in a female op for the day. I doubt she's going to get any farther than Gina did, but if his current taste is in young ones, we can but try."

"Young and pretty and female and wired?"

"That's the idea," Angelo said. "See if we can entrap him into some unaffianced type proposals that we can get on tape to play to the daughter."

"One day soon Marie will be able to do that kind of work," the Old Man said.

"She's only fourteen, Poppa."

"So not today. But it's expensive, hiring outside ops."

The outside op was a failure and knew it after a day. "No interest at all. I felt I would have had better luck at Madame Tussaud's," she said. "I'm happy to go back tomorrow to try again but I don't want you to waste your money."

"You should meet my father," Angelo said.

"Only if he's easy," the girl said. "My confidence is shattered."

Just then Salvatore returned to the office.

At dinner Angelo passed on Salvatore's report that he was fed up. "He feels we're getting nowhere," Angelo said.

"So where is this Salvatore that's got opinions for us?" the Old Man asked. "I thought he was eating here tonight."

"He got inspired to do some painting," Gina said. "But he thinks we're going to have to tell the client that this Franklin is not as bad as he thinks and that he should tough it out. Or that we might try to buy Franklin off."

"That's possible," Angelo said. "But we'll need the client's approval before we try it. Has anybody else got another suggestion?"

Gina, who often had ideas, was blank this time.

The Old Man was basking in the idea of maybe meeting the wired female op.

Rosetta was out with her fiancé.

David and Marie were just out.

"So, is nobody going to ask me?" Momma said after suffering through a long silence.

"Momma, if you have an idea of what to do . . . ?"

"I don't know about fiddly this or that," Momma said. "But I tell you something for nothing. You want to get the dirty laundry on a boy? The place to go is his mother."

Angelo prepared a couple of ways to get Felicity Franklin to talk about her son but they never left the rehearsal hall. Felicity Franklin needed no excuse to talk about anything.

"Coffee, Mr. Lunghi? Would you like some coffee?"

"That would be nice, thank you."

"Only the instant. My finances don't run to anything else, but, you know, I always think about coffee that unless you're going to have cream with it, I mean good rich double cream, like Guernsey cream, then it tastes just as good, or just as bad depending how you think, to have instant anyway. That's what I think. Of course," she added with a long-suffering tilt of the head, "I can't afford the cream either."

Finance proved to be a major theme in Felicity Franklin's conversation. As was the subject of her ungrateful only child.

"You, a child?" Angelo asked. "No! You're too young! You must have been a child yourself!" But the pump had hardly needed priming.

Felicity Franklin explained in great detail what a disappointment Maurice was to his widowed mother. Top at maths in primary school he had spurned all that and become "a so-called artist." It was clear that there was no money in being a so-called artist.

As well the son never telephoned or wrote or visited. "And now he's got some rich little bint on the boil. Not that I hear from his own lips, but I have a few friends to tell me, even now, in my distress. But will I see a penny if he hooks her? Not in a month of Saturdays. I say 'Saturdays' rather than Sundays because I've always liked Saturdays better than Sundays. You know?"

"So I got flirted with too," Angelo said when, finally, he returned.

"This time of night it might have been more than a flirtation," Gina said. But she was wearing her special nightie and she had that rare quality of complete confidence in her man.

"I got more than flirtation, all right," Angelo said. "I got an idea."

Heyward Notice was on time the next morning and struck Gina as having a strange look on his face, somehow a mixture of tension and expectation that seemed dangerous. But perhaps she was thinking too much of the threat to Maurice Franklin that Notice had made so readily in his last visit to the office.

This time when the client took off his overcoat and sat down, Angelo got quickly to the matter in hand. He said, "Mr. Notice, just how serious are you about wanting to prevent a marriage between your daughter and Maurice Franklin?"

* * *

The wedding took place the next Saturday. Angelo and Gina served as witnesses but came home straight afterwards. Not that they missed anything. There was no reception. Nor, indeed, did the happy couple plan a honeymoon.

But the couple was happy, no question about it.

Felicity Franklin could hardly get the words "I will" out of her mouth for thinking what to spend her new lifetime income on. And Heyward Notice, if not exactly wreathed in smiles, certainly felt relief and satisfaction that he had succeeded in preventing Barbara from *marrying* Maurice Franklin. Even though to do it he had had to marry Franklin's mother himself.

"So, is there nothing they could do about it, even though they aren't related in any way at all?" Marie asked. "They" being the new couple's respective children.

"As long as the parents remain married there is too great a degree of 'affinity' between the children and marriage is legally prohibited."

Rosetta was reading from a note that had been provided by Walter, who was always referred to as her fiancé even though legal niceties might suggest that Walter had too great a degree of "affinity" to his wife for Rosetta to be considered "affianced" in law. Walter was a solicitor and provided the family with legal information when needed.

"Oh that's *sad!*" Marie said. "That's really *sad.*"

Gina studied her daughter, but said nothing.

Angelo said, "They *could* go to their M.P. and have him introduce an Act of Parliament to allow it. It does happen, special laws to allow specific couples to marry. But that's not our concern. We've done what our client wanted, which was to make sure there was no way the children could get married in a hurry."

"Has he paid his bill?" the Old Man asked.

"He paid it before the wedding," Angelo said.

"Ah, weddings," Momma said.

"It isn't going to be that kind of marriage, Momma," Gina said.

"Who knows, who knows," Momma said mistily. "Maybe she'll whip him into shape."

Angelo and Gina exchanged smiles. "Somehow I doubt it, Momma," Angelo said.

"You never know," Momma said irrefutably. "So, what do you think Salvatore's up to tonight? What's this detective girl *like?*"

Reginald Hill has been busy entertaining us with his supense fiction for over twenty years. The author of such Superintendent Andrew Dalziel and Sergeant Pascoe of Yorkshire novels as *A Clubbable Woman* is also the hand behind Patrick Ruell's works. He has written a most unusual tale of revenge. The revenge in this story is at once so . . . civilized . . . in its form and structure, while remaining so savage and utterly lethal in its intent that the act and the narrative explicating the act transcend one's expectations of the limits of revenge. In this tale reprinted from *New Crimes 2,* Hill makes his perpetuator/protagonist so real that we suggest you hold onto your sympathies. But his greatest victory here is his ability to keep us wondering if what we fear is actually happening, as the inexorable scenario unfolds before our sorrowed eyes. Altogether, it's a marvelously controlled performance.

Proxime Accessit
REGINALD HILL

Proxime accessit.

"He nearly made it."

The story of his life.

School saw the start of it. Collecting the tatty certificates while others strode off with the silver cups. Left in the shallows with a ripple of applause while others bore out to sea on a great surge of cheers.

University the same. Redbrick while his classmates were Oxbridge. A sound second while dimmer men got fortunate firsts. A teaching diploma while they did research degrees.

Once established, the pattern was unbreakable. Or so it seemed to Dennis Platt as his forties darkened to fifty. Here he was, still in his home town of Dunchester, deputy head of the same school he'd almost succeeded at as a boy, with seventy-five failed applications for headships behind him, and a man ten years his junior over him.

Even his family seemed to fit the pattern. There was nothing wrong with them, and yet . . .

Pamela, his wife, had aged quite well, but somehow her dress sense hadn't matured with her figure. She was a good plain cook who had a habit of overreaching into disaster whenever they entertained. And she had more or less retired from sex after the birth of their third daughter. These were doubt-less not uncommon flaws in Dunchester domestic life, hardly tragic in their scope. But Dennis knew, though he never shared the knowledge, that it was Lucy, her gorgeous younger sister, he had longed for, lusted after, and lost. Pamela was simply a consolation prize, the vellum certificate not the silver cup.

He had hoped for a son and got three daughters. The youngest had just left home to join her sisters as a London secretary. Dennis had not been heartbroken to see any of them go. He was sure he would die in their defense, but he was less certain that he could argue for their survival in a balloon debate. Though not dull, they rarely sparkled; though not ugly, they erred on the Wimpey estate side of homely; and though not unmarriable, they re-mained steadfastly unmarried.

All this might have been endurable—indeed passed in a humdrum pro-vincial Dunchester kind of way for enjoyable—if his bright young dreams had followed a natural course and faded completely, leaving his dusty middle-aged memory to the usual task of readjusting past targets so that present torpor might figure as some kind of success.

But how to adjust, how to forget, when day after tedious day, year after empty year, he saw his hoped-for life, his *true* life, the life in which all those bright young blossoms ripened into golden fruit, being lived before his eyes?

True tragedy lies not in missing your targets, but in having a best friend who hits them, every one.

It had been Tom Trotter who pipped Dennis for most of the school prizes; Tom Trotter who read Ancient History at Oxford while Dennis did modern history at Reading; Tom Trotter whose first play was instantly ac-cepted by the same TV company who not only turned down Dennis's, but lost the script. Soon Tom was appearing on chat shows, at media events, in color supplements, and out of stretch limos at openings. He was prolific and ener-getic. He wrote plays, novels, short stories, travel books and film scripts. He produced and directed. He won a Special Prize at Cannes and the lion's share in an Oscar. He bought a London penthouse, a California beach house, a Tuscan villa, and a Polynesian atoll.

Normally such success would have provided not only the reason for friendship to die, but the opportunity. The rising spiral moves ever more distant from the plane circle whose path it shared for a little while. But families are more cohesive than friends, and at the dark heart of Dennis's discontent lay the fact that Tom Trotter was his brother-in-law. He it was who inevitably had won the lovely Lucy, leaving his discomfited rival (whose awkward diffidence was such that no one actually noticed he *was* a rival) to salve his wounds by pretending that it was Pamela he'd been after all along.

Lucy Trotter was a nice girl whose niceness had survived the sudden inrush of wealth and fame. After a sojourn in California or Cannes, after shooting on location in Tijuana or Taiwan, her heart's desire was ever to return to Dunchester where her family and the friends of her youth still lived. Nor was Tom averse to modestly parading his success and honors down the thoroughfares of his childhood. Weddings, christenings, birthdays, funerals; none was forgotten and as many as possible were actually attended, while it was a sweetly proud boast of Lucy's that no matter what the distance or disarrangement involved, she had never missed a Dunchester family Christmas in her life.

Thus for Dennis there was no forgetting. He was a man who felt himself twice wronged. Not only had his "true" life been stolen from him, but worse, instead of the peace of the grave which is the murder victim's usual consolation, he was condemned to watch the thief flaunting the usurped existence before his unavertable eyes. When the Trotters weren't actually in town, the local media provided an endless flow of news items about them, while a whole wall in the Platt kitchen was papered each year with Lucy's postcards from exotic places. And what visual detail her dense scrawl had perforce to miss out was mopped up by her video camera, to be laid before the family as a postprandial Yuletide treat.

"Now this is a little party we had on the beach, that's Tom talking to Steve Spielberg, he wanted to help me edit these things properly but I said no, the folks back home prefer to see it just like it comes, warts and all, and there, if you look over Neil Simon's shoulder, there's Clint with the beer stein, he doesn't often show at these things, whoops! now we've jumped, this is Paris, no, it's London, of course, our apartment, a little dinner, I just couldn't resist taking a few shots through the door when I went to get the coffee, there's Margaret Drabble passing the After Eights to Harold Pinter, and that empty seat next to him, that's where Tony was sitting but he was in the loo being sick, and there's Vanessa and there to her left, with the big black beard, believe it or not, that's Salman!"

And Dennis would sit in the flickering shadows with a twilight song of hate keening in his heart, but when the show was over, he was always the first in his expression of admiration and interest, for he had long since realized that in this regard at least there must be no question of *proxime accessit*. Never by word or deed, by gesture or expression, by nod or by wink, had he given anyone the satisfaction of knowing the depth of his resentment. He was in all outward appearances Tom Trotter's greatest fan. He had first editions of all his books, videos of all his films, autographed first night programs of all his plays; and if anyone in Dunchester dared to hint criticism of the Trotter lifestyle or oeuvre, Dennis was down on them with a discipular fervor.

Nor were these attitudes altogether assumed. This, after all, was Dennis's "true" life that Tom was living, and though a man may detest the thief who steals his jewels, the jewels themselves remain precious, whoever is wearing them. And Tom himself was not intrinsically dislikeable. A moment usually came on his visits when, unbuttoned and embeered, he would confide to Dennis that in the wilderness of hype and hypocrisy he now inhabited, his old friend's words were the only totally honest and unself-interested utterance he ever heard; and at such moments Dennis sometimes came close to forgiving the man his crime. Close, but no cigar, for there was always Lucy to remind him of the greatest theft of all; and yet it would have required a blindness darker than Cupid's not to see that her happiness was so inextricably bound up with Tom's that hatred of him must in some measure be hatred of her also.

So was struck a delicate balance of envy and admiration, of resentment and regard, of loathing and love, which looked to have a fair chance of bearing Dennis's painful double life undetected to the grave.

But it is strange what good a man may do in an existence he regards as wasted. Perhaps in an attempt to blot out the infinitely renewable pain of loss, Dennis Platt had resisted few calls on his time and energy in what he thought of as his shadow life. His work in the fields of youth clubs, young people's charities, and education in the widest sense, had won him golden opinions which he hardly noticed or, if he did, regarded as a kind of subtle mockery.

Until one day his headmaster said to him, "Dennis, you realize that this year marks the twenty-fifth anniversary of your appointment to the staff here?"

"Good Lord. That long? If you add the seven years I was here as a kid . . ." Dennis shook his head, realizing he was drifting perilously near open bitterness, managed a laugh instead, and said, "It doesn't bear thinking about."

"On the contrary," said the head. "Lots of people have been thinking about it a great deal. Let me put you in the picture. Your colleagues had the bright idea of giving you a commemorative award at Speech Day. There was great enthusiasm in the school, and the governors and the old pupils association got in on the act too. Things snowballed. It seems half of Dunchester are mad keen to contribute congratulations and cash! So get your thinking cap on, or come Speech Day, you could end up receiving the biggest clock you've ever seen!"

Dennis was genuinely dumbfounded. He felt moved, disturbed, even ashamed. Could it be that all this time he had possessed a pearl worth all his tribe without realizing its value? Was it possible that his shadow life had real substance? Here was a prize he had not striven for, and would not have felt cheated of if it had passed him by, and it was being offered, gratis and unsolicited, by his grateful fellow citizens.

For the first time ever he weighed solid civic virtues and values in the balance against the tinsel triumphs of Tom Trotter's world, and saw his "true" life fly high, with no weight or substance whatsoever.

"I'm bowled over," he said sincerely. "I never thought . . . it's most kind . . ."

"No one deserves it more," said the head heartily. "It'll be a great occasion both for you and for the school. Oh, and just to put the gilt on the gingerbread, and I know how much this will please you, I've asked your old chum, Tom Trotter, to present the prizes and of course your award, and he has said he'll be delighted."

A pearl dissolves in wine, they say, but it dissolves even more quickly in gall and wormwood, leaving only its seed of grit on the tongue.

Dennis smiled, and smiled, and bent all his resources of mind and will to make that smile genuine. It was *his* award, he told himself. It was being given for *his* services to *his* school, *his* town. It was going to be *his* day.

But he knew in his heart that though the occasion might glitter, it would not be with his effulgence; though the cameras might click, it would not be to record his image; though paeans might be composed, they would not be in his praise.

Worst of all, Tom would do his best for him; and by his fulsome tributes win applause for his own generosity; and by his modest withdrawal take with him the best part of the media presence. So in the annals of great Dunchester occasions, it would go down as the day Tom Trotter presented the prizes, not the day Dennis Platt received one.

Tom rang from India to say how delighted he and Lucy were about the award and how thrilled he would be to present it. It was three o'clock in the morning, but Dennis dropped no hint of this as he expressed enthusiastic gratitude in a wide-awake middle-of-the-day voice, adding the hope that Tom wasn't going to disorder his far more important affairs for such a relatively trivial matter.

"Come off it!" said Tom. "You don't think I'd miss something like this? In the world I live in, everyone's giving everyone else awards all the time. You've no idea what a pleasure it will be to present one that really matters to someone who really deserves it."

Dennis recognized a rough-cut of the central theme of Tom's presentation speech. By a gentle rubbishing of his own success, he would attempt quite sincerely to emphasize the importance of Dennis's achievement. But it is not by conjuring up images of glittering Oscar ceremonies that you persuade people they are better off in a Dunchester school hall.

By the time he put the phone down he felt genuinely wide awake. He made himself a cup of coffee, sat at the kitchen table and looked at his life. Or rather his lives.

It seemed to him that he was approaching a watershed. Some discontents may be divine, but at this moment he knew that his conviction that Tom Trotter had somehow stolen his "true" life was merely destructive. He could not rid himself of what he recognized as a totally illogical sense of deprivation, but he could at least acknowledge that there was no way in fact or fantasy for him to regain what he felt he had lost.

That admitted, would he not do well to seek to be satisfied with what he had got? And was it so bad? He tried to reconstruct his feelings on first hearing about the special award, before his thoughts were muddied by news of Tom's involvement. He had felt good. He had felt complete. He had felt as a Dunchester deputy-head with a faithful wife, three sturdy daughters, and the goodwill and high regard of his fellow citizens ought to feel.

In fact he had felt like an achiever.

And it seemed to him, sitting in that cold kitchen at the dead hour of the night, that if only he could be allowed to enjoy that award, that ceremony, that day, unsullied by any reminder of that other lost life, he might be able to go forward as a whole man into a useful maturity and a serene old age.

He rose and rinsed his coffee cup. He felt strangely calm. God was showing him that happiness or at least contentment was still a possibility. All it needed was Tom's absence from Speech Day. And surely when it came to ways of stopping a man in India from getting back to England, God was spoilt for choice. Airline strikes, mechanical breakdown, earthquakes, typhoons, civil unrest, contractual obligations, Delhi-belly—the list was endless. In fact, even without God's active opposition, the journey seemed almost impossible!

In the weeks that followed he was a new man, or rather he was more genuinely than ever before the man he had always contrived to appear to be. When his wife said to him, "This award really means a lot to you, doesn't it, dear?" he was able to reply with genuine affection and no hint of irony, "Yes, it does. But only because of what it means to Dunchester." And when the headmaster informed him that contributions to his award had topped the four figure mark, his response was equally sincere and altruistic.

"I can't accept this," he said. "A token is all I require, a memento of people's kindness. But the bulk of the money I'd like to plow back into the community. That minibus we use for the disabled kids' trips, it's a disgrace. I've spent more time fiddling with that engine than the kids have spent at the seaside. It's time we had a new one. When the people of Dunchester realize it's not just my beer money they're contributing to, we'll see how truly generous they can be!"

And they did. The money poured in. And even the news that Tom had rung the local press to say that he would personally double the total public donation cast only a temporary shadow over Dennis's new found happiness.

For he knew what no one else did, that he and God had an arrangement whereby Tom Trotter was not going to make it to Speech Day.

His confidence held till eight o'clock the night before.

Tom had said they should arrive by six-thirty, and with every minute that passed, Dennis offered silent thanks to God.

Then at eight the doorbell rang.

"That'll be them now," said Pamela putting down her knitting.

"I'll go," said Dennis with the serene certainty of one who knows it's the Jehovah's Witnesses or (just as unpalatable) some friend of his daughters, who had arrived earlier from London and gone out almost at once.

He opened the door.

"Evening, squire," said Tom. "Sorry we're late. Bloody brakes started playing up on the motorway."

Years of role-play kept Dennis's face welcoming and his voice lightly concerned as he said, "Good Lord. That could have been nasty. What was the trouble?"

"God knows. You know me, can't tell a plug from a piston. Can't have been much. The hire firm sent a grease monkey out and he soon fixed it. Lucy, get a move on with those cases! I've done my back. Daren't risk the strain."

"I'll help her," said Dennis.

He joined his sister-in-law at the open boot. Tom didn't own a car, merely hired whatever was fast and comfortable wherever he went.

"Dennis, how are you? Big day tomorrow. I'm so glad they're appreciating you at last. You really deserve it."

They kissed, a friendly family peck.

"It's great of you to make the effort to come," said Dennis.

"We wouldn't have missed it for worlds. We know how much it must mean to you."

For a mad moment Dennis toyed with the idea of telling Lucy the truth and inviting her cooperation in keeping Tom from the ceremony.

But how could he make her understand? And even if he succeeded, why should he imagine that her loyalty to Tom, not to mention her sister and her nieces, would allow her to join what must seem a pathetic, indeed paranoiac conspiracy?

He picked up the cases and carried them into the house.

After supper Tom said, "Now what's the game plan tomorrow?"

"It's quite straightforward," said Dennis. "The platform party assembles in the head's study at two o'clock, downs a quick glass of patriotic sherry, then processes to the hall where the drill will be much as it was in your time, Tom. Except that this time you're presenting prizes, not getting them."

"They wanted to have a civic lunch beforehand," said Pamela. "But Dennis said no, he didn't want that."

Dennis shrugged modestly. The truth was he'd seen his wife's proposed outfit and felt that the less public exposure it got, the better. He looked at Lucy, contrasting her elegant cat suit with the fussy cocktail dress Pamela had felt was a suitable garb for serving a disastrous boeuf en croute. And then, as evidence of the genuineness of his conversion, or reversion, to full-time Dunchester man, he felt a pang of guilt.

Lucy smiled back at him and said, "Oh you should have gone the whole hog and had the lunch, Dennis."

"Just as well he didn't, as we couldn't have been there," said Tom.

"Now that would really have spoilt the mayor's day," murmured Dennis.

Lucy gave him a slightly puzzled look and he realized he had come close to letting his number-one-fan mask slip. Injecting a dose of lively interest into his voice, he said, "You've got something on in the morning, have you?"

"You know me. Always improving the shining hour," said Tom. "You remember those short stories I did way back? The ones set locally, about the two town lads who get caught scrumping apples by the old farmer, and then a relationship develops between them and the farmer's family?"

Dennis remembered them well, remembered especially that the initial story had been loosely based on an episode in their own young lives, except that his own fortitude and Tom's tearful terror had somehow got reversed in their fictional equivalents.

"I remember," he said. "They were really good. I always thought that they could have been developed into a great TV series."

"I've always said you should have been my agent, Dennis," exclaimed Tom. "That's exactly what's going to happen. Now, the town sequences are easy. Good old Dunchester doesn't change. But we thought we needed a bit more of a contrast in the country scenes. I mean, it's really a bit scrubby round here and the local farmers look like supermarket managers. So I thought, let's widen the gap. Boys a bit scruffier, and the farmer an old-style landowner, perhaps with a title. And not a farmhouse they get taken to, but more of a country seat. And then I thought of Purbley Grange."

He looked around triumphantly.

Pamela said, "But that's fifty miles away up on the moors."

"My dear Pam, all we need is an electric point or two to plug our equipment into, and at a pinch we don't even need that," mocked Tom. "It's years since I've been there, but I can't imagine it's changed, except maybe to crumble away a bit more. It's so dramatically situated. And that dried up moat with the bridge and the arch! It's perfect, or at least so my memory tells me. But before I prise the money men out of their upholstery and ferry them up here, I thought I'd better take a look for myself and make sure memory wasn't deceiving me. It's empty at the moment and I've got the keys from the agent, so we'll be going to check the place out in the morning. And don't worry, Pam. I'll test the electricity supply!"

"I think," said Lucy, "that Pam was more concerned about tomorrow's timetable than your series, dear."

She reached across the table and squeezed Dennis's hand.

"Don't worry," she said reassuringly. "I'll guarantee he'll get to the ceremony on time. I'll even take our togs along so we can change en route if we don't have time to get back here."

Dennis smiled his gratitude, but behind the smile a wild sea of thoughts was surging.

Lucy's assurance itself was enough to have set a weaker man screaming. He already knew beyond all doubt that Tom's mere presence at the Speech Day would relegate his own leading role to a supporting part. But the presence of Tom preening himself at his own perspicacity after a successful visit to Purbley Grange, and bubbling over with the news that he was going to turn Dunchester into a prime time telly town, would wipe Dennis off the cast list altogether.

But this was no longer the worst of his fears. Even if he got through Speech Day without running mad; even if he dug down deep and found strength enough to maintain his resolve to spend the years ahead giving substance to his shadow life, despite not having the longed for launch-pad; what hope was there of success if this proposed TV series took off? He had seen how these things could spawn an infinity of follow-ups. He knew areas which TV notoriety had turned into a tourist attraction. There could be coach-loads of visitors, souvenir shops, postcards, T-shirts. Dunchester could—God help us!—become the capital of Trotter Country. There could be magazine articles, TV documentaries. There could even—most terrible of thoughts—be a moment when he would be expected to emerge smiling from behind a screen to pour his pot of sentimental syrup into the glutinous gunge of *Tom Trotter— This Is Your Life!*

It must not be. It was no longer enough for Tom not to be present at the Speech Day. He must never be present anywhere again.

He looked at Lucy. For a second the old feelings of love and longing squeezed his gut. Then he saw her as what she would be without Tom—an even more potent threat to the new, worthwhile, honest relationship he was establishing with Pamela.

It no longer felt unfortunate that Lucy would have to go too; it felt necessary.

That night as the Trotters slept the sleep of the jet-lagged and the Platt females slept the sleep of the just, Dennis slipped out of the house into the garage where he picked up his bag of tools and inspection light. Do-it-yourself mechanics was a skill proper to a Dunchester man; only those who had made it into the "real" world of executive jets and stretch limos could afford to boast their ignorance.

Tom's description of the trouble he'd had on the motorway had given him the hint. A car with a recent record of brake failure; a trip to Purbley Grange; the two things chimed perfectly. The road out to the Grange was a long uphill drag with not much reason for braking. But coming down . . . There were straights long enough for a man in a hurry to get up to eighty. And Tom would be in a hurry, wouldn't he? Lucy might nag him to give himself plenty of time, but Tom would leave it to the last possible minute, and then be determined to make the school with time to spare so he could proclaim, *look, I was right, as usual!*

So, eighty down the straights, braking hard into sharp bends with steep fell on one side and a rocky slope into a deep gill on the other; accelerate, brake! accelerate, brake! accelerate . . .

It wasn't murder. God could choose to let the brakes fail as he backed out of the drive, or as he parked at Purbley Grange, or He could steer the car past the boulders and let it come to rest, no harm done, beside the chattering beck. God's choice, not Dennis Platt's.

He switched off the inspection light and slid out from under the car. Five minutes later he was slipping back into bed beside his gently snoring wife. He dug her in the ribs and she stopped. Then he closed his eyes and drifted smoothly off to sleep, knowing that he had done everything a man could be expected to do.

The following morning he woke, alert and refreshed, to the sound of a gusting wind blowing handfuls of rain against the window pane. There was a heart-stopping moment at breakfast when Lucy wondered whether it was wise to be driving to the Grange in such conditions, but Tom said, "Non-sense. This is exactly the weather to see the place in. Don't forget your video camera. We'll have them drooling into their daiquiris in London."

"Bye bye, Dennis," said Lucy as they left. "See you at the school. And don't worry, I'll get him there if I have to carry him!"

By two o'clock when the platform party began to assemble, there was no sign of the Trotters. At ten-past-two, the headmaster discreetly enquired if Dennis knew any reason why Tom should be delayed. Dennis explained that Tom had gone off to view Purbley Grange.

"Something to do with a TV film, I think," he said vaguely. "I'm sure he'll be here any minute now."

He saw the head rejoin the mayor and murmur reassurances. The sherry was recirculated. Another ten minutes passed. The head renewed his enquiries, this time less discreetly.

"Is there any way we can try to contact Trotter?" he asked across the room.

"I suppose you could ring Purbley Grange though I'm not sure if there's anyone living there just now," said Dennis dubiously.

"What's he want to go out to a godforsaken place like that for on a day like this?" asked the mayor, who worked at being a down-to-earth man of the people.

"Well, you know how it is in the media world," said Dennis. "Tom's awfully thorough when it comes to business. He likes to see everything for himself. And we shouldn't complain, not when it gets him into our neck of the woods for an occasion like this."

It was a subtle reproof, defending Tom, but at the same time suggesting that the main reason he had come north was not the Speech Day but his own TV business.

The school secretary, dispatched by the head to try and contact the Grange, announced that the phone there had been disconnected. An envoy from the staff on supervisory duty in the hall looked in to say that a first attempt at a slow handclap by the impatient pupils had been quelled, but with even the parents and front row guests beginning to shift impatiently, he feared a second insurrection could not be so easily put down. Dennis moved among the platform party defending Tom vigorously and declaring that special allowances had to be made for the artistic temperament, and that of course it wasn't spoiling his own great day. Behind him he left a trail of admiration for his loyalty, sympathy for its betrayal, and indignation at the shabby treatment he was receiving from his so-called friend.

Finally the mayor approached him.

"Look here, Dennis," he said. "We can't hang about for ever. The head-master's asked me to take over the prize-giving. I know it's a bit of a come-down, and that you in particular will be very disappointed not to . . ."

"No, no," intervened Dennis. "It'll be an honor and a privilege to receive my award from you, Mr. Mayor. In some ways, to be honest, I'll prefer knowing I'm getting it from someone with a true appreciation of what civic service means to folks up here in Dunchester."

"Well said, lad! It's big of you to take it like that. And you're dead right. At least I can guarantee that whatever I say will come from the heart, and I'll not be thinking about some half-baked television program while I'm talking. Right, let's get to it."

The applause which greeted the platform party was close to the threatened slow handclap, but disappointment at Tom Trotter's absence was clearly diluted by relief that at last the show was under way.

The school prize-giving was got through with such élan that when a fourth year divinity prize winner missed his name, his New Testament was given to the next on the list, a surprised-looking Muslim mathematician, and thereafter everyone got the wrong book. But that could be sorted out later, and now the mayor was launching into his encomium of Dennis. Curiously it followed much the same lines as Dennis had anticipated from Tom, except that, couched in the mayor's honest earthy language, the argument that Dennis's station and achievement were much more admirable and praiseworthy than the passing triumphs of the media world rang out with real conviction and got the audience applauding Dennis for five minutes, then themselves for another five.

Dennis stood there, clutching the carriage clock he had accepted for himself and the large cheque he had accepted for the new minibus, and for the first time in decades felt totally himself with no tinge of a Trotter presence. Below him even the cameramen who had stayed in the hope that Tom would yet arrive, were carried away by the wave of local chauvinist feeling inspired by the mayor's speech, and clicked and whirred as if some great media celebrity were indeed standing before them.

Slowly, reluctantly, the applause faded and Dennis stepped forward to utter his thanks.

"Mr. Mayor. Headmaster. Ladies and gentlemen," he said brokenly. "This is a moment I shall never forget . . . never . . ."

He was right. He never did forget it.

A door opened at the side of the stage and a buzz of interest arose in the hall which had nothing to do with Dennis. Out of the corner of his eye he glimpsed a uniformed figure intruding upon the platform. Even Mark Antony could not have competed with such an interruption, and, wisely, Dennis let his emotional pause stretch into infinity. The policeman was bending over the headmaster, whispering in his ear. The headmaster did not move after the policeman finished, and the officer held his stooped position as though in expectation of a whispered response. Together they formed a tableau which any Victorian narrative painter would have seized on with delight and entitled NEWS FROM THE FRONT. Then slowly the headmaster rose and with a stricken expression advanced toward Dennis.

"I'm sorry," he said. "It seems there's been an accident."

The clock in Dennis's hand suddenly felt very heavy. He turned to place it on his chair, but it slipped from his fingers and crashed to the floor. The glass case shattered and the hands fell off. The audience exhaled a uniform gasp but the head cut it off like a double-glazed window simply by raising his hand.

"Ladies and gentlemen," he intoned. "I regret to inform you I have just heard there has been a serious motor accident involving Mr. Tom Trotter, who should have been our distinguished guest today, and his wife. In the circumstances I think we must consider these proceedings at an end and I would ask you to leave the hall as quickly and quietly as you may."

Suddenly a woman's voice rang out behind him.

"Dead? I don't believe you. Not dead!"

It was Pamela. At last her three daughters came in useful and as she collapsed in hysterics they led her away, leaving the other guests able to join the gentlemen of the press in demanding confirmatory detail from the messenger policeman.

"It was a farmer who got there first," he said, relishing his role. "He were up on the fellside with his sheep when he saw the car, going like a bat out of hell, he says, like the driver were in a desperate hurry to get somewhere. He could hear the brakes scream as he took the corners. Then suddenly the car were belting down to this sharpest bend of the lot and the brakes didn't scream. The driver, Mr. Trotter that'd be, swung the wheel hard over, and he almost made it, the farmer says. But the car were sliding sideways on the bend, the road was narrow, and suddenly he was over the slide. Not a big drop, but unfortunately there was a fire . . . If there hadn't been a fire, or if the road had been just a bit wider . . . he almost made it, the farmer says . . ."

His moving narrative was interrupted by the sound of high keening laughter.

It took Dennis a little while to realize the noise was coming from him. "I'm sorry," he gasped. "It's just that . . . *he almost made it . . .*"

After the funeral, where the family mourners had to play a very subsidiary role to the few celebrity guests and the many celebrity wreaths, Dennis and Pamela re-entered their house in silence. Pamela went straight upstairs and Dennis went into the lounge and poured himself a whiskey. So far he had refused to let himself know how he felt. Now for the first time he cautiously lifted the cover on his feelings and peered inside.

There was something down there, but he couldn't quite make out what. Cautiously he began to prod at it with the memory of these last days—the presentation, the news of the accident, the inquest, the funeral . . .

"Dennis? Are you all right?"

It was Pamela, with more of impatience than curiosity or concern in her voice.

"Yes, fine," he said, slamming down the lid. She hadn't taken off her coat, he noticed.

He said, "Are you cold? Shall I turn the heating on?"

"I'm leaving you," she said.

His mind tried to pretend it hadn't registered the words but his eyes had already taken in the packed suitcase on the floor behind her.

"I'm sorry," she went on. "But after what's happened I can't stay."

For a second he was certain she meant she knew what he had done to the brakes. The shock must have shown on his face for now she said with faint surprise, "You look upset. Why? It can't be a total surprise, not after all this time. I've never been all that good at hiding my feelings."

"What feelings?" he asked in growing bewilderment.

She considered, then said, "Disappointment, I suppose. Dennis, this isn't a judgment session. It's not your fault. I opted for you in the first place. I thought, he'll be the one. Tom was flashy but flighty. You'd be the one with staying power, I thought. And so you were. But it was power for staying in Dunchester, I should have realized that. It's all you ever wanted, isn't it? To be someone here in Dunchester. I can't imagine you anywhere else, and I can't imagine how I ever could!"

"What the hell are you talking about?" he cried, baffled.

"I told you. Disappointment. And boredom," she said. "I know I've let it show. You must have noticed. I'm sorry. I just sometimes felt so stifled in this world of yours. But as long as Lucy and Tom were alive, it seemed bearable. They were news from another world, proof that there was life after Dunchester. But now they're gone. And the girls have voted with their feet, haven't they? Now it's my turn. Don't make a fuss. You'll be better off without me, Dennis. Just think, you won't have to be embarrassed by my clothes or my cooking any more."

"Where are you going?" he asked desperately, trying to collect his thoughts.

"I'll stay with the girls till I get something sorted out," she said. "Lucy's left me a bit of money, so I won't need to trouble you much. I think that's my taxi now. Goodbye, Dennis. Take care. Dunchester needs men like you, and that's not a crack."

She kissed him on the cheek, a friendly peck, and then she was gone, before he could say anything, offer her any of the million revelations and explanations tumulting in his brain.

And yet what was there to say which would not be too little too late, or too much too soon?

He poured himself another scotch and sat in complete passivity for a while. No need now to lift the lid and poke at the thing in his mind any more. He knew why it wouldn't stir. It was dead. His life, his "true" life, had died in that burning car on the high moors road.

And what of his shadow life? To live it out now without Pamela meant that it was going to be merely the shadow of a shadow.

Should he have told her what he really felt?

What he had really done?

He shuddered at the thought. There was a noise in the hall and he rose almost in terror at the idea that she'd returned. But it was only the local paper.

They had an account of the funeral on the front page. There was a single reference to himself and they'd spelled his name wrong, as they'd done in the passing reference to his award presentation in the account of Tom's death. As for all those thousands of frames of film taken of him during the ceremony, not one had ever appeared.

Until now perhaps. When he opened the paper, he discovered and elegiac double photo-spread of scenes from Tom's triumphant career. And there, leading the rest, surely that was a shot from Speech Day?

The bottom left hand corner of the picture was filled with a very out-of-focus human ear which Dennis was pretty sure he recognized as his own.

But what the photographer had been aiming at, and what he'd got with great clarity, and perhaps just a bit of touching up, was one of the Roll of Honor boards which lined the walls of the School Hall.

This one, in letters of gold on vanished mahogany, listed the prize winners for the year 1959.

Highlighted was the school's premier award, *The Bishop Blaxton Cup for All-Round Merit*. Alongside it was the name *Thomas Trotter*.

Beneath this, not at all highlighted and in much smaller letters but still legible to the sensitive eye, was another name and inscription. *Dennis Platt. Proxime Accessit.*

Ed Gorman was recently called "one of the most distinctive voices in today's crime fiction" by the *San Diego Union*. Here he offers us this piece, which is a poignant, sensitive tale of humanity discovering itself and also a finely wrought thriller.

The Wind from Midnight
ED GORMAN

Even with the windows open, the Greyhound bus was hot inside as it roared through the rural California night.

Plump ladies in sweat-soaked summer dresses furiously worked paper fans that bore the names of funeral parlors. Plump men in sleeveless T-shirts sat talking of disappointing baseball scores ("Them goddamn Red Sox just don't have it this year; no sir they don't"), and the Republican convention that had just nominated Dwight Eisenhower. Most of the men aboard liked Ike, and liked him quite a bit. These men smoked Lucky Strikes and Chesterfields and Fatimas, and more than a few of them snuck quick sips from silver flasks at their hip pockets.

In the middle of the bus was a slender, pretty woman who inexplicably burst into tears every twenty miles or so. It was assumed by all who watched her that she was having man trouble of some sort. A woman this pretty wouldn't carry on so otherwise. Probably heading home to her parents after her husband walked out on her.

Traveling with the pretty woman was a sweet-faced little girl who was obviously her daughter. She was maybe five or six, and wore a faded white dress that reminded some of First Communion and patent leather shoes that reminded others of Shirley Temple. For the most part she was well-behaved, stroking and petting her mother when she cried, and sitting prim and obedient when mama was just looking sadly out the window.

But fifty miles ago the little girl had gone back to use the restroom— she'd had a big nickel Pepsi and it had gone right through her—and there she'd seen the tiny woman sitting all by herself in one corner of the wide back seat.

All the little girl could think of—and this was what she whispered to her mama later—was that a doll had come to life.

Before the bus pulled into the oceanside town for a rest stop, the little girl found exactly four excuses to run back and get another good peek at the tiny woman.

She just couldn't believe what she was seeing.

A lot of the passengers hurried up to get off the bus fast so they could stand around the front of the depot and get a good look at her. In the rolling darkness of the Greyhound, they hadn't really gotten much of a glimpse and they were just naturally curious.

She didn't disappoint them.

She was just as tiny as she'd seemed, and in her plain white blouse and her navy linen skirt and her dark, seamed hose and her cute little pumps with the two-inch heels she looked like a five-year-old who was all dressed up in her mama's clothes.

Back on the bus they'd argued in whispers whether she was a dwarf or a midget. There was some scientific difference between the two, but damned if anybody could remember exactly what that was.

From inside the depot came smells of hamburgers and onions and french fries and cigar smoke, all stale on the still summer air. Also from inside came the sounds of Miss Kay Starr singing "The Wheel of Fortune." Skinny white cowboys clung like moths to the lights of the depot entrance, as did old black men the color of soot, and snappy young sailors in their dress whites and hayseed grins.

This was the scene the tiny woman confronted.

She walked to a nearby cab and climbed into the back seat.

The cabbie knew where the carnival was, of course. There would be only one in a burg like this.

He drove his rattling '47 Plymouth out to the pier where the midway and all the rides looked like the toys of a baby giant.

He pulled right up to the entrance and said, "That'll be eighty-five cents, miss."

She opened her purse and sank a tiny hand into its deep waiting darkness. She gave him a dollar's worth of quarters and said, "That's for you."

"Why, thank you."

She opened the door. The dome light came on. He noticed for the first time that she was nice looking. Not gorgeous or anything like that, but nice-looking. Silken dark hair in a page boy. Blue eyes that would have been beautiful if they weren't tainted with sorrow. And a full mouth so erotic it made him uncomfortable. Why, if a normal-sized man was to try anything with a tiny woman like that—

He put the thought from his mind.

As she started to leave the cab, he just blurted it out. "I suppose you know what happened here a month ago. About the—little guy, I mean."

She just looked at him.

"He stole a gun from one of the carnies here and raced back to his hotel room and killed himself." The cabbie figured that the tiny woman would want to know about it, her being just like the little guy and all. To show he was friendly, the cabbie always told colored people stories about colored people in just the same way.

The cabbie's head was turned in profile, waiting for the woman to respond.

But the only sound, faint among the *crack* of air rifles and the roar of the roller coaster and the high piping pitch of the calliope, was the cab door being quietly closed.

A lady with a beard, a man with a vagina. A chance to get your fortune told by a gypsy woman with a knife scar on her left cheek. A sobbing little blond boy looking frantically for his lost mother. A man just off the midway slapping a woman he called a fucking whore bitch. An old man in a straw hat gaping fixedly at a chunky stripper the barker kept pointing to with a long wooden cane.

Linnette saw all these things and realized why her brother had always liked carnivals. She liked them for the same reason. In all the spectacle— beautiful and ugly, happy and sad alike—tiny people tended to get overlooked. There was so much to see and do and feel and desire that normal people barely gave tiny people a glance.

And that's why, for many of his thirty-one years, her brother had been drawn to midways.

He'd told her about this one, of course, many times. How he came here after a long day at the typewriter. How he liked to sit on a bench up near the shooting gallery and watch the women go by and try to imagine what they'd be like if he had a chance to meet them. He was such a romantic, her brother, in his heart a matinee idol worthy of Valentino and Gable.

She'd learned all this from his infrequent phone calls. He always called at dinner time on Sunday evening because of the rates, and he always talked nine minutes exactly. He always asked her how things were going at the library where she worked, and she always asked him if he was ever going to write that important novel she knew he had in him.

They were brother and sister and more, which was why, when he'd put that gun to his head there in the dim little coffin of a room where he lived and wrote—

Linnette tried not to think of these things now.

She worked her way through the crowd, moving slowly toward the steady cracking sounds of the shooting gallery. A Mr. Kelly was who she was looking for.

A woman given to worry and anxiety, she kept checking the new white number ten envelope in her purse. One hundred dollars in crisp green currency. Certainly that should be enough for Mr. Kelly.

Aimee was taking a cigarette break when she happened to see Linnette. She'd spent the last month trying to forget about the dwarf and the part Ralph Banghart, the man who ran *The Mirror Maze*, had played in the death of the dwarf.

And the part Aimee had played, too.

Maybe if she'd never gotten involved, never tried to help the poor little guy—

Standing next to the tent she worked, Aimee reached down to retrieve the Coke she'd set in the grass.

And just as she bent over, she felt big male hands slip over her slender hips. "Booo!"

She jerked away from him. She saw him now as a diseased person. Whatever ugliness he had inside him, she didn't want to catch.

"I told you, Ralph, I don't ever want you touching me again."

"Aw, babe, I just—"

She slapped him. Hard enough that his head jerked back with a grunt of pain.

"Hey—"

"You still don't give a damn that little guy killed himself, do you?"

Ralph rubbed his sore cheek. "I didn't kill him."

"Sure you did. You're just not man enough to admit it. If you hadn't played that practical joke on him—"

"If the little bastard couldn't take a joke—"

She raised her hand to slap him again. Grinning, he started to duck away.

She spit at him. That, he didn't have time to duck away from. She got him right on the nose.

"I don't want you to come anywhere goddamn near me, do you understand?" Aimee said, knowing she was shrieking, and not caring.

Ralph, looking around, embarrassed now that people were starting to watch, shook his head, muttered profanely, and left, daubing off the spittle with his soiled white handkerchief.

Aimee started looking around for the dwarf woman again. She had this sense that the woman had somehow known the little guy who'd killed himself.

Aimee had to find her and talk to her. Just had to.

She started searching.

* * *

Mr. Kelly turned out to be a big man with an anchor tattoo on his right forearm and beads of silver sweat standing in rows on his pink bald pate.

At the moment he was showing a woman with huge breasts how to operate an air rifle. Mr. Kelly kept nudging her accidentally-on-purpose with his elbow. If the woman minded, she didn't complain. But then her boyfriend came back from somewhere, and he looked to be about the same size but younger and trimmer than Mr. Kelly, so Mr. Kelly withdrew his elbow and let the boyfriend take over the shooting lessons.

Then Mr. Kelly turned to Linnette. "What can I do for ya, small fry?"

Linnette always told herself that insults didn't matter. Sticks and stones and all that. And most of the time they didn't. But every once in a while, right now for instance, they pierced the heart like a fatal sliver of glass.

"My name is Linnette Dobbins."

"So? My name is Frank Kelly."

"A month or so ago my brother stole a gun from you and—"

Smiles made most people look pleasant, but Mr. Kelly's smile only served to make him look knowing and dirty. "Oh, the dwarf." He looked her up and down. "Sure. I should've figured that out for myself."

"The police informed me that they've given you the gun back."

"Yeah. What about it?"

"I'd like to buy it from you."

"Buy it from me? What the hell're you talkin' about?"

Mr. Kelly was just about to continue, when a new pair of lovers bellied up to the gallery counter and waited for instructions.

Without excusing himself, Mr. Kelly went over to the lovers, picked up an air rifle, and started demonstrating how to win the gal here a nice little teddy bear.

"A dwarf, you say?"

Aimee nodded.

"Jeez, Aimee, I think I'd remember if I'd seen a dwarf woman wanderin' around the midway."

"Thanks, Hank."

Hank got kind of flustered and said, "You think we're ever gonna go to a movie sometime, Aimee, like I asked you that time?"

She touched his shoulder tenderly and gave him a sweet, quick smile. "I'm sure thinking about it, Hank. I really am." Hank was such a nice guy. She just wished he were her type.

And then she was off again, moving frantically around the midway, asking various carnies if they'd seen a woman who was a dwarf.

Hank's was the tenth booth she'd stopped at.

Nobody had seen the woman. Nobody.

*   *   *

"So why would you want the gun your brother killed himself with, small fry?"

From her purse, Linnette took the plain white number ten envelope and handed it up to Mr. Kelly.

"What's this?" he said.

"Look inside."

He opened the envelope flap and peeked in. He ran a pudgy finger through the bills. He whistled. "Hundred bucks."

"Right."

"For a beat up old service revolver? Hell, you don't know much about guns. You could buy one like it in any pawn shop for five bucks."

"The money's all yours."

"Just for this gun?"

"That's right, Mr. Kelly. Just for this one gun."

He whistled again. The money had made him friendlier. This time his smile lacked malevolence. "Boy, small fry, I almost hate to take your money."

"But you will?"

He gave her a big cornball grin now, and she saw in it the fact that he was just as much a hayseed as the rubes he bilked every night. The difference was, he didn't know he was a hayseed.

"You damn bet ya I will," he said, and trotted to the back of the tent to get the gun.

"I'll need some bullets for it, too," Linnette called after him.

He turned around and looked at her. "Bullets? What for?"

"Given the price I'm paying, Mr. Kelly, I'd say that was my business."

He looked at her for a time, and then his cornball grin opened his face up again. "Well, small fry, I guess I can't argue with you on that one now, can I? Bullets it is."

The carnival employed a security man named Bulicek. It was said that he was a former cop who'd gotten caught running a penny-ante protection racket on his beat and had been summarily discharged. Here, he always smelled of whiskey, and Sen-Sen to cut the stink of the whiskey. He strutted around in his blue uniform with big half-moons of sweat under each arm and a creaking leather holster riding his considerable girth. His best friend in the carny was Kelly at the shooting gallery, which figured.

Aimee avoided Bulicek because he always managed to put his hands on her in some way whenever they talked. But now she had no choice.

She'd visited seven more carnies since Hank, and nobody had seen a woman dwarf.

Bulicek was just coming out of the big whitewashed building that was half men's and half women's.

He smiled when he saw her. She could feel his paws on her already.

"I'm looking for somebody," she said.

"So am I. And I found her." Bulicek knew every bad movie line in the world.

"A woman who's a dwarf. She's somewhere on the midway. Have you seen her?"

Bulicek shrugged. "What do I get if I tell ya?"

"You get the privilege of doing your job." She tried to keep the anger from her voice. She needed his cooperation.

"And nothing else?" His eyes found a nice place on her body to settle momentarily.

"Nothing else."

He raised his eyes and shook his head and took out a package of cigarettes.

Some teenagers with ducks ass haircuts and black leather jackets—even in this kind of heat for crissakes—wandered by and Bulicek, he-man that he was, gave them the bad eye.

When he turned back to Aimee, she was shocked by his sudden anger. "You think you could talk to me one time, Miss High and Mighty, without making me feel like I'm a piece of dog shit?"

"You think you could talk to me one time without copping a cheap feel?"

He surprised her by saying. "I shouldn't do that, Aimee, and I'm sorry. You wanna try and get along?"

She laughed from embarrassment. "God, you're really serious, aren't you?"

"Yeah, I am." He put out a hand. "You wanna be friends, Aimee?"

This time the laugh was pure pleasure. "Sure, Bulicek. I'd like to be friends. I really would. You show me some respect and I'll show you some, too."

They shook hands.

"Now, about that dwarf you was askin' about."

"Yeah? You saw her?" Aimee couldn't keep the excitement from her voice.

Bulicek pointed down the midway. "Seen her 'bout fifteen minutes ago at Kelly's."

Aimee thanked him and started running.

Linnette had a different taxi driver this time.

This guy was heavy and Mexican. The radio played low, Mexican songs from a station across the border. The guy sure wore a lot of after-shave.

Linnette sat with the gun inside her purse and her purse on her lap.

She looked out the window at the passing streets. Easy to imagine her brother walking these streets, always the focus of the curious stare and the

357

cold quick smirk. Maybe it was harder for men, she thought. They were expected to be big and strong and—

She opened her purse. The sound was loud in the taxi. She saw the driver's eyes flick up to his rearview mirror and study her. Then his eyes flicked away.

She rode the rest of the way with her hand inside her purse, gripping the gun.

She closed her eyes and tried to imagine her brother's finger on the trigger.

She hoped that there was a God somewhere and that all of this made sense, that some people should be born of normal height and others, freaks, be born with no arms or legs or eyes.

Or be born dwarfs.

"Here you are, lady."

He pulled over to the curb and told her the fare.

Once again, she found her money swiftly and paid him.

He reached over and opened the door for her, studying her all the time. Did it ever occur to him—fat and dark and not very well educated—that he looked just as strange to her as she did to him? But no, he wouldn't be the kind of man who'd have an insight like that.

She got out of the cab, and he drove away.

Even in a bleak little town like this one, the Ganges Arms was grim. "Fireproof" was much larger than "Ganges" on the neon sign outside, and the drunk throwing up over by the curb told her more than she wanted to know about the type of people who lived in the place.

She couldn't imagine how her brother had managed to survive here six years.

Linnette went inside. The lobby was small and filled with ancient couches that dust rose from like shabby ghosts. A long-dead potted plant filled one corner, while a cigarette vending machine filled the other. In the back somewhere a toilet flushed with the roar of an avalanche. A black and white TV screen flickered with images of Milton Berle in a dress.

A big woman in a faded blouse that revealed fleshy arms and some kind of terrible rash on her elbows was behind the desk. The woman had a beauty mark, huge and hairy, like a little animal clinging to her cheek.

She grinned when she saw Linnette.

"You don't have to tell me, sweetie."

"Tell you?"

"Sure. Who you are."

"You know who I am?"

"Sure. You're the little guy's sister. He talked about you all the time."

She leaned over the counter, hacking a cigarette cough that sounded sickeningly phlegmy, and said, "*Linnette*. Right?"

"Right."

The woman grimaced. "Sorry about the little guy."

"Thank you."

"I was the one who found him. He wasn't pretty, believe me."

"Oh."

"And I was the first one who read the note." She shook her head again and put a cigarette in her mouth. "He was pretty gimped up inside, poor little guy."

"Yes. Yes, he was."

The woman stared at her, not as if Linnette were a freak, but rather curious about why she might be here.

"I was just traveling through," Linnette said quietly. "I thought I might stay here tonight." She hesitated. "Sleep in my brother's room, perhaps."

Now the woman really stared at her. "You sure, hon?"

"Sure?"

"About wantin' to take his room and all? Frankly, it'd give me the creeps."

Linnette opened her purse, reached in for her money. "I'd just like to see where he lived and worked."

The woman shrugged beefy shoulders. "You're the boss, hon. You're the boss."

Kelly was arguing with a drunk who claimed that the shooting gallery was rigged. The drunk had been bragging to his girl about what a marksman he'd become in Korea and wanted to do a little showing off. All he'd managed to do was humiliate himself.

Aimee waited as patiently as she could for a few minutes, and then she interrupted the drunk—whose girlfriend was now trying to tug him away from making any more of a scene—and said, "Kelly, I'm looking for a woman who's a dwarf. Bulicek said he saw her here."

The drunk turned and looked at Aimee as if she'd just said she'd seen a Martian.

Aimee's remark unsettled the drunk enough that his girlfriend was now able to draw him away. They disappeared into the midway.

"Yeah. She was here. So what?"

"Did you talk to her?"

"Yeah."

"About what?"

"What the hell's your interest, Aimee?"

"Kelly, I don't have time to explain. Just please help me, all right?"

Kelly sighed. "Okay, kid, what do you want?"

"What'd she say to you?"

"Said she wanted to buy a gun."

"A gun? What kind of gun?"

"The gun her brother stole from me."

"My God."

"What's wrong?"

"Don't you see?"

"See what, kid? Calm down."

"If she wanted to buy the gun her brother stole from you, then maybe she plans to use it on herself just the way her brother did."

Kelly said, "Shit. You know, I never thought of that."

"So you gave her the gun?"

Kelly seemed a little embarrassed now. "Yeah. Gave it to her for a hundred bucks."

"A hundred? But Kelly, that gun isn't worth more than—"

"That's what she offered me for it. So that's what I took, kid. I never said I was no saint."

"Where did she go?"

"Hell, how would I know?"

"Didn't you notice the direction she was going?"

He shrugged. "Down near the entrance, I guess." He looked chastened that he hadn't paid attention.

"Thanks, Kelly. I appreciate it."

And before he could say another word, she was gone, running fast toward the front of the midway.

There was a card table sitting next to the room's only window. It had the uncertain legs of a young colt. He'd put his portable typewriter on it—the one she'd bought him for his birthday ten years ago—and worked long into the night.

The room had a bureau with somebody's initials knifed into the top, a mirror mottled with age, wallpaper stained with moisture, a double bed with a paint-chipped metal headboard, and linoleum so old it was worn to wood in patches.

She tried not to think of all the sad lives that had been lived out here. Men without women; men without hope.

She made sure the door was locked behind her, and then came into the room.

She could feel him here, now. She had always believed in ghosts—were ghosts any more unlikely than men and women who only grew to be three and a half feet tall?—and so she spoke out loud to him for the first time since being told of his suicide.

"I hope you know how much I love you, brother," she said, moving across the small, box-like room to the card table, running her fingers across the indentations his Smith-Corona had made on the surface.

She decided against turning the overhead light on. The on-and-off red of the outside neon was good enough.

"I miss you, brother. I hope you know that, too."

She heard the clack of a ghostly typewriter; saw her brother's sweet round face smiling up at her after he'd finished a particularly good sentence; listened to the soft sad laughter that only she had been able to elicit from him.

"I wish you would have called me. I wish you would have told me what you had in mind. You know why?"

She said nothing for a time.

Distant ragged traffic sounds from the highway; the even fainter music of the midway further away in the darkness.

"Because I would have joined you, brother. I would have joined you."

She set her purse on the card table. She unclasped the leather halves and then reached in.

The gun waited there.

She brought out the gun with the reverence of a priest bringing forth something that has been consecrated to God.

She held it for a time, in silhouette, against the window with the flashing red neon.

And then, slowly, inevitably, she brought the gun to her temple.

And eased the hammer back.

At the midway entrance, Aimee asked fourteen people if they'd seen the woman. None had. But the fifteenth did, and pointed to a rusted beast of a taxi cab just now pulling in.

Aimee ran to the cab and pushed her head in the front window before the driver had stopped completely.

"The dwarf woman. Where did you take her?"

"Who the hell are you?"

"The woman. Where did you take her?" Aimee knew she was screaming. She didn't care.

"Goddamn, lady. You're fucking nuts." But despite his tough words, the cab driver saw that she was going to stay there until she had her answer. He said, "I took her to the Ganges Arms. Why the hell're you so interested, anyway?"

"Then take me there, too," Aimee said, flipping open the back door and diving in. "Take me there, too!"

Linnette went over and sat on the bed.

This would make it easier for everybody. The mess would be confined to the mattress. A mattress you could just throw out.

She lay back on the bed.

Her shoes fell off, one at a time, making sharp noises as they struck the floor.

Two-inch heels, she thought. How pathetic of me. Wanting so desperately to be like other people.

She closed her eyes and let the sorrow wash over her. Sorrow for her brother and herself, sorrow for their lives.

She saw him again at his typewriter, heard keys striking the eternal silence.

"I wish you would have told me, brother. I wish you had. It would have been easier for you. We could have comforted each other."

She raised the hand carrying the gun, brought the gun to her temple once again.

The hammer was still back.

"Can't you go any faster?"

"Maybe you think this is an Indy race car or somethin', huh, lady?"

"God, please! Please, just go as fast as you can."

"Jes-uz," the cab driver said. "Jes-uz."

Linnette said a prayer, nothing formal, just words that said she hoped there was a God and that he or she or it or whatever form it took would understand why she was doing this and how much she longed to be with her brother again and that both God and her brother would receive her with open arms.

She tightened her finger on the trigger and then—

—the knock came.

"Hon?"

Oh, my Lord.

"Hon, you awake in there?"

Finding her voice. Clearing her throat. "Yes?"

"Brought you some Kool-Aid. That's what I drink all summer. Raspberry Kool-Aid. Quenches my thirst a lot better than regular pop, you know? Anyway, I brought you a glass. You wanna come get it?"

Did she have any choice?

Linnette put the gun down on the bed and pulled her purse over the gun.

She got up and straightened her skirt and went to the door.

A long angle of dirty yellow light fell across her from the hallway.

The woman was a lot heavier than she'd looked downstairs. Linnette liked her.

The woman bore a large glass of Kool-Aid in her right hand and a cigarette in her left. She kept flicking her ashes on the hallway floor.

"You like raspberry?"

"Thank you very much."

"Sometimes I like cherry, but tonight I'm just in a kind of raspberry mood. You know?"

"I really appreciate this."

The woman nodded to the stairs. "You get lonely, you can always come down and keep me company."

"I think I'll try and get some sleep first, but if I don't doze off, I'll probably be down."

The woman looked past Linnette into the room. "You got everything you need?"

"I'm fine."

"If your brother's room starts to bother you, just let me know. You can always change rooms for no extra cost."

"Thanks."

The woman smiled. "Enjoy the Kool-Aid." She checked the man's wristwatch she wore on her thick wrist. "Hey, time for Blackie."

"Blackie?"

"Boston Blackie. You ever watch him?"

"I guess not."

"Great show; really, great show."

"Well, thank you."

"You're welcome. And remember about keeping me company."

"Oh, I will. I promise."

"Well, good night."

"Good night," Linnette said, and then quietly closed the door.

Ten minutes later, the cabbie pulled up in front of the hotel.

As always, this street reminded Aimee of a painting by Thomas Hart Benton she'd once seen in a Chicago gallery, a place where even the street lamps looked twisted and grotesque.

Aimee flung a five dollar bill in the front seat and said, "I appreciate your speeding."

The cabbie picked up the fin, examined it as if he suspected it might be counterfeit, and then said, "Good luck with whatever your problem is, lady."

Aimee was out of the cab, hurrying into the lobby.

She went right to the desk and to the heavyset clerk who was leaning on her elbows and watching Kent Taylor as Boston Blackie.

The woman sighed bitterly, as if she'd just been forced to give up her firstborn, and said, "Help you?"

"I'm looking for a woman who just came in here."

"What kind of woman?"

"A dwarf."

The desk clerk looked Aimee over more carefully. "What about her?"

"It's important that I talk to her right away."

"Why?"

"Because—because she's a friend of mine and I think she's going to do something very foolish."

"Like what?"

"For God's sake," Aimee said. "I *know* she's here. Tell me what room she's in before it's too late."

The desk clerk was about to respond when the gunshot sounded on the floor above.

Aimee had never heard anything so loud in her life.

"What room is she in?" she screamed.

"208!"

Aimee reached the staircase in moments, and started running up the steps two at a time.

An old man in boxer shorts and a sunken, hairy chest stood in the hallway in front of 208 looking sleepy and scared.

"What the Sam Hill's going on?"

Aimee said nothing, just pushed past him to the door. She turned the knob. Locked. The desk clerk was lumbering up the stairs behind her.

Aimee turned and ran toward the steps again. She pushed out her hand and laid the palm up and open.

"The key. Hurry."

The desk clerk, her entire body heaving from exertion, dropped the key in Aimee's hand and tried to say something, but she had no wind.

Aimee ran back to 208 and inserted the key. Pushed the door open.

The first thing was the darkness; the second, the acrid odor of gunpowder. The third was the hellish neon red that shone through the dirty sheer curtains.

Aimee was afraid of what she was going to see.

Could she really handle seeing somebody who'd shot herself at point-blank range?

She took two steps over the threshold.

And heard the noise.

At first, she wasn't sure what it was. Only after she took a few more steps into the dark, cramped room did she recognize what she was hearing.

A woman lying face down on the bed, the sound of her sobbing muffled into the mattress.

The desk clerk came panting into the yellow frame of the door and asked, "She dead?"

"No," Aimee said quietly. "No, she's not dead."

And then she silently closed the door behind her and went to sit with Linnette on the bed.

* * *

Aimee had been with carnivals since she was fourteen, when she'd run off from a Kentucky farm and from a pa who saw nothing wrong with doing with her what he'd done with her other two sisters. She was now twenty-eight. In the intervening years she'd wondered many times what it would be like to have a child of her own, and tonight she thought she was finding out, at least in a curious sort of way.

It was not respectful, Aimee was sure, to think of Linnette as a child just because she was so little, but as Aimee sat there for three-and-a-half hours in the dark, breathless room holding Linnette in her lap and rocking her as she would an infant, the thought was inevitable. And then the wind from midnight came, and things cooled off a little.

Aimee didn't say much, really—what could she say? She just hugged Linnette and let her cry and let her talk and let her cry some more, and it was so sad that Aimee herself started crying sometimes, thinking of how cruel people could be to anybody who was different in any way, and thinking of that sonofabitch Ralph Banghart spying on the little guy in the house of mirrors, and thinking of how terrified the little guy had been when he fell prey to Ralph's practical joke. Life was just so sad sometimes when you saw what happened to people. Usually to innocent people at that—people that life had been cruel enough to already.

So that's why Aimee mostly listened, because when something was as overwhelming as the little guy's life had been—

Sometimes the desk clerk made the long and taxing trip up the stairs and knocked with a single knuckle and said, "You okay in there?"

And Aimee would say, "We're fine, we're fine." And then the desk clerk would go away and Aimee would start rocking Linnette again and listening to her and wanting to tell Linnette that she felt terrible about the little guy's death.

It occurred to her that maybe by sitting here like this and listening to Linnette and rocking her, maybe she was in some way making up for playing a small part in the little guy's suicide.

"Sometimes I just get so scared," Linnette said just as dawn was breaking coral-colored across the sky.

And Aimee knew just what Linnette was talking about, because Aimee got scared like that, too, sometimes.

The Greyhound arrived twenty-three minutes late that afternoon.

Aimee and Linnette stood in the depot entrance with a group of other people. There was a farm girl who kept saying how excited she was to be going to Fresno, and a Marine who kept saying it was going to be good to see Iowa again, and an old woman who kept saying she hoped they kept the windows closed because even on a 92-degree day like this one she'd get a chill.

"You ever get up to Sacramento?" Linnette asked.

"Sometimes," said Aimee.

"You could always call me at the library and we could have lunch."

"That sounds like fun, Linnette."

The small woman took Aimee's hand and gave it a squeeze. "You really helped me last night. I'll never forget it, Aimee. Never."

Just then the bus pulled in with a *whoosh* of air brakes and a puff of black diesel smoke.

In one of the front windows a five-year-old boy was looking out, and when he saw Linnette he started jumping up and down and pointing, and then a couple of moments later another five-year-old face appeared in the same window, and now there were two boys looking and pointing and laughing at Linnette.

Maybe the worst part of all, Aimee thought, was that they didn't really mean to be cruel.

The bus door was flung open and a Greyhound driver looking dapper in a newly starched uniform stepped down and helped several old ladies off the bus.

"I wished he could have known you, Aimee," Linnette said. "He sure would've liked you. He sure would've."

And then, for once, it was Aimee who started crying, and she wasn't even sure why. It just seemed right somehow, she thought, as she helped the little woman take the first big step up into the bus.

A minute later, Linnette was sitting in the middle of the bus, at a window seat. Her eyes barely reached the window ledge.

Behind Aimee, the door burst open and the two five-year-olds came running out of the depot, carrying cups of Pepsi.

They looked up and saw Linnette in the window. They started pointing and giggling immediately.

Aimee grabbed the closest one by the ear, giving it enough of a twist to inflict some pain.

"That's one fine lady aboard that bus there, you hear me? And you treat her like a fine lady, too, or you're going to get your butts spanked. You understand me?" Aimee said. She let go of the boy's ear. "You understand me?" she repeated.

The boys looked at each other and then back to Aimee. They seemed scared of her, which was what she wanted.

"Yes, ma'am," both boys said in unison.

"Then get on that bus and behave yourselves."

The boys climbed aboard, not looking back at her even once.

Aimee waited till the Greyhound pulled out with a roar and a poof of sooty smoke.

She waved at Linnette and Linnette waved back.

"Goodbye," Aimee said, and was afraid she was going to start crying again.

When the bus was gone, Aimee walked over to the taxi stand. A young man who looked like a kid was driving.

Aimee told him to take her to the carnival, and then she settled back in the seat and stared out the window.

After a time, it began to rain, a hot summer rain that would neither cool nor cleanse, and the rest of the day and all the next long night, Aimee tried to keep herself from thinking about certain things. She tried so very hard.